Darkest Fears Ti

Fallen
For Him

Clair Delaney

REVIEWS FOR FALLEN FOR HIM

'The story just pulled me in, so sexy! I need more. Can't wait to read the others…' **Apple iBooks**

'What a wonderful read! The story is so compelling and captivating. I can't wait to get started on the next book in the trilogy…' **Apple iBooks**

'Loved it! Couldn't put the book down…' **Amazon**

'This book is amazing! I didn't want it to end. I can't wait to read the next one. I would recommend this book to everyone. It's fantastic!' **Amazon**

'I absolutely love this book! It's a must read. I'm going onto the second book as it's got me gripped!' **Amazon**

'Well written amazing storyline, characters you can relate to on so many levels. Great start to a trilogy. Can't wait to start book two!' **Scribd Library**

'Loved it! I couldn't put this book down, absolute page turner. Have bought book two and it just keeps getting better.' **Scribd Library**

'This is now one of my romance favourites. I am loving the ride I am on with Coral and Tristan. I'm so glad there's more to come!' **Barnes & Noble**

'This book pulled on my heart strings, can't wait to read the next one…' **Kobo**

'This is awesome!' **Kobo**

'This romance was very real, very raw, and very readable…' **Goodreads**

'I was totally involved from front to finish…' **Goodreads**

'A captivating, heartfelt and deeply intriguing story…' **Goodreads**

ALSO BY CLAIR DELANEY

Freed By Him
Darkest Fears Trilogy Book Two

Forever With Him
Darkest Fears Trilogy Book Three

A Christmas Wish
Darkest Fears Christmas Special Book Four

CONTENTS

Prologue	1
Chapter One	15
Chapter Two	24
Chapter Three	34
Chapter Four	41
Chapter Five	48
Chapter Six	58
Chapter Seven	66
Chapter Eight	76
Chapter Nine	85
Chapter Ten	95
Chapter Eleven	105
Chapter Twelve	120
Chapter Thirteen	133
Chapter Fourteen	153
Chapter Fifteen	167
Chapter Sixteen	179
Chapter Seventeen	194
Chapter Eighteen	210
Chapter Nineteen	224
Chapter Twenty	240
Chapter Twenty-One	269
Chapter Twenty-Two	288
Chapter Twenty-Three	304
Chapter Twenty-Four	319
Chapter Twenty-Five	340
Chapter Twenty-Six	368
About the Author	395

PROLOGUE

I WAKE UP IN MY BED - I am thirsty. It is dark outside. I rub my eyes and call for Daddy, but he does not come to me. Mommy is working at the hospital tonight, she is a nurse; she makes people feel better. I climb out of bed and walk along the hallway to Mommy and Daddy's bedroom. Daddy is not in bed. I hear Daddy laugh loudly, I like Daddy's laugh; it makes me smile. I'm not allowed to go down the stairs on my own in case I fall, but I want some water, so I stand at the top of the stairs.

"Daddy?" I shout.

Daddy does not hear me, so I hold on to the bannister as I walk down the stairs. I watch my feet as I take each step and when I reach the bottom I'm glad I didn't fall, Mommy would be upset.

"Daddy?" He still doesn't come to me.

The light is on through the gap at the bottom of the door. I walk over and push the door open. Daddy has a lady with her, she is sitting on the kitchen counter, she has her legs around Daddy, and he is kissing her – I don't understand?

"Coral!" Daddy turns, walks over to me and picks me up.

"I see what you mean," the lady says. "Eyes like the sea."

I don't like the lady she is looking at me funny.

"What are you doing up?" Daddy asks.

"I'm thirsty," I whisper – Why is the lady still looking at me?

"How old is she?" The lady asks Daddy.

"Four," Daddy says. I turn my head away from her and hide on Daddy's shoulder.

I put my thumb in my mouth and suck – it makes me feel better.

"Alright beautiful, water and back to bed." Daddy walks us over to the kitchen sink and fills my special cup with water, then he puts the special top on, and hands it to me.

I take a long drink, I am very thirsty. Daddy carries me out of the kitchen, up the stairs, and into my bedroom. He switches on my special lamp that glows orange, I like it a lot. He puts me into my bed and sits next to me. I drink some more of the water.

"Ok baby, that's enough." Daddy takes the cup off me and puts it on my dresser.

I look up at Daddy, his eyes look funny; they are red and squishy.

"Who is that lady?" I ask.

Daddy looks sad. "She's Daddy's friend from work. Now, no more sneaking downstairs from you young lady, it's time for bed." Daddy is a Salesman. I don't know what that means. Daddy pulls the covers over me and kisses me good-night.

I AM COLOURING IN the dinosaur pictures that Daddy bought for me. It is morning time, but Daddy is sleeping; he said he is tired. I am waiting for Mommy to come home from the hospital. Mommy said we can have pancakes for breakfast because it is a Saturday, and I don't have to go to Nursery.

I hear Mommy open the front door. "Mommy," I call out. Mommy comes into my room. She is wearing her Nurse uniform, she comes and sits next to me and strokes my hair.

Mommy looks tired. "Hey baby-girl, what are you doing in here by yourself?"

I look up at Mommy. "Daddy is tired."

Mommy looks mad. "Ok baby. Stay here for a minute and then we can go and make pancakes ok?" I smile at Mommy, I love pancakes. Mommy said we can only have them sometimes because they are not good for you. I don't understand. She says green vegetables are good for you, but I don't like them, I like pancakes.

I stop colouring - Mommy is shouting at Daddy, Daddy is shouting at Mommy. It makes me upset, they are always shouting. It makes me feel sad. I don't think Mommy and

Daddy love each other anymore. I hear crashing, and I cover my ears, the loud banging keeps going on and on. Mommy is crying and screaming at Daddy.

The door bangs open making me jump, I hide under my bed. I see Daddy walk past my bedroom. He throws a big bag down the stairs making it crash loudly at the bottom. Mommy and Daddy are shouting again, so I cover my ears. Daddy comes back, this time he has an even bigger bag; he puts it down and comes into my room.

"Coral?" He peeks under the bed and pulls me out. I try to stop him. Daddy scares me when he shouts. "It's ok baby. I'm not mad at you." Daddy hugs me hard, he is hurting me. "Daddy has to go away for a while," he tells me.

"Ok, Daddy."

He kisses me lots of times.

"I love you Coral, more than life itself, understand?" Daddy says.

"I love you too Daddy." Daddy kisses me on my head.

"Bye baby-girl. I'm so sorry."

"Bye Daddy." Daddy walks away and picks up his bag.

I AM EATING MY PANCAKES in the kitchen. Mommy is on the phone. She is speaking to my big sister Kelly, she is fifteen. She has a different Daddy to me. Mommy is smoking her cigarettes again and is drinking Daddy's wine.

"Kelly, I mean it. Come home now!" Mommy shouts and shakes her head. "I don't care what fucking rave it is, I have to work tonight. You need to look after Coral."

I don't like it when Mommy shouts, so I eat my pancakes.

Mommy turns and smiles at me, but I don't think Mommy is happy.

"Fucks sake Kelly, now or you're grounded for the rest of the year - Capiche?" Mommy slams the phone down.

We have a swear jar, sometimes I say the bad words that Mommy and Daddy say and I get into trouble. "Mommy, you said a swear word."

Mommy smokes more of her cigarette. "I know baby, naughty Mommy."

"You have to put ten pence in the swear jar like Daddy does," I tell her.

"Yes baby, I will," Mommy says.

MOMMY HAS GONE to the hospital. She has left me with my big sister Kelly. She doesn't like me. She scares me because she hits me when she is mad. Mommy made me Macaroni Cheese for my dinner. Kelly slams the plate down in front of me.

"Eat it!" she shouts.

I pick up my special fork and put some in my mouth. "Ouch!" I spit it out, it burns.

"God, you're disgusting!" Kelly slaps me around the head, hard. It makes my nose touch my Macaroni Cheese. It burns and stings so I rub it hard.

"Oh fuck this!" Kelly walks out of the kitchen. Kelly said a swear word, but I won't tell Mommy because Kelly will just hit me harder.

I am hungry. I blow on my dinner like Mommy showed me. I try again, but it's still too hot. Kelly comes back into the kitchen. She slams her bag down on the kitchen table. She is wearing a sparkly silver top and a little skirt. She's got lots of make-up on, her eyes are very black. She takes Daddy's wine bottle out of the fridge and starts drinking it.

Kelly looks down at me and starts laughing. "Well, at least you now know what it's like to be abandoned." Kelly drinks some more of Daddy's wine.

I don't understand - What is abandoned?

"You're on your own tonight little fucker. There's no way I'm missing this rave." Kelly grabs my hair. "If Mom calls, you tell her I'm in the bath, understand?" I start to cry, she is hurting my head. "Understand!?" she shouts.

"Ok." I fall off the kitchen chair. I bang my head and my leg.

Kelly picks up her bag, and I hear her slam the front door. *Mommy, Daddy, where are you?* I am scared, so I go upstairs and hide under my bed. I don't like being alone, the house makes scary noises.

When I wake up, my belly rumbles. I am hungry. I remember my Macaroni and Cheese. As I walk downstairs, I hold onto the bannister. I walk into the kitchen, it feels cold. I sit in my chair, my dinner is cold, but I am hungry, so I eat it. I go back to sleep after my dinner, I don't like playing on my own.

MOMMY WAKES ME UP. She looks tired, and her eyes are red, she is crying.

"Come on baby-girl, we have to go." Mommy picks me up into her arms, I am still sleepy. Mommy puts my coat on, and we leave the house. It is dark outside.

"Mommy, where are we going?"

"To the hospital," Mommy says.

I smile, I like going to the hospital with Mommy. She sits me in the car, puts on my seatbelt, and squeezes my hand.

"I'm sorry your sister left you on your own." I stare at Mommy, she is really crying. "Kelly is sick baby. She took something that made her bad, it's called Ecstasy, you must never take it. Do you understand?" Mommy shouts at me.

"Yes, Mommy." I am scared, so I suck my thumb.

We are in the hospital. Mommy is gone, but Nanny is here, and she is angry.

"Damn stupid girl." Nanny looks down at me. "Well let's hope you don't end up like Kelly eh? Although, the way things are going…."

I don't understand what Nanny means?

Mommy is in the corridor, she is walking slowly, and she is crying a lot. Mommy falls to the floor. Nanny gets up and goes to over to her, she shakes her head at Nanny, she looks really sad.

We all go home, but Kelly hasn't come home with us.

I AM FIVE TODAY. Mommy has brought me some roller skates, she says we can go to the park later and play with them. Daddy has been gone a long time now, and he hasn't sent me a birthday card. I don't think Daddy loves me anymore. I think it's my fault Daddy left, maybe I wasn't a good enough girl, maybe Daddy thought I was bad? I hope Father Christmas doesn't think I am bad, or he won't come either. That will make me very sad, just like when Daddy left. I like Christmas and presents. Mommy said Daddy might come to see me today on my birthday.

Kelly won't see me though because she is in heaven.

Mommy is on the phone, she is shouting, she has Daddy's wine in her hand and is smoking again.

"How could you-you fucker! It's her birthday…No…What!?…No you can tell her that!" Mommy calls me over. "It's your Daddy." Mommy hands me the phone, she puts it to my ear. "Like this baby," she shows me.

"Coral?" I hear Daddy's voice, I am sad he is not here.

"Hi Daddy, when are you coming home?"

"Happy Birthday darling, how old are you now?"

"I am five," I tell him.

"Wow, such a big girl!"

"Where are you, Daddy?"

"Working baby."

I don't understand. Daddy doesn't normally work on Saturday.

"Aren't you coming to see me, Daddy?"

"No baby-girl, not today."

I start to cry.

"Don't cry, baby. Put your Mommy back on." Daddy sounds angry.

I give Mommy the phone and go up to my room. I want to do some colouring in, when I do that, I don't think about Daddy or Kelly.

MOMMY HAS FOUND a babysitter for me. Her name is Jessica – I don't like her, she scares me. She smells funny and sends me to my room, and she doesn't cook me my dinner – I am always hungry. I don't think I like Mommy anymore either, she is mad all the time. I run and hide from her when she is trying to smack me.

I am hungry again. Mommy has been downstairs for hours now. I can hear the loud music and people laughing. I am still wearing my pretty, white frilly dress that I wore to Nursery, and I still have my shiny red shoes on. They are like Dorothy's in the Wizard-Of-Oz. If I click them together, I can disappear into a magical place just like Dorothy.

My belly rumbles again – it hurts. I go to find Mommy.

I walk down the stairs. The living-room door opens, and a man walks out, he is naked. Sometimes Daddy is naked when he comes out of the shower. He is tall like Daddy. He has lots of hair on his face and a furry body.

He smiles a big smile at me. "Well, well, well. What do we have here?" He kneels down to me. "And what is your name little one?"

I look down at my shiny shoes. Daddy said I shouldn't talk to strangers.

He takes hold of my hand, and he smiles at me again. "Are you scared?" I nod at him. He laughs loudly like Daddy. I smile back at him. "Well aren't you a shy little thing?" He looks at me funny and licks his lips.

He pulls on my hand, but I don't want to follow him.

"It's ok, come and meet my friend," he says.

I walk with him into the living room – Mommy is naked and asleep on a man. There are lots of people in here, some of them are kissing and doing other things. I can see a woman's boobies, the man has his hands on them. The music is very loud, and it is very smoky. The man pulls on my hand and sits down on the sofa, then he lifts me up and sits me on his lap, but he doesn't sit me down like Daddy does.

He puts his legs together and pushes my legs apart, so they are dangling from his.

I feel scared.

"John, watcha think?" He shouts.

Another man comes over and kneels down in front of me. "Wow, look at those eyes."

I suck my thumb – I don't like him.

"I know, and she's a shy one." The other man laughs.

"Even better!" He sits next to the man I am sitting on.

He whispers in my ear. "Shhh, you have to be quiet," he tells me.

His hand slides up my leg and under my dress. I don't like it. I want him to stop it. He puts his other arm around my waist and squeezes me tight. I can feel something long and hard pushing against my bottom. I shake my head and try to wriggle free. I want to run away, I don't like it.

The man starts to touch me in my private place.

No, stop it! I don't like it, let me go. Mommy!

I try to stop his hand, but the other man slaps my leg and

tells me to be quiet. It stings, he hit me really hard. The other man won't stop touching me.

"Oh, she's perfect." He says to the other man sitting next to him, he is breathing really loudly in my ear – *Leave me alone! Mommy, Daddy!*

I start to cry. I feel really strange, my belly hurts.

He sighs heavily and stops. "We have to tell Jessica," he tells the other man.

MOMMY IS TRYING to get me to put my white dress on, but I don't want to. I don't like wearing dresses anymore.

Mommy has Daddy's drink in her hands, but she keeps falling over.

Mommy slaps me around my face. "Put it on you little bitch!" She shouts.

I shake my head at her and suck my thumb.

"Oh fuck it, put what you want on." Mommy tries to walk away but keeps falling against the wall. When she has gone, I put on my dungarees and my favourite t-shirt. It has a picture of Super-Man on it. He can fly in the sky and out into space.

I wish I could fly away like Super-Man.

THE BAD MEN ARE BACK. I don't know where I am. Jessica brought me here today, Mommy is not here. There are lots of men and women here, watching. They are making me do bad things, I don't like it. The bad man has a video camera. He points it at me, and he makes me do things with a boy. I think the boy is scared. He won't do what they want, I tell him to, or they slap you hard. I am scared, so scared…*I wish Daddy would come home.*

The man with the hairy face is on top of me again, he has put something inside me. It hurts so much. He tells me I'm a *'good girl'* – I don't like it. He is heavy, his big hairy chest is nasty, and he smells funny. He hurts me so much. *Daddy where are you?…Please make him stop!*

I AM HOME. I have had another nightmare about the bad men and wet the bed. It is dark outside. I go to Mommy in her bedroom. Mommy won't wake up. I climb up on her bed and get under the cover. Mommy is sleeping on Daddy's side of the bed now. I close my eyes and suck my thumb. The sunshine wakes me up. I like the sunshine, it is happy, but I am scared and hungry. I don't feel very well, so I try to wake Mommy up.

"Mommy?" I try to shake her, but she won't move.

I climb off the bed and suck my thumb.

I stare at Mommy, she looks a funny colour, and she is cold.

"Mommy?" She doesn't open her eyes.

Daddy said if anything happened to Mommy or Kelly and he wasn't home, I should use the telephone. He showed me the number, I have to press 999 three times. I walk down the stairs, holding onto the bannister.

I pick up the phone and push the button three times like Daddy showed me.

"999, what's your emergency?"

"Mommy won't wake up."

"Oh!...Ok sweetheart, what's your name?"

"Coral."

"That's a pretty name. How old are you sweetie?"

"Five."

"Can you tell me your address sweetie?"

"Um…"

"It's ok, I can get it, stay talking to me, ok?"

"Ok."

"Where's your Mommy?"

"In bed."

"And where's your Daddy?"

I start to cry. "Daddy left."

"Ok sweetheart. It's alright, don't cry. I'm going to send someone over. Can you open the door for them?"

I shake my head. "I can't reach it," I tell her.

"Do you know your Daddy's number?"

"No, he's gone."

"Do you have any brothers or sisters?"

"Kelly is in heaven."

The lady makes a sad sound. "Any brother's?"

"No."

"What about Granny and Granddad?"

"Just Nanny."

"Do you know Nanny's number?"

"No."

"Ok, now listen to me sweetheart, the nice policeman is going to have to bang the door open, ok? Don't be scared, I'll stay right here with you."

"Ok."

"I'm going to send an ambulance too. They will take care of your Mommy."

"Mommy is a Nurse," I tell her.

"Is she?"

"Yes."

"Do you know which hospital sweetheart?"

"The big one," I tell her.

"Ok, keep talking to me Coral. The policeman is there, he's going to bang the door, ok?"

The door bangs loudly three times then it falls open.

I am scared, I suck my thumb.

Two big policemen come into the house - I don't want them to hurt me like the bad men did.

"Coral can you hear me?"

"Yes."

"Ok then, the policeman will call your Nanny and your Daddy for you now. Can you give him the phone?" I hand the phone to the policeman.

The other policeman tries to take my hand, but I don't want him to touch me.

"Come on sweetheart," he says.

"No!" I scream and try to run away, but he catches me and picks me up.

No! I don't like it, don't touch me...don't touch me...Daddy!

I AM IN THE HOSPITAL. There is a lady with me, and she is asking me all kinds of questions. She is very pretty. She tells me that Mommy is sick and I have to go and live somewhere else. She says she doesn't know where Daddy is, but Nanny is coming. Nanny is old and smells funny. I don't think she likes me. She is arguing with the nice lady. I want Daddy, but he doesn't love me anymore.

I HAVE LIVED WITH NANNY for a while now. I don't like it. My bedroom is cold, and all Nanny does is smoke and watch television, she won't play with me.

"Coral. Wake up." I open my eyes.

Nanny is dressed, and she has my bags packed. "Get up girl, time to go."

I brush my teeth and get dressed.

Nanny is waiting for me downstairs with another lady.

"You remember Gladys?"

I nod my head. Gladys has come to visit me three times. I don't think she's bad like Mommy.

"You're going to go and live with her," Nanny says.

I start to cry.

"It's alright sweetheart," Gladys kneels down and smiles at me, she has kind eyes. "I live by the sea Coral, would you like to come and stay with me for a while?"

I suck my thumb and shake my head.

"We can go and play on the beach," she tells me.

I don't know what the beach is.

"I'd really like you to come and stay, see if you like it." Gladys wipes away my tears with a handkerchief. I don't mind her touching me – I think she is nice.

"Ok," I cry.

Gladys holds out her hand to me, so I put my hand in hers. Her hand is big and warm.

It feels safe.

WE ARE TRAVELLING ON the train. Gladys tells me to keep looking out the window because I will see the sea soon – I have never seen the sea.

"Look Coral, can you see it?" I look out the window, and I see something big and blue. It is very sparkly, I like it a lot. It is very pretty.

I walk with Gladys from the train station.

We stop outside a big house with lots of pretty flowers outside.

"This is your new home Coral. Do you like it?" I look up at Gladys, she is smiling at me. I smile back. I think I might like it here. Gladys doesn't seem bad, not like Mommy.

Gladys shows me my room. It is pretty, and I can see the sea from my window.

"Are you hungry Coral?" I nod my head. "Come on then sweetheart." Gladys holds her hand out to me, so I put my hand in hers. It is big and warm.

We walk down the stairs into the kitchen. It is pretty with lots of flowers.

Gladys has made apple crumble and custard. It is delicious.

"Shall we go down to the beach?" Gladys asks when I finish my second bowl.

I smile and nod my head.

Gladys has another little girl, her name is Debbie. She is ten; she is nice to me too. I like her already. Gladys takes us both out to the beach, and we play all afternoon. I have never played on the beach before, I really like the sand and the pebbles.

Debbie shows me how to make sandcastles.

I like the sea and the waves, but it is cold and makes my feet tingle.

I HAVE LIVED HERE for a while now. Gladys is always nice to me. She is big and cuddly, and she smiles all the time. Debbie is my new big sister - she doesn't hit me like Kelly did. She is nice and shows me how to play new games, and is always happy.

Today I met a new lady called Joyce – she is Gladys' friend.

She has a man with her called John.

He tried to hug me, but I wouldn't let him.

Everybody got upset.

I ran into my room and hid under my bed.

Gladys came and talked to me until I was brave enough to come back out. She held my hand and told me it was ok, and that she wasn't mad at me. She said that she knew someone had hurt me and that I didn't need to worry anymore, because she would never let anything bad happen to me, ever again.

Gladys told me I will stay with her forever now if I want to.

I have never been so happy before.

I tell Gladys I never want to leave.

I think I love my new family.

But the bad men are still here.

When I go to sleep at night, they come into my dreams and scare me.

Gladys is always there when I wake up. She makes me feel a little better.

But she can't make them go away; she'll never make them go away…

CHAPTER ONE

IT'S THE START OF ANOTHER working week after a quiet, restful - if I'm honest; boring weekend. As usual, I am sat at my desk eating my bowl of muesli after my early morning swim. It's hard to imagine that I have been working here for so long.

It's fifteen years today since I first started here, and I can't believe how fast the time has flown by, but I love my job. It's all thanks to Gladys of course; she stood by everything she said to me all those years ago.

After being expelled from school, I studied at home, took my exams, then Gladys got me a position here as a legal secretary at Garland & Associates, one of the most prestigious Solicitors in Brighton, which just happens to be run by her best friend since school days - Joyce Garland.

Joyce is an awesome boss, and I have come to regard her as more of an Aunty, but that probably comes down to the fact that I see her on weekends as much as I do Gladys. They are firm friends and partners in crime and are so much fun to be around. They are like two naughty schoolgirls when they get together, drinking cocktails and joking about all the silly things they used to get up to in school.

I sigh inwardly. The last few months have been so hard, Joyce recently lost her husband. One day he's sitting in the garden with her eating his Chicken Caesar Salad, the next he's as dead as a doornail on the floor, heart attack wiped him out.

I don't think it's hit her yet; she was straight back into work the day after the funeral, said she didn't want to be rattling around at home, it's understandable I guess.

I suddenly feel my throat tighten up on me, the very thought of one day losing Gladys, which I know is inevitable grips me, and panic takes over. I close my eyes to try and push the feeling away, *Gladys is fit and healthy*, I tell myself.

Ever since that scare four years ago, she went crazy on exercise. She takes water aerobics at the local leisure centre three times a week, and has joined a local rambling club - so now she's always out and about.

Gone is the big, cuddly woman I used to know – who looks and acts just like Ma Larkin from The Darling Buds of May - now there's a slimmer version, but everything else about her has stayed the same – I hope I've made her proud.

Joyce walks into the office; she's been coming in earlier and earlier since John died.

"Morning Joyce." I smile up at her.

"Morning Coral." She looks tired. "Any messages?"

"Yes, on your desk. Just a couple, a Mr Freeman seems desperate to get hold of you?"

"Oh…good, that's…yes…" Joyce frowns deeply, smiles awkwardly at me, and then walks into her office, closing the door behind her.

Well, that was odd?

I jump up from my desk and knock on her door.

"Come." I tentatively walk in.

Joyce has been a little sharper with me lately, but I'm letting it all go, considering the circumstances.

"Can I get you anything Joyce?" I ask softly.

"Tea please, Coral, and get the boardroom ready. We need to cater lunch for five; they'll be here at 12noon." She orders.

Five? Who the hell is coming today? There's nothing in the diary.

"And when you've done that I need to speak to you," she adds.

Fuck! Panic washes over me –What if I'm losing my job or something? I mean I know the economy is shaky and everything, but…I can't lose this job!

I love working on my own, I love the peace and quiet, but most importantly I love working with Joyce. And it still feels like I just bought my very own apartment, my first place, even though I've had it a couple of years.

If I lose this job, I'm fucked!

"Of course," I answer and scuttle as quickly as I can out of her office.

I wander into the staff kitchen in a daze and prepare her pot of tea, trying my best not to let my worst thoughts go racing through my head.

When Joyce's tea is ready I walk back into her office without knocking - this is normally ok, considering I'm holding a tray - but she looks up and glares at me, halting her conversation on the phone.

I quickly place the tray down on her large mahogany desk and dash back out.

What the hell is going on?

I decide the best thing to do is get to the tasks in hand, take my mind off it all. I check the company diary and see the meeting room is free, so I block it off for the rest of the day. Then I call up the catering company and place my lunch order.

"Coral." Joyce's voice booms through the intercom system on my phone making me jump. I sigh inwardly. Like it or not I'm going to have to face the music. I quickly stand, brushing down my light blue suit trousers as I do - in an attempt to look as presentable as possible - and knock on Joyce's door.

"Come." I enter her large office, which is five times the size of mine and sit down on the chair opposite her.

Joyce is still typing, her fingers making quick work on the keyboard.

I close my eyes and take a deep breath in, trying to slow down my erratic heart, repeating the same mantra over and over in my head. *Please say I have my job! Please say I have my job!*

"Coral." I look up at Joyce and try to sit still. She looks every bit the strict boss I used to be so intimidated by. What with her glasses perched on the end of her nose, her shiny, short blonde hair immaculately styled, her suit a silver grey, her makeup impeccable. You would not think she had recently lost her husband of thirty years.

"Coral, I have some sad news." *Holy Fuck! No, no, no please don't say it!*

I swallow hard. "Ok," I manage to squeak out.

"I'm selling the company."

Selling the company!? No, you can't! What the fuck does this mean?

Joyce sighs heavily, leans back against her chair and stares out of the window for a moment. Then she looks back at me, takes off her glasses and leans forward onto her desk; I stare back at her my eyes wide with fear and try to swallow.

"Coral, I want you to know that your job is safe. One of the conditions, when I sell, will be that you keep your position. You have worked here for a long time, and you're an extremely valued member of staff," she tells me. "My most valued," she adds.

I am silent, dumbstruck. I feel all the chemical reactions one might feel to cry, but no tears come to the surface – I'm very good at blocking it out.

"I'm sorry Joyce." I offer, not knowing what else to say.

She finally smiles at me, but it doesn't reach her eyes.

"Coral, I am sorry I hadn't warned you earlier, but in all honesty…well, the offer has only just been put to me. I hadn't even thought about it until Mr Freeman made the suggestion, then I spent a few nights thinking about it. John and I built this company from scratch and…he's everywhere I look…," she says, choking back tears as she takes a handkerchief out of her clutch bag. "I'm sorry," she trembles.

For a moment I feel lost, I don't quite know what to say or do, she is my boss after all. Then I remember her singing and laughing with me on the karaoke machine last Christmas; we were all so happy.

I launch myself out of my chair and place my arms around her shoulders.

"Oh Joyce…I'm so sorry," I offer. I can feel her pain and hurt rolling over me like waves hitting the shore.

She squeezes my hand and closes her eyes, trying to gather herself together.

"It's for the best," she sighs. "My sister wants me to join her in Florida," she adds.

I smile back at her. "Maybe it's a good move," I say, but inwardly I'm freaking out. Joyce knows me; she knows what I'm like, what if my new boss isn't happy with the way I am?

"Yes, well that's what Gladys said, a new chapter in my life."

Shit! Gladys knows, and she didn't tell me!

I feel my jaw tense, and my teeth clamp together in anger.

"Now don't get that look in your eye," she scolds.

I frown in return. "Sorry," I mutter sitting back down in the chair.

"I only discussed it with Gladys this morning. She wanted to tell you, but I said I would." She leans back in her chair and runs a hand through her hair. "Coral, the deal hasn't been made yet. But that doesn't mean it won't go ahead. Mr Freeman is very keen; I need you to promise me you will keep this to yourself."

I swallow hard. "Is that who's coming in today?" I ask tentatively.

"Yes. Mr Freeman runs three very successful branches. One in London, Birmingham and Leeds. Apparently, he's been wanting to open a south based branch for a while now, and when he heard what happened to John, he made me an offer. A very good offer," she sighs.

I swallow hard again. *Don't panic!*

"Joyce, I really won't lose my job, will I? I mean, I've just bought my first place and with the mortgage' – "Coral, you have my word, you have no need to worry at all, but can you promise me you'll keep this between us?"

I sigh heavily – This was not what I was expecting when I came into work this morning!

"Yes Joyce, of course. I won't mention a thing." I try to pull my lips up into some semblance of a smile. "Well, I'd better get back to it. Do you need anything Joyce?" I add.

"No thank you Coral that will be all." I stand as gracefully as I can, my legs shaking from the adrenalin pumping through my system, and walk out of her office. *I'm so glad I have my training session with Will tonight; I am so fucking pissed right now!*

Closing the door behind me, I race over to my desk, fire up Google and start my search. I want to know what Mr Freeman looks like. I have to know, if he is in any way creepy I am out of here. I can't work for a pervert, and there's already a few male solicitors in this building that I purposely avoid. I try a deep breath in and out, but it brings me no relief. I am not happy, in fact, I'm trying so hard not to freak out - I have never wanted, and never will want a male boss.

Fuck, what am I going to do?

I remember the woman who called for Joyce was from the company Freemans & Co. I quickly type it in, and their website appears. I have no idea what Mr bloody Freeman looks like, so I search the website for some photos. As I'm scanning the webpage, I notice all the buildings are the same, white stone and tinted windows, very smart and business-looking.

I scowl at the screen. *Who gives a fuck what the buildings look like!*

Finally, I find his name – Tristan Freeman – *No fucking way!*

I gasp, pulling my hand to my mouth. Tristan and Isolde; only my favourite movie of all time. I love their story. I choke back a nervous giggle - *Get a grip Coral!*

I backspace out of the site and put his name into Google. There are tons of posts. I click on the first one; it's a page from The Independent. I start to read the blog...

'Millionaire Mogul Tristan Freeman in talks with the local council attempting to gain planning permission for his new offices in Leeds' – Boring!

I come out of that one, and see the blog was a few years ago, guess he got permission. The second blog is from a site called Property News. I click on it and find out Mr Freeman is not only interested in the Law, but also property development. I start reading...

'Mr Tristan Freeman is pleased to announce his decision to turn an undeveloped area of the city centre of Birmingham into bespoke apartments. The run-down area of Birmingham mostly abandoned warehouses; will be demolished and replaced with plush new apartments. But Mr Freeman insists they will be made affordable housing. "It is my belief that the more money generated into an area, especially a run-down area as this, has the capacity not only to reduce crime but to make the area a more pleasant environment to live in. Which means less poverty and more help for those who need it; it also enhances the general area, enticing other developers to join in its redevelopment.'

Hmm...so Mr Moneybags wants to help renovate poor areas, I wonder why? I shake my head in wonder. Why the hell are people so obsessed with getting rich? They always seem so miserable to me.

I backspace out of the blog and click on images. It's bound to have some photos of him. My screen suddenly fills with the most handsome man I have ever seen. *Fuck, this is not good!*

I pull my hand up to my constricted throat and try to

swallow. I click on an image; he's at some swanky black tie do, and his suit looks...well...totally and utterly 'wow' on him, and I don't think I've ever seen shoes so shiny. I am trying as hard as I can to be practical, logical, but the fact that my heart just stuttered, stopped then began beating rapidly again is not helping - It's only a picture for god's sake!

Damn, he looks fine!

I can see by his stance that he is oozing with confidence, his body looks rigid and hard. He's got to work out, surely. His shoulders just look too...well...big to be natural. And he's got to be at least 6ft - *Damn it, me and my tall men syndrome!*

I close my eyes and try to reign in my overactive imagination. Fuck he's hot, really, really hot, just the body alone – *Stop Coral!*

I open my eyes and zoom in on the photo. I want to get a good look at his face.

Jesus Age Christ!

I am breathless. He's male model swooning, dark knight, shining armour, handsome. I shake my head at my wayward thoughts and clear my throat. Then I take a deep breath, slowly blow it out and resume my ogling.

The first thing I notice is that he has the nicest, deepest chocolate brown eyes I have ever seen which surrounded by thick brown eyelashes. Which is weird, I'm normally attracted to blue eyes. And it's weird that I find them so, so...soulful?

His eyebrows are full, and his forehead is strong and smooth. He has a straight Roman nose, his cheekbones are high and pronounced, and his lips are full. They look very, very kissable. He also has the cutest little sticky out ears; he's totally endearing.

His hair is medium brown and styled into place to match the mogul that he is, and I can see he's recently been away, his slight tan showing a few freckles across his nose. The sun has also tinged his hair, showing natural copper highlights from where it's bleached it. *I wonder if it would be delectably soft if I ran my fingers through it?*

I backspace out of the photo and stare at all the different pictures of him. Then I notice something odd; he's not smiling at all, in any of them. His jaw is set; he looks as though he is grimacing. *There see, miserable bastards with tons of money!*

Maybe he has really bad teeth or something? I chuckle to myself. Bloody gorgeous though – *Stop Coral!*

I quickly get rid of Google, lay my head back in the chair and close my eyes. Taking a deep breath, I try to work out why I'm feeling like this. I decide it may have something to do with the fact that I haven't had sex in two years...I shudder, remembering the reason why.

I swallow hard at the bile that's trying to rise into my throat and blank the memory, the feelings, so in the end, I only feel numbness. But that's always been my way of dealing with things - block it out, repress it until it stops coming back.

Satisfied that the memory is gone, I open my eyes and sit forward at my desk. I dash a look across the room at the clock on the wall, only 9.15am. I am fidgeting all over the place, my leg is bouncing up and down, and as I look down, I realise I am chewing my fingernail. *Shit not good! Maybe I should see if I can get an appointment with George tonight?*

He's my therapist – my wonderful therapist. I shake my head at myself in frustration, this guy has got me feeling off the hook, all out of sync, and I haven't even met him yet!

I pick up the phone and call George, only to be informed by his partner Phil that he is at a function this evening. Otherwise, he would have fitted me in, but he can schedule me in for an earlier appointment tomorrow.

"No thanks, Phil I'll keep it at six," I grumble.

"Ok, you have a good day." He tells me perkily.

"You too." I put the phone down and pinch the bridge of my nose.

Come on Coral you can do this!

Rob, that's who I need, my best friend. My gay best friend, ever since my female best friend, Harriett, decided it was ok to be shagging the one and the only guy I ever fell for. I quickly shut the door on that thought, pull my mobile out of my bag, and text Rob.

In trouble big time, call me!

I leave my mobile on my desk and get to the rest of my work, which I have been ignoring for the last half hour. This is not me. I am fast, efficient and on time. I would normally have had all these letters typed up, signed by Joyce, and in the post by now.

This guy has got my head in a mess, and I don't like it.

I have to have control. I have to have a routine. I have to know exactly how each day is going to go, no hidden surprises. Boring I know, but I need predictability, I need stability, I crave it like a drug – *Control freak!*

CHAPTER TWO

AFTER TWO HOURS of typing and correcting the tons of spelling mistakes I have made, because I keep seeing a pair of dreamy chocolate eyes staring back at me, I finally wander into Joyce to get her signature and approval.

"Are you alright Coral? I know it's a shock, but you seem out of sorts." I shrug and try to smile. I have to remember compared to what Joyce is going through right now; my life is peachy.

"Really Joyce, I'm fine. A little shocked, but fine." I say trying to placate her.

"You're chewing your tips." She tells me.

I pull my fingernail out of my mouth. Old insecurities, I don't think they'll ever go away.

"Are you still seeing Dr Vickers?" Joyce knows this about me because she supported Gladys when she told her she wanted to adopt me. But I guess she didn't think she was going to get such a fuck up that needed constant therapy.

"Yes." I grimace.

"Maybe you should arrange to see him' – "I tried," I interrupt, feeling sheepish. "He's at a function tonight. I'll see him tomorrow, as usual."

"Good. In the meantime, my door is always open." Joyce smiles and hands me back the signed letters. I don't move from my seat opposite her. "Ok, out with it missy! What's on your mind?" I cringe at the fact that I haven't had to say anything, Joyce knows me that well.

"I was wondering...?" I squeak.

"Yes." Joyce cocks her head to the side.

"Mr Freeman. Well, is he...?" *Why can I never get the words out that I want?*

"He's a good man Coral. Apparently, his staff love working at his companies. He pays well; they have quarterly staff outings. Each of his buildings has a cafeteria, a gym, a swimming pool and free parking." She tells me.

I can't help feeling a little better; I love swimming.

"He's no ogre Coral; I think you'll find' – "I've never wanted a male boss Joyce, you know that." I snap a little more harshly than I should. "Sorry," I whisper feeling instantly ashamed.

"Coral." Joyce stands, walks over to me and taking hold of my hand; she guides me over to the sofa. "Sit." She orders and I do so. Joyce gracefully sits down next to me. "Darling girl," she tucks a strand of my hair that's come loose from my bun behind my ear. "At some point, you have to stop running and hiding from life. It'll get you in the end you know," she says with worried eyes.

"I just' – "I know you don't want a male boss, I won't say I understand why, but I think you should give him a go, at least try it for a while. I think he'll be good for you."

I look away from Joyce; she has no fucking idea why I don't want this – I swallow hard.

"Look, he's a hard worker. He'll expect the best from you, give him that and you'll be fine. I meant what I said Coral; you're the hardest working, most efficient, competent member of staff that I've ever had."

"Doesn't make it any easier," I sigh, feeling myself withdrawing. I just want to curl up into a ball and pretend like this isn't happening.

"Coral, life isn't always what we want it to be...I never imagined my life without John and now...' – Joyce takes a breath – 'point is, things come up that we don't expect and the true character of who we are is shown to us by how we deal with those situations."

I nod, knowing exactly what she means. George is always on to me to take more risks, more challenges - drives me nuts!

"Look, it will take some getting used to, I know that. But if you find after a few weeks it's not for you; I'm sure Mr Freeman will understand and work with you to find something else within the company."

I nod back at her. "I guess..." I murmur.

I must admit, I never looked at it like that. I suppose I could move to a different department, but I like that it's just Joyce and me, I don't have to make stupid, idle, same-o conversations with the rest of the secretaries and listen to them bitching about each other.

I like me and my thoughts - without any other invaders!

"Well, back to your desk Coral. They'll be here soon; we want to make a good impression."

"Yes, of course." I stand and walk towards the door.

"Coral," I turn and look back at Joyce. "Everything will be alright; you'll always have me to talk to, even if I'm in Florida."

"I know Joyce, thank you," I say and throw in a fake smile for good measure. I pull the door closed, lean my head back against it and close my eyes.

So, he's a nice guy huh? Yeah right, they always are until they show their true colours. My mobile buzzing on my desk pulls me from my musing. I dash over to it and see that it's Rob.

"Ola!" He cries in an absurdly Spanish accent!

"You, me, cocktails tonight at Iguanas – my treat," I say quickly and sharply.

"Who's got your knickers in a twist?" He titters.

An image of Mr Moneybags flashes in my minds-eye – *Fuck!*

"I'm sending you an image," I snap.

"Oh Goodie, is he hot, handsome and rich?" He chuckles.

"Yes, to all three, and my new boss!" I spit in defiance.

"What!?" Rob gasps - "Coral is the meeting room ready?" Joyce asks through the intercom.

"Damn, Joyce is calling me I have to go."

"What time tonight?"

"I have Will tonight, say 7.30pm?"

"I'll come to you first."

"Cool, see you later."

"Ciao!" Rob chuckles.

I hang up and answer Joyce. "All ready just waiting for lunch."

"They're leaving it a little late, aren't they?" She questions sounding concerned.

"No Joyce, they like to deliver fresh, and they haven't let us down yet. Don't worry they'll be here."

"But it's twenty-five to!" She argues, no doubt feeling nervous about the upcoming deal.

"I'll call them," I offer.

TEN MINUTES LATER I am following the two delivery guys from Lunch Ideas up the stairs and into the boardroom. *God, it's hot today!* I fan myself as I watch the two men place the trays of food down on the back table, then nod politely and leave. I turn the air conditioning on to help cool the room down then make my way back to my desk.

I call Joe on reception.

"Hi, Cori." She squeaks. She's nice, but a bit dim and always gets my name wrong.

"Joyce has visitors at 12, call me when they arrive?"

"Sure thing." She answers.

"Thanks, Joe."

"No problem Cori." *Grrr, why does she always call me that!*

"It's Coral Joe, I - never-mind." I sigh, then hang up and carry on with my work, and as I do, I remember to send the photo of Mr Mogul to Rob.

Two seconds later, my mobile buzzes. I check Joyce is still on the phone and open the text.

Delicious darling, don't eat him up all at once ;-)

Grrrrr, that's not why I sent it! - I open my top drawer, throw my mobile in and slam it shut in a temper. Then, deciding I had better take a quick pit stop before they all arrive, and to try and calm myself down, I make my way to the ladies.

Once I'm finished, and I'm drying my hands I take a good look at myself in the mirror. My dark brown hair is still pinned in place with a bun, as I do every morning. I'm wearing very little makeup; mascara, blusher and a little lip-gloss. I attract enough attention as it is without heavier makeup, but in all honesty, I have George to thank for that.

A lifetime of self-degrading, damaging thoughts can wreak havoc on the self-esteem. George has managed, somehow, to help me finally accept that I'm as pretty without makeup as I am with it, so I guess I'm getting better, bit by bit.

I sigh heavily and stare back at my reflection. My coral-blue eyes are wide and full of fear, like a deer staring at a pair of headlights. I have to wonder if it has anything to do with Mr Moneybags, with feelings that I know are trying to surface.

I mean, I have to admit it, I loved my ex-boyfriend Justin, probably to the point of obsessively, but he never knew how I felt about him. Always too afraid to show my real feelings, I kept my heart on my sleeve and the sleeve very tightly wrapped up. One of the reasons he fell into Harriet's arms was that I didn't let him in, I wouldn't let him get close to me.

Well, that's just tough. I can't operate any other way, take me or leave me I told him and well…he left – with Harriet. I shake my head at myself. *You cannot allow any man to get under your skin Coral, not ever, you hear me?*

I nod vigorously in agreement with myself, take a deep breath, square my shoulders and march out of the ladies.

I QUICKLY SCUTTLE BACK to my desk, sit back down and check to see if Joyce has sent any updates across to me – nothing! I feel agitated that I haven't got something to do to take my mind off things. My leg starts doing its involuntary jig; I clamp my hand down onto my knee to stop its rapid movements.

My phone rings, I look down and see its Joe from reception – *Fuck they're here!*

"Joe," I answer sharply, even though I don't mean it.

"Hi Cori, Mr Free' - "I know who it is Joe, I'll be right down." I snap, feeling annoyed she's getting my name wrong again and hang up.

Then I call through to Joyce to let her know they are here; she instructs me to show them straight up to the boardroom. *Crap!* Joyce knows I'm no good at this, meeting new people, especially men. I hope I don't have to shake hands with any of them. *Panic tries to grip me!*

I hang up, stand quickly, and march away from my desk.

If I keep moving, I'll keep calm.

I walk along the hallway, down the small flight of stairs and into the reception area. Mr Freeman hasn't noticed me; he's busy talking to some leggy blonde, all high heels and the tightest pencil skirt I think I have ever seen. I notice he's in a dark blue pin-stripe three-piece suit, with a light blue shirt to match, and a deep red tie.

I nod politely to the three other men who have noticed me and ignore the usual stares. *Yes, yes, it's just a face!*

Leggy Blonde smiles sweetly at Mr Mogul, and gestures that I have come to meet them, that's when he turns and looks at me - I instantly stop walking towards them.

I think my heart has relocated itself somewhere in my throat, and I have the strangest feeling spreading within me, like every single cell in my body has awoken. And there's this weird, magnetic pull – I feel as though my body is involuntarily being pulled helplessly towards him. *What the fuck is that?*

I frown at the floor and place my hand on my stomach – *Am I getting sick?*

As I look up, I see he is frowning deeply at me in the most peculiar way, and as we stare at each other, I'm overwhelmed with the strangest feeling of all - I feel like I'm finally home – *Whoa!*

I feel like my world has just tipped upside down. I shake my head slightly to try and get myself together, and when I do, I notice they are all staring at me, and then back at him in wonder. Especially the leggy blonde, she doesn't look happy at all. *Maybe she's shagging him?*

His eyes narrow for a moment, his gaze intense, I feel like he can see straight through me. He clenches his jaw, then walks graciously towards me.

Oh God, my legs feel like jelly! I can't breathe!

"Coral?" His voice is low and husky, yet soft.

"Yes," I answer breathlessly. *Why is my heart beating so erratically?*

"Tristan Freeman." He holds out his hand for me to shake it – *Shit!*

I hesitate for a moment, frightened by the prospect of it, it's almost as if I know that if I do, that will be it, that this will be the end of life as I know it. I look down at his hand, shakily reach out and place my hand in his. His breath catches with the contact. My eyes shoot up to meet his, and I'm surprised to see his eyes widen, his chocolate eyes growing darker in colour – *Ok, that's weird, what is that?*

A strange, wonderful, exhilarating feeling is raging through my system, making all coherent thoughts disappear, except for what it would feel like to have his lips brush against mine - *Fuck, this isn't good!*

Looking away from him, I try to pull my hand out of his, but he just tightens his grip. My eyes shoot back up to his - He's triggering my flight response, and he doesn't even know it. *Please let me go!* I beg internally, and almost as though he can read my mind, he drops his hand and takes a tiny step back.

"Forgive me," he murmurs. *Holy crap, his voice is so silky, yet deep and manly.*

I nod my head and turn to look at the rest of his team. I can see they're all amused and trying hard not to show it, which annoys me.

I clear my throat and finally find my voice. "If you would all like to follow me, I'll show you to the boardroom." I'm answered silently by smiles and smirks, except for the Leggy blonde who is glaring at me – *What's her problem?*

I turn around and try not to march away too quickly - as would be my usual response to anyone who threatens my equilibrium - but as my right foot takes the first step on the stairs, I notice he's at my side, taking the steps at the same time as me. I instantly get a whiff of aftershave and something else – but I can't work out what it is.

He smells so good!

I take a cautious look across at him, just as he looks at me – *Fuck!*

We both look away as quickly as we can. I feel like a complete idiot! *Oh, Rob's going to have so much fun with this, I know he is.*

"Did you know Mr Garland well?" *What, did he just ask me something?*

As we reach the top of the stairs, I stop and look up at him. Leggy blonde has to take a step around me, so she doesn't bump into me.

"Sorry?" I answer a little bewildered.

"I asked, did you know Mr Garland well?"

I frown at the reminder. "Um yes, John was like an uncle to me."

His eyebrows shoot up in response. "An Uncle?" *Was that a question?*

I guess I better explain. "Joyce, Mrs Garland, her best friend is my adoptive Mother." I offer feeling myself pale a little. "We all spent a lot of time together," I add.

"Ah," his frown deepens. Then he turns from me and stares straight ahead as though he's deep in thought. "My condolences," he adds.

I nod, look away from him and continue walking down the hallway, only this time I don't stop. I silently walk all the way up the first flight of stairs and straight into the boardroom. I check everyone has what they need, tea, coffee etc. and try not to watch as Mr Mogul takes his suit jacket off, revealing the body I pretty much thought would exist.

I quickly turn to leave so I can let Joyce know they are ready and waiting, and so I can avoid Mr Moneybags. He's a complication I do not want or need.

"Coral…" His voice stops me. *What does he want?*

I feel my legs go to jelly again. I slowly turn and look up at him.

"May I accompany you?" He politely asks.

I frown and nod silently to him. *Please leave me alone, oh this is not a good start, not a good start at all!* We walk silently down the stairs, turn to the left and head towards my desk.

"This is where you work?" He asks looking around the room.

It's a nice room with a big bay window letting in lots of light. Ok, it's old and nothing like his buildings and simply oozing with wonderful architecture, but I love it, I love its charm. Built in the 1820's this three-story house was bought by John and Joyce with a view to converting the first floor to offices, which they did, and used the next two floors as living accommodation.

As the years went by the company grew, and eventually, the whole place was converted into office space. With the added perks of two bathrooms with showers, a large rest area with comfy sofas and a big modern kitchen, Joyce likes to eat fresh every-day; and there have been plenty of occasions when someone has had a big case on, and they have slept at the office.

"Interesting." He murmurs, then turns and smiles at me - *Holy mother of God!*

His teeth are perfect, as is his smile.

I think he's finding my gobsmacked expression amusing

because his grin widens, making his nose and eyes crinkle in the most delectable way, which makes me catch my breath. I quickly sit down in my chair before my legs give way. *Jeez, I could stare at that face all day.*

"Coral?" I hear, rather than see Joyce standing in her doorway, but I can't take my eyes off Mr Mogul.

"Err…yes. Sorry Joyce, Mr Mo' – *Shit!* – 'Mr Freeman wanted to see' – "Joyce, how are you?" he interrupts, saving me.

I watch him greet Joyce, softly kissing each of her cheeks and I'm amazed to see a slight blush appear on her cheeks. *So, it's not just me!*

As I sit there, totally mesmerised by him, I'm drawn to the track that Classic FM has started playing – James Lasts, Cavalleria Rusticana Intermezzo – It's one of my favourite classical pieces. I close my eyes for a moment, imagining myself dancing and swaying with Tristan, as his strong arms hold me close to his delectable body. Which is weird, I've never thought about dancing with a man before - but who am I kidding!

Yes, I want something mind blowing and amazing, especially with someone like him, but it's not on the cards for me, I realised that a long time ago. People who are in love are open, intimate, they are not afraid to show their vulnerability to each other, and that, unfortunately, is something I cannot and will not ever do - It's too scary even to begin thinking about.

I push the stupid thought aside, and as I open my eyes, I see they are talking in hushed voices. Tristan is holding Joyce's upper arms, and she has her hands resting on his forearms. Joyce suddenly glances across at me, interrupting my melancholy thoughts, and giving me a look that speaks volumes. Great, now I'm in trouble for not *immediately* telling her that he was here!

This day just keeps getting better!

I scowl at my keyboard, wiggling the mouse to wake up my desktop and pretend that I am typing something, they move closer to me.

…. "Of course," he coos. "Coral showed me." He smiles at Joyce then at me.

I look up at him not wanting to seem like I'm rude, and plaster a fake smile across my face – *I will never go to heaven, no way, hell has a seat waiting for me!*

"Shall we begin?" He asks and holds out his arm for Joyce.

How Gentlemanly of him - How old school!

"Thank you, Tristan." Joyce places her hand in the crook of his elbow, as he leads her past my desk, I can tell she's putting on a brave face. God, this must be so hard for her to do. I wonder whether John would be happy with what she's doing?

"Coral." I look up at Joyce. "The meeting may run late, but you can still leave at five."

"Are you sure?" I answer my voice a high octave.

I swallow hard and attempt to get my normal voice back.

"Yes, I have sent across what needs completing." I nod, knowing my inbox may be overflowing, but I welcome the work, anything to take my mind off what's happening.

"Of course, Joyce, I'll get right on it."

I really, really try not to look at him, at his solid manly body, but as he walks away, I find my head involuntarily craning over my desk to try and get a good look at him.

Damn, he is one fine specimen!

CHAPTER THREE

I AM DEEP IN WORK, trying as fast as I can to get all the letters typed up for Joyce when my mobile starts buzzing in my top drawer. I quickly pull it out and see that it's Debbie, my adoptive sister. She's blonde, bubbly and flirtatious, and she hasn't got a care in the world – I spent most my childhood wishing I could be more like her.

"Debs," I answer briskly.

"Hey trouble, how are you?"

"Good, busy," I answer abruptly.

"Just called to remind you, its Lily's birthday party this weekend," she says.

Damn it, forgot about that!

Debs married Scott ten years ago, and despite my reservations, they are still together. They had Lily five years ago; she's spoilt but sweet.

"Of course, I remember!" I offer as innocently as I can. *Shit, what am I going to get her?*

"Ok, well it starts at 12noon, Saturday." Oh God, a garden full of screaming five-year-olds, I have to take Rob with me for my sanity.

"Can I bring Rob?"

"Of course, you can," she sniggers. "No new man on the scene then?"

"Debbie," I growl - *I don't need this right now!* She's always on at me about moving on from Justin; she has no fucking idea about anything, which winds me up even more!

"Ok, ok! I'll shut up!" She sniggers some more.

"So what kind of thing is a five-year-old into nowadays?" I casually ask.

"You haven't got her anything?" She barks.

"Um...no, not yet, I was going to ask you about it." I retort.

"You forgot!" She snaps.

"Did not!" I snap back.

"What's up with you? You're not your usual self?" She asks half-heartedly.

"Nothing...I'm fine, just busy," I snap again, feeling agitated she caught me out.

"Coral?" She drawls.

"I'm fine!" I huff.

"Ok, just asking. Right then, as far as Lily goes anything that's Arts and Crafts, she loves making things."

"Oh, ok, well that's easy enough. I'll go shopping on my lunch tomorrow. I'll call you to make sure I don't duplicate anything."

"Roger that. Lily misses you we haven't seen you in ages."

"I know, I've just been really busy with the move."

"Coral, that was two years ago!" She bites. *Ok, so I'm a crap aunty.*

"Debs I'm sorry, it's just...' – "Justin?" She interrupts.

"Yeah..." I sigh in agreement, although it's far from the truth.

I hate lying, but it's easier this way. When Justin and I were together, we spent a lot of weekends with Debs and Scott. They became pregnant not long after the split, and even though it's been more than five years, it still brings back memories of him; and I will avoid anything or anyplace that does that.

"That bastard!" Debs spits.

"I know," I sigh.

"It'll get easier," Debs says.

"Ya think?" I answer sarcastically.

It annoys me when she says things like that, Debs has never had to endure heartache, she met Scott at College twenty years ago, and they've been together ever since.

"Ok smartarse, I'm going, see you Saturday," Debs says.

I grit my teeth in frustration - I hate taking things out on her.

"Sorry Debs," I whisper.

"Don't worry about it." I can tell she's smiling.

"Talk tomoz?" I ask.

"Yep, see you." I hang up, put my mobile back in my desk drawer, and continue with the tasks at hand.

IT'S 5.20PM, AND I'VE JUST finished typing up the last letter for Joyce. I print it off, add it to the pile, take them into her office and place them on her desk, ready for her to sign. While in their, I stop for a moment and take a look around the large room. It's going to be so strange not seeing Joyce here every day. I'm going to miss her so much.

My stomach twists with anxiety at that thought. I know this is going to take its toll on me, at least for a while. I make a mental note to ask George to schedule me in for two sessions a week. I don't think one session is going to be enough with everything that's going on - I don't do change well.

Feeling melancholy, I head back to my desk, shut down my computer and throw my bag over my shoulder ready for the long walk home. As I head down to reception, I see that Joe has already gone. I smile and wave at Tom, the security guard, and push the double doors open to the outside world. *Whoa! It's hot!*

I didn't realise how nice it had been out today, and at that moment I am thankful I am wearing my strappy wedges, I don't think my feet would take the heat in stilettos. It's been an unusual summer so far this year, especially for the UK. Last year all we had was rain, rain and more rain, this year though, it feels like the sunny days are going to keep on coming. I smile at the thought and find my Oakley sunglasses out of my bag (a present from Gladys for my 30th last year) and slip them on.

As I start my usual walk down Eastern Street, I find my Cowon MP3 player out of my bag and pop my headphones in. Despite what's happened today, I feel summery, so I choose Rihanna.

Diamonds start pumping through my ears, and as I keep walking, I pull the pins and hair band out of my hair and run my fingers through it - it feels so good to be out of the bun - finally letting it cascade down my back and across my shoulders.

As I pick up walking speed, I feel the warm breeze blowing through my hair and across my skin. I take a deep breath in, the intoxicating combination of city traffic, the food from the cafés and pub's, and the smell of the sea make me smile.

I love this place so much.

As I look up above me, I see several seagulls circling the café's just waiting for their opportunity to get some more food – *Gannets!*

I feel a sudden rush of excitement knowing I am out tonight with Rob; we always have such a good time together, and I know he'll help me make sense of everything. If there's one thing Rob's good at doing, it's not taking life too seriously, and I do he tells me, way too seriously.

Just as I'm passing the County Hospital, I have a strange creeping sensation come over me, making all the hairs on the back of my neck stand on end. I frown trying to work out why I'm suddenly feeling like this; when I notice in my peripheral vision that a shiny black car is slowly crawling next to me, I can hear its throaty engine bouncing off the tall buildings.

Someone is stalking me, holy crap!

My heart starts rapidly beating, my hands start to shake, and I feel a cold layer of sweat cover my body. I try to swallow but my throat is tight, and my mouth feels like all moisture has been extracted from it – *Fuck!*

I wonder whether I should dash to the nearest store and hide until it disappears? But that will make me late for Will - he doesn't do late - being ex-Military makes you very disciplined about timekeeping.

Shit, shit, shit what should I do?

I think of George's words of wisdom, *'face the problem head-on, don't keep running'* so I take a deep breath and stop walking, turning slowly to see if the car stops too. But when I turn my head, the last thing I expect to see is Mr Mogul sat in a brand-new Jaguar F-Type. I instantly know it's the V8 5.0 litre, supercharged model. *Damn bastard, he has my dream car!*

He stops the car, having no reservations about holding up any traffic, yet he just sits there, roof down, aviator sunglasses on, looking as sexy as hell. *Oh no!*

I swallow hard and turn to walk away, but he holds his hand up in a sort of weird wave thing, he looks dead serious, his jaw set, his brow furrowed. So, I replicate his action, turn around and continue walking at an even more hurried pace, desperate to get away from him.

I expect to see him pass me, there's not much traffic to stop him, so when he doesn't, I decide to be brave. Taking a quick peek behind me, I see he's pulled into a parking space and is getting out of the car, and he hasn't taken his eyes off me.

Oh, holy crap! What does he want?

"Coral!" I hear him shout my name over Rihanna blasting in my ears, and because he's soon to be my new boss, I feel I have no choice but to stop and turn to him.

I stand stock still watching him approach me, a man of purpose and poise, his steps determined. He is every inch the cool, confident alpha male - *No doubt gazillionaire!*

But I can't help feeling annoyed and antagonistic towards him. *Why can't he leave me alone?*

I have nothing to give him.

Finally, he reaches me, stopping about a foot away. It's like he knows not to invade my space, then he takes off his aviators. I take one of my headphones out, push my sunglasses up onto my head and look up at him, not knowing what the hell to say.

"You have lovely hair," he offers. "You should wear it down more often; it suit's you like that." *Ok, that threw me. I wasn't expecting that at all.*

"Um....thanks," I mumble, quickly looking away because he's making me feel shy and exposed.

"Sorry," he frowns. "I didn't mean to make you feel'– "Did you need something, Mr Freeman?" I interrupt. *Will's going to kill me!*

"Don't you have a car?" He asks throwing me again.

I frown back at him - *What the hell has that got to do with him?*

"No." I sigh and wrap my arms around myself. My foot starts tapping involuntarily.

"Would you like a lift?" He asks, his voice high pitched and light, though his face is still deadpan.

I try as hard as I can to hide the fact that I would love nothing more than a spin in that racy little number, but I know it means he will see where I live, and I don't want him to. So how do I say thanks but no thanks, without it coming out wrong?

"No thank you, I like to walk." There, that should pacify him.

"Do you have far to go?" His expression looks bleak as he scans the street ahead.

What is his problem?

"Why?" I ask, frowning up at him.

"I just thought..." He stops, and runs a hand through his hair, he looks...frustrated, lost for words maybe, I don't know.

"I need to get going," I tell him. "I have an appointment."

His eyes pop open in wonder. "An appointment?"

"Yes."

"Where is it?"

"Excuse me?"

"Maybe I could drop you there?" He offers warmly.

"Um no, it's ok thanks, I have to get home first."

"Please, let me take you?" He says, his expression torn, his eyes penetrating all the way down to my dark soul. *What the hell is with this guy?*

Then it dawns on me, there is a possibility that Joyce has told him a few things about me. Maybe he is being generous and polite because he wants me to see he's a nice guy, and nice guys make sure you get home ok.

Well I don't need or want that, I have lived in this city since I was five and nothing bad has ever happened to me, except for that one incident, and besides that, I feel safe here. I am safe here. I don't need anyone looking after me. I can look after myself!

"I'm fine Mr Freeman," I say, staring down at the ground.

"Tristan, call me Tristan..." He says.

I look up into his warm chocolate eyes feeling mesmerised for a moment.

"Ok...Tristan." I get a very odd feeling as I say his name.

"So, no lift?" He asks again.

I shake my head at him.

"Maybe another time?" He questions lightly.

I shrug my shoulders, not knowing what to say to that. *You're going to be late!*

"I have to go," I tell him. "See you."

He nods his head in defeat.

Turning quickly on my heel, I scurry away, quickening

my pace as do, then I pull down my sunglasses and pop the headphone back in. As I'm speed walking away from Tristan, I wonder for a moment if he's still stood there watching me walk away.

I glance behind me and see he's getting back into his car. *Phew!*

My player flips to the next track - Stay, one of my favourite Rihanna songs. I listen to the words and think how ironic - they are reflecting my emotions completely. I like Tristan Freeman – a lot. But there's no way anything can ever happen between us. Besides the fact that he's far too good for the likes of me. But deep down on some subconscious level, I want him to stay.

Then, just as Rhianna sings the chorus, I see his car cruise slowly past me, my steps falter, I sneak a peek at him, but he doesn't look up at me, and I'm instantly flooded with a feeling of dread. *Oh god, what have I done? He's my new boss, and I've pissed him off! Way to go Coral!*

Then I'm hit with the strangest, bleakest feeling - that in reality, I did want to get in that car, and that watching him drive away without even looking back at me was like being stabbed in the heart with a knife. Like losing something I never even had in the first place. I clutch my hand to my chest and try to ease the strange aching sensation.

What the hell is this guy doing to me?

CHAPTER FOUR

I FINALLY REACH THE END of Eastern Road and make a right turn onto Arundel Street, then left onto Marine Drive, then I make a U-turn and start zigzagging my way along Marine drive until I finally turn right at Undercliff Walk. Passing Marina Car Wash I give a wave to Rob's friend Pete, he's been working at the Car Wash for two years now and always gives Rob a discount.

I think they like each other, but Robs been married since he was twenty-five. He simply went abroad for two weeks to Spain and came back with a gorgeous Spanish man in tow called Carlos; they married a couple of years later. I love him as much as I love Rob; they are perfect for each other.

I happened to meet Rob a couple of years ago when he came wandering into the gym with a swollen black eye. We got chatting straight away, and he advised me of being jumped on by a gang of pissed-up men. I told him about my personal trainer Will, he teaches combat training incorporated with boxing; and now he's Rob's trainer too. It's hard work, but confidence building and definitely worth the effort. My body looks leaner than it has ever done, and I no longer worry when I'm walking the streets alone. I know I can take care of myself.

When I reach the steps taking me down to the Concourse on Brighton's Marina, I can't help but smile. I still can't quite believe I own my property. I mean yes, I had to live with Gladys for a long time, and I had to save like crazy to get here, but it was so worth it.

It seems like it took forever to get here, but every time I got miserable about it, Gladys reminded me that it would all be worth it when I finally put that deposit down. Besides, she refused to let me rent; she said it was money being flushed down the toilet. She did the same with Debs too, let her and Scott live together in the house saving up all their wages, all we had to contribute to was food; Gladys took care of the rest; she really is the most wonderful woman I have ever known.

As I walk along the sundeck towards my floating studio, located on the Western Concourse in Brighton's Marina Village, I'm reminded of the look on Gladys's face when I said I wanted to buy the property...

"But it's a floating studio darling; It's just so tiny," Gladys says as she scans the tiny living-room/kitchenette.

"But I love it, Gladys; it's right on the water."

We turn in unison and look at the stunning views of the Marina, and the boats lazily bobbing up and down on the water.

"It is lovely," she anxiously agrees. "I just think you could get so much more for your money."

I sigh heavily and follow her back outside.

"Coral, it looks like one gust of wind and the whole thing will come crashing to the ground." Gladys looks up and down the long stretch of yellow and white studios neatly packed together. I think there's about fifteen all in all.

"You don't like it?" I say, my voice sounding sad.

"It's not that," she says. "They look like they're made out of corrugated cardboard, such an eye-sore," she adds – I chuckle because I don't care what it looks like, but she is right, from the outside they don't look so great – I'll give her that.

"Yes, you're right, they don't have curb appeal, and you don't get much for your money, but I don't have much choice." I remind her.

"Stay with me for another couple of years' – "No!" I bark, interrupting her.

I need my own place. I need my independence. My 29th birthday is only two months away. I don't want to be still living with Gladys by the time I hit thirty – It's too depressing to even think about.

"Gladys, we've spent three months searching now, how many studios have we looked at?" I question. I've lost count.

"Lots darling," she says looking up at the structure.

"Point is, for one hundred and twenty-five grand, I don't have much choice. It's either here, or a dark, dingy studio in town. Gladys, we both know if I choose town I get traffic all night, drunken idiots making loads of noise, or trains going by every five minutes."

She's nodding in agreement, so I carry on.

"All the studios we have looked at don't come near this place. I don't want to live in a dark, dingy place in town; some of them have been so awful..." *I stop talking because Gladys is tapping the outside wall in confusion. Why I don't know, she knows nothing about construction and neither do I.*

"I'm surprised they sold at all," I mumble to myself.

I wait for what I have said to sink in with Gladys. I mean yes, this place is tiny, but it's so light and airy and has wonderful views. The air is fresh from the sea every morning, and it's quiet, really, really quiet and peaceful. But most importantly, I feel safe here, and Gladys knows how important feeling safe is to me. But then it hits me that she'll probably be like this whatever place I buy. She worries about me and is no doubt feeling a little sad that I'm moving out, just as I am.

I walk over to where she's standing and wrap my arms around her waist. "I know this is tough for you," I whisper and hug her tighter.

Gladys wraps her arms around me and squeezes me tight, kissing the top of my head. "I'm going to miss you so much," she chokes.

"Me too," I offer. "But I won't be far away, and you know I'll be home on Sundays for one of your Roast Dinners." I smile broadly at her, hoping her opinion is swaying.

"You really like this place?" She questions.

I nod frantically at her. "I feel safe here Gladys, it's so quiet and peaceful, and you know how much I love boats and the water, it's idyllic. Plus, I have the gym and the supermarket, so you know I'll never go hungry and I..." I stop for a moment, a blast from the past igniting my memories. "We used to spend hours down here when I was little," I add, feeling some of those old emotions resurfacing.

God...I felt so lost back then. I still do if I'm honest.

"Yes, we did, you even loved it back then," she says, gazing warmly at me.

I nod in agreement. "I need you on my side with this Gladys. I need to know you're ok with it and that you're happy."

"Oh, darling girl, if you're happy, then I'm happy." Yes!

"Thank you, Gladys." I kiss her cheek, clap my hands together in glee, and run off to find the agent...

AS I REACH MY STUDIO, I pull my keys out of my bag and unlock the patio door that looks out at the Marina. Walking inside, I'm instantly bowled over by the heat sapping at my skin, making my hair feel damp and sweaty.

Whoa! It's only the beginning of July, and it's already scorching!

I smile to myself as I think about my upcoming birthday in August. I must ask Gladys if we can have a barbeque at hers. She loves entertaining, and she especially loves Rob and Carlos, she knows they are good guys and take care of me.

I turn and dump my bag and keys on the sofa, and head up the tiny staircase to my bedroom that has an open gallery view of the lounge. I quickly strip my work clothes and put them straight into the laundry basket - If there's one thing about having a small space is that it makes you tidy, even when you don't want to be!

I open the built-in wardrobe doors and find my clean training gear. I quickly dress in my full-length Lycra leggings, my support bra with extra support - if there's one thing that's totally annoying about having large breasts, is them bouncing all over the place when your training - and pull my training vest over the top.

Slipping my feet into my trainers, I take a quick look in the mirror. I see a toned, fit, 5ft 4ins curvy woman looking back at me. *God, I'm such a short arse!*

My mind wonders for a moment if I'm actually Tristan's type. From all the photos on Google, he seemed to have tall, leggy blondes hanging off him, not short arse brunettes. I shake my head at myself, find a hair tie and scrape my sticky hair up into a ponytail.

Once I've opened the bedroom window to let some air into the place, I run back down the stairs and fill up my water bottle. I know I'm going to sweat buckets tonight, so I better make sure I'm hydrated, especially as that's one of Will's bug-bares. Then I open the downstairs bathroom window, leaving the door open, so it helps the breeze flow through.

When I'm satisfied I'm ready, I pick up my gym bag and pull it over my shoulder. Picking up my MP3 player, I pop the headphones back in and make my way out onto the sundeck. My next-door neighbour Bob is sitting at his little table, his head buried deep in his newspaper. He's been living here since they built this place. He's old, sweet and winds me up a treat sometimes, but I really get along with him.

"Hey, Bob," I call out.

"Evening Coral," he answers but doesn't look up from his paper. It always makes me smile.

"Beautiful day," I offer.

"It's hot!" He moans.

I smile and shake my head at him. "See you later Bob," I shout.

"You off out again?" He whines.

"The gym," I say smiling at him.

"Don't think so," he teases. "Not with your keys still sat on the sofa." *Shit, my keys!*

"How did you' – "Nothing gets by me young lady." He looks up over his newspaper and smiles, tapping his nose at me. I never do things like that. *What's wrong with me?* I think I know the answer to that, but I am not going there.

I smile back at him, but it's forced, then I head back inside and pick up my keys, shaking my head at myself as I do. As I come back outside, I decide it's probably best to leave the patio door open as I'm sure it will be baking by the time I get back.

"Hey, Bob," I say.

"Yes." He drawls the word out slowly. I can't help chuckling.

"You mind keeping an eye out? I want to leave the patio door open."

He looks up from his newspaper, looks me up and down, then he scowls at me. "Why d'ya spend so much time at the gym Coral? Your figure looks just fine to me."

"Well, it's not really the gym," I answer. "It's combat training." I know this will get his attention.

"As in military training?" he asks, putting down his newspaper.

I figured Bob to be in his seventies when I first met him. I was so shocked when he told me he was ninety-three, and that he was twenty when he was drafted into the second world war. He's as fit as a fiddle for a man his age.

"Yes, and my instructor doesn't like it when I'm late, so I'd better go." I walk over and kiss him on the cheek. "Thanks, Bob, I owe you one." I look down and see he's gone as red as a beetroot.

"Go on, you'll be late," he says, ushering me away.

As I turn and wave goodbye, I make a mental note to invite him to Lily's birthday party, he doesn't get out much, and I want him to have some fun.

AS I HEAD WEST ALONG the concourse, I take out my MP3 Player and hit shuffle. Puddle of Mud starts playing Blurry, the words hitting me sharply, reminding me of Justin and how I fucked it all up by not being open and honest and well, *'emotionally available'* George calls it.

I grit my teeth in anger at myself for being this way, but I know that's not good for me, so I take a deep breath and try to be positive about it all, to do what George tells me to do, and look at it as a learning curve. I sigh inwardly; sometimes I think I'm getting better, then I think of the fact that I haven't had a date in five years - well apart from that one – I stop walking and steel myself.

Don't think of it, block it out!

It takes a while, but when I'm satisfied the horror of that night hasn't entered my mind, I continue walking. The truth is, the split with Justin hit me hard and made me withdraw even deeper into myself. Because for me, Justin was the closest I've ever got to someone - well as close as I can get to someone.

I opened my heart, eventually, and he got a knife, stuck it in, and ripped it open by doing the one thing he told me he would never do - cheat on me - which triggered all my trust issues all over again.

But when I really think about it, when I go into the deepest darkest part of my soul, and I ask the same question over and over again - Do you want to be alone? - The answer is that I don't, I hate it, but I just can't get past my demons, my fears, my insecurities.

I know I'm standing in my own way, but it's like I'm hitting my head against a brick wall. I want to feel deeply connected to someone. I see it all around me, people happy and in love, but the fear of being hurt, lied to or abandoned, take over the fear of being alone. George calls it a vicious circle, one that only I can break, but I don't know if I'm even ready to, or even willing to do that - So this life I have will have to do - for now anyway.

Feeling melancholy from running it all through my head again, I take a deep breath and decide to run it out. As I pick up my pace, I quickly reach the steps up from the concourse and jump them two at a time. I pace even harder as I head past McDonald's, its greasy smell wafting through my nostrils, I don't know how anyone stands to work in there all day, it would drive me nuts.

Healthy eating has been part of my regime for as long as I can remember. I'm good 70% of the time and semi-naughty for the rest. I learned long ago from Joyce that food can affect moods, and I try everything I possibly can to keep my moods balanced and in check.

I turn the corner and eye the prominent David Lloyd Leisure club. I slow my pace down and walk across the car park to the entrance, pulling open one of the glass front doors, I walk straight in and head to the gym department.

I locate Will chatting with one of his colleagues, he glares at me when he sees me, but quickly finishes his conversation and walks over to me. His 5ft 10ins, slim, extremely toned stature stands in front of me, his dark brown eyes and shaved head make him seem extremely intimidating.

He crosses his arms and stares down at me. "You're late." He states.

"Yes." I smile, trying to placate his mood. "My boss kept '–
"No excuses Coral." He holds out a hand to shut me up.

"Sorry." I offer.

He shrugs nonchalantly at me. "It's your time." He snipes.

"Well let's get to it then." I march away from him and turn to see a slight smirk appear on his face.

CHAPTER FIVE

THIRTY MINUTES IN AND I'm already flaked out. Even though this place has air conditioning, it still seems so hot. Will and I are busy practising combat moves when I swear to god out of the corner of my eye, I see Tristan go speeding past the ceiling height windows – wearing only a pair of swimming trunks. His hair is soaking wet, his muscles rippling as he walks...*Oh!*

"Ouch!" I cry out as Will slams me down onto the mattress. I feel all the air leave my lungs.

"Where's your head at?" He shouts. *Jesus Christ Will, calm down!*

He pulls me up by my hand, my feet leaving the floor for a moment.

"Sorry," I mumble back.

"Coral, how many times do I have to tell you? An attacker ain't gonna wait for you to be ready, you need to have your head in the game at all times." I pull my hand around to my ribs where I hit the floor, I feel winded. "Ok, that's enough." He barks.

"What?" I screech.

"I dunno where your heads at, but it's not here. Go home Coral, I'll see you Thursday."

"No!" I shout stamping my foot on the floor. "I need this Will, especially today. Please just...can we just do some bag work, or sparring...please?" I plead.

He stands staring at me with his hands on his hips. "Alright," he says shaking his head as he walks away.

I follow Will to one of the sparring mats, he starts putting on his hook and jab pads. I dash to my gym bag and pull out my boxing gloves, getting them on as quickly as possible.

We stand face to face. Will has his arms down by his sides, the moment he raises one of them, that's the one I'm supposed to hit. He lifts his right hand and with lightning quick speed, I launch into an overhead, right-hand hook.

Pushing all my body weight against it, I slam my fist into the pad.

"Good," he shouts. "Again!" ...

An hour later and we are finished. I feel exhausted. Although, I know a quick cold shower will invigorate me so I can get out and down a couple of yummy cocktails with Rob, then hit the sack. I say goodbye to Will, and he seems in a better mood than earlier. I think he realised in the end that I needed to get rid of some pent-up frustration.

As I drag my tired ass back home, my belly starts frantically rumbling, reminding me that I haven't eaten since breakfast. I must remember to have a snack at Lag Iguanas. One the many reasons I work out so hard, besides from wanting to protect myself, is that I love food - except when Moguls are buggering up my lunch pattern and making me forget to eat...

HALF AN HOUR LATER I have showered, and I'm sitting on my bed with my towel wrapped around me, staring into space... *What is wrong with me?*

I should be getting ready, but I feel immobilised by the pair of dreamy chocolate eyes and full lips that keep pouting at me, pulling me in – *God damn it!*

I am pulled out of my reverie by a knock on the patio door. I hear it slide open and panic for a second, then I hear Rob's voice call up to me.

"Are you decent darling?" He shouts.

"Yes!" I shout down to him, chuckling as I do. Feeling relieved, I throw my towel on the floor and pull my summer robe around me. His footsteps come barrelling up the stairs, and when I see him, I notice he's looking very summery tonight.

He's wearing a light blue cheese-cloth shirt, baggy dark blue jeans and a pair of dark blue flip-flops. He's mixed race, but more like his mother, very light skin, yet he has his father's height. At 6ft 3ins he seems to tower over everyone, especially my short arse, and to make him look even taller he's skinny to boot - well not so much skinny now he's done all that training with Will - but he still looks really slender to me.

In fact, now that I can study him, I'd say he's lost some weight.

"I have no idea how you live in such a tiny place." He states collapsing onto my bed.

"Knackered?" I ask, knowing he's just spent a week in London with the most awful woman he has ever met. Rob's an Interior Designer; he's got himself a fantastic reputation and charges a fortune to anyone wishing for his simplistic, yet beautiful designs.

"God, she was a fucking nightmare!" he scowls. "Changed her mind every five fucking minutes, it was hell on skates! I could really do with this tonight. I need to let off some steam." He turns on his side and eyes me sitting on the bed next to him, my hair still dripping wet.

"You're very sweary tonight." I smile.

"Yeah well..." He frowns deeply then starts picking at the throw he bought me. "This is for winter you know," he tells me.

"Yes, I know. I've been taking it off every night."

"Well, why don't you just put it away?" He bites. I look around the room as though I'm trying to find something that is lost; he rolls his eyes at me.

"You know, I think I would, only I can't seem to find a spare cupboard to put it into," I say sarcastically.

"Come on!" He snaps again, jumping up off the bed. "I need a drink, hurry up and get ready woman."

"Hey," I stop him from walking away from me. "There's wine in the fridge, and some tequila left from last Saturday if you feel you need an instant hit. Although I'd prefer if you told me what's really wrong?" I stare up at his face, he smiles weakly at me, but I can see the pain behind his black eyes.

"Carlos and I..." He stops talking and shakes his head.

I gasp and bring my hand to my mouth. "You haven't?" I whisper hoping beyond all hope they haven't split. I have never known them fall out or go through hard times. They really are perfect for one another.

"No, but let's just say it's not going so well." He sits on the edge of the bed and sighs deeply.

"Oh, Rob!" I sit next to him, put my arm around his shoulder and squeeze as tightly as I can, feeling my heart constrict for him. Then I take his hand in mine and squeeze that too. "Have you tried couples counselling like I said about?"

He smiles awkwardly at me. "No, but I think Carlos is finally willing to try it. He says he doesn't want to lose me, but he just keeps snapping at me and being really argumentative, it's not like him."

I smile, feeling relieved. They'll work it out, I know they will.

"Hey, chin up mister. You'll get through this." I offer.

Rob snorts with laughter. "Says she who doesn't date or have a significant other!"

I cock one eyebrow up at him.

That was a low blow, and it hurt.

Of course, Rob doesn't know my real reasons for my behaviour towards men, he just thinks I had my heart ripped out by some cheating scumbag, and well I did, but...

"Hey, I'm sorry that was uncalled for. I'm just feeling all stressed out." He says flying his hands around.

"Get us both a shot Rob. I'll be down in five." I say, still feeling wounded.

I watch Rob walk away. The moment he does, I throw my robe to the floor, pull on a pair of boy shorts, then my white linen trousers, followed by my strapless bra and my mint-green camisole. I rummage around my cupboard, find my matching green wedges and slip my feet into them.

Then I roll my deodorant under my arms and spray myself with my favourite perfume - Absolutely Irresistible. As I wander downstairs with my wet towels, I notice Rob isn't in the lounge, he's outside talking to Bob. I spot the two shot glasses sitting on the side, then quickly shoot into the bathroom and hang up my wet towels.

When I turn and catch my reflection in the mirror, I stare at myself for a moment, coral blue eyes encased in thick dark brown lashes and eyebrows. High cheekbones, full lips, decent nose. And the same question is raised again. *Who would want you?*

I quickly look down to the sink and try to push the thought aside. I hear Rob and Bob laughing outside, and it helps me focus on the now, on getting ready for tonight.

Taking a deep breath, I look up and decide that my wet hair can air-dry; it's far too hot to use a hairdryer. So, I grab my coconut oil off the side, squirt some into my hands and scrunch it into my hair. As I pull my head back up, dark silky waves fall across my shoulders and breasts. *Yep, that will do.*

Next, makeup! As I lean forward, I see I have a few stray eyebrow hairs - I pick my tweezers up, and I'm about to pluck away when Rob comes into the bathroom.

"Stop!" he squeals.

I pull my hand away and stare back at him. "What?"

"Darling you know what your skins like, you pluck now, and you'll have bright pink brows for the rest of the night!" I chuckle remembering the last time I met him at Iguanas and had plucked before leaving, he almost had a heart attack when I approached him. He thought I'd been attacked by some beauty salon newbie.

"What, so I should just leave them?" I question.

"Here, let me see." Moving closer he takes my face in his hands and starts inspecting the stray hairs, pulling funny faces as he does, making me laugh out loud.

When he's done, he stops and looks down at me. "Leave them!" He shouts, throwing his hands in the air. "Onwards darling, onwards - Hurry with the makeup!" he teases and leaves the bathroom doing a little dance.

I really giggle at him, then turn to the mirror and frantically begin applying a little blusher, some mascara and some nude lip-gloss. When I'm done, I walk back into the lounge and stand next to Rob who has my shot glass in his hand. He toys with me for a moment, moving it each time I reach out.

"Rob!" I scold.

"Here." He chuckles handing one to me.

"Cheers," I say tapping his shot glass.

"Cheers. To wild cocktail nights and sexy men!" He chuckles, exaggerating each word, as though he's about to get the most passionate night of his life, then knocks his shot back.

I chuckle hard, still myself and take the shot in one.

"I've ordered the taxi," Rob advises. *Damn it! I forgot to do that, where's my head at?*

I think I know the answer to that, I immediately shut down that line of thinking.

"Great," I reply, still shivering from the tequila hit.

"Right, ready?" Rob asks.

"Yep, got bag, got keys," I say shaking them in the air.

"Condoms?" He snorts. I look up and see he has a ridiculous grin spread across his face.

"Rob!" I slap him lightly around his bicep with my little carry bag.

Then I check everything is as it should be and walk outside. Rob follows me out, and as I lock the patio door I can feel the slight buzz of alcohol kicking in – *Whoa tequila!*

I turn and link my arm in Rob's, and we walk back along the Concourse towards the gym. It's been a tradition ever since we became friends. Sometimes, when I see people looking at us, I'm sure they think we look like a couple in love, well, that is until Rob does something totally gay with his hands or his body movements.

As we reach the Gym car park, we see Will leaving for the evening and wave to him as he gets in his car. A black cab pulls up, Rob gives him his name and opens the door for me and just as I'm about to get in, I'm momentarily spooked again when I think I hear Tristan's V8 engine rumbling.

I quickly search the multi-storey car park opposite us and the roads, but there's no sign of him. I suddenly feel really glum – I'm about to question why, but I don't want to go down that road because I think I know the answer – *Pandora's box Coral, don't open it!*

I nod in agreement with myself and step into the taxi.

As we make our way west on the A259, I watch all the people out and about enjoying the warm summer evening, the sun sparkling against the sea, the boats lazily bobbing about out on the ocean. I suddenly get that warm holiday glow flow through me, I just can't get used to the lovely weather we are having. I usually freeze with the slightest of breezes, but tonight - I don't even have a coat, which makes me feel even more summery.

"Can I ask you something?" Rob asks, interrupting my mellow thoughts.

"Sure." I turn and smile at him.

"You don't have to answer if you don't want to."

I immediately feel defensive. "Shoot," I say. It can't be that bad, right?

"It's just something I've always wondered about you?" He turns and looks at me, his eyes wary.

"What do you want to know Rob?" I ask a little defensively.

"Well…it's just…you never wear skirts or dresses, and I think you'd look really pretty." He says.

I am silent. *Breathe Coral!*

"And you have great legs," he adds.

I snort with laughter at that one. "I don't think so, chunky legs maybe."

Rob rolls his eyes at me. "You have really great muscle definition Coral, they are not chunky." He scolds.

I shake my head in disagreement.

Rob huffs at me. "What is it with women nowadays and self-esteem?"

"Maybe it's all the tall, skinny, fake looking models plastered all over magazines and billboards?" I blurt out.

"That's not the everyday woman, and blokes know that, well, real blokes do. Take Sam for example." *Huh?*

"Who?" I ask.

"Sam, one of the painters I use. His woman is all curves, she's got to be at least a size eighteen, and she's got boobs the size of melons." He says, his hands held out explaining how big they really must be, I chuckle loudly. "Real men don't want match stick women." He adds.

I raise my eyebrows at him and grin widely. I love Rob when he's like this, he raises my self-esteem, makes me feel normal.

"So…?" He drawls, waiting for my answer.

I feel myself lock up, inside and out. How do I tell him some fucking pervert changed all that for me? That I can't physically put a dress or skirt on without feeling utterly vulnerable, and shaking from head to toe.

"Um…well I… just…" I shake my head, unable to answer him.

"It's ok." Rob takes my hand and squeezes it tight. "You don't have to answer. I can see it makes you uncomfortable."

I squeeze his hand back and stare out the window, trying my best not to remember the past, and what they did to me.

As we reach the roundabout and take a right onto the A23, I turn to my right and eye Steine Gardens, I don't think I've ever seen so many people in there. Having evening picnics, walking with their dogs, kids still up playing in the sunshine; it's just lovely. We continue along the A23 then turn left onto Church Street, the bars, pubs and cafés are alive with people sitting outside having a good time, getting as much of the English summer as they can. As we turn right onto Jubilee Street, my enthusiasm for the coming evening escalates, I'm practically jigging up and down with excitement.

Finally, we pull up outside Las Iguanas. As Rob pays the driver I look up at the cream coloured building, it's all lit up and looking pretty inside, drawing in passers-by with its warmth. Initially, it's a South American contemporary restaurant, with a mouth-watering menu consisting of a mix of Latin American, Indian, Spanish, Portuguese and African influences. I always have such a hard time choosing what I want, it all looks so yummy. As I step out the taxi, Rob takes hold of my hand, and we walk through the doors. *Whoa!*

The smell of the food as you walk through sets your taste buds on fire, smells so good! And it really does feel as though you are being transported to Rio.

We are instantly greeted by the seating hostess. "Hi." She beams.

"Evening." We both reply and smile.

"I'm Shelly. Just a table for two?"

"Yes." Yet again, we answer at the same time and turn to chuckle at each other.

As we follow Shelly to our table, I notice the Latin type music that fills the air; it makes me want to do some salsa dancing. I've been thinking about doing that for a while now - something else to fill up my lonely evenings - *I wonder whether I should ask Rob to go with me?* Then I think it's just taking up more of his time away from Carlos, and I really shouldn't be doing that at the moment, so I put it on the back-burner for now.

"There you go." Shelly shows us to our seats and hands our menus to us. "Your waitress tonight will be Chloe, she'll be with you shortly." She adds and leaves us to it.

I open my menu, but I can't help looking around the restaurant, I love this place and its atmosphere. The interior is all soft glowing red and orange lighting, with dark wooden flooring contrasted with cream and red walls. The tablecloths are crisp and white, the seats are plush and comfortable, and the entire floor is dotted with small palm trees here and there.

Moments later a young girl appears. "Hi, I'm Chloe your waitress tonight. Can I get you guys a drink while you browse?" She asks.

"Definitely," I answer dryly.

Chloe checks her watch. "You can still order happy hour if you do it in the next five minutes." She says with a wicked glint in her eyes.

Rob and I turn to each other, the last time we did that we were both as pissed as farts by the time we left. "Oh, to hell with it, let's get hammered!" He says.

I shake my head and laugh at him.

"Great, what would you guys like?" Chloe asks.

"Pitcher or glass?" Rob asks me.

"Pitcher," I answer, knowing what I'm about to do is a bad idea - I don't do hangovers and work the next day - But tonight, I need to let off steam.

"What do you fancy?" He asks.

"You choose," I say, unable to wrap my head around the choice.

Rob peruses the cocktail menu for a moment then makes his choice. "We'll have a pitcher of the Iguana Cosmo."

I quickly read through what it is; Absolut Berry Acai Flavoured Vodka, triple sec & pomegranate juice with a squeeze of lime and a dash of grenadine.

"Coming right up," Chloe smiles and walks away.

I look up at Rob with wide, affectionate eyes for my best friend because he's chosen one without any kind of soda; he knows I don't drink that stuff.

I bump my shoulder into him. "Thanks." I grin.

"What for?" he chuckles.

"Picking one without soda," I exclaim.

Rob rolls his eyes at me. "Hurry up and chose your food," he orders. "Or we'll be here until midnight," he adds dryly. He knows me so well!

I chuckle and start perusing the menu, it all looks delicious. Chloe quickly returns with our first pitcher and two glasses. Rob pours a glass for us both and hands one to me.

"Cheers," he says raising his glass.

"Cheers," I reply, and we clink glasses.

I tentatively sip the cocktail; it's not one I've tried before. My taste-buds suddenly come alive with the sweet flavoured vodka and the tanginess of the lime.

"Mmm...delicious," Rob beams.

I nod in approval and take two more gulps. I want the alcohol to start swishing around my system. I need it to relax me and make me forget today.

CHAPTER SIX

TEN MINUTES INTO looking at the menu, I still can't decide what to order, and Chloe has come back twice to ask if we're ready. I know Rob is getting frustrated with me, but every time I think I've made a decision, I keep thinking of Mr Mogul and the way I felt when our eyes locked. And each time I do, my stomach does a backward flip, making my appetite completely vanish.

Chloe appears again. I sigh inwardly and look up at Rob, Chloe starts chuckling to herself, evidently finding us amusing.

"Shall I come back?" She asks smiling at Rob.

"Do you know what you want?" Rob asks sharply.

I shake my head, feeling guilty for not making a decision.

"Oh, for god's sake woman!" Rob looks up at Chloe. "Right, we'll both have the Chicken Breast Fajitas," he orders.

"Sure." She smiles and walks away.

"Hey, I wanted a salad," I argue.

Rob shakes his head at me. "You need more than salad if you're drinking," he admonishes.

I shrug, I guess he's right.

"So?" Rob beams and turns around to face me.

"What?" I ask slightly bemused and take a long draft of my cocktail.

Rob cocks one eyebrow up and gives me a look that says you wanted to come here tonight. I look into his wise eyes, being five years older than me I have always felt as though he's my older brother, protecting me in whatever way he can.

"Oh....that!" I answer, suddenly feeling deflated.

"I can't believe Joyce is selling up, so suddenly as well?" He says drinking more of his cocktail.

"Yeah...it totally sucks," I answer gloomily, and give him a summary of my talk with Joyce; he's listening intently. "Joyce knows I've never wanted a male boss...." I add, drifting off as I think about Mr Mogul's eyes again.

"Hello?" Rob moves his hand back and forth in front of my face trying to bring me back into the here and now.

"Sorry..." I mumble, frowning deeply.

"Well, her leaving isn't going to change by the sounds of it," he tells me. "You've just got to suck it up and do your best. If it doesn't work out, you'll soon find another position somewhere else."

"Really?" I squeak, taking another long drink. "With the economy the way it is, companies aren't really hiring, and I love where I work, I like not having to commute, and that it's so close to home." I take another long drink, then continue.

"I like...well everything about it, working on my own...and Joyce has been wonderful to me. Now that's all going to change, and I don't do well with change." I grumble, feeling my stomach start to tighten.

Rob takes hold of my hand. "Coral, you're a smart young woman, you'll figure it out. I know you will." He softly says.

I shake my head in disagreement. "I don't even know who I'll be working for! I mean, I know Joyce said I keep my job, but what if I'm stuffed into the main secretarial area? We both know what a bunch of women are like when they are put into a room together," I spit. "Constantly bitching about one another," I add my hand flying in the air, my voice getting more high pitched as I continue to rant. "Or worse still, I get a slimy male boss!"

I'm really not a people person.

Rob sighs heavily and tops up our cocktails. "Look, you don't even know if that's going to happen, do you?"

"No, but' - "So, right now you are unnecessarily worrying about things that haven't even happened yet." I drink more of my cocktail as I digest this information. "You might stay where you are and get another female boss for all you know, problem solved." Rob takes another drink. "You've got to stop panicking about stuff that hasn't even happened yet Coral, you'll give yourself a heart attack!"

I sigh again. "I guess..." I answer and take another long drink.

"Ok, so now that's out of the way, you want to tell me what's really going on?"

I take a deep breath and another drink of my cocktail, at this rate I'll be too pissed to eat.

"Is it this guy?" He asks softly, I close my eyes and nod freely. "Ok, so what about him?"

I shrug, unable to find the words I want to say.

"Oh...he's really got under your skin!" Rob wisely surmises.

I stare back at him with wide eyes - *How the hell does he know that?*

"How do you' - "You're off your food, your day-dreaming, I'd say you've got it pretty bad." He chuckles.

My stomach rolls just thinking about it, I suddenly feel really queasy.

"Hey," Rob checks me. "You ok?"

"I don't want to like him," I whisper.

"Tough." He answers unsympathetically.

"Well, thanks." I snap sarcastically.

"Coral!" He admonishes.

"Sorry." I squeak, feeling guilty for snapping at him. "I just...he's...the moment I saw him, Rob, I just thought wow, and then he turns and locks eyes with me and this weird feeling..." I rub my stomach remembering how it made me feel, and drift off again as I relive the moment.

"Sounds like you've fallen bad for him," Rob suggests.

"No," I answer petulantly. "I can't, he's my soon to be boss," I hiss.

"So?" Rob scoffs.

"You know he stalked me today?" I say, trying to change the subject.

"What!?" Rob almost spit's his drink out.

I tell him about the car, about Tristan stopping and talking to me, then the fact that I thought I'd seen him in the gym. I brush my hand over my ribs remembering, it still hurts.

"What?" Rob asks. I pull up my camisole, and there's a slight bruise the size of a small breakfast bowl against my ribs.

"Ouch!" Rob exclaims.

"Yeah," I grumble. "I got that when I thought I saw him walking past' - "Oh Shit!" Rob gasps interrupting me.

I look up and see that he is staring at the front of the restaurant.

My eyes inadvertently follow his, and who should be walking into the Restaurant but Mr Mogul himself, with Joyce on his one arm and leggy blonde on the other.

"Bollocks!" I hiss, a little too loudly.

The couple on a date sitting near us turn and look at me, I mouth 'sorry' as an apology and smile weakly at them. They don't look very impressed, but both turn away from me.

"What the hell is he doing here?" I hiss, trying to hide behind the palm tree that's a couple of tables away.

"Eating a meal by the looks of it," Rob answers dryly, looking totally relaxed as he drinks more of his cocktail.

"Oh, ha fucking ha!" I snap. "Why hasn't he gone home? I'm sure his business is all done here." I blurt.

Picking up my cocktail, I down the rest of the glass in one go. Which was not a good idea - I think I have brain freeze.

"Wow, Coral...I see what you mean..." I look up and see Rob is mesmerised as he watches Tristan walk across the restaurant – *Holy crap!*

"Rob!" I admonish, staring at the side of his face but he doesn't turn and look at me. I sigh inwardly and stare down at the table trying to gather myself together.

"Uh-oh!" Rob whispers, sniggering to himself.

"What now?" I snap, feeling totally harassed and agitated. I look up and see Rob waving, then I look across the room and see Joyce waving back – *Fuckety fuck-fuck!*

"Wave Coral," Rob says, smiling broadly. *Ah, Crap!*

I wave back, plastering a fake smile on my face. Then Joyce turns and starts talking to Tristan, pointing over to us as she does.

"Please don't come over here," I whisper in desperation, closing my eyes as I do.

"Alright, guys." I open my eyes and see Chloe stood in front of us with our meals, then she places them down.

"Thank you." Rob beams in appreciation. "I could eat a horse," he adds licking his lips.

I stare down at my plate; my appetite completely vanished and watch as Rob makes his first fajita up.

"Are they coming over?" I whisper, hearing the tremble in my own voice.

Rob turns and looks at me, concern written all over his face. "You want to go, just say the word," he says in-between mouthfuls. "We can get a pizza on the way home," he adds.

I try to act nonchalant, but my head is buzzing with alcohol and irritation.

"No, no. It's ok...I just..." I close my eyes to assess how I'm really feeling – all my fears kick in, and I know leaving is exactly what I want to do.

In fact, I would quite happily run full pelt out of this restaurant, leaving Rob behind. But deep down inside, I know I can't keep running from situations in life that I find threatening, this is what George and I have been working on for a while now.

I sigh inwardly, trying to block out all negative emotions and begin rolling up my first fajita. Just as I'm about to take my first bite, I look up and see a man's body standing right in front of the table where I'm eating, and I know instinctively it's Tristan's. He has the same suit trousers on, the ones that make his legs look long and lean.

I swallow hard and drop my fajita onto the plate.

As my eyes drift up, I see he has discarded his suit jacket, red tie, and waistcoat from earlier today. The crisp, light blue shirt he's wearing looks clean on, and he's rolled the sleeves up to his elbows. As I search higher, I stop breathing and freeze because Tristan has the top three buttons of his shirt undone, revealing a little of his toned chest, and as far as I can see, there's not a single chest hair – My biggest trigger!

I can't help looking further up at his face. Our eyes meet. He really does have the deepest, sweetest, most hypnotic, chocolate eyes I have ever seen. I cannot look away.

He smiles warmly at me, his eyes crinkling at the corners; making little dimples appear in his cheeks. I hadn't noticed those before, they're cute. And for the first time I see he's probably older than me - forties maybe?

"Good evening Coral." He holds out his hand to me. I don't smile back at him, I don't want to give him the wrong impression, but I take his hand and shake it, feeling that same surge of electricity as I felt earlier today; if anything, it feels stronger.

I clear my throat, relocate my heart to my chest and exhale. I hadn't realised I'd been holding my breath. "Tristan," I say more breathlessly than I want to.

He lets go of my hand and looks from me to Rob, but my brain just isn't firing right. Rob quickly stands, extending his hand to Tristan.

"Rob Delgado," he says, Tristan takes his hand and shakes it.

He must realise Rob is gay, yet it's making no difference to him, which pleases me immensely. There are so many straight guys out there that think they are less of a man if they are associated with gay guys, or back away because they think it's a disease they might catch or something. Yet, Tristan seems really relaxed about it, he seems really nice – *Stop Coral!*

"Tristan Freeman, I know you by reputation of course." He says to Rob.

"Well, that's good to know," Rob replies, simply glowing from head to toe. Sitting back down he glances once at me, his look says it all.

Yeah, I know he's pretty damn fine!

"Coral, would you and Rob like to join us?" Tristan asks politely.

What the hell is with this guy, he's all alpha male virility, walks like he has total confidence, should be a control freak, yet he seems…sweet and well mannered. Is that at all possible?

"Yes' – "Thank you," I blurt, stopping Rob. "But' – "You're going to say no to me again, aren't you?" He smiles widely at me, his dimples deepening.

I feel something deep within me flutter madly – *Damn it, stop smiling like that!*

I blink twice trying to get my brain to work again. "I'm sorry, it's just Rob is my best friend," I explain, my voice a high-pitched octave, I clear my throat and continue. "We haven't seen each other in a while and' – "Don't worry," he smiles. "I understand. You want to relax and have a fun evening out together."

He looks back at his table, my eyes inadvertently follow. Joyce and leggy blonde seem to be hitting it off together. Tristan turns and looks back at me, his expression intense; his deep frown marring his lovely features.

"I'm sure the last thing you want to be talking about is work," he says frowning deeply. He sighs heavily and looks down at our table, his eyebrows knitting closer together, then he looks up at me and something...something strange and silent passes between us, but I have no idea what it is. *Whoa! What was that?*

I squirm uncomfortably in my seat, I don't know why I'm having this reaction to him. He stares down at the table for a moment, and I don't know why, but I actually feel sorry for him. It's as though he's trying to subliminally tell me something. But what? Maybe work is all he does? Maybe he doesn't have any friends? Maybe he never gets to blow off steam and have a good time?

"Well, enjoy your evening." He says forcing a smile across those amazing lips.

"T-thank you," I stutter and hold my hand out to him.

We shake again. I feel the strange current run through me once more, his lips part as his gaze holds mine for a moment, and I wonder if I'm having the same effect on him as he is with me. His deep frown returns as we stare at one another.

I squirm again, this should feel wrong. I should be yanking my hand out of his, but I don't want to. I want to stay like this, and that scares the living hell out of me. I don't understand why it feels so right? No man has ever made me feel like this – *Jeez, I really need to see George!*

Releasing my hand, his eyes briefly bore into mine once more.

"Rob, it's been a pleasure," he says pulling his gaze away from me, they shake again. "Do you have a card? I may need your services in the not too distant future."

Rob's eyes sparkle with delight. *Rob!*

"Sure." His eyes light up even more as he digs his wallet out of his back pocket and hands Tristan a business card.

"Thank you," Tristan says, placing the card in his wallet. "Have a good evening." He nods once, his frown still creasing his eyebrows and forehead, then turns and walks away.

We both turn and silently stare at each other, Robs look says it all. He so would if he could.

I can't help the nervous giggle that escapes me. "Don't say a word!" I gasp, trying to figure out what that was all about.

I suddenly feel stone sober, all the alcohol I have had seems to have vanished out of my system. "Let's eat and leave," I say, all the blood draining from my face.

"But' – "I know you want to talk about him Rob, but I can't, not while he's in here. Let's eat and then find somewhere else to drink, deal?"

"Deal!" He beams and starts frantically shoving his Fajita into his mouth.

Really, it's not attractive.

"Nice!" I comment dryly, and even though I have absolutely no appetite whatsoever, I pick up my fajita and take my first small bite. *Ugh, takes like cardboard!*

Maybe I *am* getting sick?

CHAPTER SEVEN

ROB HAS DEMOLISHED HIS meal in record time, and we have finished the second pitcher, but I've hardly eaten a thing.

"Is that really all you're going to eat?" He asks.

I nod in reply, feeling queasy again. *Crap! I don't want to get ill, I hate being ill...it's so boring!*

"Shall we go?" Rob asks, looking disapprovingly at my plate.

"Yes," I answer far too eagerly. Rob stares down at me with a quizzical look, but I studiously ignore him. I'm so desperate to get out of the restaurant, away from Tristan's proximity; that I'm almost hopping in my chair.

As Rob calls Chloe over and asks her to get our bill ready, I head for the ladies. When I return to our table, I see Rob is beaming from ear to ear again.

"What now?" I ask totally bemused.

"It's all on him," Rob says, waving his hand in the air as he stands from the table.

"What do you mean Rob?" I huff my hands on my hips.

"Tristan," he slowly drawls his name. "Has paid our bill," he adds, his eyes smiling knowingly at me.

"What!" I hiss. I don't know why, but I suddenly feel angry that he's done that, I wanted this evening to be my treat, my way of thanking Rob for coming out with me at short notice.

"What?" He huffs seeing the look on my face.

"I wanted to treat you." I snap, wondering why I'm feeling so antagonistic towards Tristan, that was a nice thing to have done.

"Well, he evidently wanted to treat *you*," he smirks. "Come on, let's go," he adds.

"Shouldn't we say something?" I ask.

"I'm game." His eyes glint wickedly as he takes hold of my hand and starts pulling me toward their table. *That wasn't what I meant!*

"Rob," I hiss, trying to pull my hand out of his, but it makes no difference at all. *God damn it, Rob!*

"Tristan," Rob says slapping him on the shoulder. "You shouldn't have, but thank you."

"You're very welcome." Tristan stands, and they shake hands again, but his attention is on me.

I stay rooted to the spot, behind Joyce's chair, my eyes locked on his. He nods to me, and then sits back down, finally breaking eye contact with me.

Rob starts casually chatting with Joyce, they know each other well. I can't help getting annoyed with him, he's holding up the proceedings here!

Come on Rob, I want to get out of here!

As I stand there, feeling totally embarrassed, I catch Tristan staring at me from the corner of his eye. I cannot help staring back; it's as if he has some sort of hypnotic power over me. I'm mesmerised as I watch as his long fingers pick up his glass of wine, and he takes a sip – *Oh those lips!*

"Hello Coral." Leggy blonde is talking to me.

"Hi," I say mulishly. She stands and stretches out her hand for me to shake it. I lean across the table and take hold of her hand, it's so cold – That's odd, it's really warm in here.

"Susannah Johnson." Her handshake is firm, almost too firm. I don't think I like her, I can't help thinking she's got it bad for Tristan and I know that shouldn't bother me, but it does.

"Coral Stevens." I tighten my grip, she looks flustered for a second then loosens her grip apprehensively, I let go just as Rob comes and stands beside me.

Suddenly all eyes are on me.

"Umm, thank you, Tristan," I say quietly. "For the meal," I add literally squirming with embarrassment.

Why did I just say that out loud? What else would I be thanking him for? *Coral, you idiot!* Oh, I'm so embarrassed – *Rob, please get me out of here!*

Tristan smiles a slow sexy smile at me, stopping my heart and my breathing at the same time. "You are more than welcome Coral," he says in a croaky, deep, sexy voice.

I swallow hard, feeling totally flustered. Why can't I breathe? And why has my heart suddenly taken off, strumming so fast against my chest, it's humming like a bird? Frowning deeply, I pull my hand up to my throat trying to get myself together, unable to tear my gaze away from his.

I notice Susannah glance across at Tristan and then narrow her eyes at me.

Do something Coral!

Breaking eye contact, I quickly bend down and kiss Joyce on the cheek, trying to take the spotlight off me.

"Are you ok?" I whisper.

"Yes darling," Joyce replies and smiles, but it doesn't reach her eyes, so I know she's not. I make a mental note to ask Gladys to call her tonight. Rob bends down and gives Joyce a farewell kiss, and as Rob stands, I secretly tug on his shirt to let him know I want to go.

"Um well, goodnight everyone, enjoy your meals," I say, smiling down at Joyce.

We both turn to leave, but Tristan quickly stands, I stop walking. "See you tomorrow Coral, have a nice evening." He says, his eyes molten lava - *Holy crap, I'm going to see him tomorrow?*

I'm not really sure how I feel about that. And why is he so damn polite?

Shit, shit, shit!

"Tristan." I nod at him and bolt out of the restaurant.

I don't stop until I'm out of eye-view, a few doors down, then I stop and lean my head against the brick wall. Closing my eyes, I try to calm my rapid heartbeat and get some air into my lungs. I hear Rob's footsteps approach and open my eyes, and keeping my head against the wall I stand staring at him.

"Well, that was interesting?" He says a little confused.

I snort sarcastically at him. Interesting is not a word I would use for what has developed this evening. Grabbing him by the shirt, I start stomping down Jubilee Street.

"Err...where are we going?" He asks, walking fast to keep up with my rapid pace.

"Northern Lights ok with you?" I ask.

"Sure," Rob shrugs.

We walk in silence, my head filling with all kinds of idiotic thoughts like Tristan likes you, Tristan wants you – I suddenly stop and take a deep breath trying to halt the wayward chatter, the stupid thoughts.

"Sunshine! You ok?" Rob asks, wrapping his arms around me.

I silently shake my head. I have no idea what to say, and I'm definitely not ok! I change my mind about Northern Lights. I want the calmness of the sea, a relaxing mellow atmosphere.

"You want to go home?" Rob asks softly.

"No," I mumble into his chest.

"Come on." Rob takes me by the hand and ushers me into a waiting taxi. I slide over so he can shuffle in beside me.

"Where to love?" The driver asks.

"The far side of the moon," I mumble, wrapping my arms around my stomach. *Why is it fluttering so badly?*

Rob bursts out laughing at me. I'm so glad he's finding the whole thing amusing.

"Eh?" The driver turns in his seat, a confused expression slapped across his face.

"Don't mind her," Rob exclaims. "She's had too much sun today," he adds turning to me. "So where to?" he asks softly, his eyes taking on his warm I'm-your-best-friend look.

"I don't care," I answer, turning to stare blankly out the window.

"Marina mate," Rob tells the driver.

"Are you taking me home?" I question.

"No, I'm not, but I know you well, and when you look like you're looking now, you always end up drinking too much. So, we go to the Marina, get drunk trying to work all this out, and then I don't have too far to carry your arse home." Rob teases.

I finally smile and hit him fondly in the chest. "Well thanks," I admonish.

The taxi pulls out into traffic, and we head back to the Marina, a few minutes later we arrive. The driver drops us straight outside The Master Mariner, Rob pays, and we both step out.

"Fancy this place?" He asks.

"I don't care. I just want a strong drink." I need to steady my shredded nerves.

Rob follows me in, and we walk up to the bar together.

"So, what'll it be sunshine?" I glare at him even though I know he's trying to cheer me up.

"I'll take a J.D on the rocks." Rob nods to the barman. "Actually, can you make that a double?" I add knowing a single will be gone in seconds.

"And for you?" the barman asks Rob.

"I'll take a large glass of Chardonnay." I pull my purse out my bag to pay, but Rob stops me by placing a twenty on the bar, I'm too mad to argue with him.

Looking around I feel it's quiet, relaxed atmosphere begin to calm me, I like it in here. This place is all about boating, wooden beams, open brickwork and normally an open fire blazing, but I guess the good weather has put a stop to that.

Rob passes my drink to me, I take a large gulp of my J.D and swallow. I feel it hit my stomach then spread outward, warming my insides. I shiver a little, which surprises me; I didn't expect to feel cold tonight. But somehow, I don't think it has anything to do with my body temperature.

"Outside or inside?" Rob asks taking a sip of his wine.

"Um...inside I think." *Why do I feel so despondent?*

We wander over and take a window seat, Rob sits down opposite me. I can't help staring out at the view. I can tell he's watching me vigilantly, waiting for me to crack, which I have been known to do on occasions...when I've had too much to drink.

"Coral, why are you getting yourself so worked up about him?"

I sigh heavily and turn to face Rob. "I don't know, it's really weird, I feel like he can see straight through me or something?" I answer trying to get my own head around it.

"Is that such a bad thing?" Rob whispers.

"It's not that...I," I take another big gulp of J.D. "I just don't think I'm ready or capable of anything right now, not with everything going on at work..." I drift off again, staring at the boats bobbing on the water.

Rob knows nothing of my horrid past, my reasons for

dodging men and relationships. George is the only one I've ever opened up to, and even then, it took ages for me to do so.

"Look we've discussed the work thing, it's a given, right?" I nod in agreement. "Ok, good. But this guy Coral, he seems really great, and he's got it really bad for you." I go to interrupt him, but Rob holds up his hand. "Let me finish. Now I mean that as in it could be the best thing that's ever happened to you. Look, I hate to say this, but you've been on your own way too long. It'll send you mad you know."

I roll my eyes at him. "It's not that easy," I reply shuddering slightly as the memory of my last date comes unbidden into my mind.

"What's hard about it?" Rob argues. "It's simple, you like him, he likes you. You give him your number, you go out on a date...?" Rob shakes his head at me. "You know Coral, for such a smart woman you can be a real dumb ass sometimes."

My mouth pops open in shock. "Nice, thanks so much," I hiss.

"Sorry babes, but sometimes you gotta be cruel to be kind." He adds flippantly.

"So much for cheering me up tonight," I say gritting my teeth at him.

"Coral, why are you so against relationships? I've never been able to get my head around it."

I instantly feel like I'm having a session with George. "Look, if you're not going to cheer me up, I'm going home," I tell him firmly.

"Oh, come on...I mean I know about Justin, but there's got be more than that?" He asks.

"You don't know what you're talking about Rob." I spit.

He stares back at me with a wounded look – *Christ!*

I run my hand through my hair in frustration. "Rob, you don't understand, I... I'm not like other people, I don't run right, never have, never will, so a relationship is just...impossible." I stare blankly out the window.

"Why?" Rob whispers.

"It's...complicated," I whisper back, keeping my eyes on my glass of amber liquid.

"And you can't tell me?" He asks.

I slowly shake my head at him.

"Great, I'm your best friend. You should be able to tell me anything." He rightly points out.

"I know," I whisper back, feeling melancholy – I hate it when people probe, why can't he just let it be?

Rob cocks one eyebrow up at me. *Great, so much for a fun evening out!*

I go back to staring blankly out the window. Rob runs his hands through his black hair and takes a gulp of wine, then he claps his hands together making me jump, I turn and look at him.

"I've got it," he says looking triumphant. "Ok, so think about Twilight," he adds excitedly.

"What?" I ask, frowning in confusion.

"As an example," he says enthusiastically.

"Still not with you?" I say staring blankly at him.

"How many times have you watched those films?"

I grimace feeling too embarrassed to actually say out loud. "Too many times," I say squirming.

"And what is it you always say to me?" He questions.

"What?" I slap my hand on my forehead, the alcohol finally kicking in, my head feeling a little woozy. "Rob you're really confusing me," I slur.

"You always say 'I'd love a man to look at me like that like I'm his sunshine, the air that he breathes'," he says in a girly voice.

"I don't sound like that," I grumble, then I think about what he's just said. "Edward loves Bella, deeply and passionately, they are made for each other," I say as though I'm announcing it to the world – *Whoa alcohol!*

"Exactly, and that is what you always say you want." Rob takes a sip. "Well, when you're drunk you do," he adds.

"Ok back up, what the hell has this got to do with anything?" I ask totally bemused. "Besides the fact that their relationship is based entirely on fantasy, people don't actually feel like that about each other Rob, they just don't."

When I've finished my tirade, I take another gulp of J.D and congratulate myself on being honest.

"Noah and Allie," Rob pipes up. *What?*

"We're quoting romantic couples now?" I stare into his deep

black eyes as he sits there smiling goofily at me. *Ok, he wants me to play.*

"Christian and Anastasia," I retort.

Rob snorts and rolls his eyes. "Darcy and Elizabeth."

"Romeo & Juliet," I say.

"Heathcliff and Catherine," he counteracts.

"Lancelot and Guinevere," I smile – *Ok, starting to feel better.*

"Orpheus and Eurydice," Rob chuckles.

"Rose & Jack," I blurt, trying not laugh.

"Who?" Rob asks, his head cocked to the side.

My mouth pops open. How can he not know?

"Titanic!" I gasp in mock horror.

"Oh yeah...I always think Kate and Leo," he chuckles. "Garrett and Theresa," he adds, trying to keep the game going.

I squint my eyes shut trying to work out who it is. "Oh, Nicholas Sparks, Message in a Bottle, I got it," I chuckle gleefully, then frown – *Doesn't Garrett die?*

"Holly and Gerry?" I say. Rob shakes his head again. "P.S I Love You," I add. Then I frown again remembering that Gerry definitely dies, not such a happy ending.

Rob leans forward and takes my hand in his. "Tristan and Isolde," he whispers.

I cock my head to the side – *Bastard knows that's my favourite film!* I grit my teeth at him, then take a long drink of my Bourbon and stare out of the window.

"What's your point, Rob?" I bark.

"Another?" He asks pointing to my almost empty glass, avoiding my question.

"Sure." I swig the last of my drink and hand my glass to him. I suddenly remember I wanted to tell Gladys about Joyce, I quickly pull my mobile out and speed-dial her.

"Hello?" Gladys sounds out of breath – *That's odd?*

"Are you ok?" I ask feeling instantly worried.

"Oh Coral! Yes, darling...I'm fine." She pants. I pull my mobile away from my ear and check I've called the right number. *Yep, definitely Gladys!*

"Ok, I'll be quick, I'm out with Rob," I say, still a little mystified.

"Oh, lovely dear," she says, still panting.

"I saw Joyce tonight. Gladys, I think you should call her, she looked really sad. I think the deal went through, I think she's selling." I say, feeling nauseous again.

"Ah...so you know," she softly says.

"Yes," I whisper. "I'm ok," I add for good measure. I know she'll worry. "I'm more concerned with Joyce, we saw her in the Restaurant tonight, I don't think it's really hit home what she's doing." I close my eyes and bite my lip as I try not to think too hard about it.

"Leave it with me, darling, I'll call her now."

"Thanks, Gladys."

"You're such a sweetie." She gushes.

"Um, no, I'm not," I reply, feeling embarrassed.

"Yes, you are, you're always thinking of others, you have a big heart under that big sleeve of yours." *Crap, not this again!*

"Gladys, I' – "Goodnight Coral," she interrupts, I can tell she's smiling. "Don't drink too much and say hello to Rob, sleep well darling." She adds.

"Night, sleep well." Just as I'm about to hang up, I swear I hear a male voice mumble something in the background and Gladys giggle at him, then the line goes dead – *Ok, way too much alcohol, I'm hearing things now!*

As Rob sits down in front of me, handing me my second double J.D he takes a deep breath, twirls his glass round a couple of times then stares back at me.

"So, you want a man to look at you the way Edward looks at Bella?"

I shrug, he knows this is true, impossible, but true.

"Lucky, you, your wish came true."

I pull a face at him. "Shut up!" I slur.

"No, I mean it Coral. Tristan looked at you like that tonight." I stare, frozen and wide-eyed at Rob, trying to get my brain to compute what he just said.

"No, he didn't," I argue.

"Yes," Rob says so softly it's almost a whisper. "He did."

My breath leaves me in a long exhale. "You think?" I squeak.

"Coral, it was written all over his face," he says. "So, what's the problem? He's rich, handsome and has it really bad for you!" he adds.

"Well for a start you know I'm not motivated by money...."

I stop talking - *What the hell am I on about?* "He should pick someone else," I snipe. The words twisting my stomach, for some inexplicable reason I don't want him to like anyone else.

"Why?" He questions.

"Because I'll kill it before it even gets started." I snap, quickly standing. "I told you, Rob, it's...complicated." Rob eyes me suspiciously. "Loo break," I say and stomp off in the direction of the restrooms.

CHAPTER EIGHT

AS I'M WASHING MY HANDS at the sink, I hear Rob's words going over and over in my head. *'Tristan looked at you like that'* Something way deep down inside of me keeps giving me a little nudge, telling me that I should go for it, but I know it will all end badly and will be totally messy.

He is my boss for Christ's sake, and either he or I, will end up sitting in the corner of a darkened room, licking our wounds like an injured animal – It's just not worth it.

Shaking my head at myself, I take a good look at myself in the mirror.

My eyes are slightly bloodshot, and I look as though I've lost weight, like literally overnight. I move closer to the mirror, leaning forward I see my cheeks look slightly sunken too – *That's too much exercising for you!* I scold and quickly turn away from my reflection.

Sometimes, I really hate what I see staring back at me.

I close my eyes and grit my teeth at myself, I really shouldn't go down this melancholy road, not when I've been drinking – *Come on Coral!* – I take a step forward and stagger slightly, guess the alcohol is finally kicking in.

As I head back to the bar, I'm reminded of Lily's birthday party. I need to invite Rob, and I'm hoping if I mention it, we can get off the subject of Tristan.

"Hey." I sit myself down. "Before I forget, its Lily's birthday party this weekend. Are you and Carlos coming?"

"Are we invited?" Rob asks.

"Of course, you are. You came last year, and Debs said she's looking forward to seeing you both." I add, even though she didn't say that, but I know she will be.

"Well, as far as I know, we have nothing on, so yes. Count us in!"

"Great! Oh, and we'll need to go shopping for a birthday present, can you make lunch tomorrow?"

"Yes."

"Good."

"What time?"

I shrug my shoulders unsure of what will be happening tomorrow. "Can I text you?" I ask.

"Yes, that will be fine. I have nothing booked until next week anyway."

I try to hide the smile creeping across my face. "Was she really that bad?" I question.

"Who?" Rob asks.

"The evil witch in London?" I say.

"God was she! And she was more like '*Daddy has too much money for his own good*' kind of a spoilt little bitch." Rob sniggers; good he's off the subject of men.

"Nice!" We both laugh and clink our glasses together. "To spoilt bitches that earn us a living," I say.

"And rich bosses who send shivers down our spines!" *Damn it!*

I scowl at Rob, then bob my tongue out. "Enough with the rich boss thing," I snipe.

"Ok, ok. I'm done." Rob laughs, holding his hands up in defeat.

Good, now we are off the subject of *Tristan*, we can really have some fun...

I WAKE UP WITH A JOLT, my mobile buzzing loudly beside me. As I sit up and look around me, I realise I'm in my studio, and I'm on the sofa. I look down at my body and see I'm still fully dressed and I have a blanket draped over me. I do not remember getting here. *Ugh!* I feel so disorientated.

With half-closed eyelids, I fumble in my bag for my mobile and quickly answer it.

"Hello?" I croak.

"Ola darling!"

"Carlos?" I whisper - *Stop shouting!*

"Yes sunshine, it is me." He chuckles.

I look up at the clock on the wall, it's 7.35am. *Shit, I should be swimming now!*

"What happened?" I ask trying to recollect the previous evening and slump back down on the sofa. As I do, I can see a big glass of water on the side.

"I came down to pick Rob up, he was too drunk to do anything – honestly, you two when you get together, you're such a bad influence on each other! Anyway, I carried you home, made you take some Nurofen, and got you settled on the sofa."

Sweet!

"You did?"

"Yes, of course."

"Thank you," I whisper. Realising the Nurofen must be the reason my head doesn't feel too bad, my body, however, has different ideas! "Is Rob ok?" I ask.

"Still sleeping it off," Carlos advises.

"Sorry," I whisper.

"What for sunshine?"

"Taking him away from you," I croak.

"We needed the space." He tells me.

"Did Rob tell you about Lily's birthday?" I suddenly recollect asking him about that.

"Yes, we'll be there."

"Good, I miss you." I haven't seen Carlos in ages. I feel my eyes closing on me again, I really want to go back to sleep.

"You saw me last night." He chortles.

"I don't remember," I answer groggily.

"Well, either way, time to get up." I wish he would stop shouting. "Lots of water and a cold shower, you'll feel right as rain in an hour."

I snort loudly. "I very much doubt that." I turn on my side, and the room starts to spin.

Shit! Coral you idiot! Why d'ya get so messed up when you know you have work the next day?

I squeeze my eyes shut. "I think I might bail." I groan.

"Oh no you don't, come on, up!" he tells me sternly.

"My body doesn't feel like mine," I tell him.

"I'm coming over," he tells me. Rob and Carlos have always had a set of keys to my place, it means I don't have to get up and unlock the door.

"Ok," I whisper.

"See you in ten," he softly says.

"Ten," I whisper back and pass out.

A SOFT VOICE IS CALLING ME, trying to wake me from my peaceful slumber.

No! Go away!

"Coral come on, time to get up sunshine!" The voice chortles softly.

"No," I grumble and push the hand away that's trying to gently wake me.

"Coral, wake up." A stern voice tells me.

I open my eyes, blinking several times and see Carlos sitting on my coffee table, looking as handsome as ever; sandy blonde hair, blue eyes, gorgeous tan and a body to die for.

"Carlos?" I mumble. *Ugh! My mouth feels so dry.*

"Sit up." He orders and I quickly do so, my stomach objecting, my head spinning again. I wince as I turn to face him, my ribs throbbing with the movement. *Why are my ribs hurting?*

"You ok?" He asks looking amused.

He never takes my hangovers seriously. I slowly shake my head then quickly stop, everything still seems woozy, and it's so bright in here. *Who turned up the sun?*

"Here drink this." He hands me a pint glass of my pre-made vegetable juice, guaranteed to kill any hangover.

"Thank you," I whisper and drink the whole thing down without coming up for air.

"Come on, you need to shower and get ready. I'll take you to work." I lie back down and throw my arm over my eyes, trying to block out the sun that's blasting through. I just want to go back to sleep.

"Coral, seriously it's ten to eight. You're going to be late." I listen to his words, my brain taking a moment to process them and when it does, full-scale panic sets in.

"Fuck! I'm late." I shout and jump up from the sofa, swaying slightly as I do.

Carlos quickly grabs both my arms and steadies me – I don't mind Rob and Carlos touching me. "Slow down darling, you have plenty of time. I'm taking you to work," he repeats.

I swallow hard and launch myself into his muscular chest. I always feel emotionally raw the day after a heavy night. "Thanks, Carlos, I owe you, big time."

He chuckles hard and wraps his arms around me. "How do you feel?" He asks rubbing my back.

"Um...I don't know yet, my head doesn't feel too bad though, considering!" I think Rob and I must have got really hammered last night.

I feel him chuckling.

"Thanks again," I say feeling utterly grateful for last night, and him being here now.

"My pleasure. Now, go take a shower, I'll get your work clothes ready."

God, I love having gay friends.

Pulling out of his arms, I kiss him on his cheek then sleepily make my way over to my tiny bathroom. Once in there, I attempt to strip my clothing only to bash my arms several times on the shower door – *Damn it!*

I'm finding it hard to keep my eyes open; I just want to go back to bed. I wonder what time I was put to bed? Bashing my arm again, I decide it's probably best to sit down to do this, so I put the toilet seat down and gently lower myself down onto it, once there I am able to get all my clothes off me without hurting myself.

I clamber into the shower, using the tiled wall to stop me swaying and sink my head under the spray. The tepid water soaks my hair and slowly brings me back to life, but I decide it's still best to be careful, no sudden movements, and gently shampoo my hair.

I hear the bathroom door open and see Carlos walk in and pick up my clothes from the floor; he is such an awesome friend, I seriously don't deserve him.

When I'm done, I wrap a towel around my hair and another around my body and attempt to clean my teeth. I decide to avoid my tongue, I will do anything not to be sick, and the way my stomach is feeling, one stroke of the brush will start me retching.

When I open the bathroom door, Carlos hands me another glass of my veggie juice.

"Thank you." I take it from him and slowly sip it this time.

"You want some more Nurofen?" He asks.

I shake my head, the movement feeling much better than it did ten minutes ago. "I'm good, I'll take some to work with me in-case I need them later," I add.

As I stand sipping my drink, I watch Carlos transferring my mobile, keys, and purse from last night's bag into my work bag, along with a fresh packet of Nurofen. Looking up he sees me watching him, I can't help smiling at him.

"What?" He chuckles.

"How did I ever get such great friends like you and Rob?"

Carlos cocks his head to the side. "What on earth do you mean sunshine?"

I shrug; feeling slightly melancholy as is usual after a fun night out. George tells me its yin-yang, for every high, there has to be a low. *Shit!*

I have George tonight! – *Great, therapy with a hangover, what an awesome combination!*

"Are you ok?" Carlos asks, slightly amused - *Git!*

I punch him lightly on his muscular shoulder. "I have laid out your work clothes on your bed, hurry darling." I look up at the clock, 8.15am. I'm normally at work by now, even though I don't officially start until 9am.

"On it," I say slowly making my way up my tiny staircase with my glass of juice in hand.

As I look at the clothes on my bed I am in awe, Carlos has worked wonders. I would never have thought to match my gunmetal grey suit trousers with my black frilly gipsy top, which I only ever wear socially, and my black peep toe wedges, not too high, more for comfort. He knows I'm going to need it being hung-over, and I know once the outfit is on, it will totally rock. I quickly drop my towel, cream my skin from head to toe, spray myself with perfume and add deodorant under my arms.

I'm trying to move quickly, but everything seems to be going in slow motion. I find some pants then hunt for a bra, finally dressing in the outfit Carlos chose. Slipping my feet into my wedges, I pick up my juice and head back down the stairs.

"Stunning," Carlos says grinning widely.

"Thank you." I blow him a kiss as I head to the bathroom. "I love it," I add turning to beam at him – *Seriously, he should be my stylist!*

I quickly comb my hair and braid it into a bun. Then I finish the rest of my juice while applying my makeup. When I'm done, I exit the bathroom and look up at the clock, 8.35am that must officially be a record. I don't think I've ever got ready so quickly.

"If we leave now, we can get you some food inside you," Carlos says steering me out of the living room towards the patio doors, he ushers me out and passes my handbag to me.

It's all going way too fast for me to keep up.

"Rob says you didn't eat much of your fajita's last night, naughty Coral. It's drinking rule number one." He admonishes as he fishes my keys out of my bag and locks the door.

"I know," I grumble feeling guilty.

As we quickly march down the concourse, my arm wrapped in his to steady me, I can't help but feel a little better. I definitely would have bailed today, told Joyce I had a stomach bug or something and sat at home wallowing in my own self-pity…

WE ARE STOOD INSIDE a lovely little café called Munchies. We are only two doors away from Chester House, where I work, which is a small step away from Kemp Town and it's only 8.45am. I have time to eat!

I know I should be good, but I really feel like something naughty.

"What can I get you, love?" The lady behind the counter asks.

"I'll have the crispy bacon, poached egg and mushrooms on a toasted muffin – Carlos, you want something too?" I ask.

Carlos rubs his taut stomach. "I really shouldn't." He says, staring up at the menu, Carlos shakes his head, undecided.

He's as bad as me, so I ask for three of the same.

"Any drinks?" She adds.

"Three Cappuccinos and we're eating out, but can you bag two together and one on its own?" I add, handing the cash over to the woman.

"Sure," she answers pleasantly.

"Some of us have to work." I chuckle to Carlos who has been a kept man for the past five years.

The woman eyes Carlos and bats her lashes at him, which makes us both laugh – *Can't she tell he's gay?*

We both take a seat at a free table and wait for our order. "For Rob too?" Carlos asks.

"Of course," I answer, feeling more and more human as the minutes go by. "Figure he'll probably need it as much as I do." Carlos smiles weakly at me. "Hey Carlos, I know I met Rob first, and we hang out more than I do with you, but you know you can talk to me, right?"

His face drops, his smile disappearing – *Shit!*

"I... I just wanted you to know that, well, I love you both, and I'm here for you both. Anything you tell me stays with me." I tell him.

Carlos hangs his head and silently takes hold of my hand. "Thank you, Coral, you don't know how much that means to me," he says, his eyes glistening over. *Shit!*

"Anytime," I whisper.

We smile awkwardly at each other, it's obvious Carlos doesn't want to talk to me about whatever it is that's going on between them. The atmosphere suddenly feels very dense and heavy as we wait in silence for our food.

Five minutes later, I am kissing Carlos on the cheek and handing him his take-out bag and Cappuccinos. "Thank you for this morning," I say again, feeling utterly grateful.

"Stop thanking me." He leans down and kisses me on the cheek. "Get into work, or you'll be late," he tells me sternly.

"Yes sir," I mimic a soldier's salute then I hug him hard and kiss his cheek again. "Bye Carlos, thank you." I half run to the front of the building before he can tell me off for thanking him again.

As I reach the front door, I turn and give a quick wave to Carlos who I know is waiting to see if I am safely within the building. *Honestly, sometimes you would think I am a helpless woman who needs constant protection the way those two act!*

As I pass Joe in reception, who is stuffing her face with a blueberry muffin, I wave a quick hello to her. "Is Joyce in yet?" I ask as I dash past, she shakes her head, her cheeks bulging as she frantically chews – *Nice, very attractive!*

I don't think there's ever been a time when Joe isn't eating something, and she's so damn skinny, a tiny waif – *Where the hell does she put it all?*

When I reach my desk, I look up at the clock on the wall. It's five to nine, I made it. I collapse into my seat, smiling gleefully as my legs do a little jig of their own; I can eat my muffin in peace. I drop my bag on the floor, pull the wrapping off my breakfast and instantly devour it.

Carlos was right, I was starving.

When I'm finished, I take the wrapping and place it in the take-out bag, then stuffing it into my handbag, I zip it closed. Then I go over to the big window opposite me, unlock it and push it open. Grabbing the air freshener from my bottom cabinet, I spray it a few times to disguise the smell of my breakfast.

"That has to be the fastest I have ever seen anyone devour a muffin." A soft, husky voice says from behind me.

I instantly freeze on the spot. I've stopped breathing, and my heart is slamming against my chest – *Shit!*

I swallow hard, I know that voice…

CHAPTER NINE

I SLOWLY TURN WITH MY heart in my mouth and gaze into the dreamy eyes of Mr Mogul. He is leaning up against the wall, playfully smiling at me with his hands in his pockets. *Damn, he looks good!* – He's dressed in a gunmetal grey suit, a crisp white shirt and a dark blue tie, he simply looks…irresistible.

I look down at my own gunmetal suit trousers, thinking how ironic!

"I was hungry," I whisper, feeling totally embarrassed that he has just seen me, and scuttle back behind the safety of my desk, checking my mouth for any stray bits of food as I do. *Jeez, I really did stuff it down. Where the hell was he, I didn't see him when I walked in?*

"Me too," he says. "Could have got me one," he adds looking forlorn. *Oh crap!*

My eyes widen in horror as I stare back at him. Not looking after the boss is not good!

"Um…I didn't know you were' – "Relax Coral I'm just teasing," he says, interrupting me, a grin spreading across his face again. *Damn those dimples!*

"I had to be in early today," he explains. "Incidentally where did you get that muffin from?"

"Um…Munchies, it's just a couple of doors down." I say, feeling bewildered.

He nods and looks down the corridor, then turns back to me. "Care to show me?" *What?*

"Um…" *I can't just leave my desk and my work, what is this guy on?*

"Joyce won't be in today." He says, spookily answering my

thoughts. He rubs his fingers across his forehead as though he is searching for the right words to say. "She was feeling a little... well...off." He adds, frowning slightly.

I instantly feel panicked. *What's wrong with Joyce?* I have to call her!

"I need to call her," I state and pick up the phone, pressing the speed dial button for her mobile.

"Coral, she's spending the day with your mother, Gladys." He softly says.

I don't understand why his voice feels like it's soothing me, but I instantly feel relieved, I know she'll be ok with Gladys.

"Oh." Is all I can answer as I replace the handset. I still want to know why she's not in though, I run it over in my mind; I guess I can ask him. "Has she sold?" I mumble, keeping my eyes on my desk.

"Yes." He softly answers.

I close my eyes and pull my hand to my throat that has automatically tightened. I hear Tristan's rapid footsteps against the marble floor, then I feel his hand gently rest on my shoulder.

My eyes dart open. *Whoa!*

The feeling of him touching me is exquisite, sparks of electricity are shooting through me again, but it's much, much stronger than when we shook hands. And I'm amazed I'm not freaking out, I don't like strangers touching me, especially men.

"I'm sorry Coral. I know how much you care for Joyce, and how much you enjoy working with her. I'm going to try my very best to make this process as smooth as possible for you." He says.

But I can't concentrate with his hand touching me, so I turn in my chair to face him, his hand automatically drops down. I look up into his big, soft, chocolate brown eyes; they are oozing sincerity.

"Thank you." I croak knowing that he is trying, but wondering at the same time how much Joyce has actually told him about me.

Tristan gazes down at me for a moment, then turns and walks over to the window, he pulls it shut and re-locks it.

"Who will I be working for?" I ask as politely as I can. *I have to know!*

Tristan turns and gazes at me again with that deep, intense frown of his. "Me," he simply states.

My heart starts hammering against my chest. *God damn it! I knew it, why?*

"Joyce told me you're not practising law anymore," I say matter-of-factly.

"I'm not." He answers. "But I always have a P.A in every office. I won't always be here though, but that's not a problem as I know how conscientious you are about your work. I'll also be sending Susannah down to spend a week with you at some point during this month, she's been working with me in London for six years. I think the two of you will get on well and she can run through a few things with you, how I like things done."

I rack my brains for who Susannah is, it's ringing a bell but I can't...

"You met her last night." He says. He cocks his head to the side, gazing quizzically at me - *Shit I did, I remember now!*

"Oh...yeah right...Susannah, tall, slim, blonde," I blurt out, my brain to mouth filter evidently not working today. I glance up at him, feeling mortified I just said that out loud.

Tristan's eyebrows raise, and he smirks at me. "I suppose she is," he says looking amused, which irritates me, but I can't help feeling dubious - I don't think Susannah likes me. I don't think we'll get on at all.

"What?" Tristan asks, reading my expression.

I shake my head. I don't want to tell him that.

"Coral, tell me." He orders.

"I just...I don't think she likes me," I whisper. *Shut up Coral!*

"Nonsense, she has no reason not to like you." He tells me firmly, so I decide to drop it.

"So, when will the take-over happen?" I ask, wondering how long the process will take.

"About a month," he answers.

"And I keep my job?" I clarify even though he's just told me I'll be his P.A, I feel a little panicky. *What the hell does that involve anyway?*

"Yes Coral, you will keep your job."

I wish he'd stop saying my name like that; it keeps sending weird shivers down my spine.

"But what if I'm really bad at it? I know how to be a legal secretary, not a P.A."

Tristan shrugs. "It's pretty much the same thing Coral, and

like I said, I'll get Susannah to go through any programs you haven't used before. She'll be there to help train you if you need it, but I'm sure you won't." He says almost proudly.

I frown at him, I'm not really sure I want leggy blonde anywhere near me. What if she's secretly a bitch and sabotages me, so I make mistakes, then I lose my job – *Oh God!*

"Coral, what are you looking so concerned about?" *Damn him, how is he reading me so easily?*

"I don't like change Tristan, this is all...." I wave my hand in the air.

"I know, a shock," he says finishing my sentence for me. Picking up one of the office chairs, he places it in front of me and sits down. His scent wafts towards me, sending my senses into disarray, he smells divine – *What is that?*

"I'm leaving tomorrow..." He stops talking and frowns; and oddly glances at me, then quickly looks away. "My legal team will be dealing with the take-over, and I know Joyce will be back in tomorrow. You will have a whole month with her to process the change. I will be back towards the end of the month." I nod silently trying to take it all in. "I don't think I need to tell you this information is classified Coral, top secret," he says tapping his nose.

"Of course," I answer. "So, no-one else knows, not even the Solicitors?"

Tristan smiles some sort of secret smile and shakes his head at me. "Just you Coral."

I relax a little knowing Joyce has at least given me the courtesy of telling me in advance. If I'd have found out when it was announced, I think I would have had a full-scale meltdown.

"Ok," I say.

His gaze holds mine, I want to look away, but I'm finding it so hard to do. It's as though he's analysing me, trying to figure me out.

"So," Tristan says, standing and putting the chair back in its place. "Joyce said to tell you when you came in that you can take the day off, as she's not in herself."

Are you fucking kidding me, I have just dragged my sorry, hung-over ass into work only to be told I can go home!

I grit my teeth in annoyance and stare back at him. He

walks back over to me smiling widely, I think he's secretly laughing at me.

"But I really am rather hungry, so...would you mind?" he asks holding his hand out to me.

"You...you want me to take you to Munchies?" I clarify squeakily.

"Yes please," he smiles. I just stare back at him, not really knowing what to say, I don't really want to go anywhere with him, but – "And I'd also like to ask you to come to a couple of house viewings with me today," he adds.

"H-house v-viewings...?" I stutter.

Tristan nods once. "I always purchase a property close to where I work as I don't like staying in hotels, even if I'm only there a few days, and you know this area very well. Joyce tells me you've lived here since you were five?" He adds innocently.

All the colour drains out of my face. I don't like thinking about back then. When I first came here, I felt so alone, and I had no idea if I could trust Gladys. I didn't know if she was going to be nice to me, treat me well, or even if I was staying with her permanently, everything was so confusing.

"Coral!" Tristan dashes over to me and twists my chair around. Then he kneels down in front of me, so we are face to face, his features are etched with concern. "Are you ok? Would you like some water? Some fresh-air? Tell me what you need?" he asks frantically.

Why the hell is he being so attentive and nice?

I take a deep breath to steady my nerves then gaze into his warm eyes. "A brandy?" I choke, laughing nervously.

"Some water." He says ignoring my request and dashing away. Within seconds he's back at my side, handing me a cold glass of water, I take a sip.

He crouches down in front of me again. "Better?" he asks, I hand him the glass back.

"Yeah...thanks," I whisper turning my face away from him, trying to break the connection.

"Good. So, will you come with me? Help me choose a place?" He asks.

I know I should say no, my head is screaming at me to keep this professional, to run as fast as possible out the door and pray I don't have to work with him too much.

"Ok," I answer completely ignoring myself. *No, no, no this is not good, it's all going to end so badly, Coral what are you doing?*

"Wonderful," he breathes in relief, his face lighting up like a kid on Christmas Day.

In a complete daze, I lean down, pick up my handbag, then my Cappuccino and stand. Tristan gestures for me to go first, I hastily walk in front of him down the hallway.

As we reach Joe in reception, I see her cheeks blush as she notices Tristan, and she is still stuffing that muffin into her mouth...*jeez!*

I stifle a giggle, she is either a really slow eater, or she is on her second!

Joe stops chewing and flutters her eyelashes at Tristan.

"Hi Joe," I say as I reach her desk, she gulps loudly, swallowing a large mouthful. *That looked painful!*

"Hi Cori," she squeaks, looking at me for reassurance.

"Joyce won't be in today ok, so take messages." Then I think, how am I supposed to explain my leaving the office? It's not like Tristan can say anything, even though he's soon to be her new boss, he can't act like it, not yet anyway.

I quickly come up with a plausible scenario.

"You remember Mr Freeman?" I ask, she squeaks something and gazes adoringly at him.

"Hello, Joe." Tristan takes no notice of the fact that her cheeks that are now almost purple with blushing and holds out his hand for her to shake it, she blurts something, but I don't know what and holds up her hands in apology.

"Sorry Mr Freeman, my hands are a little sticky." Tristan puts his hand down without saying anything. I don't think he's impressed. *Way to go Joe!*

"Mr Freeman is a close friend of Joyce's," I lie. "And he's looking to purchase a property in the area, Joyce has asked me to show him around, so leave any messages on my desk tonight. I'll be in early tomorrow." Joe looks blankly at me. "But if there's a problem you have my mobile?" I add.

"Um..." She starts checking her computer.

"It's on their Joe," I say feeling frustrated. *What's wrong with her today?* "Just call me if you need to." I huff.

"Ok, Cori." I roll my eyes at her.

"See you later." I sigh.

"Bye." She answers dreamily.

Reaching the main door, Tristan pushes it open for me. As I look up to thank him, he winks at me, making my mind go completely blank. *Did he just...?*

I see a slight smile begin to form on his delicious lips. I quickly look away to where I am headed, and begin marching onwards; Tristan easily keeps pace with me.

"She was calling you Cori?" He frowns.

"I know." I sigh.

"Do you think Joe is efficient?" He asks, his expression not giving anything away. *Why the hell is he asking me this?*

"I value your opinion," he adds reading my thoughts again.

"I don't think I'm really in a position to make any judgement," I say soberly because, in all honesty, I'm not.

"I'd still like your opinion," he says.

I stop walking and look directly at him. Shrugging my shoulders, I figure he wants answers, I can ask questions. "Is she going to lose her job?"

"Unknown," he says his eyes narrowing. "Sticky fingers?" he says as though this should explain it all.

I narrow my eyes at him. "In that case, yes, she is efficient and good at her job," I say and begin to walk off again, but he stops me by tugging my elbow, I pull it out of his grasp.

"Why did you just say that?" Tristan asks cocking his head to the side.

I feel like stamping my feet and screaming at him. I don't want someone else's life to be affected by what I say.

"Look if you want to let her go, then do it, just don't get me involved, ok!" I retort.

"Why not, I'm only asking what you think of the quality of her work?"

I laugh sarcastically at that one.

"Something funny?" he snaps.

I shake my head in frustration and stare at the pavement for a moment, then back at him. "No... I just..." I grit my teeth in annoyance. "I just don't want to be put in this...position," I add.

"What position?" he questions.

I sigh inwardly. "I just...I know something no-one else knows' - "Enlighten me," he interrupts, his voice low and dark.

Crossing his arms, he takes a step closer to me. I take a step back wanting to keep the distance between us.

"Fine!" I bite, knowing I'm about to tell him something no-one else knows, not even Joyce. "But if I tell you this, I need to know it won't go any further, not even Joyce knows."

"You have my word," he says his expression intense. "Please, tell me Coral, it won't go any further," he adds.

I don't know why, because I don't trust people I don't know, but something about him is making me believe that I can share this with him, and it won't go any further.

I sigh heavily and begin. "Ok....do you know how old Joe is?"

"No." He states clearly.

"Twenty-nine." He raises his eyebrows at me in shock. "I know she doesn't look it at all," I say.

"No, she looks like she's still in her teens," he says.

I nod in agreement. "I know."

"And?" he prompts.

I take another deep breath, it's so hard divulging other people's secrets, and begin.

"Joe married her sweetheart from school. They have two kids, a nine-year-old boy, and a five-year-old girl. Her husband Matt, he worked in finance. He earned good money, enough so that Joe could be a stay at home Mom..." I stop and take a deep breath.

"Shortly after the crash he lost his job, he went to interview after interview, he knocked on doors, did everything he could to get another placement, no-one was hiring. I guess you could say it took away his pride. Men like to be the providers, bring the money home, right?"

Tristan doesn't agree or disagree, he's just listening, intently.

I continue. "He didn't want Joe to work, stupid I know, so in the end, he had no choice but to sign on. That's when things got really ugly..." I say not really wanting to continue.

"And?" Tristan asks his expression darkening.

"He developed a drinking habit, things got really bad. To cut a long story short, the neighbours called the police. He wasn't getting violent with Joe, but they had screaming rows that would wake up the whole cul-de-sac they lived in. Social services got involved and took the kids away."

I look away from him and swallow hard. The haunting, vivid memories are still so clear of being carted away from my mother; I don't think they'll ever go away.

"Coral." Tristan touches my arm bringing me back to him. "What happened?"

"He committed suicide," I whisper. "Left a note, chucked himself off the pier, his body washed up on the beach." Tristan's eyes widen in shock. "She needs this job, Tristan. If she keeps it for a year, shows social she can provide for her kids, that she's stable, she gets them back. That's all she wants, she only has two months left, and they go home to their mother, where they're supposed to be." I look up at Tristan, my eyes pleading with his.

"How is it you know this?" He asks grimly.

"I found her crying in the ladies, I guess she was missing her kids, I took her to lunch and she told me everything, I felt sorry for her," I say knowing exactly how those kids are feeling. "Look, I know she's a bit...well, she's not razor sharp, I'll give you that, but' – "She'll keep her job," he says interrupting me. "You have my word," he adds his cheeks puffing out as though he's been holding his breath the whole time.

My mouth gapes open in shock. "Really?" I squeak. "Just like that?"

"Yes," he states firmly. "Can I eat now please?"

"You're asking me for permission?" I laugh nervously.

"No." He chuckles.

I shake my head at him I can't work him out at all...I start walking again, feeling good that Joe will keep her job, get her kids back.

Tristan is back at my side again. "Do you always walk so quickly?" He asks staring straight ahead, his hands in his pockets, his height towering over me.

"Yes," I answer as I try not to look at how good he looks when he walks.

"Why?" *What? Why is he asking?*

"Because I always have a purpose, I always have somewhere to be," I answer quietly.

"Ah," I look across at him, I see a private smile playing across his lips, bastard!

"What?" I snap – *Careful Coral. New boss, remember!*

"Nothing..." he laughs, still staring ahead.

I feel the need to cross my arms, as I always do when someone has ruffled my feathers. But I can't as I'm holding my god damn Cappuccino!

"I'm supposed to be meeting a friend for lunch." I blurt out of nowhere.

"What time?" He asks.

"I'm not sure. I didn't know what time I would be' – "Can you cancel it?" He asks interrupting me.

"No!" I bark answering more smartly than I intended to. Then I think it's only Tuesday, I've got three more working days to find a present for Lily, and Rob will probably be like a bear with a sore head today anyway.

I stop walking, he follows suit. "Yes." I sigh. "I can cancel it."

He frowns deeply at me, almost as though he's looking straight through me again. "Is it important?" He asks, he looks so intense.

I swallow hard then take a drink of my Cappuccino. "Just shopping," I say. "It's my niece's birthday." *Why am I telling him this?*

"And when is that?" He asks.

"Um…Saturday. Why?" I ask, cocking my head to the side, trying to read him.

"Then we will shop today." He says resolutely.

"What?... No! I need to' – "You're seriously saying no to me again?" He interrupts, emphasising the word 'no' again.

Jesus Christ! I am far too hung-over for this!

"Mr Freeman!' – "Tristan," he interrupts. *For the love of God!*

"Tristan," I rephrase, trying to keep my cool. "I'd rather do it on my own. I have no idea how long it will take. I'm not even sure what I'm getting her? Besides, I don't see how we're supposed to fit it in as-well as house hunting?" I question.

"Good point," he says looking amused again. "Now can I please get some food inside me?"

I nod silently at him, he gestures for me to walk on and steps easily beside me...

CHAPTER TEN

As we reach Munchies, I inhale deeply – the strong smell of bacon, toast and coffee waft through my nose. Delicious – I love the smell of fresh coffee. There are a few tables and chairs outside, the canopy above protecting them from the blazing sun, but it makes no difference.

It's so damn hot already.

"Would you like to sit outside or inside?" Tristan asks.

"They have air conditioning inside," I answer.

Pulling the door open for me, he gestures for me to go first; he is very courteous and polite. I walk into the small café. It's very minimal, and everything is white. The walls, floor, tables and chairs, guess it makes it easier to keep clean.

As we walk up to the counter, my head starts to bang again, and I feel dog tired. *Maybe it's the heat sapping my energy?*

"Coral, can I get you anything?" He politely asks.

I shake my head at him and sit down at a free table. Opening my handbag, I pull out my scrunched-up takeout bag and throw it with accurate precision at the open bin behind me.

"Nice throw." He compliments.

I turn around and see he's sat opposite me with a fresh coffee. "Netball team," I answer artlessly, finding my Nurofen out of my bag, I pop one out of the packet. Just as I'm about to swallow it with my Cappuccino, I see Tristan smirk again. "What?" I say feeling frustrated. *Why does he keep smiling at me like that?*

"Hangover?" He quizzes.

I narrow my eyes at him. *I hate the fact that he knows that's what I have!* So, I ignore him, take a deep breath, open my throat, and swallow the tablet.

"I'll take that as a yes." His smile widens making his dimples deepen.

He picks up his spoon and stirs his coffee, then taking me by surprise, he starts chuckling to himself. I can't help staring at him, his smile is simply glorious. I don't think I have ever seen anyone's face look so lovely when they smile.

"Do you make a habit of it?" He asks, his smile instantly fading, his eyebrows scrunching together.

"Sorry?" I ask a little bewildered.

"Drinking, when you're working the next day?" I instantly panic. I don't want him to think this is what I'm like.

"Tristan…I've only ever been hung-over at work what…two, three times in the fifteen years I have worked for Joyce." I stare at him scrutinising me. "I hate it, I like having a clear head," I add.

"Not good with hangovers," he sniggers.

Against my wishes, I feel a smile begin to form. "No, I'm like a grizzly bear just come out of hibernation," I giggle back.

"I'll try to remember that," he chortles. "But I have to ask why?"

The laughter in me instantly dies a death. "Why what?" I bite.

"Why did you get drunk last night?"

I sigh, feeling frustrated. "Because I'd been told the company was being sold, and that Joyce is leaving, and…" I stop right there.

"And having a new boss?" He says, finishing my sentence for me.

I know he's digging to see if he's affected me.

"I…." I shake my head at him and glance down at the table. "I'm not that great with people Tristan, you might want to consider that."

He nods once and stares down at his coffee. *Shit! Did I really just tell him that?*

We both look up at the same time, our eyes lock for a split second, but he shoots his eyes back down to his coffee. If I knew him better I'd say he's nervous, but so am I, which is making me feel really uncomfortable. I just want to get this day over with, so I can go home and curl up into a ball feeling sorry for myself.

He suddenly looks up, his gaze holding mine. I can tell he's trying to work me out - *Why can't I look away?*

"Do I make you nervous?" He softly asks.

I sigh inwardly. I really don't want to be going down this road with him. I manage to pull my gaze away and stare down at the table, but for some unknown reason, my mouth runs away with me again.

"All men make me nervous," I whisper.

I hear his sharp intake of breath, and close my eyes, gritting my teeth at myself. *Why the fuck did I just say that out loud?*

I purse my lips in a vain attempt to stop them from blurting anything else out about myself, but I have to question - Why did I tell him that? No one knows that about me except for George. Now I'm really, really, angry with myself for sharing that with him, because I know I've just opened a can of worms. I shake my head at myself in frustration. I can't believe I just said that. I really don't function normally the day after a heavy night.

I look up at him, wondering what he's thinking, but he seems miles away. His eyebrows are creased together as he stares down at his coffee, then he suddenly looks up, and our eyes meet, he opens his mouth to speak, but I'm saved from this question by my mobile buzzing. I plunge my hand into my bag – *Coral, you need to get this day over and done with and get Tristan bloody Freeman out of your life!*

Locating my mobile, I press answer without even looking at who it is. "Coral Stevens," I bite.

"I love you." Rob's croaky voice shouts. I think Tristan heard because he suddenly looks crestfallen. "So much, do you know that?" Rob adds.

"Stop shouting," I chuckle.

"But I do," Rob croaks again.

"Why?" I snigger.

"You bought me breakfast," he sighs happily. "My stomach is so grateful," he groans.

"I'm happy that you're happy," I say feeling melancholy again.

"Ok, what's up?" He sounds so perky compared to me.

"Nothing, but I'm going to have to bail today...can we do lunch tomorrow instead?" I ask.

"Why, what's happened?" His voice is immediately concerned.

"Um...I can't really talk," I gripe.

"Ooh...is he there?" Rob teases.

"I have to go," I say, feeling panicky and shaky.

Rob starts howling with laughter – *Bastard!*

"I mean it," I snap. He keeps on chuckling so I hang up on him. I smile tentatively at Tristan and put my phone back into my handbag.

"Was that your boyfriend?" He asks all traces of humour gone.

I squirm slightly, feeling uncomfortable that he's just asked that question. I'm about to answer him when his breakfast is placed in front of him, saving me.

"One bacon egg and mushroom muffin," the woman says who served me earlier. She lingers for a second, smiling down at Tristan. "Can I get you anything else?" She asks batting her lashes at him, swaying her hips closer to his lovely, strong, broad shoulders.

I feel like slapping her down, I could be his girlfriend for all she knows yet she's blatantly flirting – I can't help raising my eyebrows at the audacity of the woman.

"No, thank you." He answers politely, keeping his eyes locked on me. She shrugs and walks back over to the counter. Tristan stares down at his muffin and takes a sip of his coffee. *So much for being hungry!*

"Boyfriend?" He asks again not looking at me, his face contorted like he's in pain.

"No." I snap, and cross my arms - *Not that it's any of his business!*

His wide grin returns, and he happily takes a bite of his muffin. I am trying not to watch, but I have never seen anyone take their time with their food as Tristan does, he seems to be really relishing it, savouring each mouthful. I can't help wondering if that's what he would be like as a lover, taking his time with each move, each body part...*Coral!*

Whoa! Where did that come from? I shut the door on those thoughts and try to concentrate on something else. The radio playing in the background catches my attention. 'Use Somebody by Kings of Leon starts playing, so I softly sing along.

"So, you don't want me to shop with you today?" He questions interrupting my humming, but I don't get a chance to answer him. "You like Kings of Leon?" He asks.

"Um...yeah," I try to hide my smile, and I don't know why I tell him, but I do. "This is my favourite song of theirs."

"Mine too," he answers frowning down at his muffin. "So, no shopping?" he repeats.

I stare back at him, drowning out the tune. "No," I answer. "I was meant to be shopping with Rob." I unintentionally blurt out.

"That's who was on the phone?" He asks still taking his time, each sip of coffee elegantly consumed.

"Yes," I huff, feeling annoyed he caught me out.

"And the guy this morning, was that your boyfriend?" I cock my head to the side and narrow my eyes at him. *He was spying on me?*

"That's none of your concern," I snap.

"Yes actually, it is." He argues.

"How so?" I swallow nervously, I don't like where this is going.

"I like to know the personal situations of all my staff Coral." He gazes at me for a moment before popping the last tiny amount of muffin left into his mouth.

"Why?" I question.

He finishes chewing and takes a sip of coffee, smiling at me as he does. "Because it's important," he answers artlessly, taking another sip of his coffee.

"Why is it?" I push, wanting an answer.

Tristan sighs leans back in his chair and crosses his legs, assessing whether or not he should tell me. "I like to know my staff. I like to know who's married, single, got kids, what kind of lifestyles they live."

"Why?" He's still not answered my question.

"I like to look after my staff Coral. When it's their birthday, I send a card. If they are getting married, I send a gift. I like to get involved, it's very important to me, you want a good team you have to show them you're interested not only in their work but their home life too."

I raise my eyebrows in surprise. "John and Joyce were never like that, and everyone seemed happy enough," I scoff defiantly.

"Maybe, maybe not," Tristan retorts.

"I still don't see what difference it makes," I argue, spinning my empty Cappuccino cup in my hand. And I think that's it, that I've won as Tristan is silent, but it only lasts a couple of seconds.

"A couple of years ago," he says bringing my attention back to him. "I had a member of staff with an excellent resume. She was punctual, had a smart appearance, she cared about her job and had a great work ethic. At the time, she was only twenty-two and had been working for me for a couple of years. Then, out of nowhere she started coming in late, her work became shabby, and most days she looked like death warmed up. Now, I could have pulled her in and given her a verbal warning, but that's not how I work. Like I said...or I'm trying to say, I actually care about their happiness." He admits looking slightly abashed.

"Oh...so what happened to the girl?" I ask totally taken in with his story.

Tristan leans closer to me, I lean closer too, we are only a few inches apart.

"Turns out her partner had left her, completely screwed her over. She couldn't afford the rent on the flat they had, and there were four months left in the agreement. She had no savings to put a deposit down for a more affordable place, so she was getting more into debt as the weeks went by. She had no help from her family, so in her despair, she started drinking."

"Oh...so I take it you didn't sack her?" I ask gripped by where the story's going.

"No. I upped her wages, she was due a pay rise. Then I paid off the balance on the agreement and secured her a more affordable apartment." He answers as though it's the most natural thing in the world for him to have done.

I swallow hard, this guy is an angel.

"And she's ok now?" I ask croakily, feeling slightly shocked and warming more to Tristan as the second's tick by.

"Karen is now my P.A in Leeds, she just needed a little help, and I like giving good jobs to good people who deserve it." He says sincerely.

"Tristan, there aren't many bosses that would do something like that..." I stop talking wondering why the hell he would do that. "Why are you like that?" I ask incredulously.

He grimaces briefly, as though he's remembering something painful. "I just am." He answers thoughtfully.

I suddenly understand why he reacted the way he did about Joe. I look away and stare out the window. Either way, my private life is not the kind of territory I should have to go into with him. I'm very private like that. I don't want him to know the status of my non-existent love-life. It has nothing to do with him.

"Well as far as I'm concerned Tristan, as long as I give 100% at my job it's no-one's concern what I do in my spare time – or who I'm seeing," I add feeling exposed and vulnerable that he would want to know any of this.

"I thought you might say that." He adds wryly and stands to leave. He holds out his hand to help me up, I ignore it.

"I'm fine, thank you," I say standing sharply. I'm quite capable of getting out of a seat by myself, even though I am feeling a little wobbly again.

As I follow Tristan and we reach the door, he pulls it open and gestures for me to go first again. I have to wonder where he gets it from. It's like he's straight out of an old black and white movie.

As I walk outside, I'm blasted by the sheer heat of the day, sapping at my skin, making my head pound even more. I look up and see the sky is blue, there's not a cloud in sight, and the sun is scorching, belting down with wave after wave of ferocious, fiery heat. I stop walking, close my eyes and pull in a ragged breath, but there's no air, it's so stifling. *Ugh!*

My head suddenly feels woozy, and I feel a little sick. Opening my eyes, I take a step forward, and that's when I feel like I'm going to pass out. My right leg buckles and I almost hit the ground, but strong arms quickly encase me from behind, gripping me tightly. I don't panic because I know from the hands that it's Tristan, and for some unfathomable reason, I feel ok with it.

I place my hands over his and hold him tightly, subliminally trying to tell him not to let go as I haven't found my voice yet.

"Do you need to sit down?" He asks his lips millimetres from my ear, his voice low and husky, the sheer proximity of him...*Oh!*

I feel a shiver run down my spine. I shake my head slowly, unable to understand why I don't want his arms to leave me.

I take a deep, ragged breath, trying to control my irrational thoughts and I'm instantly knocked over by his hypnotic scent.

It's potent, really, really potent; a scent all of its own. I know I can smell the faint odour of aftershave, but that's not what's taking over all my senses. It's him, his scent. It's sweet, sexy, and musky all at the same time. And those pheromones are racing through my nostrils and setting my blood on fire, igniting something deep within me. I feel as though I want to rip every piece of clothing off his body and make crazy, deep, passionate love to him. *Whoa! What is that?*

Tristan slowly turns me around; his arms tightly encasing me and pulls me against his chest. Then he gently moves us so that we are under the canopy and out of the direct sunlight. I keep hold of him, my hands on his upper arms; they feel so strong and bulky.

"Better?" He asks huskily, staring intensely at me.

I cannot pull my gaze away from him – *Coral what are you doing?*

"Are you alright?" He adds, his eyes examining my face.

I manage to move my head up and down once. He brings his hand up to my face and runs a cool, soft finger down my cheek, my breathe hitches at the contact.

"Are you sure?" he asks. I can feel his breath against my lips, he's that close.

"Yes," I whisper breathlessly. I almost lean forward to...

His breath hitches stopping me. "I feel it too," he whispers.

My head instantly clears. I scowl at him and pull slowly out of his arms, pushing him away from me as I do. As we stand there, silently staring at one other, I notice he looks lost, hurt, confused maybe? I feel...I don't know what I feel, which is even more confusing. He's is my boss. I can't. "You don't know what the hell you're talking about." I hiss. I turn away from him and start marching back to Chester House.

I hear his footsteps close behind me, and quicken my pace. I need to get away from him, away from his proximity, his smell, his eyes; all of him. I hear him call my name, but I ignore it and keep walking. Beads of sweat form on my brow from the relentless sun beating down on me, I take a deep breath trying to calm my thumping heart, but there's still no air, I feel faint again.

My head swims and sways as I try to focus my footsteps on getting back to work. If I weren't feeling so rough, I would be running full pelt by now.

"Coral!" He calls my name again, and it's a plea.

My steps falter, I don't know why I slow down, but I do. He reaches me in seconds and rounds on me, so he is facing me, walking backwards.

"Will you please just stop for a moment." I carry on walking keeping my eyes on the ground and stumble again, he instantly catches me, but I pull out of his arms and continue walking.

"Please..." he begs, and it's the tremble in his voice that makes me stop and look up at him.

He takes a deep breath and visibly relaxes in front of me, then reaches out with his hand, his palm open, I turn my head away and stare at the ground.

"Will you please come with me?"

I shake my head at him. I can't do this.

He drops his hand to his side. "Please," he begs again. "This heat is killing me, and I'd like to talk to you," he adds running his hands through his damp hair.

"I don't think so," I whisper.

"Coral, it's a conversation. That's it, I give you my word."

I look up at him, that same intense look is plastered across his face, his eyes tight, his jaw tense, his frown deep. My gut instinct is screaming at me to run, to get as far away from Tristan Freeman as I possibly can, but another part of me is intrigued, curious even - I cannot get my head around why he is pursuing me?

I feel like I'm being torn in two, part of me wants to take his hand and go with him, the other part of me feels like I'm being dragged along the floor against my will, kicking and screaming the whole time, my fingernails scraping along the floor trying to stop me.

"Please?" He takes a step towards me, so he is inches from my face. "I didn't mean to scare you," he says, his thumb gently brushing against my cheek.

I close my eyes in surrender. The sensation of him touching me is exquisite. No man has ever made me feel this way. I take a moment to analyse and assess my feelings. I try to think logically, sensibly about it all, but I don't think I can keep fighting it

– whatever this is, is too strong for logic or reason. But there are a few things I need answers to before I take this any further.

I take a deep breath. "Tristan, are you married?" I ask, even though there's no ring, but you never know.

"No."

"Girlfriend?"

"No."

"Anyone?" I croak.

He shakes his head at me. I see a flicker of pain flash across his face. I close my eyes for a moment, when I open them I gaze up at him, my mind made up.

"Ok. I have to be somewhere at 6pm tonight. No excuses, I have never missed these...appointments." I tell him sternly.

He looks relieved and nods once. "Again, you have my word." He holds out his hand for me to take it, I look away from his open palm. "I just want to keep you steady on your feet Coral."

I look up and see his eyes are sincere, his words a heartbeat away from making me fall...deeply...*Shit!*

"Come to the car with me?" *He's asking?* "I really want your help today," he adds, sounding nervous again.

"Ok." I croak feeling nervous too and place my hand in his.

The moment I do, I feel like there's a firework display going off inside me, one boom after the other; my body starts to tingle all over...*Whoa...so many sensations!*

His fingers slowly entwine themselves with mine, his grip is firm but gentle.

I swallow hard and look up at him.

"Shall we?" He asks, his thumb gently circling my hand, calming me, relaxing me.

"Yes." I manage to whisper, even though I'm feeling completely overwhelmed, on every level. Emotionally, mentally, physically, and at the same time, I feel really confused.

I don't know this man, yet, the feel of my hand in his feels like home.

Oh god, what am I doing...

CHAPTER ELEVEN

WE TURN AROUND AND start walking at a gentle pace. Tristan is glancing at me every now and then from the corner of his eye. I try to fathom it, to work out why I suddenly feel so peaceful, so relaxed, I've never felt like this before. I frown deeply as I try to understand it – I am walking with a man I hardly know, my hand in his, and I'm not scared - by some god damn miracle I'm not afraid of him; at all.

Tristan looks down at me and gently squeezes my hand, my heart flutters madly in response. I am astonished that I am feeling ok, no panic attack, no fight or flight reaction.

I fight back the urge to cry in relief.

We turn left and walk down the concrete steps to the underground car park, its dark, but a welcome relief from the heat of the sun; down here it's cool, comfortable.

Tristan takes out his mobile and makes a call. "We're here," he says and hangs up. *Who was he calling?*

Tristan stops walking and keeping hold of my hand, he turns to face me. "Ok?" He softly asks giving my hand a gentle squeeze.

I nod silently, my eyes perusing the car park for any would-be attackers, as I always do.

"I saw you in the Gym last night," he says. "Self-defence?" *I knew I had seen him!* I instantly remember the reason for my aching ribs. "Coral? Is it to keep fit, or to learn how to protect yourself?" He asks looking concerned.

I decide not to answer, he already knows too much.

"You're safe with me Coral." He whispers, his expression is

so profound I feel my legs start shaking. *How did he know what I was thinking?*

"I know," I whisper. Because I know it's true, that I am safe with him, but at the same time, I know I shouldn't say that. *This cannot happen; I'm not good for him.*

"I mean it." He states more firmly. "I'll protect you, no matter what." He smiles down at me, his eyes glowing with sincerity. I look up into his wide eyes – I can only see the truth.

I swallow hard against the lump that's formed, and try to make my lips smile back at him. But I'm side tracked by the male voices heading into the car park, and from all the swearing and bantering, I'd say they're roughnecks, exactly the kind of guys I avoid like the plague. Tristan cocks his head to the side, noticing my reaction and turns around to watch them. I see them enter from the far-right corner, and take a small step behind Tristan, keeping hold of his hand.

They look like builders, construction workers, I'm not sure which as they are both dressed in combat shorts and boots and their torsos are bare and very tanned. I guess that's all the good weather we've been having. And they are holding what looks like an early lunch, or late breakfast depending on how you look at it.

They both notice me as they walk towards their vehicle, I can tell they're dying to say something but with Tristan stood next to me, I guess it changes things, but I still feel nervous. I have no social skills when it comes to dealing with men like that – I just clam up.

I squeeze Tristan's hand, and he gently squeezes me back, it's as though he's silently telling me not to worry. They head straight past without a word, a wolf whistle, or some derogatory remark. I am astonished and gleeful at the same time.

God that felt good!

I have never been able to walk past a building site without something being shouted at me, it's not nice, especially for someone like me. Debs has always lapped it up when she's wolf whistled at. Personally, I think it's just asking for trouble when you jeer them on.

Tristan is still watching them walk away – I use the opportunity to study him.

He's tall, more than six feet - I think. Has long lean legs, a slim waist and very broad shoulders, I guess that's all the swimming. But there's something else about him that I'm missing, something I can't quite put my finger on?

He certainly has an air of authority about him, a knowing...I try to work it out. Is it inner-confidence? He seems very sure of himself – I wish I was confident like that. But I'm not sure if that's it? I sigh inwardly, whatever it is, I guess I'll figure it out.

Either way, standing so close to him, I feel safe and protected. I can tell he can look after himself, which means he can look after me. And I know at that very moment, he has made a fundamental difference to me.

I don't quite know what it is yet, but I'll soon find out when I see George tonight.

Tristan turns and gazes down at me, my hand still in his. I think he's waiting for something, but I don't know what.

"What are you waiting for Tristan?" I whisper feeling shy.

"The car." He explains.

"The V8?" I ask looking around me.

"You knew what car it was?" He asks slightly astonished.

I nod shyly. "You have my dream car," I tell him playfully. *What the hell - I'm never playful.*

"Seriously?" He looks at me like I've just told him I'm an alien, totally amazed.

"Yeah...F-Type, it's the 5.0 litre supercharged V8, right?"

Tristan laughs-out-loud throwing his head back as he does. It echoes and bounces off the cement walls of the car park. His laugh is simply wonderful. I light up inside. How can he have that effect on me? Then I realise, he's laughing at me, not with me.

I immediately feel defensive. I have no confidence, so I can't take a joke, whether it's at my expense or not, I really can't take people laughing at me.

"Are you mocking me?" I snap, my face losing all humour.

"No." He laughs again but emphasises his point by shaking his head. "I'm just shocked you knew which model it was." He adds still chuckling hard.

I let go of his hand, cross my arms and pout at him.

"Amazing." He mumbles to himself, then turns and holds his hand up to an approaching silver Jaguar, only this one is completely different to his.

"Where's your car?" I say feeling a little miffed that I won't be getting a drive in it.

"At the hotel." He smiles.

"Oh…" I can't help scowling.

"You wanted the F-Type?" He says, still smiling. *How does he know?*

"Which model is this?" I ask as it pulls up along-side us.

Tristan opens the rear passenger door for me, and I slip inside. The luxury leather seats immediately encase me, and I'm amazed by the amount of legroom available, and it's so cool inside; I actually shiver a little. Tristan shuts my door, and I look up at the driver, feeling a little embarrassed.

"Good morning," I say quietly.

"Good morning, Miss Stevens." *He knows my name, how?*

I watch Tristan walk around the other side and slip in beside me. I'm finding it hard to stop looking at him.

"Morning Stu." Tristan beams widely at the man behind the wheel.

"Good Morning Sir. Shall I head to the first appointment?" He asks pleasantly.

"Please," Tristan replies kindly. "Seatbelt, Coral."

"Oh…" I quickly clip it into place just as Tristan does and we head out into traffic. "He knows my name," I whisper a little shakily to Tristan, he smiles warmly at me.

"I told him to expect you. This is my driver, Stuart Riley." I look up at the rear-view mirror again, Stuart nods to me.

"How long have you known him?" I whisper not wanting to seem panicky. Trusting people is a huge issue for me. Tristan maybe winning me over, but that doesn't mean I trust others around him.

"Coral, relax, I've known Stu ten years. He's been my driver for five of those." He whispers back.

"Oh…ok," I say feeling a little more relaxed. As I look down at Tristan's legs, I see he still has plenty of room, which brings me back to my original question.

"So what model is this?" I ask again, scanning the huge panoramic tinted glass roof that extends the full length of the car, making me feel cocooned. And I'm surprised at how private the cabin area feels. I had no idea Jaguar made cars for chauffeuring.

"It's an XJ premium luxury long-wheelbase model." He answers.

"It's really nice." I offer, feeling quite spoiled that I am in being driven around in complete luxury. "What engine does it have?"

Tristan laughs loudly again.

"What?" I bark. *Why does he keep laughing at me?* I already have enough self-esteem issues.

"Nothing..." he chuckles, shaking his head in amusement.

I huff and frown sulkily at him.

"Hey." Tristan reaches for my hand, the moments our skin touches I relinquish. "I'm sorry. I don't mean to laugh...I just find it so sweet and fascinating that you like cars." He smiles down at me, then gazes out the window. "Most women don't." He adds, then taking me by surprise, he lifts my hand up to his lips, making his intention clear and lightly kisses my knuckles.

I shiver from head to toe. His lips are warm and so soft. I practically melt like ice-cream into the leather. And I'm surprised at myself, I have always thought guys that do that sort of thing are corny and are literally trying to get into a woman's knickers, but with Tristan, I can't find anything that's corny, fake or shallow about him at all.

I swear he's all heart and soul.

"So, the engine?" I ask trying to keep my voice steady.

"Not sure, Stu?"

"Sir, this is the 3.0-litre petrol V6 supercharged model, 0-60mph in 5.7 seconds."

I cock one eyebrow up and smile at Tristan. "You have a thing for supercharged cars." I chuckle.

"I didn't choose this." He says. *Huh?*

"Really?" I ask a little high pitched.

Tristan shrugs. "Well I'm not the one driving it so' – "You picked it, Stu?" I say working it out for myself.

"Yes, Miss Stevens." He says.

"Nice choice," I say. "And please, call me Coral, I don't like Miss Stevens, makes me sound like a teacher."

"As you wish."

I smile at Stu, then turn to Tristan. "So, you let your staff choose their cars?" I tease, feeling quite astonished that he does.

"No." He shakes his head to emphasise his point. "Stu was

told which model I wanted. He could choose the engine, the extras all that kind of stuff." He says waving his hand.

"Oh." I don't know why, but I feel like playing him up, teasing him. "So, do I get to choose?" I say, trying to keep the grin off my face.

"No." He snaps. "Company cars are always the same, no matter who it is."

Holy Shit I'm getting a car?

"I was only joking Tristan," I say, choking on my own words.

"I'm not." He says smartly. *What?*

Panic is rising within me – This has got to be a joke? A wind-up, surely?

I frown back at him. "Hold on a second, are you saying I'm actually getting a car?" *This is not happening!*

"Yes." He snaps staring out of the window. *Why won't he look at me?*

"Tristan!" I scold louder than I intend to.

"I want you to have one." He quietly says, finally looking at me.

"I don't want one," I snap back. "I have nowhere to store it. I would never use it. It's a total waste of money! Besides, I like walking to work it helps keep me fit." I cross my arms and glare at him, but he's staring out of the window again – Ignoring me!

"Tristan, I swear to god.... if you buy me a car I will quit, walk out today. I'm not kidding." I warn, my voice low and threatening.

He finally turns to me with a look of shock plastered across his face. "You're serious?" He breathes, his eyes wide.

"Yes," I hiss. "If I felt the need for a company car, I would have asked Joyce ages ago, in-fact she offered me one or the pay increase. I went for the money." *He so better not get me a car!*

"Why?" he asks.

I close my eyes for a second trying to reign in my frustrated temper. "Ok, not that it has anything to do with you, but for me, a car is just another expense eating into my wages. I got the job with Joyce when I was sixteen, I saved 70% percent of my wages every month, so eventually, one day, I could buy a place of my own – which I did, two years ago. I didn't equate a car into it."

"But' – "Tristan," I hold my hand up to stop him then

continue. "I have absolutely no need for a car, so please don't get me one. Higher my wages if you want to, I can put that away as savings to get a bigger place one day." I say, feeling totally exasperated.

My head is banging again. I pinch my nose and close my eyes, taking several deep calming breaths. *This guy sure does know how to wind me up!*

"Guess the first appointment is cancelled Stu, onto the next." He says.

"Yes, sir." Stu punches something into the sat-nav.

My mouth pops open in shock, I turn to glare at Tristan. "You were about to take me to get a car?" I squeak, feeling as though I'm about to completely lose it.

"Coral, as my future P.A, I may need you to travel, and the location could be at any of the other offices."

I feel a panic attack coming on – How do I tell him that I won't leave my comfort zone - and that zone is Brighton!

"Tristan, if you require me to accompany you, then I will use the train," I say, hoping he is just testing me.

"You'd rather use public transport than drive in a luxurious car?" He says incredulously.

I turn in my seat to face him. "I'd rather not leave Brighton, full stop." I snap.

"Ah, I see." He says.

"I don't think you do," I mumble.

Tristan's face contorts. "I don't want to upset you Coral if you don't want a car that's fine." He sighs.

"No, I don't." I snap back, wondering if I am pushing him too far, and he's about to sack my ass.

Tristan turns towards me, he looks like he's about to say something momentous, but he changes his mind and stares out of the window instead.

I cross my arms in a huff and stare out the window too.

We continue southeast on Eastern Road, and as we reach the end of the road, Stuart turns left onto Arundel Road.

"Where are we going?" I mumble.

"First house viewing." He quietly answers, still staring out the window.

"How many are there?" I ask.

"That depends." *Why is he so being so cryptic?*

"On what?" I question glaring at him, but he keeps his eyes focused on the outside world. "You're not going to tell me, are you?" I question.

Tristan slowly shakes his head. *Oh, that is so annoying!*

"Great," I mumble, turning to stare out the window.

We sit in complete silence. I feel moody and withdrawn that we are arguing. *Why can't this just feel like a normal, straight-forward, boss and employee relationship?*

As we reach the roundabout, Stuart takes the third exit, and we cruise along Roedean Road. Then he makes a right turn, and we cruise onto Cliff Approach, followed by a left turn onto The Cliff.

We are high up, and ironically, the Marina is right below us, although you can't see it. I start to feel fidgety that I'm so close to my place, and that Tristan will be so close to me; that's if he buys anything up here. Suddenly the big trees to my right clear...I gasp aloud and stare, transfixed by the scene unfolding before me – *Wow!*

The views from up here are incredible. All you can see is a wonderful, panoramic view of the sea. There's no Marina, no houses, it's breath-taking...I bet the sunsets and sunrises are awesome.

We continue to cruise along The Cliff, it's a long straight road with huge houses set back away from the road, concealed by high walls, wrought iron gates, and big trees. The people that live up here are rich, really, really, rich – which makes me feel very small and insignificant.

"I'm sorry," Tristan whispers so only I can hear.

I turn and look at him, only to see he's staring straight past me, transfixed as I was at the view.

"Me too." I offer. I feel myself calm a little and the atmosphere in the car lightens.

Stuart stops outside a pair of large wrought iron gates. I notice a plaque on the wall that reads Seascape – I guess that's the name of the house? I instantly like it, although, I can't actually see the house, because it's surrounded by large oak trees, giving it maximum privacy.

"Well, I guess we have a few minutes," Tristan says. "Appointments not till half-past." He adds.

"Oh...ok." I look at my watch and see it's only five past.

I bite my lip wondering what we're going to do for the next twenty minutes or so.

"Sir." Stuart pipes up. Tristan nods, and Stuart gets out of the car, leaving the engine running, so the air-conditioning stays on.

I instantly panic. "Where is he going?" I blurt.

"Ciggie break." Tristan answers.

I relax. "Oh..." *So, he doesn't mind smokers?* "Do you smoke?" I ask.

"Cigars, occasionally. You?" He asks.

I shake my head. "I used to as a teen..." I drift off remembering trying to quit, took a while, still feel the need now and again.

"Why did you start? Just wanted to try it?" He asks. *Damn it!*

"Um...I..." I turn in my seat and look up at him, he might as well know. "I had a lot of issues when I was..." I break off, shaking my head at myself – *Who am I kidding? I still do.* "When I smoked, it helped calm me down," I add half smiling.

"Issues?" He questions.

I look up at him and nod, but I can't look away – those soft, round, milk chocolate eyes of his are pulling me in.

"What kind of issues?" He asks, his head cocked to the side, his eyebrows pulled together.

His question instantly pulls me out of it. I blink rapidly, trying to get some of my equilibrium back and stare out of the window.

"Tristan, I'm very private, I'd rather not....' – "Sorry that was uncalled for. I guess I just want to know you're ok." He softly says.

I shrug my shoulders in reply. What does he expect me to say to that? Because I am far from ok.

"So, what's with the name Coral?" *Jesus, what is this, twenty questions?*

"What's with the name Tristan?" I ask avoiding his question.

"You first." He smiles.

I shake my head at him.

"Coral?" He's gazing at me quizzically again.

"What?" I snap.

"What, you can't answer a simple question?" He snaps back. *We're arguing again?*

I can't take this – I'm too hung-over.

"Fine!" I snap. "My asshole father gave me that name because he said my eyes were like the coral blue sea." I hiss, my breathing erratic, my heart hammering against my chest. I hate thinking about him, about the past.

"Hey." Tristan reaches for my hand, but I'm feeling trapped, I need to get out of the car. I pull on the door handle, but it doesn't open, my eyes widen in horror as I turn to Tristan.

"Let me out," I whisper trying to calm the full scale, anger/panic attack that's trying to break through. His face pales at my reaction. He silently reaches forward and presses a button on the centre console. I hear a loud click and launch myself out of the car, taking in a huge lung full of air.

I hear Tristan approach. "Jesus Coral, I..." He runs his hand through his hair.

"I'm sorry," I say taking several deep breaths, I squint up at him. "I don't like talking about my past." I whimper, and lean my hands on my knees; I feel faint again.

I feel Tristan rub his hand up and down my back trying to soothe me, but I feel even worse, the car was so cool and relaxing; out here feels so hot – and there's still no air.

"I think I need to get back in the car," I tell him.

Reaching out to me, he takes my hand and grips it tightly, then he places his other arm around my waist and gently steers me back to the car. He opens the door for me, helps me inside then quietly closes it. I lay my head back against the leather upholstery and close my eyes, I hear Tristan get back inside and shut his door.

I instantly feel better; the cool air is helping to calm me down. "I'm really sorry," I squeak. "No-one's ever asked me that before, beside Gladys and well, she knows my past." *Well, some of it!*

"No, I'm sorry," he answers huskily. "I shouldn't have pushed, I should have seen you didn't want to answer," he adds.

"You don't know me Tristan, so how could you have seen?"

"By being more observant," he answers back.

I open my eyes and look across at him. He's deep in thought staring out the window again.

"So, your name?" I ask. "Tristan and Isolde is my favourite romantic story you know," I add, smiling softly at him.

He raises his eyebrows in surprise and turns to me, a gentle smile playing across his lips. "Really?" *He doesn't believe me?*

"I don't lie," I tell him sternly. "Well, except that white lie I said to Joe, but I didn't really have a choice," I add.

"No, you didn't." His smile widens.

"Your name sir?" I ask sweetly.

"My mother, it was her favourite romance too, or so I was told." He tells me.

"Was?" I whisper and swallow hard, feeling all the colour drain out of my face.

"Don't look so worried," he tells me, then leaning towards me, he reaches up and softly strokes my cheek. "I never knew her, she died giving birth to me." I gasp. *How awful!*

"Tristan, I'm so sorry." I clasp my hand in his and squeeze it tight. Tristan smiles at me, but it doesn't reach his eyes, then he leans back and stares out the window. "And your father?" I whisper.

"He worked on the oil rigs, I never saw him." He says. *No Dad, just like me.*

"Do you see him now?" I ask hesitantly.

"No, he died in an accident...Oh, twenty years ago now." He says, glancing down at me. It doesn't seem to have had any effect on him, but then I think if he didn't know him, then how could it?

"So, who raised you?" I whisper.

"My maternal grandparents," he says, a sorrowful look appears across his face. I frown back at him. Why is he looking like that? *Hmm, I wonder...* I quickly do the maths in my head. Tristan's got to be in his thirties, maybe forties, so they must be in their eighties, nineties by now?

"Do you have any siblings?" I ask.

Tristan shakes his head. "You?"

"I had a sister, she was a lot older than me; we had different fathers. She went raving one night, took an Ecstasy tab. I never saw her again."

Tristan squeezes my hand. "Sorry," he whispers – and even though I know I should not say it, I do.

"I'm not," I spit. His eyebrows pull together. "She was vile to me," I add.

"How?" He questions.

I close my eyes and lean my head back against the leather seat. "She hated me, used to bully me, no torture me more like. I was just a kid, I couldn't defend myself." I tell him, opening my eyes I glance across at him.

Tristan is silently contemplating something. Maybe he thinks I'm an evil bitch for saying that? I sigh inwardly. Maybe I am?

"Ok, that was harsh," I sigh. "Of course, I didn't want her dead, I just' – "Wanted her to leave you alone." He interrupts, finishing my sentence for me.

I nod in agreement. Tristan smiles weakly at me then kisses the back of my hand again. And for some reason, I feel like it's ok to keep talking, to tell him more; which I've never done with anyone other than George.

"They kept leaving me with her, she didn't want to have to look after me all the time, which is understandable I guess, she was a teenager, she wanted to be with girls her own age. And I didn't want her with me either if she wasn't going to be nice to me. But I have Debs now, my adopted sister, she's great," I tell him.

Tristan nods in agreement, still deep in thought. But it's no good, I really want to know about his parenting, so I ask him.

"Your Grandparents?" I ask keeping my eyes to the floor. "They must be what...in their eighties, nineties by now?" I ask.

Tristan's cheeks flush red, his eyes darkening as they do. He glances across at me then stares back out the window, seemingly embarrassed. Then he closes his eyes briefly, takes a deep breath then turns to stare down at me; analysing whether he should tell me.

"I buried them both, last year," he whispers, his voice cracking slightly.

Shit! Me and my big mouth!

I squeeze my eyes shut, then squeeze his hand tightly. "Tristan...I'm so sorry. I didn't mean' – "No harm, no foul," he interrupts. *Jesus! I'm shocked.*

I didn't expect him to say that at all. I can feel his pain

emanating from him; he must miss them so much, I open my eyes and look up at him.

"I'm so sorry," I whisper again, frowning deeply. Then I think if he has no siblings, who does he have? Aunties and Uncles, surely?

"Don't be," he tells me. He leans forward and with his thumb, he strokes in between my eyebrows, causing my frown to melt away. "They were the best parents I could have ever wished for, I feel blessed to have been raised by them," he tells me.

I feel better for hearing that and less guilty for blurting out about their age.

I smile back at him. "Guess that explains the ingrained good manners," I whisper.

Tristan leans back in his seat and stares out the window. "Yes, I suppose they were from a different era...." He turns and smiles at me, then drifts off again. "They would have loved you," he says after a moment.

I gaze back at him in wonder. I don't know why he's telling me this, and I don't see how he's come to the conclusion that they would have loved me. I am not lovable, no, I'm far from it. But I feel like I should say something?

"I'm sure I would have liked them too," I say.

"What about you Coral. Any Grandparents?" he asks.

"No, I only knew my granny on my mother's side. I only met her once, and when I did, I understood why my mom wouldn't have her in our lives, she was...well horrid. She took me in for a couple of weeks before I went to live with Gladys." I cringe at the memory.

Tristan is quiet for a moment. "I'm sorry...do you see her now?" he asks softly.

"No, she could walk by me on the street, and I wouldn't know who she was," I answer blankly.

We are both quiet and contemplative for a few minutes, the silence is comfortable.

"I sometimes feel like I was born in the wrong era." I muse out-loud.

"Yeah..." Tristan is gazing quizzically at me.

I nod and lock eyes with him. "I think I would have liked the forties, you know, the way people were. Guys taking girls out dancing, the girls wearing pretty dresses. I think people had better manners and were more..." I cut myself off, feeling embarrassed.

"Go on," Tristan urges, smiling down at me.

"Well, it just seems like, I don't know...like there wasn't any of the crap that we all have to deal with nowadays." I say.

"Like what?" he asks. *Do I really want to say it?*

I sigh inwardly, then start blurting it all out. "Like it was, couples got to know one another first, you know...There was no pressure to have sex straight away or be a goddess in the bedroom, nowadays you're made to feel weird if you're not out every night having one-night stands. Men were gentleman and women were ladies. They conducted themselves in a much better manner. I guess what I'm trying to say is that they fell for one another because' – "They fell in love without the sex." Tristan says finishing my sentence for me.

I nod shyly knowing sex has been mentioned.

"That's how it was with my grandparents." He smiles widely, his dimples deepening. "My grandma always said to me 'if she falls into bed with you, she isn't worth keeping'."

"Sounds like my kind of woman." I softly say.

Tristan smiles sweetly at me, then stares out of the window again, and we sit in comfortable silence, both deep in thought, my hand still in his. Acker Bilks, Stranger on the Shore starts playing on the radio. I begin to feel tense, yet I love its relaxing melody. It's a bitter-sweet sensation. I see Tristan notice out of the corner of his eye.

"Coral, what's wrong?" He asks huskily. I turn to him and shake my head. "Tell me," he urges. I sigh inwardly then I think, what the hell, after what we've just shared.

"This piece of music," I say shaking my head, trying not to remember the nightmares.

"Do you want it turned off?" He immediately asks, reading my expression.

"No, no it's ok," I tell him. "I've always loved it, ever since Gladys introduced it to me. She used to play it to me to help me sleep. Just takes me back, that's all." I smile remembering how thoughtful and careful she was with me back then.

"She sounds pretty awesome." I turn to Tristan and smile widely at him, knowing I love that woman more than I've ever loved anyone, ever.

"She is." I acknowledge then stare out of the window. "Gladys put it onto a tape, so it played over and over all through the night, so if I woke, it would soothe me back to sleep." I close my eyes for a moment, letting its soothing tune relax me.

"You used to have problems sleeping?" He asks. *Still, do honey!* I decide not to get into that one; we could be here all day!

"I really like this tune too," Tristan says, ignoring the fact that I haven't answered him. "Very relaxing," he adds.

I smile weakly at him then close my eyes again. Out of nowhere, I get an image of Tristan and me dancing. I'm safely cocooned in his arms as he swishes us slowly around, my idea of heaven – *How odd?*

I open my eyes and look out of the window, I'm drawn to a couple strolling along with their baby in a pushchair, the woman is laughing heartily at her man as he puts his arm around her shoulders and kisses her on the lips. They look so happy.

I quickly look away. I can't help feeling bitter when I see happy families, makes me so mad to think my parents couldn't keep their shit together and make it work…

CHAPTER TWELVE

STUART STARTLES ME BY getting back in the car, just as another car pulls up behind us. I look behind me and see a short, balding man jump out. He looks flustered, and I can see from his pale pink, short-sleeved shirt; he's sweating buckets.

I instantly don't like him – he looks slimy.

"Showtime," Tristan says, smiling wickedly at me.

I smile back at him and then he exits the car. I watch him talking to the man. Then I watch the sweaty man punch a code into a security system, and the gates swing open. Tristan gets back in the car, and Stuart cruises down the short sweeping driveway, the estate agent following and brings the car to a stop. I turn in my seat and see the house. I'm instantly blown away. It looks brand new, standing two stories high. And for some reason, I think it's much smaller than what I thought Tristan would have gone for, but it is beautiful.

The house is white with a beautiful dark grey slate surround that encases the first floor, including the front door, creating a kind of open porch with enough space for a seating area, yet the owners have chosen several potted ferns instead, it looks lovely.

"Ready?" Tristan asks.

I beam at him. "It looks beautiful," I gush.

Tristan jumps out of the car races round to my side and opens the door for me. I momentarily compare him to Justin, who never opened car doors for me or any kind of doors come to think of it.

I take Tristan's hand to get out of the car thinking he'll let me go, but he doesn't. I frown again, this feels so nice – I should be freaking out about it. We walk over to the agent, Tristan shakes his hand and then he reaches out for mine, but I pretend not to notice and turn to take in my surroundings.

The small, quaint driveway is surrounded by tall oak trees, and a high brick wall, and of course, there's the wrought iron gates; all giving the house maximum privacy. The driveway looks brand new and has been laid with a beautiful choice of brickwork paving, and has enough room for at least four cars.

Then I notice a double garage set back on the right-hand side of the house, again the garage is white with a black slated front. *So much room! Does one man really need all this space?*

I'm suddenly drawn to what the agent is saying about the place...

"As you know from the brochure Mr Freeman, the house has been completely transformed by the present owner into a contemporary style home, which has been finished to an exceptionally high specification, both internally and externally. White Italian porcelain flooring downstairs and walnut flooring in the bedrooms, giving it an absolutely stunning; unique finish." He smiles purposefully at me. *Maybe he thinks I'm buying this place?*

I have to stifle a giggle, he continues...

"The property boasts five bedrooms all with en-suite, three reception rooms, open plan kitchen-diner and living area, utility room with downstairs W.C, games room, indoor pool, cinema room, gym, bespoke outdoor dining area; and landscaped gardens to rear."

My mouth pops open in shock. "An indoor pool?" I squeak looking up at Tristan, he squeezes my hand and grins so widely, I think his face is about to crack in two; he looks so happy.

"Like it so far?" He whispers.

"Yes." I choke, half laughing. *What's not to like?*

I'm really trying hard to hold back my glee that I'm going to be walking around this place with him, and that he wants my opinion, I'm so excited – I've never walked around a big house before. This is miles away from my world, especially when I think back to all the dark and dingy places I looked at when I was buying.

"Ready to take a look inside?" Tristan asks; his smile still wide.

I smile and nod frantically at him. *This is so cool!* Tristan squeezes my hand, and we walk the few steps towards the front door.

"Shall we?" The agent drawls in a posh accent, which I'm sure is put on.

Tristan nods, so the agent pulls a set of keys from his pocket and opens the front door, which is unique in itself, and three times the size of any normal front door, I think it's walnut, and it has a very long, narrow window running down the centre of it. The door opens with the grace that only a heavy door can allow, and we follow the agent into a huge entrance hallway - *Oh wow!* – This place is huge. How have they done that? It looks so much smaller from outside.

The agent continues…

"Entrance hallway leading into the social centre of the house, utility room with small W.C to your right, then into the beautiful bespoke fitted kitchen & dining area, glass doors leading to rear terrace providing panoramic views of the coast…" *Whoa!*

The first thing I notice is how light and open it is, high ceilings, white walls, very contemporary; I'm already in love with it. The second thing – this place is ginormous!

The large entrance hall expands several feet in front of us then opens out into a large, open-plan living space – I guess you could call it the living-room? Right in the centre of the room is a huge, white column that houses a large fireplace – it's new, white and silver, very contemporary, and totally gorgeous.

Surrounding that is a large white u-shaped sofa – it's so big you could fit twenty of me on it. It hugs and surrounds the column in a really cosy way, which I wouldn't have thought possible with how big it is, and I can just about make out what I think is a breakfast bar, just off to the right of the fireplace.

The entire back wall is ceiling height windows. I can see right out to the coast, the sun sparkling against the sea, the boats way out, no doubt soaking up the beautiful weather. I stand completely immobilised. The view is extraordinary, breathtaking. I think my chin has hit the floor.

I hear Tristan chuckle and look up at him. "Like it?" He asks beaming widely at me.

"Yes." I choke out. I manage to pull my gaze away and take in the rest of my surroundings.

To my left, is a wall that runs right along the length of the huge room. I see a door behind the sofa and another right behind me. The other reception rooms? To my right, is a small square shaped room. *I guess that's the utility room?*

Beyond that is a short hallway that leads to a wooden slated staircase, surrounded by beautiful glass panelling, but they head downstairs, not up - *I wonder where they lead to?* Then I remember the swimming pool, that probably where they lead to.

I have to stop myself from jumping up and down with excitement, this place is amazing! I take a deep breath trying to take it all in and slowly blow it out; it's such a huge expanse.

"State of the art alarm system..." The agent drawls pulling me out of my musing, he points to a large white box on the wall to my left. Tristan nods in approval then the agent turns to his left and opens the first door.

Tristan and I follow him inside. Ok, this room is huge, bigger than my studio.

"And here, we enter into the first reception room, the smallest of the three. As you can see the current owners use it as a study/home office."

Tristan looks around the space nodding in approval. We follow the agent out and walk diagonally over to the door that was to my right.

"Utility room, and W.C." He says. Tristan pops his head inside and nods, he seems bored with this room. *Typical!* I think it's awesome, but I don't even have space for a washing machine!

We head down the hall towards the living-room, when suddenly it opens out to the right – and there it is – the huge, bespoke kitchen. *Wow!*

White walls, black slate surfaces, chrome cooker and burners; I am in heaven. They are the exact colours I would choose for a kitchen; if I were to ever have the money to buy a bigger place. I smile inwardly, this kitchen is so big, I could cook up a storm in here. *Oh, it's so beautiful.*

"Completely refurbished, double cooker, warming drawer, large fridge-freezer, dishwasher, centre console with extra hobs and sink, surrounded by a beautiful bespoke breakfast bar. As you can see, the current owners prefer to dine here, looking out over the magnificent sea views."

I look down and set in front of the large breakfast bar is a small, round, very quaint looking antique table with six chairs. Yes – I think I would prefer the table to the breakfast bar – *Coral, what are you talking about, you're never going to live here?* I can pretend – I argue back at myself.

The agent turns, and heads back towards the living area, we walk around the sofa, and he opens the door behind it. "Second reception room." He steps back to let us through.

As I walk in with Tristan, my mouth gapes open in awe, the owners have turned this room into a library, a beautiful, cosy library. All the walls bar the one to my right, which is floor to ceiling height windows, have bookshelves that go all the way up to the ceiling, and are completely over-stocked with books, there's even a stylish ladder to reach the ones at the top. Then, set in the centre of the back wall, is a very large fireplace, it looks very old and suits the room perfectly.

There are several small, very squidgy looking sofas and four leather recliners, each of them has a reading lamp next to them. I instantly imagine myself curled up on one of the chairs, book in hand, fire blazing, feeling warm and snuggly on a cold, wet winters day. I can't believe how cosy it feels, considering how big the room is.

"Current owners use this room for relaxing and reading, they like to think of it as their own mini library." He starts laughing at his own joke, his nose making a funny snorty noise as he does.

"Very good," Tristan muses, turning to me with a look that says, don't-laugh-or-you'll-start-me-off, I tighten my lips, fighting back the smile.

"If you would like to follow me, sir," the agent says. We follow the agent out of the room and head straight past the kitchen towards another door. Just as we reach it, I notice a carpeted stairway to my right.

"Stairs to the bedrooms." The agent points to the right. "And door leading into the largest reception room." He opens the door, and we follow inside.

If I thought the other rooms were big, well I was kidding myself, you could land a jet in here. The owners have placed a long walnut table in the centre of the room, and there are at least thirty chairs comfortably seated around it. I shake my head in mock horror. This room is big enough to hold a banquet. I can't help chuckling sarcastically to myself.

Tristan cottons on and cocks his head to the side.

"Would you like some time to peruse this level?" The agent asks Tristan.

"Yes, thank you." The agent nods politely and turns to walk away. The moment he is out of view, Tristan turns and gazes down at me with dark, worried eyes. "You don't like this room?" He asks.

I snort sarcastically. "What's not to like?"

He frowns at me. "But you looked horrified, and then you laughed," he says. *Jeez, he hardly knows me, yet he has my facial expressions pegged already!*

"Well it's just...very grandiose," I murmur.

"I suppose," he smirks. I smile back at him. "And the rest of the house?" he asks.

"Gorgeous," I say.

Tristan smiles enigmatically at me, making my heart skip a beat. Then he tugs gently on my hand, and we walk back out and into the kitchen. I turn and look out at the view again, but decide I want a closer look. Moving forward, Tristan releases my hand and leisurely follows me as I skip towards the window.

I feel like I'm on cloud nine like I'm in some sort of dream. I turn and giggle at him, he shakes his head at me, his smile widening. When I reach the patio doors, I see a large balcony that juts out with tables and chairs. I instantly imagine myself sitting outside with a glass of chardonnay watching the sun setting across the sea.

I turn to Tristan and puff out my cheeks, exhaling all the air slowly. I walk back over to him and as I reach him, I know I have to ask, it's been bugging me since the door was opened, actually before that.

"Tristan," I whisper just-in-case the agent is close by. "How much is this place?" I ask with wide-eyed awe.

"It's rude to ask." He softly scolds, but I can tell he's teasing me.

"I know. I'm just intrigued. Maybe I can buy it?" I chuckle.

"It's on the market for one, seven, seven five." I look up at him in confusion. That's way too cheap; somebody must have put it up wrong. "One million, seven hundred and seventy-five," he clarifies. *Whoa!*

I swallow hard and cross my arms. "Guess I won't be buying it," I grumble as I walk over to the large bespoke kitchen, Tristan follows me. "But I'll be dreaming about this place for weeks, I've never walked around a house so big. Maybe the rich really are happy if they're living in huge places like this?" I mumble to myself.

"What does that mean?" He half chuckles.

I moan, instantly wishing I hadn't said anything.

"Nothing, just ignore me," I say wafting my hand, staring up in wonder at the spotlighting above the centre console.

"That's impossible," he whispers.

My mouth pops open in shock. I stare back at him with wide eyes.

I can't believe he just said that! *Maybe Rob is right?*

We gaze at each other for the longest time; the room seems to charge with something electrical. I feel it buzzing through my veins, heating my blood. I feel like I've been electrocuted. I suddenly feel very hot and flustered.

The agent walks back in catching us unawares. "Shall we move on?" he asks.

"Coral." Tristan holds out his hand to me again, I take it without thinking about it this time, and we head towards the stairs leading to the bedrooms. As we make our way up, I subtly shake my head and smile internally, not one of the stairs creak, not like my place; I guess it's all about the finishing touches.

As we reach the open-plan landing, the agent takes us to the left, showing us the first bedroom with en-suite, which is just breath-taking, floor to ceiling tiling, bespoke furnishings. Then back out in the hallway, he leads us forward and shows us two further bedrooms with en-suites. Both these rooms are bigger than the first, but in all honesty, all of these bedrooms are bigger than my little studio. *Oh, to have this much space!*

I'm going to feel so claustrophobic when I get home tonight. I wonder if I should stay with Gladys instead? We move on to the next bedroom which is the largest, so I'm guessing this must be the master bedroom. Then my mind confirms it. It has to be, it has a walk-in closet/dressing area. Then the agent brings us back out into the hallway, and we climb another set of stairs I hadn't even noticed were there.

As we reach the top floor, the agent opens the door. "Master bedroom, large en-suite bathroom, ceiling height patio doors, leading onto the balcony..." I gasp in shock. It has ceiling height windows too, and the view... *Wow, it's even more breath-taking up here.*

I turn around and take in the huge room, set back against the wall so you would wake up to this magnificent view is the huge bed, and either side of the bed are two doors.

The agent walks over and opens one up. "Separate walk-in closets." He closes the door, walks diagonally across the room and opens the door to my left. "Master en-suite, comprising of double shower, bespoke bath, double sinks, W.C and bidet."

Tristan lets go of my hand and follows the agent into the en-suite. I turn and stare out at the view, I'm starting to feel very overwhelmed – *So this is what money can buy?*

I take a step forward, and I'm lost in a magical world. I feel like a princess in a fairy tale who's just found out she owns a beautiful, elegant house at the top of a hill.

"Coral," I hear his footsteps approaching me, pulling me out of my secret little fantasy.

"Yes," I whisper staring out to sea.

"That has to be the most beautiful thing I have ever seen," he says.

"Yes, the views are just...stunning," I whisper, agreeing completely.

"I wasn't talking about the view," he softly says.

My breath hitches hearing him say that. I close my eyes for a moment – *Me?* He was talking about me? No, surely not? He must have blinkers on or something? I swallow hard and slowly turn to stare at him with wide, cautious eyes. He's casually leaning up against the wall with his hands in his pockets, gazing at me, looking every inch, the millionaire mogul – *Man, he's sexy.*

I swallow hard against the lump in my throat and look away, trying my best to fix my gaze out to sea. In my peripheral vision I see him walk towards me – *Oh God, what does he want?*

As he reaches me, he stands directly aside me, just staring down at me. I can hear him breathing, he's that close. He leans down towards me, and as he does, I hear his breath catch. *What's he doing?*

I keep my frozen, wide-eyed gaze, fixed firmly ahead. If I look at him, I swear I'll just become putty in his hands.

"Mr Freeman?" The agent calls out.

Tristan sighs heavily, I feel like I have no choice but to look up at him. He closes his eyes briefly in annoyance then looks down at me; his look is heated, hot - *Oh Crap!*

"Excuse me," he says, gently touching my elbow then walking off to find the agent. I exhale slowly, not realising I'd been holding my breath and try to gather my scattered thoughts.

In a daze, I head into the en-suite. It's huge, and the furnishings...they look so nice, so new. I walk over and stare down at the huge, egg-shaped bath, *oh what I wouldn't give to have a place with a bath.*

I close my eyes and imagine I'm taking a long hot soak, on a cold winters night, candles surrounding me, music softly playing in the background – I sigh inwardly, feeling melancholy about it.

"Coral?" Tristan calls.

"In here," I shout. I hear Tristan approach me, then he stops standing directly behind me and places his hands on my shoulders. I should be freaking out, why aren't I freaking out?

He chuckles lightly. "You like this bath?" he asks.

"Of course," I snort and turn to look up at him. "Who wouldn't, it's huge. This whole place is huge..." I say throwing my hands up in the air.

Tristan gazes quizzically at me, I laugh and shake my head then walk out the en-suite, back into the bedroom, and drift off towards the bi-folding door. There's a very wide balcony at this level too. Not that I'll be going out there, I'm not so good with heights. I gaze out at the view, it's just so stunning. I mean, I like boats and the sea, but all you can see up here is the deep blue sparkly ocean. I feel I'm floating up in the air somehow.

"Do you like it?" Tristan asks pulling me from my musing.

I burst out laughing at his question; it seems such a silly one. How anyone can say they don't like this house, is beyond me. Then I really start to laugh, so hard in fact that my stomach starts to hurt. Tristan soon joins in; laughter is too infectious like that.

"What's...so...f-funny?" he asks between gasps for air.

I finally stop laughing so hard, just a trickle of chuckles are escaping me. "Tristan, I think this place is magical," I say mopping up the laughter tears that are streaming down my cheeks.

"Magical?" He says, his smile disappearing and a look of confusion spreading across his face.

"Yes," I breathe. "To me, this is magical, like a dream..." I smile my first bona fide smile at him.

His eyes instantly widen, just as his lips part and his breath hitches. I can tell he's breathing heavier. The room suddenly charges, and yet again I cannot pull my gaze away from his eyes, there so...so...I suddenly become very aware that we are alone... which sends my heart into a mad frenzy.

My hands and forehead instantly feel clammy...*Ugh!*

I feel hot, agitated; unsure of what to do as we stare at one another.

Then his mobile buzzes – saving me.

He looks down, breaking the connection, rolls his eyes in annoyance, clenches his jaw and pulls his mobile out of his trouser pocket. I think he's cursing under his breath. He stabs his mobile forcefully with his forefinger, I think he's annoyed with the interruption and forces it back into his pocket.

"Sorry about that." He says as he walks over to me, when he reaches me, he silently holds out his hand for me to take it. I move forward, feeling a little apprehensive at how easy it's becoming and place my hand in his.

"Do you like it?" I ask. "After all, it's you who's got to live here." He smiles oddly at me, and we start heading down the stairs. "Tristan?" I ask, wanting to know his answer.

"I..." He turns and looks up at me, stopping on the stairs. "I... I like it has a pool," he answers soberly. "I like to swim." He adds then tugs on my hand for me to follow him.

"Me too," I smile, then frown – *Something's wrong with Tristan?*

When we reach the first floor, we walk through the kitchen, and back into the entrance hall. I clock the agent, he's beaming from ear to ear, no doubt hearing our previous fit of giggles. Then I think he's probably smiling because he thinks he's made a sale already, but with what Tristan just said...I don't think he likes it that much, which I think is weird. *How can anyone not like this place?*

Following the agent, we make our way down the set of stairs that lead to the ground floor. I'm trying as hard as I can to listen to the agent, but I'm watching Tristan intently, he seems to have withdrawn into himself. I can't help wondering why? Maybe it was something I said? Maybe there's something about this house that he doesn't like? I'm not sure, but I don't know him well enough to ask him either.

The agent continues. "Entertainment suite on the garden level with a heated indoor swimming pool which is equipped with swim against tide, cinema room, gym and bi-folding doors leading to the lawned and decked rear garden..."

I decide I have to ask, it's eating away at me what's going through his mind. And even though he's assured me I keep my job, I'm panicking I might have said something wrong, and he's changed his mind. It's also made me realise that it's going to take a very long time for me to get to know him as a boss, to trust him to be honest with me, so I don't get suddenly sacked one day for going too far.

"Tristan," I whisper and tug his hand, so he follows me out into the beautiful patio area. "Are you ok? You seem kind of... off?"

He looks down at me, and I can see the worry etched on his face. *Shit!*

"Is the company in trouble?" I blurt.

He frowns deeply at me. "No."

"Are you upset about something? Have I upset you?" I ask my voice a slight tremble. "Is' – "Coral, stop!" he bawls, making me flinch slightly. Then I see his shoulders relax a little. "It's not you or anything you've done," he adds, he seems very tense.

I look away from him, then I glare at the agent, he seems to be hovering, trying to eavesdrop. I guess he thinks we are having a fallout and he's losing his sale.

"Do you want to see the gardens?" Tristan asks, his tone clipped; his eyes dark and heated.

I shrug. "Sure, why not."

As we walk across the lawned area I look up at the back of the house, I can see what they've done with it now. From the back, you can see all four levels, but from the front, it just looks like two, it's clever, and I like it. The flooring of the alfresco dining area is a different tiling it's got a lemony colour to it, it's nice, but not as nice as indoors.

The whole area is encased in a huge ceiling that juts right out, propped up by four gigantic pillars, but as I turn to Tristan to ask him what he thinks, I notice he looks miles away, which is making me feel nervous, anxious. I bite down on my bottom lip, suddenly feeling lost and insecure. I don't know this man at all, which is making me feel increasingly uncomfortable.

I think I want to go home now.

"Want to look at the cinema room?" Tristan asks pulling me out of my musing.

I shake my head, pull my hand out of his and cross my arms, I definitely want to go home.

"Alright then. Lunch?" He asks.

I shake my head again.

"Coral, please, have lunch with me. The next viewing isn't until 2pm." I look at my watch and see it's twenty to twelve, and I already feel hungry again. I always do when I've been drinking the night before.

"Please," he begs again, his eyes going lighter, the colour of milk chocolate.

My resolve falters. "Ok," I squeak.

Tristan holds out his hand again, ready for me to accept or reject it and as I seem to feel safer that way, protected, I take it willingly. Then I think how strange it is that I'm allowing him to and that I'm willingly doing this. We head back towards the agent who is smiling nervously at Tristan, we quickly reach him, Tristan seems to be in a hurry to leave.

"Mr Freeman." He takes out a handkerchief and wipes away the sweat. I know it's hot for England but *Ew!*

"I'll be in touch," Tristan simply says.

"O-of course Mr Freeman." The agent looks crestfallen, he takes Tristan's hand and shakes it, and before I have a chance to move, he has grabbed my free hand and is shaking it.

I die a thousand deaths – his hand feels all hot and clammy, just like his hands used to when I was a child...an innocent fucking child; bile rises in my throat...*Oh no!* I think I'm going to be sick.

I yank my hand out the agent's, turn away from him, and

clamp my hand over my mouth. I close my eyes to stop the sickening, queasy feeling, then I hear Tristan walking the agent away from me.

I hear George in my head, *'Anger is better than fear. Fear will hold you back make you feel small, anger will pull you out if it.'*

I decide to get angry for a second or two, just until the fear washes over me. I clench my fists and imagine I'm sparring with Will, punching the bag as hard as I can; pouring all the rage and anger out of me.

"Coral?" I hear Tristan approach and open my eyes.

He reaches his hand up to touch my face, I take a cautious step back.

"Please...don't touch me," I beg. He immediately drops his hand and frowns down at me with a confused, shocked look. "Just... give me a minute," I whisper.

Tristan stares at me for the longest time; then he finally nods once. "Shall I wait for you upstairs?" he softly asks, yet he looks torn like he doesn't want to leave me.

I nod my head in approval.

"Alright..." His lips set into a hard line, then I watch him walk away from me.

It takes me a good five minutes for me to compose myself.

Feeling ready, I dash up the stairs two at a time and find Tristan waiting for me by the front door. He doesn't offer his hand to me, which I'm thankful for, and by the time we reach the cool comfort of the car, I'm feeling more relaxed, and back in control...

CHAPTER THIRTEEN

THE MOMENT WE ARE back in the car, Tristan gently takes my hand in his, and stares down at our fingers, deep in thought.

"Are you alright?" He asks.

I nod in reply.

"Why didn't you shake his hand?" He asks me.

"Sorry?" I ask meeting his dreamy eyes.

"The estate agent, you refused his hand when we met him, then you shook it as we left."

"No, I didn't," I argue. "*He* grabbed hold of my hand before I could pull it away." I correct him.

"So, if he hadn't taken your hand you wouldn't have shaken it?" He deciphers.

"No." I sigh and look away from him. I feel like I already know what he's going to ask.

"Why?" I knew it. I sigh heavily and close my eyes. *Do I really want him to know?*

"Some men are creepier than others," I whisper. *Shut up Coral!*

"Am I creepy to you?" He asks.

My eyes dart open in astonishment. "No!" I gasp in shock. "Tristan, are you mad?" I swallow hard, still feeling amazed he asked me that. "Tristan, you are the complete opposite of creepy. Your kind, and sweet, and genuine and I… quite honestly, I'm finding it all rather odd how comfortable I am feeling in your presence. It's quite unexpected…" I finally take a breath and exhale.

He continues to gaze at me as though he's assessing that

what I have said is true, that I'm not hiding anything. His lips twitch up momentarily, then he nods once, squeezing my hand.

"Satisfied?" I ask feeling frustrated that we are having this conversation. I'm going to have to be more careful around him; he seems to be extremely perceptive.

"I want to ask why?" He softly says, his thumb circling my hand.

"Why what?" I whisper.

"Why you're the way you are?" I stare back at him in wide-eyed, frozen silence, radiating stress.

My shoulders start to work their way up to my ears, and I feel a cold sweat break out on my forehead. I can feel the trembling start from deep within me, and my heart is thumping wildly echoing my anxiety. After what feels like an eternity, I slowly shake my head at him, warning him not to go any further.

"Let's eat," he says taking note and changing the subject.

I feel my shoulders slump back down, my heart slowing back down to its regular beat, I lean back into the seat and try to relax.

"Where can we go that's quiet and has good food?" Tristan asks in a monotone voice.

I know a few places, but they're all on the Marina, and I don't want to take him there. Then it hits me, Gladys took me there for my 30th – It should be quiet this time of day.

"There's the Smugglers Rest in Peacehaven," I reluctantly suggest. "It shouldn't be too overcrowded at this time on a Tuesday, the food's great, it's a nice place."

"How long to get there?" he asks.

"Twenty minutes," I state.

"Smugglers Rest it is then." He says.

"Peacehaven?" Stuart asks.

Tristan nods silently then seems to convert back to his previous, silent brooding. I want to shout at him to stop being like this because he's making me feel uncomfortable. But then I think if I were about to spend nearly two million pounds on a house, I would be thinking very seriously about it too.

As the car pulls away, I'm instantly drawn to the song that's playing. I love music, I have such a huge collection. "Stuart, can you turn it up please?" I ask sweetly hoping he'll do so.

Stuart looks to Tristan, who silently nods. The car is

suddenly filled with Labrinth's Beneath your Beautiful. I feel Tristan gazing at me as I softly sing along, I should feel self-conscious about singing in front of him, but I think it's beautiful and poignant, so I don't let him stop me.

When the song ends, Stuart turns the radio back down. I can still feel Tristan gazing at me, the silence seems to stretch between us, so I decide to ignore it and stare out of the window.

We turn right onto Roedean Road and descend back down towards the Marina, bypassing it completely, we head east onto the A259 towards Peacehaven.

The silence continues...

"CORAL, WAKE UP DARLING." I groan and push the hand away that's trying to gently wake me.

"Tired," I manage to whisper.

"We're here," a husky voice chuckles.

"Leave me alone Carlos." I scrunch up my eyes and attempt to turn over in bed, only to jerk awake. There is no bed, and Tristan is hovering over me, grinning widely – *Shit I fell asleep!*

"Oh God, I'm so sorry!" I gasp. *How embarrassing!* "It was the car, the journey, so smooth and I just' – Tristan holds up his hand, I stop talking. "No harm, no foul," he smirks.

I quickly pull myself up from my slumped position and smile hesitantly at him. Then I watch him open the door, jump out effortlessly and make his way around the car. I look up at Stuart and bite my lip to hide my embarrassment.

Then I wonder – If Stuart is driving us around all day, what's he supposed to have for lunch? Tristan opens my door, and as I'm unbuckling my seatbelt, I decide I'll ask him anyway.

"Stuart, did you want me to bring you something to eat?"

He turns in his seat, and I see his face for the first time. He's got a captain America jaw-line, a crooked nose that looks like it's been broken a few times, hazel eyes and short spiky blonde hair. He's actually quite intimidating now I can see him properly. I certainly wouldn't want to get on the wrong side of him, he beams widely at me.

"That's sweet Coral, but I'm fine. Thank you," he says chuckling softly, then turns back in his seat.

I shrug wondering what's supposed to be so funny and

accept Tristan's hand helping me out of the car, when I look up at him I see he's chuckling too.

"He's right," he says pulling me closer to him, taking my breath away because I think he's about to kiss me; and the scariest part about it is that I think I want him to. "You are so very sweet," he moves so quickly that I don't see it coming and kisses the tip of my nose.

Then, pulling away from me as quickly as he moved in, he takes hold of my hand, and I walk with him into the Restaurant in a complete daze, my nose still tingling from his kiss.

As we walk up to the bar, Tristan's face lights up.

"What?" I chuckle squeezing his hand slightly.

"They have Timothy Taylor." He beams.

"Who?" I ask none the wiser.

"It's a beer," he chuckles slightly. "My favourite," he adds. *Well what d'ya know, I definitely took him for a wine swisher.*

"You drink beer?" I choke. "I definitely took you for a wino," I blurt without thinking about it – *Oops!*

"A what?" he chuckles.

I look away and bite my lip feeling embarrassed that I said that out loud.

Tristan puts his forefinger under my chin and raises it, so I have to make eye contact with him. "Don't hang your head feeling guilty for being you Coral, I thought that was funny." He lets go of my chin, and I make myself blink, so I stop staring at him. "Although I have no idea what it means, I can pretty much guess," he adds.

I smile weakly at him.

"What would you like to drink Coral?" *Such a gentleman!*

I shake my head feeling unsure. "Give me a minute," I answer, wondering whether I should have coffee to wake me up or water to rehydrate me.

"I like this place," he says looking around him. It's all cream walls, with wooden chairs and tables covered in white linen cloths, and has an up-market feel to it. And the place is spotlessly clean, which is always impressive when you're about to eat somewhere.

"Gladys bought me here for my 30th," I explain.

"Yeah...did you have a good time?" he asks sweetly.

"Yes, it was great, and the food was really' - Tristan suddenly moves closer to me, instantly silencing me, and kisses me so softly on the cheek that I feel as though I'm about to pass out.

All the bones in my body feel like they have liquefied. I have stopped breathing, and my heart has stopped beating.

"What was that for?" I ask breathlessly, trying to tear my gaze away from him.

"Does there need to be a reason?" he replies.

I look away from him, it's no good. I'm going to have to give him the low-down, tell him I'm not good for him... tell him to find someone else.

Tristan quickly looks away and orders his pint of beer, when it's done the barman hands it to him.

"Here try this." He holds his pint up in front me.

I shake my head, it smells funny.

"Have you ever tried it?" he questions.

"No," I grumble crossing my arms defiantly. Knowing full well I don't touch alcohol the day after a heavy night.

"Well how can you say you don't like something if you've never tried it?" he admonishes.

I sigh heavily. I'm too hung-over for the argument. I take the pint from him and tentatively take a sip – *Uh-oh!*

"That's tasty," I exclaim, handing it back to him and wondering if the hair of the dog will actually make me feel a little better.

"Would you like one?" he asks amusingly. No way. I have George tonight, I'll need a clear head – hopefully, I'll have one by then.

"I can't," I tell him quietly.

"Why?" He looks confused.

"Because I have..." I stop, wondering to myself if I should tell him, then I change my mind.

"What is it Coral?" He's intense again.

"I have an appointment tonight." I remind him.

"So, you can't drink?" He clarifies.

"No," I whisper.

"No alcohol?" I shake my head. "What would you like?"

"A large glass of water with lots of lemon please," I reply.

"Still?" he questions.

"Yes please." I smile tentatively.

Tristan places my order and hands my glass to me, we are

asked if we are eating, and when we say we are, we are told to help ourselves to whatever table we want.

Tristan leads us to a table by a large window overlooking a beautiful garden.

"This ok?" he asks. I nod in agreement.

As I side step to my seat, Tristan is instantly there, pulling it out for me. *Why does this suddenly feel like a date?*

I sit down, then I watch him walk around the table, remove his jacket and sling it over the back of his chair, then he sits down. I place my bag on the floor and pick up a menu, my stomach rumbling at me.

Tristan takes a couple of long gulps of his beer and picks up his menu. I decide it's probably best to get it out of the way now, what I want to say to him before I eat. Taking three long gulps of water, I mentally prepare myself.

"Tristan, I have something I need to say to you."

"And I to you," he adds, this stuns me into silence. "But by all means continue," he smiles coyly. "Ladies before gentleman," he adds.

He looks down at his menu again, but I think he can tell I'm staring at him, waiting for him to look at me, when he does, he instantly places his menu down and leans back in his chair, giving me his full attention. *Shit, now I don't know what to say!*

I frown down at my fingers that are twisted together in anxiety. "You really like me, don't you?" I ask mournfully.

"I think that's a given." Tristan snorts.

"You really shouldn't," I say staring at the ice swirling in my glass.

"Why?" His voice is croaky again; I think I detect a hint of pain.

"Because I don't do this Tristan," I say waving my hand in the air.

"Well good, neither do I."

I look up and narrow my eyes at him. *How the hell is this guy single?*

"Are you seeing anyone?" I question.

"You've already asked me this. No, I'm not seeing anyone." His answer is immediate, his look screams honesty, but I just don't get it, so I decide to test him.

"I don't believe you," I choke. "You're smart, rich,

unbelievably handsome, a real catch. And you're telling me you're single?"

"Why is that so hard to believe?" He asks.

"B-because you...well, you just seem so...so lovely and normal. Somebody must have caught your eye? You must have liked someone, surely?" I blurt in disbelief.

"I've had relationships in the past, they didn't work out," he says artlessly, but I detect something in his voice.

"Why didn't they?" Tristan pulls his gaze away from me and seems to withdraw into himself and I know I've hit a nerve, but before I can say anything, he answers me.

"I...I had a very different upbringing Coral, I don't think or act like my generation should. I..." he stops and shakes his head.

"You seem perfectly normal to me." I offer.

"There's that word again," he groans. *What? Oh! It dawns on me.*

"Normal?" I hiss feeling instantly incensed.

"Yes." He answers frustratingly.

I can't help the sarcastic laugh that bursts out of me. "Believe me, Tristan, in *my* world, normal is wonderful."

"That may be so but...this is irrelevant," he snaps running a hand through his hair.

I take a deep breath to calm myself. "Tristan." He looks up at me. "Are you trying to tell me they didn't get you because you were what...different? Didn't act like other guys your age, what? Tell me," I plead, even though I don't know how it got to this, and I have no idea why I'm asking.

"Apparently, I'm...it doesn't matter," he snaps again in frustration. "My past relationships are irrelevant." I relent and sit back in my chair, sulking. "And what about you Coral?" His sharp-eyed look takes me by surprise. I immediately feel defensive, but I know he deserves an answer.

"I don't date...at all," I reply feeling embarrassed.

"What, no-one's caught your eye?" He throws my words back at me, his voice dripping with sarcasm. *Yes, you have! You lovely sexy normal man, you should steer clear of a freak like me!*

"Tristan I..." I stop and stare at the table trying to grasp the right words. "You deserve better than me," I mumble almost to myself, I look up, my eyes pleading with his. "I... I don't even know if I'm capable of anything anymore...I'm broken Tristan, a freaky fuck up. You'd stay away from me if you knew what's good for you."

"I think that's my decision to make, don't you?" He retaliates.

"Tristan!" I glare back at him. "I'm telling you this, so you'll drop it," I hiss, my jaw clenching all by itself, my stomach twisting into knots.

"So, you're saying, stop before we've even got started?" He clarifies.

How perceptive of him. "Yes."

"No." He shakes his head at me. *Damn it!*

"Look, I'm not like other people ok, I don't run right, I never will, and you seem..." I stop for a moment and take several gulps of my water, really un-ladylike, but totally necessary, and continue.

"You...you're...well, lovely and gentlemanly and sweet and attentive. You deserve someone who is capable of giving all of that back to you...I... I'm not girlfriend material." I say my voice quivering on me.

For the first time in twenty-five years, I feel like I want to cry.

I'm suddenly overtaken by this strange devastating feeling that's spreading through me, it feels like grief. *How odd?* It feels like I'm about to let something go that's more important to me than I could ever imagine. I shake my head, not understanding it. *I don't know this person!*

"I just want to be straight up and honest with you Tristan, I don't want to start something that's going to have us both hurting in the end." He goes to interrupt me, but I have to keep going. I have to let him know.

"Believe me, you really don't want to be with me, especially with the fact that you're soon to be my boss."

He glares back at me, shaking his head in disagreement, I roll my eyes at him.

"Ok, let's say we date, and it doesn't work for you, or vice-versa. Somebody gets hurt and then where does that leave us, apart from a really uncomfortable and awkward working relationship." I take another drink then stare down at my knotted fingers.

"No matter how hard you try Tristan...you and me... it's just not possible." I sigh heavily feeling weirdly satisfied that what I have said covers everything, and above all I've been open and honest with him, honesty is huge for me.

I wait with bated breath for him to say something, but he's just sat there, staring at me, running his forefinger back and forth across his luscious lips. *Please stop doing that!*

I hastily pick up my menu, squirming in my seat as I do, and start to read through its offerings.

"Coral." I look up over my menu at him.

Tristan sighs heavily and stares down at his beer for a moment, then out the window at the garden, then back to me.

"You put on a good show. But I bet you're feeling just as strongly for me as I am for you, and I'm guessing that you're scared, shit scared actually...well back at you. So am I." Tristan leans forward, I open my mouth to argue, but he holds his hand up to stop me.

"Hey, you said your piece let me say mine." I am silenced, I can't argue. Gladys raised me up to be diplomatic in all situations, I nod to Tristan.

"I don't understand why you're so adamant about not wanting to even try it, to give it a go, see how it works out. But then you say I'm about to be your boss, which I am, but I've already told you, I'll hardly be there, at the office I mean. If we actually tried...and we found it was working out, I would spend more time working from home, here in Brighton, so I could see you on an evening...." he stops for a moment, lost in thought, then continues.

"Either way, it wouldn't affect your job at all. If it didn't work out, I wouldn't sack you Coral, that's the last thing in the world I would do."

Ok, feeling a little better about him being my boss and what he wants, what I have a sneaking suspicion I want. But I'm denying it, protecting myself, protecting my already broken, tattered, ragged heart.

"And just for the record, I think you're the most attractive, the most beautiful, and the sexiest woman I have ever met. Not only that, I think you're sweet, funny, and have a heart of gold which somehow has got broken, badly. I'd love to be the man that repairs it for you, mends it, heals it, but unless you give me a chance, I can't do that. And I'm not going to push you into something you don't want to do, although it's going to kill me to walk away from you."

I swallow hard, I can't believe he just said that to me. I've known him half a day, and he's declaring himself to me like... like...

Tristan continues, shaking my thought pattern.

"But at the same time there are a lot of things you don't know about me, so let me let you in on a little secret. I spend 85% of my waking hours working, and when I'm not doing that, I'm sitting in one of my houses staring at the T.V screen attempting to enjoy the movie I'm watching; when really all I feel is this crushing, sinking feeling that I am completely alone in the world. And unless I do something about it, I'm going to end up a very sad, lonely old man."

I stare down at my knotted fingers feeling quite astonished he just shared that with me.

"Don't you have any friends?" I whisper in shock.

"Friends come and go," he adds flippantly. Immediately, a feeling of being amazingly blessed that I have Rob and Carlos washes over me.

"When I finished University, I spent all my time building a successful career for myself, then the business. I wanted to make my folks proud, and I wanted to be wealthy enough to take care of them when they got older. I wanted to give back to them what they gave to me."

Tristan sounds like he's choking up. I look up and see his eyes have reddened. I think he's fighting back the tears. He must miss them so much - *Oh Tristan!*

He quickly finishes his pint and stands, his cheeks are flushed, his eyes dilated, and I have no idea what to say to him.

"Would you like another?" He politely asks, his voice a little shaky.

I drain the rest of my water and hand him my glass. "Yes please," I answer politely, unable to break eye contact with him, I watch him walk over to the bar.

Pulling my gaze away I sit staring blankly at the table. Who'd have thought it? Tristan is sad, Tristan has no-one! My heart constricts for him. He must be so lonely? I wonder if I could just be friends with him, or whether it would still be complicated with him being my new boss?

Tristan returns and places my glass down in front of me. His scent overpowers me again, shredding my nerves, sending my senses into disarray. He sits back down and takes a small sip of his drink, then stares down at the table, instinctively I know he's not done.

"You made a comment earlier about rich people being happy if they live in big houses." *Uh-oh! It was me and my big mouth that pissed him off earlier.*

"You're right Coral, totally right. If a person is happy with a successful business and big houses, nice cars, and all the trappings that money can give you then great, and in truth, I always thought I would be, I'm not saying I don't like being wealthy." He clarifies taking another drink.

"I just didn't realise something was missing in my life, something deeper that money or wealth, cars or big houses can fill. I was happy, I had my folks, the business was doing well enough so I could spend more time with them' he pauses for a moment 'then last year when they died within six months of each other, everything came crashing down. I realised it doesn't matter how successful you are, or how much money you make, without family, without love; there's no point to it, to any of it.

"I'd been putting off meeting someone because I'd convinced myself I was ok on my own, but I'm not, at all. Losing my folks made me realise that, made me realise there was a big fucking gaping hole in my life." Tristan shakes his head and drinks some more beer.

And I'm shocked. I think it's the first time I've heard him swear.

"I turn forty this year. Not that I think age is important, I just thought I would have more in my life by now...you know a partner to spend my time with...marriage, kids maybe, I don't know..." He drifts off, frowning deeply and stares into the distance for a moment, then he gazes back at me.

"And then I met you." His eyes lock onto mine, they look so deep and soulful at that moment, that I swear he can see straight through me, right into my dark soul.

"The moment our eyes met I knew I was in trouble. You knocked me sideways, took my breath away. I felt like the earth was rumbling beneath my feet, and the sky was thundering above me. I've never felt anything that can even come close to how that made me feel' – he says a little croakily, so he takes another drink – 'when I turned around and saw you standing there, I didn't see it coming at all Coral. In an instant, I saw image after image flash up in my mind's eye, all of you and I together. And for a brief moment in time, that deep empty hole disappeared."

Shit, shit, shit! That's how I felt! *Oh, Tristan!*

"I'll give you what you want Coral, but I can't say I'll stop being protective of you, I want to take care of you." He shakes his head. "For some reason, I get the feeling that you've been through enough, and I want to make sure you're ok, in all situations."

"Tristan," I whisper breathlessly, as a warm fuzzy feeling starts to flow through me, around me, encasing me. And I'm not sure if it's Tristan, his words, the confusion about how I feel; or a combination of all three, but all I want to do is jump up from my seat and wrap my arms around him, so that's exactly what I do.

Almost knocking my chair over, I take a couple of steps around the table and launch myself into his lap. I wrap my arms around his neck and shoulders and squeeze him as tightly as I can, pressing my cheek against his.

After a moment, I feel his arms encircle me, squeezing so hard I think I may stop breathing. But I like the feeling, him gripping onto me for dear life, me comforting him. It feels so good, then I think I'm probably totally confusing him.

I pull back and look down into his warm chocolate eyes, then gently stroke his face. His skin is surprisingly soft, with only the very light tickle of facial hair coming through after his morning shave.

"I'm so sorry you're lonely...just for the record, I am too," I whisper. "And I'm not trying to confuse you. I just hate it when others are suffering. I have this incessant need to help them, to comfort them. Gladys says I've always been like it ever since I came to live with her."

Tristan gazes into my eyes and runs his finger down my cheekbone, then rubs his thumb across my bottom lip. It sends lightning bolt sparks of electricity to every corner of my body.

"Try," he whispers, and I know he means us.

I gaze at him, hypnotised again. I can feel his breath against my cheeks. His body feels warm and welcoming against mine, and his scent...*oh he smells so good*. I feel like I'm being pulled in two, one part of me wants to kiss his lips with such passion and fire, and the other part is running out the door...

"I'm sorry, I can't," I whisper and kiss him lightly on the cheek. I stand awkwardly, my legs feeling like jelly and make my way back to my seat. My head is spinning. I can't believe he's disclosed so much to me, that he likes me that much. Racking my brains for what I can say to him, I suddenly have an epiphany. Maybe a way it could work? I don't know...

"Do you want to hang out, as friends?" I ask hoping he'll say yes.

Tristan gazes intensely at me for a moment. "I'd really like that," he answers hoarsely.

I sigh inwardly, feeling relieved. For some reason I feel like I need to hang on to him, I already feel like I can't let him go.

"I could introduce you to Carlos, Rob's partner, he has a huge circle of friends, and I'm sure before you know it you'll have lots of friends to spend your free time with," I add.

But I know it's not what he really wants, and if I'm honest, it's not what I want either. I frown deeply at that thought. I don't want him going out there socialising; he might meet someone, he might fall for her! And I know deep down inside, that if I'm completely honest with myself – all I really want is the one, and I have a sneaking suspicion it's him.

Tristan gazes lovingly at me for a moment, then his expression changes, his frown reappearing. "Let's eat." He states sombrely – And I wonder if I've fucked it all up again.

Sighing heavily, I pick up my menu and start to look through it, but my appetite has completely vanished. So, I decide on a salad, it's light, and I don't have to feel guilty if I don't eat much of it.

I put my menu down, and sneak a peek at Tristan, he's still perusing the menu. This guy seems to take his food seriously. I wonder why? After a moment he puts his menu down, looks up and catches me gazing at him, he smiles back at me, but it doesn't reach his eyes.

I instantly feel gutted, I really like his eyes lighting up when he looks at me. *God, I'm so confused!*

A waiter appears out of nowhere, and I'm pleased that he's

male. I don't think I can take another female ogling Tristan. He smiles politely at Tristan then turns to me, his eyes nearly popping out; I want to roll my eyes at him.

He blinks several times then turns back to Tristan. "Are you ready to order?" He asks a little nervously.

"Coral." Tristan offers for me to go first.

I look up at the waiter with a stern face; I don't want to give him the wrong impression. "I'll take the avocado & green leaf salad, hold the dressing."

"And for you sir?" He turns to Tristan.

"Chicken Caesar salad," Tristan replies not taking his eyes off me, the waiter nods, picks up the menus from our table and quickly scuttles away. "Seems I'm not your only admirer. Do you have any idea how attractive you are?" Tristan asks me.

I frown down at the table. If he had any idea of what I think of myself… "Tristan, there are thousands of women across the world that are far more attractive than I am," I mumble, feeling shy that he said that.

"So, you have self-esteem issues too?" He perceptively says.

I choose to ignore it. "Well, the woman in Munchies couldn't take her eyes off you either," I answer smartly.

"It's just a face." He waves his hand in the air.

"Precisely," I say agreeing completely.

Tristan shakes his head and takes a drink of his beer. "So, what did you really think of the house?" he asks.

"I told you, Tristan, I thought it was magical," I say. I have no idea if we've actually come to an agreement, conclusion…

"Magical?" He beams.

"Yes," I say feeling exasperated. *How many times does he want me to say it?*

"What if I said I wanted to buy it for you, for us?" I almost choke on the sip of water I've just taken.

"That's not funny." I bark, considering the conversation we've just had.

"It wasn't a joke." He counteracts, his face deadly serious.

"Are you frigging kidding me? Tristan…did any of the conversation we just had register at all? You don't know me, and you want to buy a house for me?"

"I want you to be happy." He says with a shrug of his shoulders.

"Is that why you asked me to come with you today? To make sure *I* liked the house?"

"Yes." *Shit!*

"Tristan," I moan. My mind feels like it's going to explode, too much information in one day.

He leans forward, and takes hold of my hand, he looks like he's trying to apologise. "Hypothetically speaking. If we were dating and we moved in together, would you like that house?" *Oh my God! I would love that house, but it's impossible.*

"Tristan...please, don't make this any more difficult than it already feels," I say pulling my hand away.

"Hypothetically speaking I said." He says, waiting for my answer.

"Yes," I whisper staring at my twisted hands. "I love the contemporary styled homes; the sea views are extraordinary, and the fact that it has a swimming pool is just..." I laugh, then stare out of the window. For a moment, I imagine myself in the kitchen cooking something up, Tristan coming home, embracing me...

"Then I shall cancel the next appointment, there's no point looking at it." He states pulling me from my daydream.

"Why?" I question.

"Its old school, Edwardian. Lots of dark wood, small windows..." He answers artlessly, then reaches into his trouser pocket and pulls out his mobile. "You wouldn't like it," he adds pressing a number on his smart-phone. "Susannah, my appointment today at 2pm; cancel it, please. Get Martin to make an offer on The Cliff, come in at one-five, and see where we go from there. I want this house...yes if I have to pay full price I will but, yes you got it..." Tristan smiles warmly, then listens for a moment. "Thank you." He hangs up and places his mobile back in his trouser pocket.

"Please don't tell me you are buying that house because of me." I squirm, feeling totally uncomfortable.

"You like it," he shrugs. "A man can dream," he adds.

My jaw tenses, I shake my head at him.

"Look Coral, say for instance one day you change your mind, and I'm living somewhere that you hate. I'd have to go through the whole process all over again and to be honest, I find it all a little...boring." He admits.

I gasp in shock. "You find buying million-pound houses boring?" I'm choking on my own words.

"It is when you're doing it on your own," he answers a little glumly. "Today was the best house hunting day I've ever had, watching your face light up as we went through each room was.... magical," he says, using my words, his eyes lighting up again. "You've made me declare my hand far too early Miss Stevens." He growls playfully.

"So sorry to have done that to you Mr Freeman, but you're living in a fantasy world." I retort and cross my arms to create some sort of barrier between us.

"Coral...I'm sorry, but I had to tell you how I feel. I'm already afraid of another man coming along, and you'll say yes to him' – "Tristan," I interrupt. "Believe me when I say, there's absolutely no chance of that happening, trust me." I sigh.

"Hmm....well when I move in, I'll be fantasising about you being there with me.... every day." His eyes gleam wickedly at me, and I have to wonder exactly what kind of fantasies he's conjuring up in his mind.

I swallow hard, not knowing what to say to that.

"I'm sorry Coral, I didn't mean to make you feel uncomfortable..." Tristan drifts off, and I'm acutely aware that I'm in it, big time!

And for a tiny moment, I imagine what it would feel like to date him. To have him give me his jacket in the winter, or feel his protective arm around me in a busy bar, or curling up together in the cinema room that we didn't see watching a movie together eating popcorn, or – *Stop!* I can't allow myself to think sexually about him, it's just too intense.

"Coral?" I look up at Tristan. "You look breathless, and your eyes have dilated. Are you ok?" I pick up my water and take several gulps of it.

"I'm fine," I say breathlessly. "So, what now?" I ask feeling frustrated.

"Sorry?" Just as Tristan says that the waiter appears with our meals.

"One avocado salad," he says his eyes flirting with me, his body way too close to mine and places the plate in front of me. I frown at him in disapproval. *Back off dude!*

"Without the dressing," he adds far too seductively for my liking.

I immediately tense up, and I sense rather than see Tristan's disapproval. The waiter then turns and places Tristan's plate in front of him. "One chicken Caesar salad," he says smartly.

Leaning back in his chair with his forefinger pressed against his lips Tristan glares up at him. *Whoa if looks could kill!* The waiter looks back at him and quickly realises that Tristan is not impressed, he quickly clears his throat.

"Will there be anything else sir?" he asks, his voice a little shaky.

"Yes, the manager." Tristan snaps.

The waiter hops from one foot to the other not knowing what do to, his cheeks flame bright red, and a layer of sweat appears across his top lip, I feel bad for him, he's only a kid.

"Tristan, it's ok, you don't' – "Now." He barks to the waiter who scuttles off as quickly as he can. *Uh-Oh!*

"Tristan, you really don't need to' – "He was making you uncomfortable, I could see that, and what's more annoying is so could he. I hate blokes like that." He says, then cuts a piece of chicken and starts chewing.

Moments later a woman in her mid-fifties appears looking a little flustered. She smiles tentatively at me, and I return the smile, picking at my salad. Tristan swallows, wipes his mouth with his napkin and stands, gesturing to the woman to walk with him. They only move a few feet away, enough so that I can't hear what's being said.

I frown as I watch Tristan, I can tell he's annoyed, his hands moving around as he talks to the woman. As she listens to him, I watch her face go from pacified to her furious. She does not look like a happy bunny. Her head is nodding as she listens to Tristan, and from my bad lip-reading skills, I think she is apologising to him.

Within moments he is back at the table, and without a word, he sits down and tucks into his meal. I can't believe he just did that, just because a waiter got a little flirty! Which makes me think how he would be if I actually did go out with him? I know there is absolutely no way I could go out with a control freak, that would drive me nuts and make me feel trapped.

I look down at my salad and spear a piece of avocado with my fork.

"Are you a control freak?" I blurt. *Oh my God Coral, shut up!*

Tristan freezes. "Excuse me?"

"Well, are you?" I repeat.

"No," Tristan chuckles lightly. "You think because I made a complaint about a member of staff that I'm a control freak?"

I shrug and don't answer, feeling as though I've just dropped myself in it *again*.

"Will you tell me what you said to her?" I ask.

"No," he retorts.

"Why not?" I grumble.

Tristan stops eating and eyes me carefully. "Does it matter?" *He's trying to reason with me?*

"Yes, I want to know." I squeak my voice a little higher than I want it to be.

"Why?" He questions.

I roll my eyes at him feeling frustrated again. "Honesty is something I value, highly," I say.

"Me too," he says and continues eating.

"Just tell me," I snap, throwing down the gauntlet.

Tristan smirks, finishes chewing, uses his napkin and takes a long drink of beer. *He's teasing me!* Prolonging the agony of not knowing, he doesn't play fair.

"I'd like to go home." I sulk, dropping my fork next to my plate, glaring at him venomously.

"Are you always this argumentative?" He asks, his eyes sparkling. *Damn it!*

"No... I'm not! I just..." I purse my lips and cross my arms. I decide the best thing to do is shut up, and wait for him to finish. He's definitely not going to tell me. No-one's ever wound me up this good, yet weirdly enough, fighting with Tristan feels kind of...ok?

"Ok...if I tell you, will you agree to spend the day with me this Sunday?" He asks teasingly.

"No." I snap.

"Not even as friends?" He asks smirking at me.

"No." I pout feeling as though this is getting silly and way out of hand.

"Ok, if I tell you, can I come to your niece's birthday party on Saturday?" *What? Why would he want to hang around a bunch of screaming kids?*

"No," I answer with a nervous laugh.

"That's a lot of no's." He says smirking at me.

"I'm done," I say. Throwing my napkin on top of my plate, I pick up my bag and stomp out of the restaurant without looking back. The moment I'm outside I see the car, Stuart jumps out, looking behind me for Tristan and walks straight over to me.

"Miss Stevens?" I roll my eyes at him.

"Coral," I say through gritted teeth. "I'd like to go home," I state, my arms crossed, my foot tapping. Seconds later, Tristan comes out of the restaurant, he nods to Stuart who immediately walks back to the car.

Tristan stops when he reaches me, I glare up at him. "I'm sorry. I thought we were having fun?" He says leaning into me and running a cool fingertip down my cheek.

"No, you were being cruel, not playing fair. I don't like to be wound up Tristan."

"I can see that." He states.

My throat burns and my eyes sting, I feel like I could cry again - *What is wrong with me today?*

I mean, I know I'm normally a little under the weather after a heavy night, but I think everyone is. Today, I just feel like there's a dam waiting to burst and I haven't cried since...I close my eyes trying to push the feeling away and take a few deep breaths.

"You're a hard one to work out Coral." Tristan murmurs.

"Back at you," I whisper, keeping my eyes closed. *This is crazy!*

I need to start avoiding him as much as possible, create an impenetrable thick glass wall between us. Be smart, and not get more involved than I already am. Maybe even get another job? Then I think about never seeing him again, and I'm suddenly overtaken with a feeling of despair.

I'm having a really hard time ignoring how I'm feeling for him. A fleeting thought passes through my mind of just going for it and sleeping with him, then I remember what my last sexual experience was like.

I shiver internally. I haven't been with a man since...

"Come back to me Coral," he whispers in my ear, bringing me out of my reverie.

I open my eyes and stand there like a statue, staring up into his warm chocolate eyes. I can see now that I'm so close to him that he has tiny flecks of hazel in his eyes, and the blazing sun is making all his natural highlights shine brightly, burnt copper and a hint of reddish brown. I can't decide which one I like best?

"Come on, let's get you home," Tristan says.

Home – It's a strange word. What does it really imply? Is it the people that you love, a house, your hometown? Or is it a feeling? A sense of safety, belonging? I've never really known where home is, that is until now – I quickly push the thought aside and nod at Tristan, he puts his arm around my waist, and we head back to the car.

CHAPTER FOURTEEN

STUART DRIVES AWAY FROM the restaurant, and we head back to Brighton. I relax into the coolness of the leather seats.

"Are you going to tell me what you said to her?" I ask nicely.

Tristan turns to me and grins. "I told her that you're a food and restaurant critique, and I was simply a friend joining you for lunch. And that I would try my very best to get you to change your mind about the awful review you were going to put up, simply because the waiter was rude and flirtatious." He grins even wider, his dimples deepening.

I shake my head at him and start chuckling. "What did she say?" I ask.

"The meal was free, and that she would be having words with the waiter." Tristan smiles back at me.

"That's so cool," I laugh. "What a great story to come up with. I may have to use that one in future."

"You don't like it when you don't get your own way, do you?" He asks.

My face falls. "It's not that, I just don't like things being kept from me. I don't like secrets."

"It wasn't a secret," he argues.

"I know…I just wanted you to tell me." I offer by way of explanation. "I'm sorry I walked out on you," I add.

"Don't be." He answers.

"What are you doing for the rest of the day?" I ask casually. But what I really want to know is who he'll be with?

"Working," he tells me.

"You're going back to the office?"

"No, the hotel."

"Oh…is it nice?" I ask. Hoping he'll tell me what hotel he's staying in.

"Yes, I suppose it is," he smirks at me, his eyebrows raised - *Of course it's nice Coral!*

I try to think of the best hotel in Brighton. I wonder if it is that one?

"You wouldn't be staying at The Hilton by any chance?" I ask dryly.

"Yes." I raise my eyebrows in astonishment, I am right! And it is really nice; Debs had her wedding there.

"It's a nice hotel." I agree.

"You've been in there?" He asks a little confused.

"My step-sister had her wedding there, it was really lovely. The whole day was great, the food, the staff, and Debs said the Wedding suite was gorgeous." I look across at Tristan. "Oh…let me guess you're staying in a suite, aren't you?"

"Yes." He sighs.

"Which one?" I giggle.

"The best one." He shrugs.

"Really?" *Oh, to live in luxury!*

"Yes, the double Hilton." He sounds bored.

"Is that the top suite?" I ask teasing him.

"Yes." He sighs again.

"If you don't like hotels, why did you bother getting the best room?"

"I always book the best suite." He answers bitterly. *Ouch!*

"Sorry," I whisper.

"Let's get you home," he says. And for some reason, I know the conversation has ended for now, so I turn and look out of the window, feeling broody and confused.

We sit in silence for about ten minutes, when I suddenly realise what Tristan meant, *'let's get you home'*– Shit, he's taking me back to the Marina!

"Aren't you going to ask me where I live?" I mutter to break the silence, knowing full well we are nearly there.

Tristan silently shakes his head at me. *God damn it! He knows where I live!*

I remain silent for the rest of the journey…

WHEN STUART PULLS UP outside the gym, I quickly unclip my seatbelt, and I'm about to pull the door handle when Tristan's hand covers mine, sending tingles all the way up my arm. "Allow me," he mutters and then jumps out.

I watch him walk around the car and open my door for me, helping me out with his hand again. He shrugs out of his jacket and leaning into Stuart he hands it to him, then he takes off his tie and hands him that too, muttering something as he does. I watch in panic as Stuart pulls away, leaving me with Tristan who has taken his cufflinks off and is rolling up his sleeves.

"Aren't you going with him?" I ask breathlessly.

"No."

"Why not?" I question.

"I'd like to walk you home," he says, unaffected by my brooding.

"Tristan, I've been living here for two years. I'm fine, this place is safe; I feel safe here." I say defiantly.

"Still." He shrugs unapologetically.

"No!" I bark and step away from him.

"You don't want me to walk you home?" I shake my head at him. I don't want him to see where I live, I know it would seem ridiculously small to him.

Tristan moves closer to me again. "I know you live in one of those floating studios Coral' – "How?" I snap taking another step back.

Tristan backs off with his hands in the air. "Joyce told me," he states truthfully. "I wasn't sneaking around asking Coral. I'm not some crazy weird stalker, although I could easily get your personal details from H.R." He adds.

I sigh heavily, of course, he could, but he didn't. Then I think he will soon have access to every member of staff's personnel file, so it's inevitable that he's going to know where it is, eventually!

"Why did Joyce tell you?" I ask feeling a little betrayed that she must have been discussing me with Tristan.

"You came up at dinner last night. Joyce was saying that, well...that you haven't had it easy, and that you've pulled through really well. She was saying that she's really proud of you, and pleased that you finally got on the property market."

I feel sick. Susannah was dining with them last night.

"As you know I'm looking to buy, so out of interest I asked where you were...what?" He asks seeing the look on my face.

"Joyce was discussing my private life in front of Susannah?" I squeak, feeling mortified.

"Good god no!" Tristan pulls me into him, crushing me to his body and kissing the top of my head. "Susannah had the meal then went back to her hotel room, Joyce and I stayed on."

He pulls back and lifts my chin, so I have to look up at him. *Oh crap!* Please don't kiss me; I don't think I'll stop if you do!

"Coral don't you know? Joyce would never divulge personal information about you to just anyone. She knows I need to be filled in about the staff, you came up." He says softly.

I nod feeling a little better, but I need to get out of his arms, his lovely strong arms.

"Ok, it's hot," I say struggling out of his arms. I smile tentatively at him, then march away. "Are you coming?" I shout not looking back. Tristan is next to me again in no time at all. "I'm sorry about lunch," I say still feeling guilty.

"There's no need' – "Yes there is. It's something about me that you're going to have to get used to Tristan, as your future P.A. I do something on the fly, without really thinking it through, then I mentally castigate myself for it, the guilt trips are well..." I wave my hand in the air and laugh sarcastically at myself.

"I was the one to blame there." He argues.

"Doesn't matter who's to blame, the point is I don't think I would easily forgive someone for storming out of a restaurant on me. I'm surprised you're still talking to me, and that I still have a job. When people are nice to me after doing something bad I... I don't understand it, I don't get why they don't just tell me to fuck off out of their lives."

As we reach the steps to the concourse, I stop and look up at him. "I really did mean it, Tristan, I'm way beyond complicated. I'm a complete fuck-up, and you're a fool to want anything to do with me." I march on down the steps leaving Tristan standing there with a look of shock spread across his face.

He catches up with me again, pushing his hands into his pockets. "It is lovely here," he says sounding genuine, not commenting at all about my little outburst. "Do you like boats Coral?"

I turn and smile up at him. "I don't just like them, I love them," I answer.

"What kind do you like?" He asks.

I shrug, unsure. "All of them, I guess – I've never really thought about it, can't afford one so..." I drift off again.

"You've never been on one?" He asks.

"No." I sigh.

"Not even a dingy?" He chuckles.

"No." I try not to smile. "Why?"

"Just curious," he says shrugging his shoulders. "So, you don't know if you'd like say...a wooden schooner, a catamaran or a modern yacht?"

I stop walking and stare up at him. "No, I don't. Why are you asking?" I'm already suspicious. Tristan shrugs again. I narrow my eyes at him. "Do you like boats?" I ask.

"Yes." His tone is clipped.

"What kind do you like?"

"Yachts." *Figures! He's rich, he can afford one!*

"Let me guess, a big ass luxury one?" I question sarcastically.

"That's not a bad idea," he says, stroking his chin. *He's laughing at me.*

"Tristan!" I scold.

He smiles a slow, sexy smile at me. "If you like boats so much why haven't you taken a sailing course or something?" He questions.

My mouth pops open, he has no idea. "Tristan, do you have any idea how expensive it is?" I say my hands on my hips.

"No, do you?"

"Yes."

"How much?" he asks, his smile still visible – *Ok, I'm getting wound up again.*

"Half my monthly wage for one day out, I'm sure you know how much I earn, so work it out for yourself." I huff and walk off. *Oh, I'm mad at him!*

He thinks this is funny, well it's not – He has no idea how fucking crushing it is to have something that you really want to do, that sits in front of you every day, but can't afford to do it – *Rich bastard!*

Reaching my patio door, I unlock it and walk inside. I'm instantly bowled over by the heat. I march straight over to the bathroom and yank open the window. Tristan follows me in, casually looking over the place, his cheeks start to pink, and I wonder if he's going to pass out, he looks really hot. It feels very strange having him in here, I want to tell him to go, that I got back safely, so he'll leave, but I feel like I should refresh him with something...?

"Come outside," I say. "It's cooler on the sun-deck," I add.

Walking back outside I see Bob, he's leaning back in his chair with his sunglasses on. I can't tell if he's sleeping, and I can't believe I missed him when I got here – My brain is definitely not working properly.

"Know you're there," he shouts making me jump just as Tristan joins us.

"Bob, meet Tristan." I chuckle. Tristan wonders over, and they shake hands. "Anyone for lemonade?" Bob loves Gladys's homemade lemonade. "It's homemade," I tell Tristan, he nods in approval. I walk back inside feeling instantly zapped from the heat, get three tall glasses from the cupboard, add lots of ice from my tiny freezer, then top them up with lemonade.

Taking my wedges off, I quickly pad back outside and hand the drinks out. Bob drinks his down in one go and hands me back the glass, I put it on the little table next to him. Within a couple of minutes, Bob is softly snoring. *Guess I'll be asking him to Lily's party later then.*

"Excuse me a moment." Tristan gently touches my arm and walks back into my studio.

I watch him pull his mobile out of his pocket and make a call. I can't help wondering what that's all about? I lean on the railing and stare out at the boats. I'm so lost in thought that Tristan makes me jump when he re-joins me.

"Jesus Coral, it's like an oven in there," he says, dabbing his top lip and his brow with his hand, then he leans against the railing, his body mimicking mine.

"Well, I'm not normally home till late, and by then it's really cooled down – and I have my electric fans," I add although I'll probably spend the afternoon in the pool at the gym; it's too hot to stay indoors.

"Like that'll make much off a difference." He answers dryly.

I laugh and look out over the water - there are so many boats out today. *I'm jealous!*

"So why boats?" Tristan softly asks.

I shake my head not wanting to tell him.

"Is it that they can give you adventure, travelling to different places?" He asks.

"That's a huge bonus," I reply.

"What then, escapism?" My eyes widen. *How is he doing that?* Hitting the nail on the head all the time? He's starting to make me feel like I'm easy to read.

"That's it." He says, grinning triumphantly.

I nod solemnly.

His face falls, turning away from me he looks out at the boats bobbing on the water. "Must have been pretty bad for you to want to escape Coral," he adds darkly.

"You know why I bought this place?" I say. Tristan turns and looks down at me. "When I first came here' – I take a deep breath – 'to Brighton I mean, Gladys used to take me to all these different places, the beach, the parks, the pier, it didn't matter what she did, I was...uncontrollable. Then one day she brought me here, I remember it clearly. We sat right over there' I point to the wall 'and sat eating ice-cream, three ice-creams actually. We were here so long. Gladys was astonished, it was the only place I was calm and still, and as far as she knew...happy."

I shake my head remembering how I used to be.

"So, after that first day, we came back every day, no matter what the weather." I can't help chuckling at myself. "I think more so that Gladys could get some peace and quiet for the day, but the more she did it, the better I got. I think it's because I had my place to escape to, I would get lost in thought imagining I was on one of those boats, sailing to distant islands having an adventure. It still feels like that to me..." I drift off.

Tristan nods once, staring down at me with those captivating eyes of his. He puts his arm around my shoulder and squeezes me tight. Then leaning in, he softly kisses my temple.

I melt, that was so sweet!

"I don't want to leave you," he murmurs.

I grin widely at him. "Have you been listening to a word I've said?" I tease, bumping his shoulder, trying to ease the magnetic pull I can feel resonating from him.

"I have to go back to Leeds tomorrow, it's going to seem so dull compared to this place."

I chuckle loudly. "Yep...Brighton certainly has charisma!"

"I wasn't thinking about Brighton," he says gazing affectionately at me.

"Tristan," I admonish softly, and try to pull my gaze away, but it's just so difficult.

He's looking at me that way again, as though I'm the air that he breathes, so I give in. I close my eyes and rest my head on his broad shoulder. I really don't understand why this feels so...so, right? I've never felt this safe with a heterosexual male before, not even Justin, took me weeks and weeks before I even kissed him, and I know nobody really liked him. Gladys didn't trust him at all, even told me so *'he's not to be trusted that one, be careful Coral'* in fact, I would go so far as to say she secretly hated him, of course, she was right.

I push the memory away, I don't want to think about him, not while I have Tristan here with me, for some reason, it seems insulting to do so. A fleeting thought enters my mind – I know Gladys would really like Tristan and approve of him. I huddle even closer to him feeling safe and peaceful, knowing somehow, that he's completely and utterly who he is.

There's no mask hiding any monsters, he's honest and up front.

God, I must be confusing him so much by now...I think through the day we've had, the truths, the disputes, yet he's still here, he hasn't run for the trees, even though my behaviour has been pretty despicable. I'm reminded of my rudeness towards him on Monday night, which reminds me...

"Were you following me Monday night?" I question, opening my eyes to gauge his reaction.

Tristan shakes his head slightly. "No, I was headed to the gym."

We gaze at each other for a moment, I really like the fact he loves swimming as much as I do.

"For a swim," he spookily adds. "I wanted to offer you the courtesy of a lift." He smiles.

"But you didn't know where I lived then?" I say surprised.

Tristan shrugs. "Wouldn't have mattered, I'd have still driven you wherever you needed to be. It would have given me peace of mind to know you were safely there."

"Why?" I ask incredulously.

He stares at me for the longest time, then looks out to sea. "Honestly? I don't know." He says, shaking his head slightly. "I just wanted to make sure you were home safely," he adds.

"Oh." Tristan smiles shyly at me then gazes out to sea again.

"So where was Stuart then?" I ask a little confused. I don't get why he would bring two cars down here, seems a little over the top to me.

"At the hotel with the rest of the team," he answers.

"Oh." I whisper, trying to work it out. "So, you drove your car down?" I ask.

Tristan chuckles. "Yes...I like driving it," he says excitedly.

"And Stuart drove down alone?" I ask.

"No, he brought the team down." I quickly work it out – there were four others in his team.

"That must have been cramped." I chuckle sarcastically.

"Not really, Susannah was with me," Tristan says.

I turn and lock eyes with him, then stand up straight, backing away as realisation dawns. "She...she was in your car?" I choke, the green-eyed monster in me rearing its ugly head.

"Y-yes?" Tristan stutters, confused. I grit my teeth and go to walk away from him. "Hold on a minute," he says tugging my elbow. "Is there a problem?" He asks sharply.

"No." I bark trying to yank my arm out of his grasp.

"Coral," he admonishes. "There's nothing there, Sus'- "I don't want to know." I bite, interrupting him.

"Hey!" Tristan doesn't let go of me. "You're jealous?" He guesses, his lips quirking up at the corners.

"No," I answer sounding like a sulky child.

"You have no need to be." He softly says, trying to reassure me.

"I'm not convinced." I snap.

"Susannah is happily married," he snaps back. "And even if she wasn't, I have no interest in her."

But I still don't believe him, all those pictures I found on Google, all those tall, leggy blondes.

"You know, for someone who isn't interested in me, you're putting on a mighty fine show of being upset about other women. So, which is it Coral, either you don't care if I date, or you do?"

I'm stumped, he's caught me out. – I'm about to answer him when he suddenly looks up over my head. I follow his gaze, only to see Stuart walking down the concourse, struggling with a large cardboard box, Tristan hands me his glass and runs over to him. They both pick the item up and walk over to where I'm standing, and bypassing me entirely, they enter my studio and place it down on the floor. I follow them both in, placing our glasses on my tiny coffee table.

"What's going on?" I ask irritably.

"Where are your scissors Coral?" Tristan asks ignoring my question.

I glare back at him. "Why?" I huff, feeling aggravated.

Tristan rolls his eyes at me and starts searching in the kitchenette drawers, finally locating where I keep them. He quickly snaps the plastic binders, then he and Stuart start pulling the cardboard off, until finally, standing in my studio is a tall white electrical item of some sort? Stuart picks up all the cardboard, plastic, and Styrofoam padding, and leaves my studio, nodding once as he passes me.

"Um...what's this?" I ask.

Again, Tristan ignores me, which is winding me up a treat.

"Tristan!" I scold. "Answer me." He plugs it into the nearest empty socket and switches it on. A low humming sound fills the room, then Tristan fiddles with a couple of buttons and stands in front of it, holding his hands out, I think it's a fan?

"Marvellous," he says, grinning widely. "The joys of technology," he adds turning that dazzling smile on me. His dimples deepen again, and I can't help but smile back at him.

Curiosity gets the better of me, so I walk over to him, he pulls me in front of the machine, and I'm shocked by how cold the air is that's coming from it, and how amazing it feels to have his body brush against mine.

"What is it?" I ask.

Tristan walks over to the patio door and pulls it shut. "An air-conditioning unit." He tells me.

My eyes widen. "Aren't they really expensive?" I gasp.

Tristan shrugs. "Can't have you melting in here Coral, I couldn't bear to think about it."

I eye the machine again. My little studio is quickly dropping in temperature, becoming cooler, more bearable.

"How' – "When I made the call earlier it was to Stuart, I asked him to see if he could locate one for you."

"But' – "No buts," Tristan playfully tells me off. "I want you to have it." I pout back at him. He stands behind me again. "See how much nicer it's already becoming in here," he adds.

I nod in wonder. "Thank you," I gush. "It's great." And I have to ask myself why I didn't use my own savings and purchase one, my two electric fans weren't really doing anything.

I turn around, reach up onto my tiptoes and kiss him on the cheek. "Thank you," I say again. "It's really wonderful...and thoughtful," I add.

The atmosphere in the room charges, his eyes become intense, dilated, as he stares back at me. His jaw sets and I can see the passion swimming in his eyes, I'm sure mine are reflecting the same intensity back to him. He's dying to kiss me as I am him, but if I let it happen, I don't think I'll stop.

Tristan finally pulls his gaze away, picks up his lemonade and drains the last of it. Placing it on the kitchen counter, he silently looks back at me.

I frown when I see that his expression looks tortured.

He takes two quick strides towards me, and without a word, he pulls me into him, wrapping his one arm around my waist and his other around my shoulders, crushing me into him. After a moment, I do the same, feeling the muscles in his back ripple. It feels heavenly divine. I don't want him to let go...

"Please think about it," he whispers. I know he means us, think about us.

I look up at him, his eyes are wide and dark. He leans down and kisses my forehead...*Oh, Tristan, I'm trying, I'm really trying!*

He squeezes me one last time then pulls away, and when he does, he takes his wallet out of his pocket and hands me a card. I take it from him and look down at it. It's a business card. I can see the home line of his other houses, his mobile number and all the other numbers to reach him on at work.

"Only five people have one of these, be careful with it, I'm very private Coral. I don't want just anyone getting hold of my personal numbers."

I frantically nod, unable to speak, because I know I'm not going to see him again for...till...and my heart feels like a steel hand is crushing it, and he hasn't even left yet. I bring my hand to my mouth, trying to block out the nauseous feeling that's taking over me, literally petrifying me, my lungs feel as though all the air has been sucked out of them.

I can't breathe!

I feel like I'm free falling into some horrible nightmare, never to wake again...

"Ok?" Tristan asks, lifting my chin to look at him.

I nod silently again, trying to get my lungs to work.

"So long Coral, I'll see you soon," he says desperately, a hint of hope in his voice. Then with one last kiss on my forehead, I watch his tall, strong stature disappear out of my studio.

I stare numbly at the door. *Why do I feel so empty?*

A strange, horrible, aching feeling fills my stomach – *What is that?* I look down at the floor trying to work it out. Why do I feel like this? Why do I feel so void of all things, even myself?

You know why...

My knees buckle, and I fall to the floor, one hand gripping my stomach, the other my chest where my heart is, trying to stop nauseous feeling that is washing over me, wave after wave. I stare back at the door, and all I want is Tristan back in my arms, holding me close, protecting me, loving me... *Tristan!*

SOMETHING STRANGE IS happening to me. I have spent the last hour staring blankly at the wall. The only thing that has pulled me out of it is my mobile buzzing in my handbag next to me. I wonder if it's Tristan calling me? The moment I think that my heart slams against my chest and triples its beats, my stomach fills with butterflies, and I feel an odd ache somewhere between my heart and my abdomen.

I place my hand against my chest and try to calm my racing heart. Then I reach over and pull my mobile out of my bag. *Crap!* It's not Tristan, it's not anybody, it's my reminder for my appointment with George tonight.

I groan inwardly, I have two hours to go until I see him, and for some reason I can't quite fathom, I decide I have to see Gladys before I see the good doctor. I want to know what Joyce has said to her. Maybe I can find out what she's told Tristan about me. Plus, I want to know if Joyce will be back in tomorrow and if she's ok.

And I think, just maybe, I might ask her opinion on what I should do about Tristan, see him or not see him. I keep thinking it's just the fact that he's going to be my boss that's holding me back, but in truth, I know it's not – that's not what's really stopping me.

I jump up from the sofa and scramble as quickly as I can up the stairs, removing my clothes as I go. Pulling on my robe, I run back down the stairs, go straight into the bathroom and turn on the shower – Five minutes later I'm done.

With my skin creamed, I wrap my robe around me and run back up the stairs to dress. I pull on my grey combats, my white support vest and my flip-flops. As I'm dashing about I catch myself in the mirror, and for a fleeting moment, I don't recognise the woman staring back at me, she looks...happy?

I shake my head, turn away from the mirror and dash back down the stairs. Grabbing my bag and my keys, I stop for a moment wondering if I should leave the air conditioner on. I decide not to, I can always cool it back down when I return.

Wandering over to it, I press the off button. That was such a sweet thing for Tristan to have done. Tracing my fingertips across the machine, I see Tristan standing before it, I see his hypnotic eyes gazing back at me, his beautiful smile. And I'm daydreaming again...I have to shake my head to snap myself out of it!

Pulling the patio door shut behind me and locking it, I make my way up to the gym. I'm hoping that there will be a few taxis waiting; otherwise, I won't make it from Gladys to George's in time. Good fortune seems to be on my side. As I reach the car park, I see there's a taxi waiting, and he's free. As I scramble inside, I have a flashback from the previous night's escapades – Rob and I drunkenly trying to remember the words to the song Tequila that was done in the nineties - I think the group was Terrorvision - while we waited for Carlos to come and collect us. I can't help chuckling, feeling my mood lighten a little. Spending time with Rob will do that to a person, he's so much fun.

"Where to love?" I hadn't even noticed the taxi wasn't moving. *Not a good sign!*

"Oh...um 78 Waldegrave road please." I smile sweetly at

the driver who is eyeing me speculatively, I suppose most people don't get into a taxi and stare blankly ahead.

As we pull out into traffic, I'm drawn to the music playing. James Morrison is crooning away singing You Give Me Something, the words matching my feelings for Tristan, literally line for line. I shake my head and bite my lip, how ironic. It really seems so poignant that it's playing right now, I almost laugh out loud at the perfect timing of it all. Maybe the universe is playing a joke on me?

I frown at that thought. What if Tristan isn't real? What if none of this is and I'm dreaming it all? I pull my right hand up to my left arm and pinch myself. *Yep, definitely felt that! Then Tristan must be real...*

My lips curl up into a smile, and it doesn't leave me the whole way there.

CHAPTER FIFTEEN

TEN MINUTES LATER, I am walking up the front steps of the three-bedroom Victorian house that I grew up in. Gladys bought this house with her husband forty years ago, before Brighton really became what it is now. Gladys and her husband had only been living in it for five years when she came home and found a letter telling her that he'd fallen for his secretary, and had already left her.

With no job and no money to support herself, Gladys went a little crazy for a while until Joyce suggested renting the spare bedrooms out. So, she did, it helped pay the bills, and she made some really good friends, but she dreamed of having a family of her own. Joyce was the one that suggested adoption and went with Gladys to get her signed up. Two years later she had Debbie, then ten years later, she got me – poor woman!

I put my key into the lock and turn it. Stepping through the front door, I immediately know something is different, I can smell spicy food. Gladys doesn't eat anything spicy. As far as she's concerned a Chicken Korma is hot and foreign, she really has no idea at all.

I can also hear some strange guitar music playing, it sounds like what you would hear the street buskers playing if you were in Spain, and it's loud, really loud - I hesitantly pull my key out the door and shout hello, to which there is no reply.

I close the door behind me and make my way down the long hallway, past the living room, the dining room, and stop when I reach the swinging door that leads into the kitchen. I put my ear to the door, I can't hear anything unusual, so I push the door, and it swings open, and what I see before me is enough to make anyone's toes curl.

Gladys is sitting on the kitchen table half-naked, her silk dressing gown is falling down her back, a man's head is nuzzled between her breasts licking what I think is squirty cream off her, and she is moaning and giggling loudly... *What the...?*

"Oh my god!" I gasp in shock and spin around so I can't see anymore.

I have absolutely no idea where to put myself!

"Coral!" Gladys screams I hear them both burst into fits of giggles.

I want to run away, but my feet seem frozen to the floor, in the next second the Spanish music is switched off, and there's lots of banging and cluttering going on with lots of muffled sniggering.

Jesus Christ if I'd have known I never would have used my key!

"Coral," Gladys sniggers. "What are you doing here?" she asks breathlessly, still chortling.

I slowly turn to her, peeking with my one eye first to make sure she is covered up and thankfully she is, so I turn and face her.

The man who was in the kitchen with her seems to have disappeared.

Picking up my handbag that I dropped to the floor in shock, I glumly answer her back. "I thought I would come by and see you, ask how Joyce was," I say not knowing where to look.

I can't quite believe I have just caught Gladys in a passionate clinch, with a man I didn't even know she was seeing! In fact, I don't even know if she is seeing him, or if he's just a bit of fun? I immediately scratch that thought away. I don't even want to go there.

"You look shocked." She chuckles then hiccups. I think she's a little drunk. Her cheeks are bright red from all the extra-curricular activities, and she's swaying slightly, but as I take a closer look at her, I see her eyes are all red and bloodshot.

I narrow my eyes at her, then I notice it, a strange smell, not spices, but something else, something herby...then I clock it. A half-smoked joint is lying in a saucer on the draining board. *You have got to be kidding me!*

"Come meet Malcolm." She says all buzzy and lightheaded, still giggling.

As I look back at her, all I can see is the image I just walked in on – *Oh God I wish I hadn't come! I'll never get that image out of my mind!*

"Um...no thanks, I think I'll take a rain check," I say humourlessly.

"I'm sorry darling I didn't know' – I put my hand up to stop her. "Don't apologise for..." I stop not wanting to say the word. "This is your house Gladys you should do what you want..." I stop again feeling myself cringe, I can see Gladys is finding the whole situation amusing and is trying her best not to laugh.

After a few seconds, I finally see the funny side of it and start chuckling too, but then I think it may have something to do with the weed that's floating around the kitchen, giving me a hit.

Gladys totally loses it and almost falls over she's laughing so hard. "Oh, your face..." She roars, laughing even harder.

I instantly lose my sense of humour. "Glad you're finding this all so amusing." I bite. I almost go to bollock her about smoking weed, especially with all the grief she gave me about not taking drugs when I was a teenager. But then I think, what harm can a little joint do every now and then, she looks like she's having a great time.

I sigh heavily and walk over to her, giving her a big hug and a kiss.

She finally composes herself enough to talk to me. "Please, come and meet Malcolm."

I shake my head. She knows how I am about meeting new people – especially men. "Another time," I offer, not wanting to hurt her feelings.

"He's important to me." She says all traces of humour gone. And I know I can't let her down if that's the case, and if he is, I have to ask why she hasn't told me about him? She knows I hate secrets; it destroys trust and wreaks havoc in relationships.

I follow Gladys through the conservatory and out into the patio garden area, where I immediately spy a tall white-haired male. He's got to be at least 6ft 2ins and is only wearing a pair of what I think is boxer shorts and has the body of a fit forty-year-old, with a small amount of love handles around his waist.

"Malcolm this is Coral, Coral meet Malcolm." I take his outstretched hand and shake it quickly. His hand is cool and dry, thank god, but I'm not sure who's more embarrassed him or me.

As I take in his features, I immediately see my guesstimate was wrong. This guy has got to be in his sixties maybe seventies, judging by the number of wrinkles on his face. Looking closer I see he has kind blue eyes with lots of laughter lines around them, his face is long and weather-worn, his nose long, his lips thin and when he smiles he shows a pair of dazzling whities.

"It's a pleasure to meet you Coral, I've heard so much about you," he says in a slight South London twang.

I immediately tense up. What has Gladys told him?

"Although...I have to say," he chuckles. "It would have been nicer to meet under different circumstances," he adds laughing some more.

I look away, still too shocked to say anything. I have never, ever seen a man in this house.

"Drink darling?" Gladys asks.

"No thanks, I'm good," I state a little bitterly.

Malcolm looks from me to Gladys who nods at him. "Well, I'll leave you ladies to it," he says, discreetly taking himself back inside.

I turn and stare at Gladys in shock. "Gladys, who the hell is that?" I hiss, keeping my voice low.

"He's Malcolm..." she shrugs.

"Gladys!" I scold.

"He's from the golf club," she says artlessly.

"The golf club?" I repeat in shock.

"Yes." She sniggers. *Why is it that I feel like the adult and Gladys is the child?*

I sigh heavily. "So...you're seeing this guy?" I ask.

Gladys nods once. "I'm sorry darling, I should have told you about him, but I didn't want to until I really knew myself..." Gladys drifts off and stares, and the potted plants with a dreamy look spread across her face.

"He's important to you?" I repeat her words back to her.

"Yes, sweetheart he really is. I never thought anything like this would happen to me, well not at my age anyway." She says, and I notice she's holding her hands behind her back.

"What would happen to you?" I question cocking my head to the side, feeling my world fall away from under my feet.

"Well...he's...Malcolm's just proposed!" She squeals, shoving her left hand underneath my nose so I can see the huge diamond ring on her finger. *Jesus age Christ, this guy must be minted!*

"Oh my god!" I gasp, taking her hand and inspecting the ring.

"Don't say anything yet darling, we want to announce it after Lily's party and have a little get together to celebrate."

I look up at her in wonder. How the hell can this be? How is it I don't know any of this?

"I... I don't know what to say." I whisper.

"Be happy for me darling," Gladys says taking my hand and squeezing it tightly.

"I am... of course I am. I'm just shocked...I wish you would have told me you were seeing him, that you were happy with him. At least I would have been warned – and I wouldn't have walked in on you today." I add, still feeling sour.

"I know, I'm sorry about that. I don't know who's more embarrassed you or Malcolm?"

"Oh, I think it's me," I answer dryly.

"He likes you," Gladys says, staring at the patio door where she last saw him – she's acting like a love-struck teenager.

"So, you're in love?" I say in disbelief.

"Yes!" She beams. "I know this is a shock Coral, but it is for me too. I never expected anything like this to happen to me," Gladys repeats – So I know it must be true.

I nod silently listening to her words, this is going to change everything. And although I am truly happy for Gladys, I always kind of expected her to be on her own, always available to me.

I know deep down that sounds selfish, but she's my rock, my shoulder to lean on when it all gets a bit much, and if this new man is always going to be here, then I won't have that anymore...

"Coral," Gladys whispers and lifts my chin, so I have to look at her. "Tell me what you're thinking darling."

I shake my head, unable, yet again, to get out what I really want to say.

"You're unhappy about this?" She questions forlornly. "You don't want me to see him?"

"No Gladys, no that's not it."

"Then what darling, you can tell me."

I sigh inwardly. "It's just…you've always been there whenever I needed you and' – "That won't change," she interrupts, her voice firm. "Malcolm knows how important you and Debbie are to me, I'll never turn you away Coral."

"It won't be the same," I whisper.

"I know," she agrees. "But if I told you I've been lonely for a long time, and I am happier with Malcolm; would it make you look at things differently?"

"You're lonely?" I gasp.

"Yes, I was." She says, her eyes glistening over.

"Gladys, why didn't you tell me?" I ask feeling concerned. *How long has she felt like this?*

"What's the point in that darling? You can't magic a partner out of thin air for me; the only one that could do anything about it was me…" I continue to listen in a daze as Gladys tells me all about Joyce helping her join a dating agency, the awful dates she has had. Making some friends out of the dates that went ok, but there was no spark, to finally ditching the dating agency and joining the golf club. *So that's why she did that, not to get fit, to find a man?*

I chuckle slightly and shake my head. I must admit, it's brave for her to do that, especially for a woman in her sixties. She continues telling me all about Malcolm. Apparently, he's a property developer and a successful one too (that explains the rock on her finger) and is divorced with two grown girls, who are twins. And I know Gladys is trying to convince me that he's a nice guy, but a deep dark part of me is already worrying. What if he turns out to be a bastard and treats Gladys badly? What if he leaves her or breaks her heart? What if he seems like he's really nice and turns out to be evil just like – *No, don't think that, don't go there.*

Either way, I don't think I would be able to keep my hands off him if he hurt her, in any way.

So, I decide to question it all.

"How long have you known him?" I ask feeling like the parent.

"A year." She tells me.

"Really, that long?" I squeak.

"Oh, we were just friends at first," she clarifies. "Malcolm was very hurt when his wife left him, she told him she was in love with another man and had been for the past ten years, and the only reason she stayed was the twins. It devastated him, and he lost all trust in women, he's been on his own for twelve years now.

"And as for me...well it almost crushed me when my husband left, he was the apple of my eye. I believed he was the only one for me, and I spent many years waiting for him to come back through the door...of course he never did," she smiles hiding the pain in her eyes.

"So, when we met and told each other our stories, we decided to take it slow, start as friends. We both knew there was a deep attraction there, and that sometimes it just takes a little longer for trust to build. Shortly after six months, we went away for the weekend' – "I remember that" I gasp interrupting her. *Gladys lied to me?*

"You told me you were going away with Joyce and John for the weekend," I say. I remember Joyce talking to me about it the following Monday, making it up as she went along no doubt!

"Joyce did go away with John," she clarifies, reading my mind. "And she hated lying to you, but she was doing my bidding. I didn't want you getting upset about what was beginning to feel like such a big change if it wasn't going to work out."

"But it has," I grumble moodily.

"Yes," Gladys beams.

I can see how happy she really is. "But a year isn't that long to know somebody," I tell her. "What if he turns out to be an ogre and is horrible to you? Or hurts you, or breaks your heart? What then?"

Gladys chuckles slightly. "Oh darling, it shows how much you care about me to be thinking the worst already, but try to put your mind at rest. Do you really think I'm the type of woman who would allow a man to treat me badly? I would not stand for any kind of abuse; mental, emotional or physical. He'd have his bags packed and out the door before you could say, how long does it take to pickle onions."

Huh? I have no idea how long it takes to pickle onions.

"Besides," she continues. "I knew the moment our eyes met and so did Malcolm."

Shit, that sounds like Tristan and me.

"Knew what?" I ask in wide-eyed wonderment.

"That he was the one." She softly says.

I frown hard. "What...just by looking at him?" I ask.

"Well...yes darling. Goodness me, you must know about Soul-Mates?"

"What?" *Now I'm confused!*

Gladys chuckles again. "A Soul-Mate is something much stronger, more profound than good old regular love," she says her eyes beaming brightly.

"It is?" I ask incredulously.

"Yes," she smiles.

"So how are you meant to, you know...know that you've met your Soul-Mate?" I ask as effortlessly as I can, I don't want to give anything away about Tristan.

I see Gladys's eyes narrow slightly. "Have you met someone Coral?" She asks shrewdly.

I venomously shake my head. "No, you'd be the first to know if I had," I say, laughing a little to trying to hide the lie. Gladys stays silent and continues to look at me dubiously. "Will you tell me?" I prompt, trying to get her to stop looking at me like that.

Finally, she smiles and sits back down in her chair.

"Well it's not really the person's physical body you're drawn to, or the way they look. It's far deeper than that. It's something that you feel deep within you that you can't get away from even if you tried, and that's because it's their soul that you've instantly fallen in love with. Not their body, their mind, or their personality," Gladys takes a breath.

"It's something much more...what's the word? – "Earth shattering?" I pipe up knowing exactly how that feels and also feeling nauseous with it. *What if Tristan is the one, my soul-mate, and I'm his?*

I quickly brush the thought away. I haven't got long left, and I came here for different reasons.

Gladys laughs loudly at my version. "Are you sure you don't want a drink darling?"

"Ok, lemonade please," I say hoping she has a homemade batch left.

"Ok, darling, coming right up." She says patting my knee.

I follow Gladys into the kitchen, ignoring the food that's

scattered all over the kitchen table. I dread to think what they were doing with it. "So, what are you guys going to do? Are you moving in with him or him with you?" I ask, praying she'll say she's staying here.

"Ah, that's something I wanted to talk to you about. I was going to come and see you, but now you're here," she says passing my lemonade to me. "I can tell you now. Malcolm doesn't really like Brighton darling, he prefers Devon or Cornwall." I nod as I listen, both are cool and definitely more for the non-party type people. "And to be honest darling, I have wanted to move out of Brighton for a while now." She adds.

I remember Gladys begging me to let her sell the house when I was ready to buy, but I just thought she was doing that to get me a bigger deposit, a nicer place. Not because she wanted out herself?

"Then why haven't you?" I ask.

"Because of you darling, I don't want to leave you all on your own." She says, her eyes glistening over again.

"Oh, Gladys!" I hug her hard. "That's so daft," I say. "I'm not on my own, I have Rob and Carlos and Joyce, and Debs isn't too far away either. Worthing isn't the other side of the world; it's forty minutes in the car." I laugh trying to make her feel better.

"That's not what I meant." She says. *And I know it's coming!* "I hate that you're on your own darling, I worry about you all the time. I don't have to worry about Debbie at all, she's happily settled with a family of her own. But I can't relax and retire and do all the things I want to do because I'd be constantly thinking about whether you're ok."

I sit down, Gladys does the same, and take a long drink of my lemonade, I need a lubricated throat for this when I'm done I put the glass on the table and get to my feet.

"Gladys!" I shout making her jump in her seat, her eyes widen in shock. "I am so effing furious with you right now. I cannot believe you have been holding yourself back because of me! To be quite honest I think it's bloody ridiculous!"

"Coral!" Gladys shouts back, her voice wobbling, she's always hated swearing.

"No, I'm serious. I'm not a kid anymore I don't need you to babysit me. I am a grown woman living her own life, and I think it's about time you did the same, don't you?" I sigh heavily rubbing my fingers across my forehead, trying to push the headache away that's forming. *Delayed hangover!*

"Gladys please, you don't need to keep this house. You don't need to stay in Brighton. I think you've done enough for me already, don't you? And if you want to go with Malcolm to Devon or Cornwall, or wherever," I shout, throwing my hands up in the air. "It's fine by me, in fact, it would make me extremely happy to know that you're happily living where you want to be, doing what you want to be doing. You could be cruising the world for all I care, as long as you're happy."

I sit back down in my chair. Feeling a little calmer, I take her hand in mine.

"I'm sorry, I didn't mean to shout at you, but I had no idea you felt like that, and I guess in a way I am clingy to you, but that's just because I don't want to lose you and because I love you so very much. You saved me in more ways than you will ever know. And I will miss you every day, it'll be really strange not being able to just pop round, but there's always Skype." I say smiling broadly, swallowing hard against my tightening throat.

She shakes her head, not understanding. I knew she wouldn't have a clue – Gladys is definitely non-techno.

"It's like making a phone call, except it's on video, you can see the person you're calling."

Her eyes light up. "Oh, that's wonderful dear, I can skip you every day." She beams.

I chuckle hard at that one. "Skype." I reiterate, still laughing.

"You're taking this all too well Coral. I know you don't like change." She says watching me, assessing me.

I shrug my shoulders at her. "It's inevitable," I answer morosely. This is the second shock in as many days, I think I'm beginning to get the hang of what change is like. "Speaking of change how is Joyce?" I ask.

"Oh, you know darling, she's sad, very sad in fact."

"Are you sure that selling up is what she really wants to do?"

"I'll tell you a secret," Gladys whispers, I lean in closer. "John wrote her a letter."

"Really?" I squeak.

"Yes, not long after they married, he had it secured with their wills." I wait with bated breath for Gladys to continue, when she doesn't I'm practically bouncing in my seat with anticipation.

"So, what did it say?" I ask.

Gladys frowns, her eyes filling with tears again. "John told her if anything should happen to him, to their life together, she was to completely restart it. Move country if she wanted to, to sell everything, their belongings, their home...of course, he didn't know at the time they would have a successful business together," Gladys pauses for a moment.

"He said he didn't want her living her life in the past, regretting his death, spending too long mourning him. That life was for living, and she was to pick herself up and move on." I can't help feeling like it's getting rid of the person as though they never existed.

"And she's honouring his letter," I say, thinking how sad the whole situation is. John was such a lovely man. Why does it always seem it's the good ones that die young?

"Yes," Gladys sighs heavily. "I know you're scared of being with someone Coral, but don't waste too much time on that. Life really is for living."

"And relationships are not the be all and end all of life." I retort, wanting to get off the subject.

"Are you sure you haven't met anybody?" Gladys asks her eyes narrowing again.

"No," I reply. – *Time to leave before she really gets suspicious.* Picking up my handbag, I find my mobile and call a taxi to take me to George's, I know I won't make it on time by foot.

"Coral, let Malcolm take you," Gladys says.

"No." I hiss. I don't want him taking me to see my shrink for god's sake! "So, will Joyce be back in tomorrow?" I ask changing the subject.

"As far as I know she will."

I kiss Gladys on the cheek. "I'm really glad you've found someone," I say, hugging her again.

"Me too," she chortles, we walk arm in arm down the hallway to the front door. "Malcolm and I want to take you out for tea, so you two can get to know each other a little more. And we can tell you our wedding plans." *Jeez, they haven't wasted any time!*

"Ok, how about tomorrow?" I know I don't have anything on.

"Marvellous, we'll pick you up," she beams.

"Ok." I force my lips into a smile and kiss her again. "Bye Malcolm," I shout up the stairs.

"Bye Coral," I hear his voice shout down to me. "Nice to have met you," he adds.

I smile, feeling embarrassed again and head out the door. Stepping into the taxi, I wave at Gladys as it pulls away, and try not to fall apart...

CHAPTER SIXTEEN

I'M SAT IN GEORGE'S OFFICE, staring blankly out of the window. I can't believe Gladys has met someone. I can't believe she's getting married. I can't believe she didn't tell me any of this – I think I'm in shock.

"Coral, where are you?" George asks pulling me from my musing.

"Sorry," I mumble apologetically.

"Care to share what's on your mind?" He asks.

I look up at George, his green eyes are bright, his smile is warm, his cheeks a rosy red – I'm taken back for a moment to when I first met him. I thought I was staring at Father Christmas with his crisp white hair and beard, and his big round belly.

It was not long after what happened two years ago that I knew I needed help, that I needed to get it out and tell somebody. I spent weeks meeting lots of therapists and not clicking with any of them, then one night I drunkenly told Rob and Carlos about my search. George's partner Phil is a good friend of Carlos's, and he asked if George would take me on.

I was gutted when I was told he had recently retired, but I didn't give in. Knowing full well that I feel more comfortable with gay men than I do with straight men, I got it into my head that he would be perfect for me, and when I casually met him (of course all arranged purposely by Carlos), I begged him to take me on. Initially, he said no, so I begged and begged again until I got so annoying that he finally relented.

I am his only client, and to see him I have to get to their house on Wilson Avenue and walk through their home to his little office. I always feel very privileged that he is doing this for me.

"Coral?" He repeats.

"Um...sorry, so much has happened this week. I don't know where to begin."

George smiles warmly at me. "I always find the beginning is a good place to start." He states, handing me a cup of tea.

"Thank you." I take a sip and place it on the coffee table in front of me. "The beginning…" I sigh heavily and begin to reel everything off.

Joyce selling, meeting Tristan, how I feel about that, spending time with him, our openness to one another about how we feel. I tell him I'm worried about Rob and Carlos, I don't think I could take it if they split; they are my role models that people actually do stick together. And then I tell him about Gladys meeting Malcolm, and the fact that they are getting hitched and buggering off.

"That's a lot to contend with in one week." George clarifies.

I nod in agreement.

"Ok, well let's start with Joyce selling. You've been advised your position is safe. Do you feel that it is?"

"Yes...No... I don't know, maybe if I hadn't met Tristan I would say yes..." I say, scowling at the floor.

"Coral, it was going to happen at some point in your life," George says.

"What was?" I ask.

"Falling in love," he says, chuckling slightly.

I shake my head at him, frowning deeply. "I'm not in love," I tell him sternly.

"Really?" He says in surprise, his eyebrows rising.

"Yes," I whisper.

"Let's discuss. Tell me how you feel about Tristan?"

"There's nothing to say." I bark back at him, crossing my arms in defiance.

"Then why are you so defensive?" He aptly says.

"I can't let him in." I snap.

"Why?" George asks.

"You know why." I bite back, then instantly regret it. "Sorry."

"Coral, I've never seen you like this," George says frowning deeply at me.

I sigh heavily. "George, I... I'm not denying there's something huge there. I know there is...but I'm just...I'm not capable of having a relationship. I didn't even have one with Justin." I swallow hard. "Besides, he's about to be my new boss, and that makes for a very imbalanced, tricky, sticky mess that I don't want to get into."

"So, if he wasn't your boss, would you date him?"

I hadn't thought of that one. "I guess so...if we took it slow...I mean really, really slow..." A fleeting thought of that night two years ago comes unbidden into my mind's eye, I close my eyes for a second and clench my fists.

"Coral, replace the image," George tells me.

I take a deep breath and think of a funny moment in Ice-Age. I have a thing about animated movies. George tells me it's my lost youth, that my innocence was taken away from me at such a young age. That it's kind of like I'm re-living it, my childhood. I think I'm warped and twisted. George tells me I'm not, at all, just trying to heal the wounds of my past and that's what he's here to help me to do, to help me live my life to the best of my abilities and to enjoy it.

"Coral, what happened?" George asks his tone full of concern.

"I thought of Tristan...being intimate with him," I mutter.

"Sexually?" He questions.

If I blushed, I swear I would be scarlet by now.

"Yes," I whisper feeling embarrassed.

"And how did that make you feel?" He asks.

"I don't know if I can?" I answer.

"Justin was a long time ago Coral." He reminds me.

"I know." I whimper.

George crosses his legs, and as I look up, I see he is deep in thought. "Coral, from what you've told me, this man sounds safe, reliable, trustworthy and above all an honest gentleman. He is nothing like Justin."

I nod knowing he's right, then shake my head in confusion. "I feel like I'm losing a little of myself when I'm around him," I say.

"That's what happens when two people come together, and

they click so well. You don't really lose yourself. You just become about the two of you, rather than the self." His words make sense, yet it means I lose some sense of control over myself, my life.

"I feel like I'm losing control," I tell him.

"Coral, we've discussed this, control is an illusion. An illusion that yes, makes you feel as though you have control of everything that happens around you, but you don't, not really. The universe does all that for you. For instance, did you expect Joyce to sell?"

"No." I gripe.

"To meet Tristan?"

"No." I choke sarcastically.

"For Gladys to tell you she is leaving and getting married?"

This could go on forever. *What's his point?*

"No," I grumble.

"Control is an illusion." He reiterates.

"So, what am I supposed to do?" I ask as that familiar lump forms in my throat again. *What is wrong with me? Why do I feel like I could cry again?*

"Explore it Coral. Change happens whether we like it or not, sometimes it's good, sometimes it's bad. Life is yin-yang, for every high, there has to be a low. All I am saying is try to be brave, and find the courage to put your heart out there and give this man a chance. He could be the best thing that's ever happened to you." *Ok, that sounds like Rob!*

"But what if I can't? What if we date, and we, you know… the inevitable start to happen and I freak out? He's going to think I'm crazy and I'll never see him again…and I," I grit my teeth, close my eyes and push back the tears. "I don't know how to be intimate with someone…I… I just don't know how to do it." I croak.

"Dear girl," George shakes his head at me. "How many times have I said to you that you worry far too much about future events that haven't even happened yet?"

"I know," I croak again. "Rob's always telling me that too."

"Ok, well let's just take a moment. Have you considered talking to Tristan?"

I look up at him in confusion. "How do you mean?"

"I mean having a heart to heart with him, telling him about your past experiences, what happened with Justin."

"No. Why would I want to tell him that? It's private." I tell him.

"Yes, it is very personal to you I know that. But maybe if he knew you a little more intimately, he could make compensations, compromises, take it slow with you. And he would understand more, I'm sure of that."

"I don't think I can do that...it's...he'll think I'm a freak, I'll never see him again," I say.

"Somehow, I truly doubt that. And will you please stop referring to yourself as a freak Coral, you are anything but. You're a bright young woman with so much to offer. Open your eyes and see yourself Coral, as others do." He commands. "Or if you prefer, with your permission, of course, I could run through some details with Tristan on your behalf. I know you don't like to talk about your past, and reliving it is no good for anyone. Does that idea appeal?"

I shrug my shoulders, not really knowing what to say to that.

"Well think about it and let me know," George says.

I nod feeling a little squeamish. *Do I really want Tristan to know my sordid past?*

"I'm really confused," I say. "On the one hand I really like him, more than like him and that's what's making it feel even more confusing. I don't see how I can feel so attracted to him, so safe around him, so...." I stop before I say in-love; after all, I just denied it to the good doctor.

"I've only just met him," I continue. "And I feel really weird around him, even when I only think about him for a split second, my heart hammers against my chest and I feel this weird sickly butterfly feeling in my stomach, and an ache between my chest and my abdomen. I'm off my food for god's sake and I always eat!"

"Coral." George removes his glasses from the edge of his nose, and comes and sits next to me on the sofa. Taking my hand, he squeezes it gently. It's ok for George to touch me. "Everything you have just described to me is exactly what happens to every person on the planet when they fall in love."

I close my eyes and sigh heavily – *Fuck! I can't fall in love!*

"So, what am I supposed to do?" I groan.

"It's up to you. You have two choices, you can ignore it and continue with your life as it is, or you can go for a change and explore it?"

I sigh heavily and rub my forehead; my headache still hasn't left me. "I feel sad for Joyce, I miss John," I tell him.

"Grief is a slow and natural process, don't try to tame it. If you feel like crying then do so. As I've explained before crying is a release."

I nod knowing he's right, yet I always fight the tears, I see it as a sign of weakness, a sign of vulnerability. And I can't afford to be vulnerable. It's just a risk I can't ever take.

"So, what you're saying is relax more, go with the flow?"

"Yes." He smiles.

"Well, I think I've kind of accepted that work will change, Joyce is definitely going. And as for Tristan…I… I'm not sure about that yet." I tell him.

"Coral, there's no timescale. You don't need to rush, take your time, do your meditation, listen to your inner guide, it will always know what's best for you. Your ego will always hold you back, make excuses for you not to risk, to try something new."

I nod knowing he's right.

"But what about Gladys, I never told her, but I'm devastated she's going I… I don't know how I'll cope without her, you know being physically there to hug me when I'm feeling insecure, or a little low or…" I choke off pushing away the tears. *Everything feels so fucked up right now.*

"Coral, again it's a bitter-sweet one. On the one hand, you want Gladys to be happy?"

"Of course," I mumble.

"On the other hand, you feel what? A little lost?"

"No, not lost."

"Then what Coral, what do you feel?"

I close my eyes and go deep down, I recognise the feelings, but I don't know the words to explain them. "I feel like…like when my Mom told me my Dad didn't love me anymore, that he was never coming back. I feel numb…um, abandoned I guess?" I shake my head, that's not the word.

"Devastated, I think? Gladys means so much to me, without

her around, I don't know if I can...even function properly." I scowl at the floor.

"Coral, I strongly urge you to speak to Gladys about this, maybe even make a move with them. Start somewhere fresh with a new job. There certainly wouldn't be any denying seeing Tristan then." His eyes sparkle for a fraction of a second, and I momentarily feel like he's really pushing me to go for it.

"She doesn't want that. And I'm not a kid anymore, I may feel like it but...there has to come a point when you stop running to your momma to make everything better, right?" George doesn't agree or disagree. "I mean, Debs has always moaned at me that I run to Gladys when the slightest thing happens. She thinks I'm a crybaby."

"She may well do Coral, but she doesn't know your past."

"I know." I sigh inwardly.

"I will also reiterate telling Gladys what really happened to you when you were a child. She may understand more why you don't feel as compelled as others naturally do to find a mate."

A shiver runs down my spine. "Ok, I'll think about it." I sniff loudly, then laugh at the sound I made.

"That's good Coral, seeing life as a silly funny game, is far more productive than seeing it as a set of scary dramas that you have no control over." And there's that word again – Control. I remember asking Tristan if he is a control freak when in actual fact, it's probably me.

"George, am I a control freak?"

"Well, in the general terms of the saying, yes I would class you as one. You crave control in your life." I nod feeling stupid that I asked Tristan if he was one when he clearly is not! *Stupid-ass Coral!*

"But you're not a freak Coral," he admonishes. "So, let's work through it all. Your job is safe, it may change somewhat in the work you are asked to do, but you feel confident in that?" I nod.

"Good. Tristan, well he's completely up to you. But I would go with letting him in, telling him what happened." I bite my lip, just thinking about that conversation has me feeling nervous.

"Take your time with your decision Coral, there's no rush." I nod, knowing he's right. "Gladys, talk to her. Tell her how you really feel or be brave and let her go."

I nod knowing I'm going to have to do one or the other. *The trouble is which one?*

"Ok, so let's end with a high," George adds.

"I had a great night out with Rob last night," I chuckle remembering our terrible singing. "Did get a little too drunk though," I add feeling dog tired.

"Good, having fun with your friends is imperative," George tells me.

"I have Lily's birthday party this weekend, and Gladys and Malcolm are taking me out tomorrow night, to meet under better circumstances, they already have wedding plans." I roll my eyes at that one. I really hope Gladys doesn't ask me to be a bridesmaid.

"Good, lots of enjoyable events to look forward to," George says.

"Yep," I sigh heavily.

George narrows his eyes at me. "Ok, so what's really on your mind Coral?"

I feel all the air leave me. "I don't think I can do it again," I whisper. "I keep having nightmares, not all the time, just when..." I drift off.

"Do what again Coral?" George asks softly.

"Have sex." I tremble, my hands clenching into fists.

"Why ever not?" George asks, astonished.

I squeeze my eyes shut. I've almost told George so many times, then chickened out.

"Because of Justin?" He prompts.

I shake my head.

"Then what Coral?" He questions.

I open my eyes and stare out of the window, trying to block out the memory, the feelings, but it's no good - My stomach rolls, and I know I'm going to be sick – *Shit!*

I slap my hand to my mouth, dash up out of my seat and run flat out for the bathroom, flinging the door open I run to the toilet and vomit; over and over again, until all I'm left with is dry retching. When it finally ends I flush the toilet and head over to the sink, as I'm washing my mouth out with water, I hear George softly tap the door.

"Coral?"

"I'm ok," I answer and take several gulps off the water.

"Can I come in?" George asks softly.

"I'm coming," I answer and head out the door.

I turn to the right, to follow George back to his office and lose my balance; my head feels so woozy. George quickly catches me, then puts his arm around my waist and leads me back into his office, sitting me down he hands me a glass of water.

"Thanks." I croak my throat feeling burned. *Stupid Coral!*

I'm never drinking again when I have George the next day. Hangover, no food, hot weather, finding Gladys with a man, and Tristan making me feel all funny is not a good combination.

George sighs heavily and sits down opposite me. "Coral, why do I get the feeling I don't know everything? That you're holding something back?"

I frown deeply, staring at the glass in my hand. "I made a mistake," I tell him. *And it was a mistake, a huge mistake!*

"We all do." George offers.

"A stupid one, one that cost me..." I add.

"And the mistake is?" George asks.

I shake my head again. I don't want to talk about it.

"Coral, I can't help you if you don't' – "I can't ok!" I shout.

George is silent, he knows how to deal with my little outbursts.

"I've got to go!" I tell him, quickly scrambling up to my feet.

"Coral," he admonishes. "You know you shouldn't' – "I know." I stop and stare back at him. Shouldn't leave a session on a downer, it should always be an upper. "George," I whisper.

"Yes." He answers softly.

"One day," I tell him.

George nods silently. I know he knows what I mean, that I'll tell him when I'm ready.

"See you next Tuesday then?" He asks.

"Actually, with everything going on I was going to ask...I feel bad though..." I say, my hands twisting together anxiously.

George smiles broadly at me. "You want another session?" he says.

I nod in agreement. "You don't have to George, you're retired for goodness sake, you shouldn't have to...." I sigh heavily. *Why oh why do I always feel guilty - about everything?*

"It's absolutely fine Coral."

"Really?" I squeak.

George looks solemnly at me again. "I'll agree on one condition."

"You want me to tell you." I guess. "Ready or not?"

"Yes," he answers sternly. "That's my condition."

I actually think twice about it for a second, then I think about the number of things going on, and how much better I feel having someone to talk it all through with, someone that doesn't think I'm a lunatic.

"Ok." I sigh.

"Good." George sternly says.

I look up at him again, he looks mad. *Great!*

"I have to say Coral, I'm not very pleased that there's something you've kept from me." He says, spookily answering my thoughts.

"I'm sorry," I whisper.

"Well, I suppose, whatever it is I'll soon hear about it." I frown again and feel my lips clamp together. "Right then, this week or next?" He asks sharply.

Oh, which lonely evening shall I pick?

"Can you...this Friday?" I ask my voice barely audible. "I finish early at 4pm."

"I'll see you here 4.15 sharp." He tells me.

I tremble inside. "Ok, thank you, George," I whisper and turn to walk out of his office.

"Coral." I look back at him, he sighs heavily, pinches his nose for a moment, then puts his glasses back on. "I want you to forget about what you're going to tell me, and focus Coral, focus on what we have talked about today. Think about talking to Gladys and Tristan, concentrate on that." He softly says.

"Sure doc," I answer numbly, my mind already elsewhere…

AS I HEAD SOUTH DOWN Wilson Avenue, in the direction of the Marina, I feel like I'm in someone else's body. Like someone else is making my feet take each. I feel better after talking to George, but if I'm completely honest with myself, I still feel a little shell-shocked. I can't quite get my head around the fact that Gladys is re-marrying.

And as for her moving away…

As much as I know she isn't purposely doing it, I feel as though she's abandoning me, which is completely ridiculous; I am a thirty-year-old grown woman. I should be able to deal with life's ups and downs by myself now, and I should be living a life of my own, as most people do, away from their parents. Most people at my age have husbands and wives and children...but all that just seems so impossible for me to even attempt to do. I have nothing to offer anyone, nothing but fears, insecurities and zero self-esteem.

Without realising it, I find myself standing outside Pizza-Express staring blankly ahead. Then I hear my stomach rumble, and I realise I have been subconsciously heading here for comfort food. I think back to what I've actually eaten today. Muffin for breakfast, I didn't really eat much salad at lunch – *Hmm...*

Deep down I know I really shouldn't, its naughty food, but I have nothing in the house that I fancy. I turn and face the Restaurant, and as I do I see it's packed outside, I hadn't even heard the low rumble of people talking, laughing, knives and forks clicking against plates – *What is wrong with me?*

I sigh heavily and make my way inside...

TWENTY MINUTES LATER I am back at my studio. I go straight to the oven switch it on low, and place my pizza inside to keep warm while I change, then I turn the air-conditioning unit on to cool the studio down. As I stand in front of it thinking about Tristan, tears pool in my eyes, making my vision blurry.

Holy crap! For the first time in twenty-five years, I am crying!

I really don't understand it, why I'm feeling so emotional. I'm never like this. Shaking my head at myself and dashing the tears away, I slowly make my way up the stairs, one foot in front of the other; my legs feel like they have lead weights attached to them.

I head to my closet, pull out a pair of sweats and change into them. Then I make my way back down the stairs and go straight into the bathroom. In a daze, I wash my face and clean my teeth as my mouth still feels rancid from being sick. When I'm done I stare at myself in the mirror, I can see it right there behind my eyes – the fear.

I can feel it building within me. I squeeze my eyes shut

trying to push it away. I shiver slightly. I don't think I can take any nightmares tonight. Maybe I should have a glass of wine before I eat, it might help me relax and sleep better, no nightmares...

AN HOUR LATER I have had two glasses of cold chardonnay and half the pizza. I am lying on the sofa watching the movie Taken – I love that Liam Neeson is a kick-ass Dad who'll do anything to protect and save his baby girl – *Why couldn't I have got a Dad like that?*

I quickly push that thought away. Normally if I watch a movie, it's a romance. Crazy right, fucked up girl who can't stand men, can't have a relationship, yet she's a born romantic – *I'm so fucked!*

I stare back at the screen, not wanting to go down that line and try to clear my head. I get a flash image of Tristan, standing in the car park with me, telling me he'll protect me, no matter what. I grit my teeth and try to blank him out – I don't want to be reminded of Tristan. I don't want to think about anything, I just want all my thoughts to disappear, to go away.

I AM DREAMING I'M IN a hotel room. Someone is with me, I turn around to see who it is and I'm instantly filled with dread and fear – It's not a dream but a memory, reliving itself.

Coral get out, wake up!

I try to run, but my legs don't make a move.

No! Not him!

He is smiling at me, a look of approval stretched across his face; he is leading me into his hotel room, just for a drink he said. He is kissing me and getting forceful, aggressive, my worst nightmare come true...I don't understand. Why is he doing this, he likes me, we have something special going on, he told me so.

We've spent hours together, no sign of this ever happening!

"*No!*" I tell him as he tries to squeeze my breasts, grab my ass.

"*Yes!*" He growls.

And this is my warning; this is my cue that it's all going horribly wrong.

"*I said No!*" I bawl totally incensed. I try to push him away, but he's too strong.

He grabs my hands and pins them behind me, in an instant he has picked me up and thrown me onto the bed, covering me with the weight of his body. He rips my t-shirt as he pulls it up and yanks my breasts free from my bra.

"*No!*" I shout - I am now in full-scale panic mode.

I try to get my hands free as I kick at him and frantically buck my body up and down in an attempt to get him off me. It doesn't work. He raises his arm, clenches his fist and brings it down, hard, slamming it into my right cheek. I see stars; my eyes are trying to roll into the back of my head.

I feel like I'm going to pass out...

I WAKE UP GASPING FOR AIR – *Fuck!* – I can't breathe. I fall from the sofa onto the floor trying to get some air into my lungs, my head is banging, my body shivering, my heart is hammering so fast and heavy against my chest, I think I can hear it. *Get out of my head!* – I scream internally. My stomach rolls, the memory is still reliving itself, he's ripping my clothes off – *Oh fuck not again!*

I run to the bathroom and vomit, violently – *Oh God! Please help me, make it go away please I'll do anything...*

The dry heaves eventually stop. I curl up next to the toilet shivering, I'm so cold. My muscles are still in spasm, my fists clenched tight, and at that moment, all I want to do is call Tristan and have him come sit with me, hold me tight, warm me up and make it go away, make me feel safe. But it's impossible, I know it is – *Why the hell would he want this?*

As the fear starts to ebb away, the anger starts to take over which quickly turns to tears, like my anger is directly attached to my tear ducts, I fight back at it. Then I think about what George has said over and over again, to let it all out, to cry if I need to, so I do.

Heavy, wreaking sobs burst out of me. I let my body go limp, my torso hitting the bathroom floor, my cheek against the cold tiling. I've never allowed myself to cry about it before; I've never let it out - I cry and cry and cry; I don't seem to be able to stop. *Oh, when will this end?...*

I DON'T KNOW HOW LONG I'm there for, but as the tears die down, I slowly become aware of the movie that's still playing; I hear gunshots, shouting, Liam Neeson no doubt kicking the shit out of someone. The pain starts to wash away as well as the anger and the fear, but now I feel really cold and dirty – I need a shower.

I sit up, and pull my legs up to my torso, wrapping my arms around my knees to try and generate some heat, but it doesn't seem to be working. *Why am I so cold?* I wonder for a moment if I'm actually becoming hypothermic? *Not good!*

I quickly stand, my muscles protesting and turn on the shower, my teeth are chattering like crazy, my body is actually starting to feel painful. *Why? Why am I so cold?* It suddenly dawns on me, air-conditioner!

I run into the living room, which is so cold you can see my breath and switch it off. *Jesus! It's like the god damn Arctic Circle in here, Christ!*

At least I know it works! I roll my eyes at my own stupidity and head back into the bathroom. Stepping into the shower, fully clothed, I crouch down onto the floor, allowing the hot water to cascade all over me, I grip my arms around my legs and pull in tighter.

Slowly but surely, the shivering dies off, and my teeth stop chattering. When I'm satisfied that I'm warm enough, I slowly stand, making sure all my muscles are working properly and strip my wet clothing from me. I decide to leave them in the shower; I can't be dealing with them now, all I want is my bed and sleep; no nightmares.

I step out of the shower, wrap a towel around my head, and then one around my body, pulling it tight to keep the warmth in. I quickly dry myself off, rubbing my skin harshly, so the blood keeps pumping. Then I dash upstairs and pull out my winter pyjamas.

Quickly dressing, I grab my hairdryer and blast my hair on the hottest setting; it doesn't take long to dry. Moments later, I am back downstairs with my wet towels. In a daze, I reach the bathroom and hang them up to dry, then I go to the patio door, unlock it, and open it a little, letting the warm breeze flow into the studio and warm it back up.

My head is still banging, so I decide to take some Nurofen.

I walk over to the cupboard under the sink and fall to my knees, I still feel so weak; I guess that's having no food in my system. I find my little medicine box and open it up, and there staring at me is a brand-new bottle of Night Nurse. I always have some just-in-case I catch something in the winter, it's really good at knocking you out, so you don't wake up coughing or sneezing, which gives me an idea!

I know I shouldn't, but I do. I grab the bottle, snap off the plastic safety cap, twist the top off and take several glugs, it actually tastes quite nice and soothes my burning lungs from being sick so much. I know I shouldn't take it for any other reason than sickness, but I'll do anything not to re-live that, I don't want another nightmare about it, I don't think I could take it.

Figuring I have about half an hour before it kicks in, I decide to eat the rest of my pizza, I carefully reheat it in the microwave, and grab a carton of coconut milk – very good at settling the stomach – and curl up on the sofa. I eat and drink in a daze, barely aware of the film still playing. When I'm done, I lock up and take my sorry ass up to bed.

CHAPTER SEVENTEEN

I WAKE UP ABSOLUTELY sweltering; the sun has risen and is blasting through the studio. I must have climbed into bed last night with my P'J's still on, and my king size quilt is completely wrapped around me. I quickly scramble up, kicking my feet to free myself from this unbearable heat. *Oh my god, I'm melting!*

I decide to try the air-con out again, but this time on a lower setting. Running down the stairs, I turn it on low and feel it start to cool the room, then I tiptoe back upstairs. As I reach my bed, I glance at my alarm clock. 5.04am, only another couple of hours to go and I'll be swimming.

I strip my P'J's and leave them on the floor – *Boy I'm getting untidy!* – And get back into bed, as I do, I have to smile – No nightmares, a restful sleep, I feel so much better for it.

I turn on my side to go back to sleep, five minutes later I am turning on my other side. Five minutes after that I am flat on my back staring up at the ceiling. All I see every time I close my eyes are images of Tristan, the way he looks at me, how his eyes light up, his mannerisms, his thick dark hair, his soulful eyes, his protective way around me.

I shake my head at myself and run my hand through my hair, trying as hard as I can to hide the stupid grin that is spreading across my face. Joyce is going to think I'm a complete lunatic walking around smiling all day, I hardly ever smile at work – *Oh! That's not good!*

I wonder for a second if I actually come across as a miserable cow that everyone avoids. I mean, none of the other secretaries have ever offered for me to go out to lunch with them. And I know they all get together once a month on a Friday for a girl's night out, they've not invited me to that either. I snort, wouldn't go anyway!

Precisely so what are you going on about Coral?

Feeling too hyped up to sleep, I decide to go for an early morning run on the beach. Dressing in my training gear I head downstairs, clean my teeth, wash my face, and for a fleeting moment I stare back at the woman in the mirror, I don't look so good. Look at the state of my eyes. They are so puffy that I don't think I'll be able to wear any mascara today – *Great!*

That's it! No more stupid crying, especially if this is what it does to you – *Oh no!*

Joyce is going to know I've been crying, which means she'll call Gladys, I know she will, and then Gladys will call me, and she'll be all upset – *Double Crap!*

As I turn to head out the bathroom, I spy my wet clothing still in the shower, and I'm instantly reminded of why they are there. I still myself and close my eyes – *It's ok, he can't hurt you, he's gone, he's not here!*

I take a deep breath in, then exhale slowly as though I'm blowing the memory out of me, another trick from good old George. Bending down, I pick up my soaked clothing, squeezing as much water out of them as I can. I decide to hang them outside on the railing, they shouldn't take too long to dry in the sunshine…

AS I PACE ALONG THE beach my mind wonders over everything that's happened over the past couple of days. Honestly, I'm dreading Friday, I don't want to have to tell George anything, but on the flip side, I know I need help, I can't keep letting it haunt me. I push the thought away and pace harder, the sun is already scorching, almost burning my bare shoulders and I'm sweating buckets. I stop for a while before I take another sprint and stare at the ocean, watching the waves rolling in and out.

I wish I could be like a wave, each one completely different from the one before, everything new and fresh. I inhale deeply, I love the smell of the sea, it's the best smell in the world – well it was until – *Stop!* – Don't think about him, I chastise.

I decide to have a pit stop and sit down on the pebbles.

I pause my MP3 player that's been blaring Funhouse; my favourite pink album and place it down in front of me. As I sit there assessing my emotions, the one that seems to be the most prominent is anger, so I decide to question it. *Ok, so why am I angry?*

Well I guess I'm pissed Joyce is leaving, I'll miss her like crazy, I love working with her. But more importantly, I'll be losing a family member, a beloved Aunty, and I've already lost a beloved uncle. Tears prick my eyes; just thinking about John's funeral is enough to make me start blubbering again. God knows how Joyce is feeling - *What else?*

I search the inner recesses of my mind, nothing seems to come up about Tristan that's making me angry, so I move on – *Gladys?*

Yep definitely pissed about that, even though I know I shouldn't be, but why am I? Ok so weirdly enough I think there's a little jealousy going on there – *Why?*

I shake my head at myself because deep down inside I know it's because I feel like it's the wrong way around. Surely it should be the kids getting married first, like...well, it should be me getting hitched and not Gladys. It should be me finding the one, not Gladys – *That's ridiculous!*

I castigate myself harshly – *Be happy for her Coral, it's not her problem you're a fuck-up who hasn't...*I stop myself there – *Ok so get rid of the stupid jealousy!* I nod in agreement with myself.

Squinting my eyes from the glare of the sun, I stare out onto the sparkling ocean and take another deep breath before continuing – *What else?*

I sigh heavily, life is changing. I evidently can't let myself in with my key anymore. The kitchen scene from last night at Gladys's comes brightly and vividly into my mind's eye. *Ew!*

I immediately try to replace it, takes a while. I think it will haunt me forever!

But most importantly, I won't see Gladys every day. I won't be able to hug her, or laugh with her, have a lazy Sunday roast or...I sniff loudly and swipe at my tears. *Stupid god damn tears! Why the hell am I crying so much?*

Ok, so I'll miss her, like crazy, like I wouldn't believe. I already do, and she hasn't even gone yet, so I assess again. *What's so bad about her moving away, what am I so afraid of?*

Pain! – The answer is clear and immediate.

I don't want the pain and the heartache I already know I'm going to endure when she's gone. The emptiness, the hollow feeling that I have no family because I know that's how it's going to feel. Just like it did when I no longer had either parent anymore. I felt abandoned and unwanted. I take a moment to calm myself down.

Anything else?

Of course, Gladys is getting hitched. When Debs got hitched, I was a bridesmaid for her, after months and months of her begging me to do it – *"You are my sister, my best friend. The one person in the world I will always love above all others. Please baby sis, do it for me…"*

Her constant whining had me crumbling in the end, and I wore her stupid dress. Actually, it was a very beautiful dress, midnight satin blue, fitted bodice and deep flowing skirt – I still have it, that's how much I liked it, but I didn't like wearing it. *Oh ok, so that's pissing you off too!*

I have an epiphany! - I do want to wear skirts and dresses. I always push it off like it doesn't really bother me, but it does. I want to feel pretty and feminine without the trembling body and the hyperventilating that goes with it, I just want to feel normal.

Ok, this is good, this is progress, and definitely something I should discuss further with George on Friday. I swallow hard, it's nerve wrecking just thinking about it, and I have no idea why, but Susannah comes into my mind's eye with her pencil skirt that's so tight it looks like it's been painted on, bet her husband loves that. *Fuck!*

Men do like all that kind of stuff, sexy dresses, skirts and heels. Tristan's face comes into my mind. I can't help wondering if he's a skirt and heels man? I shake the thought away – *Concentrate Coral!*

Ok so I've got the heels part down to a T, seriously if I buy any more heels I'll need to start renting a garage to store them all in – I just need to sort out the skirt and dresses part. Feeling satisfied that I've run through everything that I need to, and feeling less angry and fearful about it all, I pop my headphones back in.

I still can't believe I caught Gladys in the kitchen smoking a joint and doing the deed with a guy, sounds more like what a teenager would be up to rather than a woman in her sixties. I giggle aloud and stand up, ready to take my next sprint - *God life is so strange!*

Getting back to my studio after being out in the hot morning sunshine and not sweltering to death was, quite frankly, wonderful. I have to find some way to really thank Tristan. And I'm also quite annoyed with myself for not getting one anyway. Why melt when you can be cool? I hear Tristan's voice echo in my head *"The joys of technology"* Indeed, I couldn't agree more…

AS I HEAD OUT THE patio door for my walk to work, I see Bob's already out there with his morning paper.

"Hey, Bob." I chirp cheerily as I lock the patio door.

"Morning, Coral." He actually pulls his paper down and smiles at me.

I am grateful my sunglasses are hiding my puffy eyes. "Bob, would you like to come out for the day on Saturday?"

"With you?" He asks a little shocked.

"Yes," I chuckle.

"Any man that says no to you is a fool," he croons. "If I were your age, you'd be in trouble young lady."

I raise my eyebrows at this little declaration. "Thanks, Bob," I chuckle. "But it's not just me, it's for Lily's birthday. Rob, Carlos, Gladys and Joyce; they'll all be there." He's met them all before at Christmas and at Gladys's Sunday roasts, he shakes his head at me. "Too noisy?" I ask.

"How old is she?" He grumbles.

I swallow hard. "Five," I answer, and try not to think about what happened to me at that age.

"Means I have to go shopping, get her a present," he grumbles. "I hate shopping."

"No, you don't," I chortle. "I'll get it for you. That's what I'm doing on my lunch today. So, will you come? It'll be a fun day out!" I can see it's not working.

"Gladys hasn't seen you since Easter, and you keep saying no to her Sunday roasts. I think she'll be very upset if you don't come along," I say. "And so, will I," I add sweetly.

And that does it, his blue eyes sparkle and I know I have him.

"Alright then," he drawls.

"Excellent." I beam and kiss him goodbye, his cheeks flush as usual. I can't help chuckling as I walk away...

I AM SAT AT MY DESK eating my muesli. As usual, I am early, but this morning I am especially early. After running for so long I decided to ditch swimming, I didn't really want to do both, but I'll get back to it tomorrow. Besides, I think I needed it, the fresh sea air, the sun on my face – the time to think and assess.

And earlier, when I attempted to put some makeup on, I could see my shoulders had caught the sun; in fact, if it's still this nice on Sunday, I may take my butt off to the beach for the day, catch some rays. I rarely sunbathe, I get too bored.

Tristan comes to mind again. I don't understand why I keep thinking of him, he keeps randomly popping into my head. I know I'm denying it to myself, well trying as best I can to deny it, but the truth is, I miss him. I miss his face, his smile, his smell.

I decide to go to the Google page I saved. I click it open, and all his pictures fill my screen. I swallow hard. What is it about this guy that's got me feeling so twisted up inside? I feel like there's an eternal battle raging.

Staring at one of the photos, I feel my stomach swarm with butterflies. I instantly lose my appetite – "Coral?" I turn and see Joyce stood there staring at me with her mouth half open.

I finish chewing, swallow hard, and as quickly and discreetly as I can, I close the page. "Yes," I whisper back, wondering what I must have done wrong for her to be looking at me like that.

"Come into my office." She orders, her face stern.

I put down my muesli and follow her in.

"Shut the door." She tells me, so I do – *What have I done now?* I wonder for a moment if Tristan had made it all up yesterday and I was supposed to be at work.

Joyce puts her briefcase and handbag down, then turns to me with her hands on her hips, scrutinising me. "What on earth has happened?" She asks.

I look from left to right trying to get my brain to find the right answer. "Um...I'm not really sure what you mean Joyce?"

"Your face?" She says.

"Huh?" I quickly pat my face with my hands. Have I got muesli on my cheek or something?

"How long Coral?" *Ok, I'm getting annoyed now.*

"Joyce, I'm sorry, but you've really lost me?" I answer incredulously.

She sighs and shakes her head at me. "Follow me."

I frown back at her but do as she asks and follow her out of her office, down the corridor, past the restrooms and straight into the bespoke kitchen.

"Sit down." She tells me sternly pointing to one of the breakfast stools. I silently do as I'm asked and watch as she marches over to the fridge and pulls the door open. "Tell me you already know this one Coral?" She says as she takes out a cucumber.

I have to chuckle at that one, I have no frigging idea what she's on about.

"Sorry, still lost!" I laugh.

With a slice of cucumber in-between each manicured fingernail, she walks around the breakfast bar until she is stood in front of me. Sighing heavily, she stares back at me with a painful look of regret in her eyes.

"What's wrong?" I ask, ignoring the cucumber altogether.

"I didn't think you would take it so hard," she says wearily. "Here, close your eyes." I do as she asks, then I feel cool cucumber being placed over my eyelids.

"Wow!" I gasp. "That feels great, really cooling."

Joyce sighs again. "Hold them in place," she says. I hear her step-up and sit on the stool next to me. "You didn't know cucumber is fantastic for puffy eyes?" She asks a little exasperated.

"Um...no," I answer. "Should I?"

Joyce laughs at that one. "Well I suppose if you visited the beauty salon more often you would know these things," she says artlessly. "So, you want to tell me about it?" She softly adds.

"Sorry?" I'm lost again, too busy thinking about how cool cucumber is, well I know it's cool, but it literally feels like it's taking the puffiness away – *Amazing!*

"Coral," she admonishes. "I've never seen you with swollen

eyes, which can only come from crying darling...and for a long time too." *Shit!*

"Oh!" I whisper.

"Yes, oh!" she repeats wryly. "I'm so sorry, I didn't think you would take it so hard," she says gloomily.

"Take what so hard?" I ask dumbfounded.

"Stop being obtuse!" She barks, making me jump a little.

"I'm sorry Joyce, but I don't know what you mean," I say.

"You were crying?" She whispers.

"Yes," I whisper feeling embarrassed.

"Last night?" She asks.

"Yes," I confirm.

"Because of what's happening here?" She questions.

"Oh! No, no Joyce..." Ok, now I'm upset that she thinks she has caused this to happen to me, that I'm stuttering as I'm trying to get my words out. "Joyce no... I mean, of course, I'm upset you're leaving. I...I'll miss you like crazy, you...your family, m-my family...my Aunty," I choke. "But that's not why I was crying." I finish.

"Oh, darling!" I can hear it in her voice; Joyce is shocked, I feel her wrap her arms around me and squeeze me tight. "I'll miss you too darling girl." She says I hear a little sniff.

"Like you wouldn't believe," I chortle trying to lighten the mood.

Joyce lets go of me, I hear her step down and walk back over to the fridge. Then I hear her heels clicking as they reach me again. Her fingers gently peel away the cucumber; she looks so tired, so sad. "Want to talk about it?" She asks, hesitating slightly.

"No thanks," I answer staring down at the floor.

"Is it Gladys? She called me and said that you had...well, met Malcolm." My eyes dart up to meet hers. I can tell she's trying really hard not to laugh about it, which makes me burst out laughing.

"I...c-can't...believe...t-that h-h-happened," I laugh, at least I can see the funny side of it now.

"Neither can I," Joyce chuckles. "I bet you didn't know where to put yourself."

We really start laughing, so much so that my belly is hurting.

I can see Joyce is trying really hard to compose herself, but it's just not happening.

"I don't know who was more embarrassed, Malcolm or me?" I titter.

Joyce chuckles some more, it's nice to hear after all she's been through.

"Well, the cats out of the bag now!" She says, sighing again.

"Sure is," I say, trying to keep this light-hearted.

"How do you feel about it?" She asks.

I shrug. Joyce scrutinises me again – I don't want to talk about it. I think she picks up on that because she nods and hands me the new slices of cucumber.

"Here, keep putting them on, replace them once they get warm'– "But this is your cucumber," I argue.

"Well, I can always get another one!" She says rolling her eyes at me.

"Ok, ok!" I give in as I always do with Joyce, but I can tell she has more to say.

"So, it's not me, and not Gladys?" She questions narrowing her eyes at me.

I shake my head. I know she's digging, but I can't talk to her about it.

"Want to talk about it?" She asks again.

"No... I'm good," I say swallowing hard. "I think I just needed a good old cry," I say brightly. "I'm ok now."

"Are you sure?" She asks scrutinising my expression.

"Yes," I smile. "Really, last night was...well once the crying was done I ate my pizza, had some wine and an early night." I omit the part about taking cold medicine.

"Sure?" Joyce asks again, she is so watchful of me, always looking for hidden clues or signs that something more might be wrong. "You can take the day off if you want to?" She adds.

"No, really I'm fine. I'd like to stay, but thank you anyway." I say hoping this will placate her and she won't send me home.

"Alright then, as long as you're sure?" She says still eyeing me speculatively. "If you change your mind though...?" She adds.

"I won't. I'm fine. Oh, but there was one thing," I say remembering my lunch date with Rob. It's strange that I haven't heard from him. I wonder if he's remembered? "Is it ok if I take a half hour off my lunch tomorrow and snag it onto today?" I roll my eyes. "I have to shop for Lily's birthday, Rob's meeting me," I add.

"Coral, take two hours. You can get something from me too." Joyce replies.

"Oh ok, thanks." I beam brightly.

"And you don't need to take it off tomorrow's lunchtime." She sternly adds.

"Yes boss," I giggle. "What did you want me to get for Lily?"

"Something pretty, a nice dress…" Joyce looks lost for a moment. "Have my card off me before you go." She adds.

"Ok, I will." She smiles at me, but it doesn't reach her eyes. Then she takes my hand in hers, squeezes it once, then turns and walks out of the kitchen.

I still have the new pieces of cucumber between my fingers, so without a second thought, I slap them both on…

THE MORNING HAS FLOWN by and before I know it, Joyce is handing me her card so I can go shopping. Plus, earlier today I had a text from Rob asking what time to come and meet me, so at least he remembered.

"Hey, trouble," I say as I bound into reception and give Rob a big hug.

"Happy today?" He asks.

"Yes, Joyce has given me two hours for lunch, so we can take our time." I beam, I hate rushing around trying to find gifts for people.

"So, what's new?" Rob asks as we head out into the sunshine.

"Loads," I answer, not really wanting to think about it all. "But let's shop first, then we'll talk over lunch."

"Cool." We link arms and make our way over to Rob's car. "So where to?" he asks.

"Churchill," I say. "But can we make a stop at North Laine too?" I have no idea what to get Tristan, but I'm bound to find some inspiration there.

"Shall we have lunch there too?" Rob questions.

"Yes, good idea!" I answer.

We make our way over to Churchill Square Shopping Centre in complete silence, I've tried making conversation, but he seems miles away.

"You ok?" I ask turning to face him as he parks the car.

Rob shrugs solemnly – *Uh-oh!*

"Things still rough with Carlos?" I ask, hoping he'll say no.

"Same-o, same-o," he says, but there's an odd look behind his eyes, one I can't get the meaning to.

I frown back at him.

"Come on, we haven't got long." He says, changing the subject altogether.

I shrug. "Ok." I step out of the car and decide its best left alone if he wanted to share he would. Rob's never been one for holding back…

FORTY MINUTES LATER we have successfully reached our goals. I have found a pretty dress in Next for Joyce, got a big box of crayons from Bob – You can never have enough crayons when it comes to Lily – and Rob has bought her a Magnetic Tile Art Gift. Debs is going to love that one, I can already imagine the fridge freezer covered in Lily's designs, and I have bought her a Babushka Russian Doll Painting Kit, I hope she likes it.

As we wander down North Laine trying to decide on where to eat, I am suddenly captured and have to stop. I am staring at a very large painting of an old E-Type Jaguar, the artist has captured it effortlessly and set the scene so you can just imagine yourself stepping out of the car and having a lazy evening picnic. Set high on a cliff with the sun setting and the sea for a background, the green Jaguar looks lovely, almost as though it's bouncing out of the picture, begging you to take her for a drive.

I don't know why, because it's not Tristan's model, and I have no idea if he likes the classics, but something deep within me tells me to buy it. I know it will be a one-off and would look lovely hung in the main living area, above the over-large sofa. That's if he buys that place!

"Coral?" Rob pulls me from my thoughts. "You ok?"

"Uh-huh," I nod. "I'll be back in a minute," I say.

I walk into the gallery and enquire about the price. Thankfully, it's not so expensive that I can't afford it, but it will still make a dent in my savings. I quickly put a deposit down, explaining to the woman that I want to have lunch first, then come back to collect it and pay the remainder, she is animated and evidently happy for the sale.

"What was that about?" Rob asks a little tersely as I walk back over to him.

"It was for Tristan," I tell him matter-of-factly.

Rob beams from ear to ear, pulls me into him and squeezes me tight. "I knew you'd come around," he chuckles.

"No," I bark. "You've got it all wrong."

"Have I?" he snaps back, I frown at him. "You should go for it with him Coral I really want you to try. I'm tired of seeing you on your own."

"Not you too…" I groan.

"Me too?" he questions.

"Yes, you, George and Gladys, telling me I need to find someone," I mumble.

"Well, he is rather delicious," Rob states. "And you're a fool if you don't," he adds tersely.

I shake my head at him and roll my eyes.

WE FINALLY FIND a place to eat, and decide to sit outside – it's too nice to be indoors. We place our orders with the waitress, and I watch Rob pour cold, still water into both of our glasses.

"So, what's your news?" He asks even though he looks distracted.

I explain all about my day with Tristan, about him buying me an air-conditioner, and my thought of buying him a gift to say thank you, and that it can be a welcome to your new home present.

"So, he's bought it?" Rob asks with renewed vigour.

"I don't know, but does it matter?" I say shrugging my shoulders.

"I guess not…" he sighs drifting off.

I stare back at him, he really doesn't seem right today. I can't help watching him observe everything that's going on around him like he's sucking it all up for the last time, he looks kind of…sad?

"I have other news," I say hoping to bring him back to me.

"Yeah?" He smiles back at me, but it doesn't reach his eyes.

Our salads arrive, and as I tuck into mine, I notice Rob

is just picking at his, so something is definitely off. I feel my stomach drop fearing the worst – then I take a deep breath and remember that I shouldn't be doing that, thinking that way, or worrying about the future. I really need to put into practice everything George, and I have been working towards, so I carry on with what I was about to say.

"So, Gladys is getting hitched!" I say cheerfully.

Rob's mouth drops open, he is speechless – *That's a first*.

"And she's leaving, going to Devon or Cornwall," I add and take a big mouthful of my salad. Rob is glaring at me now, he looks really mad. I quickly chew and swallow. "Hey," I reach over and touch his hand. "You ok?"

Rob swallows hard and shakes his head. "I can't believe it," he whispers.

"Well, neither could I," I bawl and launch into an animated story of finding Gladys with her new man. I use lots of humour and dry wit, but there's nothing, just nothing. Now as much as I'm really trying not to think the worst, I know whatever is wrong with Rob must be really bad, because I know Rob so well, and he would be rolling on the floor with laughter at that one, especially with how embarrassed I was through it all.

I clear my throat and stare at my salad. "Rob, what's wrong?" I look up at him, he shakes his head at me. Still not ready to talk then? I sigh heavily. Isn't that what friends are for, to always be there for each other, in their times of need?

"You'll tell me though when you're ready?" I add. I get nothing, so I try a different tack. "Look whatever it is, we can sort it, I know we can. I'll always be here for you, whenever you need me." I tell him softly.

"It's not really something you can help me with." He croaks, his eyes glistening over - *Oh no!*

"Oh Rob, won't you tell me?" I beg.

He silently shakes his head. I squeeze his hand again, trying to make him see I'll always be here, he's always got me.

"I can't believe Gladys is leaving you," he whispers.

I frown at him. "Well, she's not really' – "I mean, I get that she's getting married, not wanting to be on her own and all that. But why move away, why leave you?" He bellows.

I turn and look at the people walking by us, who stop and stare at Rob's little outburst.

"Rob! It's ok. I talked it all out with George last night." He doesn't look convinced. "Really, it's ok. She wants to move away and have a new life with Malcolm. It's not like I'm a kid anymore, she doesn't need to stick around for me."

Rob clenches his jaw and stares blankly ahead – *Why's he getting so worked up about Gladys?* It doesn't make sense, I decide to get off this subject.

"Hey, I was going to ask you…I've been thinking about doing something regularly, but I need a partner for it."

"What is it?" He asks, his voice flat.

"Salsa dancing," I say. I know Rob loves dancing, I'm confident he'll say yes.

"I can't commit to…anything at the moment Coral." He stares out into the distance again.

"Oh, ok." I look down at my salad.

"I don't want to hurt you or let you down." He adds.

I nod silently. The rest of the meal continues in awkward silence. I want to ask him if it's me if I've done something wrong, but deep down inside I have a feeling this is all about Carlos, and nothing at all to do with me…

WE WALK IN SILENCE back to the Gallery, and I pick up the painting for Tristan. Rob carries it back to the car for me. As we drive out of the car park, Rob finally speaks to me.

"How are you going to get all of this home?" he asks.

"I'll get a taxi," I mumble.

"Want me to drop it off at your place for you?"

I turn and smile at him. "Really, you wouldn't mind?"

He rolls his eyes at me. "No, I don't mind, and I'll drop the other presents off too."

I frown at him. "The other presents?"

Rob stares ahead, his face blank. "Yeah…something's come up, I won't make it Saturday." He looks sad again.

"Oh…ok." I don't really know what else to say, not if he won't talk to me.

"Tell Lily I'm sorry." He adds.

I nod silently as Rob pulls up outside work. "See you soon then?" I whisper.

"Sure…" He stares straight ahead, still deep in thought.

I lean across and peck him on the cheek. "Here for you, always."

His eyes glisten over again – *Crap!*

He turns slightly and gives me a weak smile.

"Love you," I whisper and step out the car with the dress I purchased for Joyce.

I wave at Rob as he quickly pulls away, he half waves back to me with a stony face, and I'm left standing on the street feeling totally gutted, and sad – sad for my best friend. He's going through something, and I don't know what to do about it, but if he won't talk to me, there's not much I can do about it…

I HEAD BACK TO the office feeling sombre. What a change from this morning. I actually felt like I was dealing with everything, and now I just feel lost. Back at my desk, I check to see if Joyce is on the phone, the line is clear, so I knock on her door.

"Come." I plaster a fake smile on my face and buoyantly walk in.

"Joyce, I got a lovely dress," I say handing it over with her card. She pulls it out of the plastic bag and smiles.

"Lovely choice Coral, Lily will look so sweet in this." I nod in agreement. "Thank you for doing that. With everything that's gone on…I completely forgot to get her something."

"Joyce, it was my pleasure, and like you say you have enough going on."

Joyce stands from her desk, walks around it and hugs me, kissing me lightly on the cheek, so as not to smudge her perfect lipstick. "Your eyes look better." She softly says.

Oh yeah, forgot about that! – I feel even more melancholy now because I know Rob must be feeling really, really bad because he'd have drilled it out of me as to why I'd been crying.

"I know," I say making my lips smile. "I'll definitely use that trick in the future," I add. I go to walk out, then I remember there was a question I wanted to ask her. I stop and turn around.

Joyce is already back in her seat; typing at full speed.

"Um…Joyce." I stare down at the floor.

"Yes, dear?" She looks up at me.

"Can I ask you something? It's not work-related."

"Of course, you can." She smiles.

"Well...I wanted to ask, you've met Malcolm?" I question.
"Yes."
"Do you think...um...I don't know how to put this?" I bite my lip. "Is he...do you think Gladys will be happy with him, do you think he's a good man?" I blurt.
"Yes," she clearly states. "I do."
"Ok." I go to walk out.
"Coral, you're worried?"
I stop and turn around. "Yes."
"Malcolm *is* a good man. And don't forget they're not love-struck teenagers. It's different when you get to our age. Most people are very sure of themselves, of who they are and what they want. I think they'll make each other very happy." I feel better hearing that and decide to really give Malcolm his chance tonight, but above all to be happy for them both.
"Thanks, Joyce I'll get back to my work. Can I get you anything first though?"
"No, I'm fine. Thank you." I smile back at her and skip out of her office, feeling a little lighter than before, but when I sit back at my desk and begin going through my inbox, my mind wanders back to Rob, and that sinking feeling in my stomach reappears. *Don't think the worst Coral!*

Then I panic. How am I supposed to get to Worthing for Lily's party? I was supposed to be going with Rob and Carlos. I sigh inwardly; guess I'll have to get a lift with Gladys. *Oh god! I hope they're not all mushy with each other in the car!*

CHAPTER EIGHTEEN

JUST AS I'M FINISHING off for the day, I get a call from Gladys.
"Darling, what time shall we pick you up?"
"I don't mind," I answer.
"Shall we say seven?"
"Sure." *Great two hours of hanging around not doing anything!*
"Lovely, we'll see you then." Gladys sounds giddy with excitement.
"Ok." I almost hang up when I hear Gladys call me.
"Coral, dress smart darling. We're going to the Hilton."
I raise my eyebrows in surprise. "Oh, ok." *Wow, dining in style.* Funny how things change, Gladys always used to like The Katarina Harvester at the Marina. "I'll meet you at the Gym," I tell her.
"Ok sweetheart, see you soon." I frown deeply wondering why Gladys has changed from her usual restaurant, then shrug it off, maybe Malcolm prefers fine dining…

I AM STANDING OUTSIDE the gym, waiting impatiently for them to collect me. Although I shouldn't be as I'm fifteen minutes early. I don't understand why I feel so nervous? My foot won't stop tapping, and I'm chewing my tips again.
Ugh! Stop it Coral!
I yank my finger out of my mouth and scan the road for them again, no sign. I take a deep breath and try, for the millionth time today to clear my mind of all things Tristan. I have wondered far too often about him today. His eyes, his lips,

his chiselled cheekbones, his shiny dark hair, and whether he's thinking of me like I'm thinking of him – *It's ridiculous!*

I knew the moment I got back to the studio I had to do something. I wasn't going to give myself any more spare time to daydream about him, and I couldn't sit in the studio waiting around, twiddling my thumbs, so I grabbed my gym bag and spent an hour in the pool. My shoulders feel sore for it, but the water was so cool and inviting – I didn't want to leave.

Reluctantly I did, and took a long lazy shower, then dressed in my best. Actually, I feel like I'm going to work because my best consists of my dark-blue pin-stripe work trousers, and my short-sleeved, light blue blouse – I wish I were in a dress, a really beautiful, long, fitted, summery dress. I shake my head at myself – *Get a grip Coral!* – I take a deep breath and try to calm my anxious mind.

As I look up again, I finally see them. Malcolm is waiting for the traffic to clear so he can turn right into the gym car park. I'm surprised by his choice of car, I thought he would be in an executive car, you know, a flashy Merc or a BMW, but no. He's in a silver Toyota Land Cruiser.

Gladys is waving at me with a wide smile stretched across her face. I lift up my hand, plaster a smile on my face, and wave back. *Why am I nervous?*

Malcolm pulls up beside me, then leaving the engine running he exits the car. I raise my eyebrows in surprise. He's impeccably dressed in a smart, light beige suit and a crisp white shirt, he scrubs up good. He smiles broadly at me, with kind, gentle eyes. I can already feel myself warming to him and relaxing – *Maybe this won't be so bad?*

"Good evening Coral." He smiles deeply and leans in to kiss my cheek. I'm surprised that I don't feel weird about it.

"Hello Malcolm, nice ride." I smile, but I quickly notice he looks just as nervous as I feel. No doubt still embarrassed about the last time we met. Malcolm opens the rear door for me. I'm impressed, the guy has manners. I slip inside the sumptuous beige leather seating and lean forward to kiss Gladys.

"Hello, darling." She smiles warmly at me.

"Hi." I lean back in my seat and put my seatbelt on.

Malcolm gets back into the car, and we are soon heading west on the A259. No-one is talking, but surprisingly enough the atmosphere in the car feels really calm and relaxing. I'm trying not to notice the loving glances they keep giving each other or the fact that Malcolm has been holding Gladys's hand above the centre console, squeezing it every now and then, at least I don't have to endure the loved-up couple for too long.

Ten minutes later we are parked at the Hilton Metropole. I instantly think of Tristan – I wonder if he's up there? Then I remember he said he was going back to Leeds. I wonder if that's where he's permanently based? I shake my head at myself – *Forget him, tonight's important, concentrate Coral.*

Right, concentrate! I look up at the building, last time I was here was for Debbie's wedding. I start getting flashbacks, all the preparations, Debs walking down the aisle, Scott's face when he saw her in her dress, the meal, the after party.

"Coral?" I hadn't even noticed Malcolm had opened my door for me again and is standing there with his hand held out to me.

"Sorry Malcolm, miles away," I say and place my hand in his. As Gladys reaches me, she wraps her arm around my waist, squeezes me and then winks playfully at me.

"Shall we ladies?" Malcolm gestures for us to go before him and we head inside....

I AM COMPLETELY WON OVER. Malcolm is charming, warm, witty, sweet, and he seems to think the world of Gladys. I finally relax knowing that Joyce was right; they really do seem like a perfect match for one another. Inside I'm gushing with happiness, I have never seen Gladys so happy and buoyant, it's like she's got this fire lit inside her. I can see it so clearly, the glow and twinkle in her eyes give it all away. How strange it feels though, I always thought she was really happy anyway, Gladys has always been a fun, positive person to be around but now she just seems so, so – alive?

After an hour of drinking, chatting and laughing we have finished our starters, which were delicious, and the wine is going down a treat. In fact, I think Gladys is getting a little tipsy, she seems nervous.

As the waiter clears our plates, Gladys turns to me and

squeezes my free hand. "So darling, we have something very important to ask you." She says. *Uh-Oh!*

My stomach flips. "Ok," I whisper and take a gulp of wine – *Please don't ask me to be a bridesmaid!*

"Well, it's about the wedding." She says glancing at Malcolm.

I try not to frown.

"We'd like to do it sooner rather than later," Malcolm says, seeing that Gladys is struggling a little.

"Ok." I shrug nonchalantly.

"We've got a date in August," Malcolm adds.

My eyebrows rise, I stare back at him feeling a little surprised – *Christ that is soon!*

"And we'd like to have it here," Gladys adds. "Debbie's wedding was such a lovely day."

I nod in agreement.

"But the only date they have left' – Malcolm says – 'Is the 8th August." He takes another swig of wine and looks across the table to Gladys. *My Birthday!*

Gladys pipes up. "We're only asking darling, we don't want to spoil your day if you don't want it then' – "Stop," I tell her. "Let me think." I quickly run it over in my head and instantly relax. I wasn't going to be asked about bridesmaids after all. I can't help smiling at that one. I can see Malcolm and Gladys visibly relax before me.

Then I think about their request. Am I really that bothered? My birthday is a Thursday this year, and I wasn't planning on doing anything special. I was going to ask for a barbeque the following Saturday, so what difference does it make? *Decision made!*

"Ok, well first off, no I don't mind at all, but it's a Thursday? Don't you want your wedding to be on a Saturday? Isn't that when people traditionally get married?" They both chuckle.

"No darling, we're not worried about all of that. We were just going to go to the registry office and have a little party back at the house, but then we came here for a meal a few weeks ago, and I was telling Malcolm all about Debbie's wonderful day here' – "And I insisted we book it." Malcolm interrupts beaming at Gladys again, then taking her hand in his, he raises it to his lips and tenderly kisses it - Gladys melts and goes all gooey-eyed.

"Well, I think it's a fabulous idea," I say excitedly. Then I frown, Joyce will be gone by then, what if I can't get the time off?

"What's wrong darling?" I'm surprised it's Malcolm asking me and not Gladys.

I already feel like I've known him a very long time – *Huh! Who'd have thought it, maybe I'll get a father figure after all?*

"Joyce will have sold by then. I just hope my new boss gives me the time off?" I say.

"Tristan!" Gladys beams, blinking rapidly. "Of course, he will be darling." She adds flippantly, as though it's a no-brainer. Anyone would think she's a close and personal friend the way she's acting!

I roll my eyes at her. "Gladys, you don't know him, so I don't know how you can say that?"

"I know more than you think." She says winking at me. *What? What does that mean?*

I blink several times trying to get my brain to work again. I really want to ask her what she knows, but if I do, she'll get suspicious, and I can't handle her questioning – I'm not even sure how I feel about him yet. I guess Joyce must have told her a lot about him.

God damn it, I really want to know!

I sigh inwardly. "So, you think he will give me the time off? I just think with the take-over, it might not be such a good time." I foolishly add.

"Nonsense, I'm sure it will be fine." Gladys soothes patting my hand. "So, you really don't mind?" She queries.

"No," I chortle. "It will be a lovely day," I add feeling all warm and fuzzy inside.

"Thank you, Coral," Malcolm says, smiling warmly at me.

I shrug, it's no big deal. "Are you planning on having a big wedding?"

"Oh no!" They both answer. Then smile at one another – *Ok, the lovey-dovey looks are actually starting to gross me out a little bit!*

"Just family and a few close friends," Malcolm clarifies.

I nod and drink some more wine.

"Now," Gladys says in a very business-like manner. "Bridesmaids."

My face falls, and my heart sinks.

They both start sniggering. *Oh great, make fun of me why don't you, yep lap it up!*

"We're not having any," Malcolm chuckles, and Gladys bursts out laughing – Oh I get it, they knew I'd be freaking out about it, so decided to wind me up!

I instantly relax then see the funny side of it. "Oh! Very funny you two," I chortle. – *Phew! Off the hook!*

"Sorry darling, we just couldn't resist." Gladys chuckles.

"Evidently!" I snort and shake my head at them both…

AS WE DRINK MORE WINE and browse the menus for our mains, my mind keeps rushing forward to their wedding, my birthday – I still don't know if I can get the time off, and I like things to be set in stone. I mean, I'm pretty sure Tristan will say yes, but I just want to be sure. In that very moment, I feel his card glow red inside my purse, begging me to call him. In fairness I've been waiting for an excuse to hear his voice since he walked out my door yesterday afternoon, so much seems to have happened since then.

I debate for a good five minutes about calling him, yes –no, yes-no; until I just can't take it anymore. I pick up my handbag and excuse myself from the table. Once inside the restroom, I get myself into a stall, lock the door, put the toilet lid down and sit.

My leg instantly starts jigging up and down – I'm so god damn nervous.

Taking a deep breath, I open my purse and pull out his card. I run my fingers over his name. I feel my stomach flip over then start fluttering madly. The card in my hand is rapidly shaking, giving away my nerves – *God damn it!*

Trying to ignore all my body's reactions, I take a deep breath, fish my mobile out and punch in his mobile number. I take another deep breath and press dial, it starts ringing.

My leg goes into full-scale jigging mode, and I am biting my bottom lip in nervous anticipation.

It only rings three times.

"Coral." He sounds relieved.

I frown deeply. *He knew it was me!*

"H-hi," I stutter a little astonished. "You knew it was me?" I gush, all the air leaving my lungs.

"Yes." I can tell he's smiling. "It's good to hear your voice," he adds sleepily.

"Did I wake you?" I gasp.

"No," he chuckles. "I was relaxing on the sofa, reading."

"Oh!" I answer breathlessly - *Come on Coral, you can do better than that!*

"To what do I owe the pleasure?" Tristan's voice is husky and soft and sexy all at the same time.

Is that even possible… or legal?

"Um…I was," I stop for a moment. *Where do I start, so much has happened?* – "So, Gladys is getting married," I say. "You know my adoptive mother?" I add.

"Is she?" He asks his voice full of surprise.

"Yes, I only found out yesterday. We're at the Hilton, they're having the wedding here, next month."

"Wow, that's…quick." Tristan still sounds shocked.

"Tell me about it, I didn't even know she was seeing anybody," I answer dryly.

"Are you ok?" He instantly sounds concerned.

"Um…quite honestly, I don't know…well, yeah I guess. I'm happy she's happy and has found Malcolm' – "Malcolm?" Tristan interrupts.

"Yeah, the guy she's going to marry. He's nice." I say trying to placate him.

"Hmm." Tristan doesn't sound convinced.

"Honestly…he is," I sigh. "I feel comfortable with him… which is surprising." I roll my eyes. "And you should see the way they keep looking at each other, all gooey-eyed and loved up," I add dryly.

"That's good though right?" Tristan says still sounding concerned.

"Of course, I'm…h-happy for them…but," I break off. *Why do I feel the need to spill my guts to him?* I was only supposed to be checking it would be ok to get the time off!

"I'm coming to see you," he says, his voice low, but full of a deep and profound promise.

And I believe him. I think if I asked him, he would come to me. I can hear his footsteps moving quickly across a wooden floor. Then I think about the guilt I will feel afterwards, the fact that I just need someone to lean on because I don't have anyone right now.

"No Tristan, don't. I..." He sighs heavily. I can no longer hear his rapid footsteps across the floor. "I'm ok." I try to sound convincing, then I sigh feeling the weight of my words.

"I'm not convinced." He states.

"It's just all...a bit of a shock," I croak.

"I'm sure it is. Have they known each other long?"

"A year, Gladys didn't want to tell me until..." I sigh again feeling a little of the betrayal I initially felt when she told me.

"Until what?" Tristan asks a little annoyed.

"She wanted to wait until, well, that they were both sure. I guess they were just careful, they've both been hurt in the past." I say I don't mean to sound gloomy.

"Well that's understandable," he says. I wonder for a moment if he's, actually right?

"Either way, the Wedding isn't the worst part of it," I say sombrely.

"Then what is?" He asks.

"Oh, they're leaving," I croak, my eyes filling with unshed tears - *What's going on? I was fine a minute ago!*

"Leaving?" He says his voice low and dark.

"Yeah...Gladys wants out of Brighton. Malcolm likes Cornwall or Devon, they're not sure which yet." Tristan is silent, I hear nothing, and I wonder if I've lost signal. "Tristan?"

"I'm here." He answers.

I take a deep breath and compose myself. "So anyway, the reason I was calling is to see if it would be ok to get the time off." He doesn't say anything, so I continue while I can. "For the wedding...I mean...it's going to be on a Thursday, the 8th August' – "Your birthday?" He interrupts.

He knows when my birthday is too?

"Um...yeah, I... well that's why I'm calling...will I be able to get the time off?"

Tristan is still silent. *What's wrong with him?*

"Tristan, are you there?" I ask.

"Yes." He exhales loudly like he's been holding his breath for a long time. "Of course, you can have time off," he adds, sounding annoyed.

"Well, I just thought I'd check...you know with the take-over and everything..." I say scowling at the floor.

"It's no problem at all Coral; you shouldn't even have had to ask." He scolds.

"Sor-ry!" I bite back.

"No... I didn't mean..." Tristan exhales in a rush. "I really would like to come and see you, see for myself that you're ok." I close my eyes and swallow hard, my throat seems so dry.

Get off the phone Coral!

"I have to go," I tell him. "They'll be wondering where I am."

"Can I call you later?" He asks his voice a sombre whisper.

"Sure," I reply before I've even thought about it – *No Coral, what are you doing?*

"I'll let you go...I miss you." He whispers then hangs up.

I stare at my mobile in disbelief. Did that conversation really just happen? Did he really just say I miss you?

I feel a strange fluttering in my belly – "Coral?" *Shit, Gladys!*

"Yeah...I'm here!" I scramble out of the stall.

"We were wondering where you were?" She says, her cheeks a little flushed.

"Sorry," I mumble and walk over to the sinks to wash my hands.

"Darling, are you really ok with the date?" She looks so worried.

I quickly dry my hands and hug her hard. "Yes, I really am. I'm not just saying it." I feel her shoulders relax. She hugs me back for a second then pulls back with her hands still on my shoulders, studying me intently.

"Who were you talking to?" She quizzes, her eyes narrowed – *Shit!*

"Rob," I lie. "Something's really wrong with him." I frown hard. "He won't tell me what it is, and he's not coming on Saturday, which reminds me, can I get a lift with you and Malcolm?"

"You don't need to ask that." Gladys softly scolds.

I pull my lips up to smile. "Bob's coming too," I add feeling a weird fluttering race up and down my body, and I know it's because I'm going to hear Tristan's voice later.

"Oh lovely, haven't seen him in a while." She says warmly.

I nod with more enthusiasm that is necessary and pull my lips up to smile again, it feels odd.

"Come on, let's get back to Malcolm, he's going to think I've deserted him." She chuckles.

I follow Gladys out of the restroom and back into the main restaurant…

MALCOLM HAS WALKED me back to my studio. He was insistent, even though I told him I was fine at the car park, I unlock the door and smile up at him.

"Thanks, Malcolm."

"My pleasure," he smiles. "Now go on, get yourself inside and lock up behind you." He adds.

"I will," I say, pulling the patio door open.

Malcolm watches me lock the door behind me, smiles and then waves as he walks away.

Well, that felt nice, how protective of him – Then I realise how hot it is.

Dashing over to the air-con, I switch it on high to cool the room down. I feel exhausted, my belly is full, and I've had far too much wine. Kicking off my stilettos, I pick them up and make my way up the stairs. My head is swimming again, so much is happening, I don't even know where to begin trying to assimilate it all.

As I'm getting changed into my sweats, I feel my heart start fluttering, like a bird in flight – which is very worrying – because I know it's because I'm going to hear Tristan's voice soon, that's if he calls.

I sigh inwardly and head back down the stairs. I decide to call Carlos, Rob's been on my mind since this afternoon, I've been trying to work out how I can reach him, so I can find out what's wrong, maybe Carlos can shed some light on the situation?

I check the time 10.20pm, it's not too late, so I call him, but I get no answer, which is strange, Carlos always answers his mobile. I check the number to make sure I got the right one and press call again, only this time it goes straight to voice-mail.

I instantly feel angry, he knew I was calling and pushed

me to voice-mail - *Arghhh!* – I chuck my mobile on the sofa in frustration. *Why won't they talk to me?*

I AM STOOD STIRRING my cup of hot chocolate when my mobile starts ringing. I spin around and dash over to it, hoping it's Carlos calling me back, but it's not, it's Tristan.

"Hello," I mumble feeling a little deflated.

"Convince me not to come down there and see you." He replies sharply.

"Um..." I pinch my nose trying to think of something to say. "I'm really ok," I say.

"You don't sound it," he states sternly.

"Ok...ok," I sigh heavily. "I'm not 100%, but I need to learn to stand on my own two feet Tristan, that much is evident." I huff.

"Coral, having your family around you to be there for you in times of need doesn't mean you can't stand on your own two feet. You seem very capable of doing that to me."

"Look, it's just' – I sigh again – 'there's just a lot going on right now and..." *Why am I telling him this?* – I exhale loudly. "It just feels like my life has gone from being very organised and balanced, too messy and complicated in a Nano-second. It's a little disorientating that's all."

"Spill," he orders.

"I... I" I stop there. I don't need any more complications right now – *Especially with him.*

"A friend in need is a friend indeed," he reasons.

I sigh again, and against my better judgment, I start babbling it all out.

"Ok, well my job is changing. I'm losing Joyce, Rob's weirding out on me, Carlos won't answer my calls, and then I find out Gladys has kept this relationship a secret and well, I'm happy for her of course I am, but I'm so gutted she's leaving. Gladys and Joyce are my family, and in one foul swoop they're gone, just gone..." I stop and think about what I'm saying. That must have been what it felt like to Tristan when he lost his folks, well his grandparents. "Incidentally, how did you know it was my birthday?" I say changing the subject.

"Had something planned," he tells me.

"You...what? Why?" I gasp trying to get my head around it.

"It's not a problem, I can move it. Do you have any plans the Saturday after?"

"Um...I..." My head feels scrambled. *He had something planned?*

"Coral?" Hearing his voice pulls me from my musing. I think back to what Malcolm told me while Gladys was in the ladies, "I'm *taking her to Bali, she's always wanted to go, we leave Saturday after the wedding.*"

"Why?" I ask, wondering what he has planned. I'm not so great with surprises.

"Believe me, you'll love it," he says with full confidence.

"You don't know me Tristan so how can you say that?" I argue.

"Are you free?" He asks again changing the subject.

I give in, I'm too tired to argue. "I guess, but I warn you...I'm not too good with surprises."

Tristan chuckles. "How did I know you were going to say that?"

"When's *your* birthday?" I ask wondering who he'll be spending it with now that his folks have gone. My mind instantly speeds forward to Christmas. Who will Tristan spend it with? And what about New Year? He can't be alone, that's just... just awful...

"Coral, I heard you gasp then, what's wrong?"

"I... nothing, when's your birthday?" I ask again.

"November," he tells me.

I roll my eyes. "What *date* in November?"

"25th" He answers.

"Do you have any plans?" I ask sweetly.

"It's a little early to be' – "Do you?" I ask more forcefully.

"No actually, I don't."

"What did you used to do?" I enquire.

"Not much. I don't really agree with the western way of thinking...you know the age thing."

"Age is just a number baby." I giggle.

"Exactly," he says in agreement.

"What about Christmas and New Year? What did you use to do then?" I question.

"Hold on a second I thought this conversation was supposed to be about you?"

I ignore that one. "Please," I whine. "Answer me this one, and we can go back to me," I say with my fingers crossed.

"Fine!" He barks, then he's silent for a long time. "I'd.... be with my folks," he answers sombrely. *I knew it!*

"I guess this year's going to be pretty rotten huh?" I say my voice sounding a little sad.

"I was planning to go abroad actually, as I did last year, completely forget the holiday season," he says.

"Really?" I squeak. "Where to?"

"Oh…I don't know…somewhere warm and tropical, not really sure yet." His voice sounds wistful.

"Sounds delightful…" I'm already day-dreaming about it.

"Want to come?" Tristan asks playfully.

"Can't, Gladys would never forgive me if we weren't all together for Christmas. So, I'm officially inviting you, I don't want…I don't think you should be on your own at Christmas Tristan…that…it's just…wrong." I stutter.

"Is it now?" I can tell he's smiling again.

"Yes, it is!" I state.

"Well, thanks, I accept your offer if I don't go away that is."

My eyes start to feel heavy, the evening's events catching up with me. "Well, I better go." I stifle a yawn.

"Am I boring you?" He chortles.

"No. Just tired, it's been a long day." I offer.

"I'm sorry Gladys is leaving," he says.

"It's ok," I yawn again. "I've got Rob and Carlos and my sister." *Well, I think I have Rob!*

"And me," Tristan says.

I frown at the explosive feeling that begins fluttering away in my stomach.

"Have you thought any more about us?" He whispers.

"Yes," I answer breathlessly.

"And?" His voice sounds hoarse.

"Look, Tristan, there's a few things I need to sort out, get straight in my head, I…" I instantly think of George's words *"talk to Tristan"* I shake my head, it's just too hard.

"So that's not a no?" He questions.

I sigh heavily. *Is it?*

"It's not a yes either," I mumble.

"I can live with that," he croaks sexily. *God damn it, please stop doing that!*

"I... I have to go." I breathe.

"Coral, I'm here for you either way, whatever you decide, you need someone to talk to, a shoulder to cry on. I'm here." He sounds so determined.

"That's sweet Tristan, and very kind of you, considering we don't know each other," I say, my stomach twisting at his words.

"Getting there though." I can tell he's smiling again.

"Goodnight Tristan," I say, shaking my head at his confidence.

"Goodnight Coral, sleep well beautiful." *Damn it!*

"Tristan!" I moan.

"What?" he chuckles. "I can't call you beautiful?"

I shake my head at him. "Never mind. Night, I'll see you when I see you."

"Sooner rather than later," he teases and hangs up before I can say anything.

I growl at my mobile. *What the hell does he mean by that? –* Oh god, I hope he's not coming back down here. I don't think I could take it. I close my eyes and try to blank him out of my head, but all I keep picturing is him smiling at me – That smile of his gets me every time! *Stop it Coral, you and him, it's never going to happen you know that!*

I nod in agreement with myself, pick up my hot chocolate, switch off the air-con, and drag my tired butt up the stairs...

CHAPTER NINETEEN

THE ROOM IS FLOODED with sunshine, but I can't work out where I am. I turn around and realise I'm somewhere strange, a place I haven't been before, and the strangest part about it is the earth isn't still. I am moving back and forth even though my feet are on solid ground. I hear Tristan call me, I walk forward trying to locate his voice, and as I do, I look down at my feet. No shoes? – My toes look brown, and my toe-nails are pink like I've been sunbathing. *How odd?*

As I walk forward, I catch my reflection in a mirror. I'm in a khaki bikini, and my body looks tanned and healthy. As I stare back at myself, I don't recognise the girl staring back at me, I look so happy. I hear Tristan call me again, his voice connecting with me on some deep elemental level. It floods me with a feeling of complete and utter peace. I feel so content, and I don't feel afraid anymore, just blissfully happy – very strange!

Tristan calls me again, I try to locate his voice, it seems to be coming from above me; I step forward and climb a small, wooden staircase. As I reach the top, I am blinded for a moment by the sunlight. Tristan comes into view, he's stood there with his hand held out to me, he has his aviators on, and he's wearing his sexiest smile. He's dressed in a pair of navy combat shorts, no shirt and his feet are bare – *Wow!*

Reaching out I take his outstretched hand and look around me, and it's at that moment I realise we are on a boat, that's why the earth is moving. We are moored in a little cove, surrounded by a beautiful rocky landscape. The sea is twinkling sweetly, the sky a perfect blue and the sun is high in the sky.

I turn around again to look at Tristan. He is beaming at me, a smile so wide; his dimples are deeper than I've ever seen them, he leans down and kisses the back of my hand.

"Mrs Freeman," he croons and leans in to kiss me...

I AM RUDELY AWOKEN by my alarm clock buzzing loudly at me. I jump up in shock and slam my hand over the top of it – *Oh My God! What the hell was that?* I run my hands through my hair and stare blankly at the wall trying to work it out. *I... what?* Mrs Freeman? I was married to him in the dream? *But I, Noooooo, that's just ridiculous!*

I shake my head in wonder. I have never in my life imagined myself getting married. I don't even believe in marriage, I don't believe it has any value; my parents are a good example of that. So why am I dreaming I was married to him? I shake my head, trying to work it out. When Debs got hitched, she told me it was all coming true, how she had dreamed it would be as a little girl. What her dress would look like, the church, all the bells and whistles.

I shake my head in confusion. I've never done any of that, ever - *How odd?* I lie back down and stare up at the ceiling, trying to remember more about the dream. Then it comes to me, that peaceful feeling, almost as though it was a knowing like I knew that there was no more pain, no more fear. That I was ok, actually happy, really happy - *Weird!*

I decide it's best not to be thinking about a silly dream for too long, it's not healthy, it's never going to happen and it's not reality. The reality is that I have to get to the gym and do my morning swim, go to work, and then tonight I have training with Will.

Just another ordinary day. Nothing special, nothing new.

The peaceful feeling quickly dissipates and is replaced with a deep longing, a feeling of wanting something, and wanting it so badly. It's always been there, for as long as I can remember, but now it feels more profound.

I just wish I knew what it was, so I could get it and make the longing go away...

THE REST OF THE DAY passes by in a blur; I cannot seem to concentrate at all – I just keep getting the boat dream with

Tristan playing over and over in my head. Joyce pulled me up on it several times, and I apologised several times. And as for the walk home…well, I don't even remember doing that.

After training with Will, and getting knocked on my ass far too many times. I decided to have an early night. I know it's weird – but I wanted to watch Twilight again. So I quickly showered – wishing I was actually in that egg shaped bath, soaking my aching muscles – dressed in my pyjamas, and took my laptop up to bed with me. I don't know how far I got in the movie before I drifted off, but I remember the dream.

I was stood in the middle of a dark green forest, it was misty and cold. I could hear the rain crashing down on the canopy of branches above me, the air thick with the smell of pine.

Edward was stood in front of me, then he blurred and changed into Tristan. He looked so sad as he held his hand out to me when I looked down to place my hand in his, a red apple appeared, and I looked up in confusion. He lifted the apple up between his long fingers and stepped closer to me.

"Take a bite," he whispered.

I tried to step forward, but I was being held back by some invisible force. I pulled against it, desperate to get to Tristan; I wanted to reach out, to touch him, but I couldn't free myself.

The more I struggled, the stronger the force became until eventually, I had to watch Tristan slowly morph from a solid human form to a cloudy mist, whispering my name just before he completely disappeared…

I AM STARING BLANKLY at my computer; its 3.45pm and its Friday. I know I should be bricking it about seeing George, but I'm not – All I have done all day is daydream about the dream I had Wednesday night, just like yesterday. *I feel like I'm losing my mind!*

I don't know why I can't stop thinking about being on that boat with Tristan, and every time it comes to me, I keep getting that Coldplay song Us Against the World playing in my head. I don't get it at all, and I certainly cannot understand the marriage part.

I've been trying to convince myself that it's because Gladys is getting married, and I'm subconsciously thinking about it, but then I thought no, that can't be right. I didn't think about getting married when Debs did, and I was far more involved with all the wedding shenanigans than I am now – *No, there has to be some other explanation for it all.*

But more than that, more than the whole married thing, every time my mind has wandered to the dream, I have felt the same sense of peace wash over me and quite frankly, I've loved it, so I've purposely allowed it.

I have never felt like that before, ever – "Coral?" I look up in a daze.

"Yes Joyce," I answer dreamily. I hadn't even noticed her standing there.

"Are you sure you're alright? You've been very pre-occupied this past couple of days." *Uh-Oh!*

I panic for a moment and quickly run through my in-box – *No, I have definitely done all my work!*

"Have I?" I sigh.

Joyce rolls her eyes at me. "Well, I'm leaving now, so you can do the same," she tells me. "I'll see you tomorrow," she smiles.

"Ok, see you tomorrow," I answer already on autopilot.

Joyce walks off shaking her head at me.

I go through the motions of shutting my computer down and heading out for the evening, all the while thinking about that wonderful peaceful feeling...

I HEAR DOGS BARKING, in a daze, I look up and realise I have reached George's house. I ring the bell, and after a moment, I hear George's partner Phil, telling his two Maltese dogs to be quiet. He opens the door and smiles widely at me.

"Hello Coral," he says and ushers the dogs back inside.

"Hey, Phil." I follow him in and shut the door. Phil air kisses both my cheeks. "You look well," I tell him.

"No!" He says flicking his hand – he's so girly. "Although, I have just come back from the Spa," he says, smiling sweetly at me.

"Ooh, lucky you," I chuckle and almost go to say 'lady of leisure' but stop myself just in time.

"My weekly massage, full body and face. You should try it, makes you feel amazing," he glows.

"It shows," I say and bend down to greet Tinkerbelle and Princess, they're totally adorable, fluffy little pooches. After licking me to death, I follow Phil into the kitchen.

"You're a little early," he says.

I shrug. "I know. Joyce let me go early."

Phil suddenly narrows his eyes at me. "You look different," he says observantly.

I shrug again. "Do I?"

"Amour," he says, with a twinkle in his eyes. *Love?* "That'll do that to you," he titters.

I smile weakly at him. "I don't know what you're talking about!" I say feigning innocence.

He gasps. "You have! You've met someone!" He says with animated glee. If I blushed, I swear I would be purple right now. *Is it really that obvious?*

"Kind of..." I say, not really sure what I'm talking about.

He slaps his hands to his face and squeals, his eyes twinkling. "How marvellous!"

I smile weakly at him.

"Tell me everything," he says, leaning on the kitchen counter, his chin cupped in his hands. He's dying to know, but I don't know what to say. Thankfully the phone starts ringing; saving me.

Phil pulls a sad face. "Back in a sec," he says and skips out of the kitchen.

I start day-dreaming again. I'm pulled out of it by George placing his hand on my shoulder. I jump a mile and have to calm my heart down. "Wow George, don't do that to me," I scold.

"Are we in the land of the living?" he asks dryly.

I pull a face and silently follow him out of the kitchen. As we pass Phil who's gossiping on the phone, I mouth 'sorry' to him – I know he'll want all the juicy details when I've finished with George, 'later' he mouths back; we smile at one another.

I sit down on the couch and wait for George to settle himself. Sitting in his leather chair, he takes out his notepad and pen, pops his glasses on, and smiles down at me – *Ok, here goes!*

"So Coral, how's the rest of your week been?"

"Um...good," I say.

"You seem...relaxed." He quickly assesses.

"Yeah, I guess." I shrug non-committed.

"Care to share?" George asks.

I stare down at my fingers - I'm not sure I want to share the dream. It felt so private so...like it was just mine and Tristan's.

"Coral?" George prompts.

I sigh in resignation. "I had a dream," I confess, keeping my eyes on my hands that are now twisted together.

"And?" George says. I decide to tell him about my conversation with Tristan first, about asking for the time off and Gladys's news about the wedding. "And his reaction?" George asks.

"Shocked," I answer. "And worried, for me," I add.

George chuckles, my eyes dart up to meet his.

"Why is that funny?" I ask a little sharply.

"I think it's quite obvious he's already developed a deep connection to you." George states.

I shake my head at him. "Doubtful, he's very caring about his staff, that's all," I answer.

George studies me for a moment then crosses his leg. "Men are very different to women Coral. Do you think he's organised birthday surprises for his other members of staff? Or offered to drive goodness knows how many miles to come and see you, because he simply *'cares about his staff'* no, I don't think so." I frown at George not knowing where he's going with this.

My leg starts jigging up and down, a sure sign that I'm nervous.

"So tell me about the dream," George adds.

I exhale slowly, my cheeks expanding and stare out of the window. "I kind of don't want to tell you...it felt like...well like it was private," I say looking back at him.

George shakes his head at me. "Nothing's private Coral, not when you're in therapy." He tells me softly. *Grrrrrrr!*

"Fine!" I snap and reel off how the dream went, how it made me feel. When I finish George doesn't say a word, he's frantically taking notes on his pad.

Finally, he looks up at me. "It's not something we've ever covered Coral, so I'm intrigued, do you want to get married?"

I vehemently shake my head. "No. It's never been on the cards for me." I state firmly.

"Yet, you felt contented, peaceful?" He queries.

"It was just a dream," I answer dully.

"I'd like you to consider that possibility for yourself."

My eyes shoot up to his – *Is he joking?*

I snort sarcastically at that one. "George, I don't believe in it ok. I don't think marriage has any value, so there's no point asking me to consider it."

"Why?" He asks cocking his head to the side.

"Because...I...I just don't," I shrug. "Look, I get what you're saying, I really do. But I can't even imagine myself in a relationship, so I think throwing marriage in there is a bit...well silly." I say, feeling a little resentful.

"One step at a time Coral, I would strongly suggest you consider it as being a possibility in your future. I really want you to start opening yourself up to all possibilities. You have just as much right to the deep happiness you felt in that dream as anyone else on the planet."

"Fine," I say wanting to get off the subject. "I'll consider it," I add rolling my eyes.

"Good," George says. "Now, how did your evening go with Gladys?"

"Fine," I answer.

"That's a lot of fines," George scolds. "Elaborate please, Coral."

"There's not really much to say. Gladys is happy, Malcolm is nice, really nice actually' – I scowl at the floor – 'they're getting married on my birthday."

George raises his eyebrows. "And how do you feel about that?" he asks.

"Quite honestly, I don't care. It's the middle of the week. They just want a small gathering, and that's the date the Hilton can get them in." George nods as he listens to me. "You know, I've thought about a lot of things this week. And as far as Gladys is concerned, it was going to happen someday, right? And I guess I'm trying to do what you tell me to do. To be less afraid of change, to understand that I can't control everything, and as sad as I am that both Joyce and Gladys are leaving, there's not much I can do about it, so I'm rolling with the punches."

"I'm very glad to hear you say that Coral, that's a very positive reaction." George smiles warmly at me. "And like it or not, I think deep down, way down there in your subconscious you're not feeling so afraid because you already have someone else to lean on, someone you know you can depend on."

I frown back at him. "I know I have that, I have Rob," I state.

George shakes his head at me. "I wasn't talking about Rob, I was talking about Tristan."

"Tristan. Is. My. Boss." I hiss, enunciating each word – *Honestly, can't he get that?*

"That may be so, but I think you'd better start letting your real feelings for him come to the surface Coral."

"What real feelings?" I question, laughing sarcastically at him. He cocks his head to the side, folds his hands in his lap and waits patiently for me - *Argh!* I stand up and start pacing the room.

"Coral, please sit back down." I cross my arms in a huff and sit back down on the sofa.

"What I am trying to say to you is that you wouldn't be having the type of dream that you had unless you are fighting how you truly feel for him. So if I was to ask you to be brutally honest with yourself, and say it out loud' – "I can't," I shout, interrupting George. "It doesn't matter how much I like him. It doesn't matter that I have dreamt about him. It doesn't matter that he's the best man I've ever met in my entire life. I'm not good for him!" I yell, thumping my fist on the sofa and choking back the tears that have thickened my throat.

"Yes you are," George says in his quiet, calming voice.

I squeeze my eyes shut. I feel guilty for shouting at him. "Sorry," I whisper.

"No need." He says.

I sigh again and open my eyes. "George," I say softly. "He's a good man who deserves a happy, healthy, emotionally balanced woman by his side. You know what I'm like, I self-destruct everything…"

"That's your fears talking." George retorts.

"I know it's my fears," I bark back, gritting my teeth.

"Coral, I really want you to answer the question. How do you feel about him?"

"I love him!" I shout. "Is that what you wanted to hear? I'm already in love with him, and I've only spent a few hours with him and I…" I stop myself there. "It's best left alone," I snap.

"Good, well done Coral." George praises.

"How is that good?" I mumble.

"It's good because once you open yourself up to the possibility of a relationship with him, your subconscious will start to work in your favour. You want him, you love him, but your fears are holding you back."

I shake my head in wonder. "Why would he want me?" I snap. "I'm nothing, a broken, empty vessel. I have nothing to offer him. How can he want someone who doesn't love themselves, it makes no sense at all. Why the hell would he want this?" I spit, gesturing to all of me.

"Coral!" George gasps. "I thought we had made progress in this area? Do you still feel like that? Are you still suffering from self-abhorrence issues?" George looks horrified.

I squeeze my eyes shut. "Yes...no," I take a deep breath. "He'll leave me," I whimper. "I know he will."

"You can't know that," George argues. "And there's no guarantee in any relationship Coral. They take work, love, openness and commitment, and even then it's not set in stone. When a person enters into a relationship, they do so with a factor of risk. They could be very happy, yet their partner leaves them or vice-versa, nothing is guaranteed in this life, and nobody can say for sure that they will be together until the day they die." He softly says.

I swipe at the angry tears that have started to fall down my cheeks, one after the other.

"Coral, I need you, to be honest with me. Are you still in the place you were when we started your sessions? Do you really feel that way about yourself? Have we made no progress at all?"

I sniff loudly and shake my head at him. "I am a little better George, which has only been possible with your help. I guess what I'm trying to say is, I know me, I know what I'm like. The closer I get to him, the more I'll start pulling away...." I shake my head and grit my teeth. "I don't want to hurt him," I whisper.

George is frantically writing again. "So what you're saying is this isn't about self-abhorrence, it's about your worth and your fears of him leaving like your father did?"

I look up at George with wide, tear stained eyes and slowly nod.

"Darling girl, you have to start to understand that a

relationship with a lover is very different to a parent. If you dated Tristan and he decided it wasn't working for him; he won't just disappear like your father did, it doesn't work that way. And you are worthy." He adds.

I sob into my hands – *This is too heavy, I can't do this.*

"Coral, I suggested talking with Tristan. I'm going to set that as part of your therapy. Like it or not, I want you to start opening up to him. I'm not asking you to tell him everything, just a little bit at a time. Maybe start with your fears, your fears of him leaving, the fear of self-destructing the relationship. When one is armed with information, it is so much easier to look at it from a solution base rather than a preventative base."

"You're setting me an assignment?" I gasp in anger; my tears come to an abrupt stop.

"Yes," he answers firmly.

"No," I bite back, shaking my head in disapproval – *I can't do that.*

"Coral, I can only help you so far. And quite frankly, I think you need the push, especially in this direction."

"I won't do it," I sulk, crossing my arms in defiance.

"Then you leave me no choice but to halt out sessions for now." I glare back at him.

"Well that's just great," I snap in exasperation.

"One step at a time Coral," he reiterates.

"Fine," I snap back. "I'll try telling him...something," I blurt, my hand flying in the air.

"Good, now our agreement." He says calmly, watching my reaction.

I close my eyes and squeeze my hand into fists. I take a deep breath and exhale slowly. *I have no choice now, I have to tell him.*

Swallowing three times, I hear the words come out of my mouth. "I was raped," I whisper. I hear George gasp, and because I'm worried about his reprimand; I keep my eyes closed.

"When?" He whispers.

"Two years ago," I answer my voice flat. It doesn't sound like me.

"But...but that's how long you've been seeing me?" He says disbelievingly.

"Yes," I whisper. "That's why I initially started seeing you, but every time I got close to telling you, I chickened out." I keep my eyes closed, for some unexplainable reason, it's helping to keep me calm, and stopping me from imploding.

I hear George stand, seconds later I feel the sofa sag next to me as he sits down, he takes one of my hands in his. "Darling girl," he softly says, gently squeezing my hand. "You said on Tuesday you made a mistake?" he says bleakly.

I nod my head and finally open my eyes, then turn and meet George's shocked expression. "I know I should have told you...before, I'm sorry." I croak.

"Being raped isn't a mistake Coral." He softly says.

I sniff loudly and swipe at the silent tears – *Fucking tears they're pissing me off now!*

"It was for me. I was stupid, I never should have..." I cringe as I recall that fateful night.

"No sweetheart, that's not how it works. I take it you said no, rejected him in some way?" I nod silently. "Then you didn't make a mistake, he forced himself on you." George takes a deep breath in, slowly blows it out and continues. "Did you report it?" He softly asks.

I close my eyes and silently shake my head, I hear him gasp.

"Why ever not?" he says in disbelief.

I squeeze my eyes shut tighter, remembering why. "Because he scared the life out of me George, I thought, well, I was worried that he knew where I lived, and to be quite honest I've never seen a pair of eyes with such malicious intent. What happened to me as a kid was bad enough, *his* eyes were pretty terrifying, but this guy, maybe because I'm an adult now, I don't know... he told me he'd kill me," I whimper. "George I was so scared." I choke back the tears, my hands balling into fists, makes me so fucking angry thinking about it.

"Give me a moment." George softly says and leaves the room. A minute later he's back at my side, I open my eyes, and he hands me a large glass of amber liquid. "Courvoisier," he explains.

I take a sip and swallow, feeling it warm my insides as it smoothly makes its way down to my stomach. I take another sip, then decide to take a gulp which I know you shouldn't do with Brandy, but I know George is going to want details, and I think it's going to help me get it all out; it really burns as it trickles down.

"Want to tell me about it?" He softly asks.

"Not really," I choke, even though I know I should.

"I understand," George coos.

I turn and look at him, he looks really shaken. "Are you ok?" I croak.

"No," he answers sternly. "I'm not."

"Oh George, I'm sorry I didn't tell you' –"I'm not upset with you Coral, I'm upset with myself..." He stares blankly ahead, deep in thought.

"Don't," I whisper. "I'm very good at hiding things George; don't punish yourself for not seeing this."

His eyes dart up to meet mine. "But I should have seen," he chastises. "I'm a therapist, I've dealt with so many women who've been raped. I've always known, seen it before they've admitted it...but with you..." He drifts off again, rubbing his fingers across his forehead.

"Please George, I don't think you realise how accomplished I am at keeping my emotions at bay. I always have my game face on, my mask, as I call it. I'm very good at pretending everything is ok when it's not. Remember how long it took you to get me talking about my childhood?"

He slowly nods his head. "It's like keeping it in my head, doesn't make it real, saying it out loud does." Amazingly, I start to smile. "Just like you getting me to admit how I really feel about Tristan, I know things will be different now, so please George, don't feel bad." I plead, squeezing his hand back.

Then I have a moment of clarity. If I tell George what happened, he might be able to help me, and the nightmares might stop, and in all honesty, I'm tired of being scared of it.

"I have nightmares about it," I whisper.

George squeezes my hand. "I'm sure you do," he whispers back.

"Last one was on Tuesday night. When you worked out that I was holding something back, and you said I had to tell you about it. I felt so fearful, so vulnerable that it came to me again, I woke up in such a state; it makes me feel so dirty, and every time I wake up from it I throw up, I don't know how much more my stomach can take." I take a deep breath, then continue.

"And I cried George, for the first time in twenty-five years, I cried. It felt very cathartic like you said it's a release, but I still feel like I shouldn't cry, that it's a sign of weakness, but I did, I let it all out." My eyes fill with unshed tears again. I chuckle to myself. George smiles softly at me and squeezes my hand. He's so good to me, so patient.

"It happened about a month before I bought the studio. As you know, Gladys and I had been looking for studios for a while, but nothing was coming up that I really liked. I was feeling really melancholy, the very thought of still being with Gladys when I hit thirty was depressing me, I was feeling so miserable that I was never going to find anything, and I was still hurting about Justin. I had no friends, no social life and to make matter worse, Gladys had gone away for the weekend. One the one hand I loved having the house to myself, but on the other, I was lonely, I felt empty, scared, and vulnerable. So, to try and take my mind of it all I decided to go for a run on the beach. That's when I met him." I take a deep breath and try to stay focused.

"Let me get you another," he whispers taking my empty glass off me. When he returns, I notice he has one too. Sitting next to me, he smiles weakly at me and hands me the glass.

"Thanks," I whisper and take a sip. "So I'm running on the beach, and I notice this guy, he's running too. When I stop to take a breather, he comes over to me, and we start talking. We had so much in common and before I knew it an hour had passed and it only felt like five minutes. He told me he was from London and had come down for a long weekend, he said he'd split from his girlfriend, he seemed genuinely cut up about it. I told him about Justin, it felt like we were kindred spirits, you know…" I take a deep breath and another swig of brandy.

"I relished the company, having someone to talk to, someone my own age. Anyway, he asked to see me that night, I was so excited I really thought there was some potential there. I thank god every day that I decided to meet him in town, he wanted to pick me up at the house, but my instinct was telling me not to do that. I thought that tiny nagging feeling of fear was just my usual self-protectiveness coming through, but I guess I was picking up on the fact that he was dangerous, that I should be careful." I take another drink.

"We had a great night, I felt very connected to him on every level, we laughed, we talked non-stop; I was fascinated with him. When the pub closed he asked me to take a walk with him along the promenade, he took my hand in his he couldn't stop gazing at me. I felt like there was something really big there, he told me he wanted to see me again the following weekend, I agreed, and that's when he kissed me; he was so gentle, it was such a sweet kiss. We didn't want to leave one another, so I agreed to go to his hotel for more drinks.

"When the hotel bar closed, he asked me to come up to his room, I told him I wasn't that kind of girl, but he assured me it was just for another drink. He's been a perfect gentleman all evening, so I didn't see any harm in it, and I certainly didn't see any danger. Hand in hand, we walked up to his room chatting the whole time. He opened the door and gestured for me to go first, which I did, but when he closed the door behind me, he turned into a monster." I drain the last of the brandy.

"He grabbed me from behind and started groping me, I was shocked, totally stunned. I told him no, and again that I'm not that type of girl, I tried to push him off me, but that just made him more aggressive. I managed half a scream before he covered my mouth with his hand, I tried to fight him off again, but he was too strong. We fell to the floor, I begged him to let me go, he laughed at me, said it was all my fault that I'd led him on. I screamed at him that I hadn't done that, but that made him angrier. He started swearing at me, calling me a whore, a dick-tease. I couldn't see how I'd given him that impression, which made *me* angry, so I shouted *'go fuck yourself'*, and that's when he punched me in the face, right here, see." I point to the tiny scar that's across my right eyebrow.

"He'd knocked me out, so when I came round, I found myself on the bed, my hands were tied to the post, and he was striping my jeans off me. I tried to kick him off, but he punched me again, right in the jaw, I could taste blood swimming in my mouth. I was in so much pain, I could hardly see out my right eye, and I knew, I just knew what he was going to do, it was inevitable." I take another deep breath.

"I thought about trying to buck him off me, but my past reminded me that doing that only makes it more painful, so I went limp and withdrew, just like I used to, and let him have his way with me. He was so rough with me, he was spitting vile, repulsive things at me the whole time, I can still feel…" I close my eyes to try and compose myself, I swallow hard and continue.

"When I have nightmares about it, it's the ripping and the pounding into me that I remember, it makes my pelvic muscles go into spasm, he just didn't stop. It felt like it went on and on, I thought it was never going to end, he threatened to kill me, and in all honesty, I wanted him to, I wanted it to be over." George gasps again and squeezes his eyes shut.

"I don't know how long it went on for, but in the end, I passed out in pain." I stare blankly ahead, amazed I managed to get it all out, and I'm surprised at myself, I thought I would be upset, crying even, but I just feel numb; like I'm listening to someone else tell the story, totally void of myself. I turn and stare at George, he looks like he's going to be sick and he's so pale.

"George?" I prompt.

"That was very brave of you Coral, well done for being honest and telling me what happened. How do you feel now you've told me?"

"Numb," I answer my voice sounding void of all emotion.

"That's understandable," he says.

I laugh sarcastically, then out of nowhere, the numbness disappears, and I feel overwhelmed with fear, I feel it shake and rattle my body. I guess reliving it again, saying it out loud… unwelcome and unbidden tears start to cascade down my cheeks.

"Coral!" George gasps and wraps his arms around me.

I finally crack, the levees bursting on me, and I crumble into his arms. I wrap my arms around his waist and sink my head into his chest. He gently rocks me, trying to soothe me with gentle words.

"You're safe now," he whispers. "Nothing can happen to you."

I hear his words of comfort, but they make no difference. I cannot stop the tears. I cry long cathartic sobs, soaking his shirt. I take a ragged breath, trying to calm myself down, and it's at that moment that I realise a shocking, unwelcome truth.

I want Tristan; right here, right now. I want his strong arms around me, his scent invading my senses, his lips pressed hard against my forehead, his proximity even; that would be enough.

I mean, George is wonderful and sweet and is trying his best to comfort me, but he can't make me feel safe, he can't protect me, he can't…he can't…finally, it hits me, what I've denied to myself; he can't love me like Tristan can.

I squeeze my eyes shut, trying to block out this revelation. I sit up from my slumped position and try to catch my breath. "I'm sorry," I choke, looking down at George's shirt; it's covered in black mascara.

"No need," he soothes. "Would you like another?" he asks gesturing to my empty glass.

I look up at the clock on the wall, my hour is up. "The time George, I don't want to keep you," I sniff.

"Nonsense," he barks. "Would you like to use the bathroom?"

"Please," I croak.

George helps me to my feet, my legs feel all shaky. "It's the adrenaline," he explains. "Let me help you." George guides me to his downstairs bathroom, once inside he tells me to take my time and shuts the door behind him.

I grab a load of toilet tissue, and blow my nose several times, throwing the paper into the toilet, I press the flush. In a daze, I turn to the sink so I can wash my face - *Jesus, what a mess!*

I have mascara streaks running down my cheeks, my eyes are really swollen, and my nose is bright red – *Great!*

I fill the sink with cold water and plunge my face in. It shocks me for a second, but I stay under holding my breath, after a minute I pull back up. I stare back at my reflection, water dripping down from all over my face. Surprisingly, I feel better than I thought I would, just saying it out loud feels as though a small weight has been lifted from my shoulders.

I start laughing at myself, my eyes look like pandas, and I have black mascara streaks running down each cheek; I look like something out of a horror movie. I notice there's a hand-wash on the sink, so I squirt some onto my hands, and wash away the mascara, refreshing my face again with more cold water, I can't believe how much better I feel - I shake my head at myself - *Should have done this ages ago!*

I dry my face and stare at my reflection, wondering if the tears are going to come back, but surprisingly they don't. I make myself smile trying to perk myself back up, then chuckle at myself – *You idiot!*

Taking a deep breath, I square my shoulders and head back to George's office…

CHAPTER TWENTY

I WALK BACK INTO GEORGE'S office and sit on the sofa next to him. He smiles softly at me and hands me another Brandy. "Thanks." I take another sip.

"I wish you would have told me Coral." He softly scolds.

"I know, I was just thinking the same. I actually feel better for telling you."

"A problem shared..." George cocks an eyebrow up at me in disapproval, he's not happy with me.

"I'm sorry. It wasn't something that was easy to say, and I didn't want to..." I break off.

"Didn't want to what?" he asks, his head cocked to the side.

I take another sip. "Lots of things, I didn't want you to be mad at me for not telling anyone, or going to the police, or..." I stop for a moment. "I was scared and ashamed," I whisper.

"I understand," he softly says. "But I wouldn't have been angry with you, at all." He admonishes.

My head starts banging. I haven't had much food today, so the alcohol is going straight to my head. I place my glass down and pull the pins and bobble out of my hair, then run my fingers through my scalp to try and ease the tension, letting my hair fall across my shoulders and down my back.

"Do you remember his name?" George asks.

"Yes, but I don't think it was his real name."

"How did you get out?" I shudder and take a gulp of brandy.

"When he finished with me, he fell asleep. I think I kept drifting in and out of consciousness, the pain was...horrendous. The next time I came round I could see it was light outside, I remember him waking up, so I pretended to be asleep. I heard him go into the bathroom, he locked the door and turned the shower on; I knew it was my only opportunity to get out, I had to take it.

"When I sat up, I realised my hands were free, I don't remember him untying me, so I grabbed my bag, jeans and t-shirt and fled out of the room, completely naked. I ran to the stairwell, pulled on my jeans and t-shirt and ran home. My feet were so messed up by the time I got back. I don't know why I didn't pick up my shoes, I think they were wedges, I guess they wouldn't have been any good for running in, I just had to get out of there. I was so scared he would catch me leaving," I clench my fists as I recall running back to the house.

"I bled for two days George, and I know he didn't use protection. I was so scared that he'd given me an STD, but he hadn't thank god."

"You got tested?" He questions.

"Yes, I went to the genitourinary clinic, gave a fake name. Test results came back clear."

"What did you tell Gladys, you must have made some excuse up?"

"Yes I did, and I hated lying to her...but, it was just too hard to say. I felt ashamed, embarrassed, and I think I was still in shock. I told her I'd gone for a run and I got jumped on by some drunken bum. I'd taken myself to the hospital before she came back, so I had a couple of stitches on my eyebrow, I was pretty messed up.

"She almost had a heart attack when she walked through the door, she wanted me to go to the police, but I said I didn't even know what he looked like, so she dropped it. She and Joyce took care of me that week, Gladys was still working part-time then so they took it in turns. I'll always be eternally grateful to them both for that, they'll never know how much it meant to me."

"And I take it you remember his face?" I instantly know where George is going with this.

"I'm not going to the police George. I won't have it all dragged back up."

His lips set into a hard line; I can tell he doesn't agree with me.

"Ok, say I report it, and they find him, it's my word against his, and there's no evidence. And don't forget, I know this industry. I know how long these things take. It will take years to go through the system, to finally get to court, which means I'd have it hanging over me for what another two, three years. I won't do that George, I won't put myself through it, and I know it sounds bad, but I'd rather just work on getting better."

George frowns at the floor, deep in thought.

"And now you know..." I stare back at him with wide eyes. "You can help me right?"

"Of course," George whispers and knocks back the rest of his brandy. "So that's why you're so nervous about Tristan?" He surmises.

"No...well sort of," I answer taking another sip. "I'm terrified of having sex again and it all coming back to me. It's hard enough having the triggers that I already have, to having this on top of it as well..." I shake that thought away. "I'm scared of how strongly I feel for Tristan, but I'm even more scared of him turning away from me when he learns who I really am, what I really am.

"Gladys and Joyce moving on has made me realise that unless I exorcise these demons, once and for all, then I'm going to be alone, completely alone, and that...*that* scares me more than anything else ever has." It's weird, now it's out there, now I've said it out loud. I feel ready, I feel really determined, and I know I'm strong, that I can get through this. I just need some help.

"So let's get to work," I say resolutely.

"Well, you've already taken the first step towards healing," George smiles.

"Because I've told you?" I question, he nods once. "Ok, so what else can I do?" I question.

"Well, you have several options. We can keep the sessions at twice a week, and there are several support groups for women, which I think you would find very beneficial. I have dealt with many patients in the past that have been through the same trauma, and when I've directed them towards these support groups, they have all said that having likeminded women around them, who have been through the same thing and are supporting each other, has greatly improved the healing process.

"Now, having said that there have been several patients who

have not gone down that line, they have chosen instead to go to the root of the problem by having sex again. It can be a way of freeing themselves of the panic, the fear. Some wait until they are in a relationship, some are brave enough to pick a guy up, gaining confidence as they do and some, well, some have used male escorts, no ties, just sex."

I gasp in horror. "Are you friggin kidding me? You want me to go out and have' –"No," he laughs. "I'm not telling you to do anything Coral. I'm just explaining to you how other women have dealt with the trauma of it."

"I'm not a victim," I spit rising to my feet - I refuse to be, shit happens, and you just have to deal with it the best way you can, my hands start to shake, a delayed reaction to talking about it.

"I didn't say you were." George scowls.

I sigh heavily and sit back down – *Calm down Coral!*

"I'm sorry George," I close my eyes for a second then look across at him. "Ok, so support groups. Aren't they for women who are being abused by long-term partners though?" I question.

"Some are, others are for women who have basically had the same thing happen as you have. Would you like me to inquire for you?"

"Yes please, I'll try anything," I say, George, grins broadly at me. Then I remember what I thought of the other day. "You know, I was thinking about a lot of things the other day, running them over in my head, and I'm tired George, really, really, tired."

"What of?" He questions.

"Everything," I scoff. "I'm tired of being scared all the time. I'm tired of feeling vulnerable. I'm tired of my associations with men – not all men are bad, I know that. I just don't know how to change how I feel about them, and I want the sex thing sorted, so I'm not freaking out about it. But there are other things too…" I swallow hard surprised by my own candour – *Where's this all come from?*

"Go on," George prompts.

I sigh inwardly and continue. "I want to feel feminine; I'm tired and fed up of wearing trousers and jeans all the time. But I don't want to go through the feelings I get when I put a skirt or dress on, it's too…I feel too vulnerable and out of control. It's exhausting feeling like you're constantly in fight or flight mode.

I want the choice, it was taken away from me, and I want it back." I snap.

George still looks deep in thought. "Well, there is one other option, I hadn't considered it before, but it may work," he muses.

"Whatever it is, I'll try it," I say.

George starts grinning from ear to ear – *What is he smiling about?*

"George!" I scold.

"Sorry, it's just such a pleasure seeing you so ready to try' – George sighs – 'Normally you don't want to work on anything, you just want consistency. It's wonderful to see you so enthusiastic to work on your fears rather than hide behind them." *Jeez, I just want to wear a dress!*

"So what is it?" I ask with bated breath.

"Hypnotherapy," he says.

I scowl at him. "Seriously?" I squeak.

"Yes, it's worked for many of my patients, with excellent results." I light up inside.

"So, you're saying it could what; help me with sex and dresses?" I question.

"Coral, it's certainly something we could try, you never know."

A big smile starts to spread across my face. "Really?" I squeak – *Now I'm excited.*

"Yes," he chuckles.

"Let's go for it." I push.

"Alright then, I know a fantastic therapist in this field, she's expensive though," George tells me.

"I'll dig into my savings," I say – *This is going to work; I have a good feeling about it.*

"Alright then," George says with satisfaction.

Then I panic. "Er…George?"

"Yes."

"I don't like the idea of a stranger having control over what they put in my head. So will you come with me, or can we have the sessions here?"

George cocks his head to the side and raises his eyebrows. "I can do that Coral, but you know what that sounds like?" he says. I already know the answer.

"That I'm a control freak," I answer gloomily. "But you just told me one step at a time, so once I feel comfortable with the Hypnotherapists, I can go without you," I say, feeling triumphant in my reply.

"So I did," he replies, smiling at me again. Then he picks up my glass and walks out the room. He returns moments later with another brandy for us both.

"George, I'll be wobbling home at this rate," I say.

"I don't want you to be alone tonight Coral." He says sitting next to me.

I stare back at him in confusion. "Why not?" I chuckle.

"Because you've just re-lived a trauma! For goodness sake Coral, are you saying you're happy to be on your own after what you've just revealed?" He asks rather astonished.

I shrug and take a sip of Brandy. "George I've been living with this for two years, I'll be fine," I clarify.

"I'll be fine is your answer to everything," George says sarcastically.

"Well I will be," I squeak taking another sip – *Damn this Brandy is nice!*

George shakes his head at me. "Really Coral, in all seriousness I would rather you weren't alone tonight, it will give me peace of mind." I frown and take another drink. "What about staying with Rob?" He asks.

"Can't he's' – I stare down at my hands wrapped around my glass – 'he and Carlos are having some troubles," I say feeling guilty for sharing their secrets.

"Oh?" George cocks his head to the side.

"Rob was acting weird when I saw him on Wednesday, and Carlos won't answer his mobile," I growl remembering him pushing me to voice-mail.

"Gladys?" he asks.

I snort with laughter. "What, and sit in all night with the love-birds?" I blurt. "No thanks, I'd rather be on my own, besides I'll only get hounded as to why I've been crying," I add tersely.

"There is that," George agrees. "How about staying here for the night?" He says, smiling gently at me.

"I-I can't do that," I stutter in amazement. "You…you're my therapists?"

"That I am, and as professional as I should be…well, you feel like family to me. And it's not as if we haven't socialised with one another. We do have mutual friends after all." I nod in agreement, we do, and we have socialised plenty, but wouldn't it be – well wrong?

"That's sweet George, I think of you as family too." I smile tentatively.

"Well then, that's settled. I'll get the spare room ready for you…Oh! And Phil is making his famous Moules Marinieres spaghetti dish' – his eyes sparkle and he claps his hands together – 'and he always makes too much." I can see he really wants me to stay. "And we have a lovely crisp Frascati to go with it." He adds cheerfully.

"But' – "No buts," he says holding up his hands. "For us, Friday nights are about great food, great wine, and a good old movie; how about it?"

"What about Phil? Maybe he wants a romantic night in," I say, feeling a little embarrassed.

"We have all the time in the world for romance darling," George says wistfully.

"I-I just don't know…" I say feeling confused. Then I question – Do I really want to be on my own tonight, glugging more Night Nurse to chase away the horror? I'm sure it's going to come back again.

"I don't want to pressure you Coral, I just don't want you to be on your own." I think about George's offer for a moment, the food sounds amazing, and I already know how much of a wonderful chef Phil is, but wouldn't it just feel really awkward staying here? I decide it would, but then I think it would be rude to say no – *What to do?*

"Ok, I'll be honest. I don't want to stay. I never sleep too well in other people's beds, but I think most people like the comfort of their own bed." George nods in agreement. "But I'd love to stay for the meal and a movie if that's ok, I mean that's not rude is it George?"

George starts chuckling at me. "Oh Coral, you are such a sweetie."

I frown at him, shake my head in disagreement and sip more brandy.

"Now, I'm going to inform Phil we will be three for tea, then I'm taking the dogs for an evening walk. Would you like to join me?"

I nod my head. "Yes please."

"Alright, back in a moment," George says and steps out of his office.

Whoa! That was a weird session. Ok, I got it out about being raped, but I'm more mind blown about Tristan – *Am I in love with him? Do I really want to date* – "Coral." George calls, pulling me from my musing. I drain the last of the brandy, put down the glass and skip out of his office.

Half an hour later we step back into the house. The walk was quite refreshing and blew the cobwebs away. George hasn't asked me anymore about what I told him, which I'm grateful for. In fact, he and Phil seem to be in fine form, and are determined to make this a fun, relaxed evening…

I AM FULL TO THE point of bursting. I ate far too much Moules Marinieres – George was right, Phil did way too much – and I ate far too much French baguette too, but dipping it in that delicious sauce that Phil made was just too good to resist – A lot like Tristan.

I haven't gone too mad with the wine. I don't want to embarrass myself in front of George, and I already have enough brandy swishing around inside me. When I've finally helped Phil clean up in the kitchen – after a lot of arguing and debating whether I should – he tops up all our wine glasses and I guiltily follow them into their snug. George turns the ambient lighting down low as Phil switches on the T.V and the DVD player. I instantly feel as though I'm intruding.

"Um…I think I might' – "Sit down." George barks.

"Honestly woman, you should do as he says," Phil says winking at me.

I smile back at him and curl up on the end of the large, plush leather sofa. Phil and George get comfy too, both propping their feet up onto the matching leather footstool. Then the movie starts, and I'm instantly surprised. For some reason, I was expecting the latest blockbuster, but no, it's a black and white, something called 'The Shop Around The Corner'.

"Heard of it?" Phil asks. I shake my head. "Well you know, You've Got Mail?"

"Tom Hanks," I nod. "He's awesome." I roll my eyes at

myself – *Of course, you think he's awesome Coral, he's your favourite actor!*

"Yes," Phil smiles. "This is the original," he says then turns back to the face the screen. *Well what d'ya know, you learn something new every day.*

As the movie begins I already know that the main actor is James Stewart, but I'm not sure of the woman and I should, I've watched enough black and whites with Gladys in my time.

"Who's the actress?" I whisper to Phil.

"Margaret Sullavan," he whispers back. "She didn't make many films, preferred the stage."

"Oh!" That explains that then. I relax back into the sofa, slowly sipping my wine and completely lose myself in the movie…

TWO HOURS LATER the movie ends. I sigh blissfully, stretching my legs as I do.

"Enjoy that?" Phil asks. I nod vigorously.

"Yeah, it was really good, you can't beat the oldies." I chuckle.

"I quite agree." Phil turns to George who is softly snoring on the sofa and leans down to wake him.

"Don't wake him," I whisper.

"Ok, you sure you won't stay? You're more than welcome."

"No Phil, but thank you. I had a lovely evening, and the meal was delicious." I rub my belly in appreciation.

He chuckles at me. "I'm glad you liked it."

I silently follow him out of the snug. Once we are back in the kitchen, Phil calls me a taxi while I check my mobile for messages – *Nothing! Damn it, Rob, why haven't you called or text me?*

I try not to get angry at him or think the worst, but we keep in constant contact, and I haven't heard from him for two and a half days now – that just isn't Rob's normal behaviour! I decide after Lily's party, I'm going up to their place and knock down the door if I have to – I want some answers, I can't go through this worry if there's no need.

As we are stood in the kitchen waiting for the taxi, Phil

hands me his cucumber eye gel, which he has been getting me to apply all evening. Apparently, it takes away puffy eyes.

"Take it," he says. "Put a load on before you get into bed, and in the morning when you wake, no-one will know," he adds.

"Thanks, Phil." We hear the taxi pull up, Phil opens the door and air kisses both my cheeks again. I get into the taxi and wave happily at him as the car pulls away...

WHEN I GET BACK to my studio, I instantly dive towards the air-con and switch it to full. Today has been swelteringly hot and going straight to George's from work has allowed the studio to get toasty. I feel dog tired again, and I'm surprised that when I check the time it half-past twelve.

I really feel like a long hot shower to relax my aching muscles from swimming hard this morning, and I know it will help me feel better. But I also have a nagging feeling that the nightmare might return, and the last thing I want to do is turn up at Lily's birthday party, looking and feeling like shit.

So, against my better judgment, I pull out the bottle of Night Nurse and take two large glugs of it knowing full well that by the time I've showered, and curled up in bed it will have kicked in, and I'll be out for the count. I dash upstairs, strip my clothing, pin my hair up and pull on my robe.

In the shower I take my time, letting the hot water cascade across my tense shoulders, down my back, turning around I let it warm my breasts and my slightly swollen abdomen.

Tutt, Tutt naughty Coral! *That's too much bread and pasta for you!*

I chuckle back at myself – *Yeah but it was so worth it!* I think I may have to ask Phil to show me how to make that dish, then I think it might be dangerous, I may make it too often and turn into a big fat bloater.

I chuckle again and turn off the shower. Just as I open the door and reach for my towel, I feel myself wobble slightly – *Uh-oh! Drugs kicking in!*

I carefully step out, dry myself off as quickly as I can, wrap my robe back around myself and head out the bathroom. As I pass the air-con, I decide to leave it on low for the night. I'm going to give myself a rare lie-in tomorrow, and I don't want the heat waking me up.

I groggily make my way back up the stairs, unpinning my hair as I go, feeling more and more sleepy with each step I take. As I reach my bedroom, I strip my robe off me and collapse onto the bed.

Curling up, I pull my quilt over me so that it's covering my torso, leaving my legs free and slip easily into a deep and dreamless sleep...

I HEAR A STRANGE knocking noise. I turn over in my bed trying to make the funny noise go away, but it won't. I hear it again, the strange tapping noise. I groan and slam my hand over my alarm clock, but that makes no difference either. My eyes flutter open, sunlight is flooding into my bedroom. I'm totally disorientated, and I still feel so sleepy.

I turn over and hide my head under the duvet, I just want to go back to sleep, but I can't help glancing at my alarm clock, 10.15am – *Shit! I'm late for work!*

I go into a full-blown panic attack and scramble out of bed, stubbing my toe in the process. "Shit!" *Ouch, that really hurt!*

I start hopping on one foot, then I freeze, I can hear voices down on the sundeck.

"Coral, can you hear me, darling?" *Knock, knock, knock.*

"Gladys?" I question, not understanding why she's here. Then it all comes flooding back to me, it's Saturday – *Shit Lily's party, Gladys is picking me up, shiiiiit!*

I grab my robe; wrap it around me, and dash down the stairs. I am mortified. Gladys and Malcolm are stood on the sundeck, and they look like they are being baked alive – *How long have they been there?*

I scramble for my keys out of my bag, dash over and unlock the patio door, yanking it open in the process, the heat almost knocking me over as I do.

"Sorry, sorry...come in," I usher with my hands. "Mornin' Bob," I grab hold of him and pull him in too, as he's stood there looking as though he doesn't know what to do with himself.

I slam the door shut, and then I dash over to the air-con and switch it onto full power. As I turn back around, I see Malcolm and Bob exchange a smirk.

"What's that?" Gladys asks, fanning herself.

"Air-con' it'll soon cool down," I say feeling guilty. "Sorry, overslept, help yourselves to drinks," I say as I walk into the bathroom and slam the door behind me. *Oh god, how embarrassing!*

Then I see myself in the mirror – *Holy crap!*

My hair literally looks like I've been electrocuted, it's sticking up all over the place –What the hell did I do in my sleep last night? *No time - no time to think about that, shower Coral* – Right yes shower! Just as I turn it on another thought comes to mind – *Damn it!*

I yank the bathroom door back open and see that Malcolm is already making drinks for everyone.

"Coffee Coral?" He's trying so hard not to laugh.

"No thanks – Gladys!" I screech.

"What!?" She jumps half a mile and stares back at me in wonder.

"I didn't wrap the presents!" I bellow.

"Coral!" She softly scolds.

"I know, I know, terrible aunty and all that. But it's not just mine," I say, lifting the bags that hold the presents from the side of my sofa. "It's mine, Bobs and Rob's," I squeak.

"Alright darling calm down, I'll wrap, you shower." Gladys soothes.

I finally breathe. "Oh…good…ok, thanks, Gladys," I say my heart settling down. I hand her the wrapping paper, sellotape and scissors.

"Which is which?" Gladys asks, I quickly point out who's bought what, then dash over to the kitchenette, grab a large glass and fill it with my pre-made veggie juice.

"That looks disgusting." Bob pipes up.

"It good for you," I bark back.

I hear him chuckling hard as I dash back into the bathroom and slam the door shut. I have the quickest shower on record, cream my skin from head to toe, apply my makeup, and add coconut oil to my hair. Pulling my robe back on, I exit the bathroom, noticing that Gladys, Malcolm, and Bob all seem very relaxed as they sit discussing the merits of air-conditioning, and how useful they are. I panic for a second, I hope Gladys doesn't ask me anything about it. I don't think I'll be able to hide the fact that Tristan bought it for me.

Pushing that thought aside, I dash up the stairs.

Twenty minutes later I am ready and making one last check in the mirror. I've decided to go casual because it's a kid's party, and well truthfully, I need to take a visit to the launderette. So I pulled on my only pair of jean shorts that I've had forever, as it's too hot for jeans, a t-shirt and my flip-flops. Grabbing my hoody just in-case it gets chilly later, I make my way down the stairs.

"Ready," I say still feeling flustered. Malcolm and Bob both stand, I walk over to them, giving them both a kiss on the cheek and a normal un-rushed good morning, and then I turn to Gladys and hug her hard. "Thank you," I say again.

Gladys chuckles and pats me on the back. "Well come on then, we're late as it is."

I grab my bag and my keys and leaving the air-con on low we all usher out of the studio. I notice Malcolm has hold of the presents – I roll my eyes at myself, that would have been the next thing I would have forgotten –locking the door behind me, we all turn to make our way to the car.

Walking in front of me Gladys links her arm in Malcolm's, and for a moment I feel a pang of jealousy – *Why can't I be that free and happy?*

I guess Bob must have picked up on it because he stops, and holds his arm out to me with a big smile on his face. I smile back at him and curl my arm around his; I'm instantly surprised by how firm his arm feels.

"Bob, do you work out?" I ask, finding my sunglasses and popping them on.

"Yes, every morning." He smiles.

"Really, what do you do?" I ask feeling quite shocked.

"Calisthenics." *What?*

"Oh!" I say not wanting to say I don't know what that is. But Bob is too wise for that, he chuckles again and pats my hand.

"Squats, press-ups, crunches, that sort of thing," he says. I decide the moment I'm home I'll check it out on the web.

"Cool, good for you. You can tell," I say squeezing the muscle on his arm.

"A compliment," Bob says raising his chin in the air. "Sure feel proud to have you on my arm Coral." He's such a smoothie.

"Ah Bob, me too," I say and kiss his cheek again. *I wish he were my Granddad!*

We make it to the car at a much slower pace than we would have done, Bob maybe fit, but he doesn't walk as quickly as he used to.

"Gladys, have you told Debs yet?" I ask wondering if she's shared their news.

"No darling, taken the ring off," she says wiggling her hand at me.

"Oh, ok!" I frown, wondering why she hasn't, it seems a little odd to me. "When *are* you going to tell her?" I enquire.

"Soon," she answers. *Humph!* "Gosh, isn't it such a beautiful day for the barbeque," Gladys smiles, changing the subject.

"Barbeque?" I frown.

"Yes dear, you know what they're like. Debbie asked Lily if she wanted sandwiches, ice-cream and jelly and she said no, she wanted Daddy's burgers," Gladys chuckles. "Ten years older than she is that one!"

I roll my eyes. If it had been my kid, they would have got what they got. *What are you talking about Coral? You're never going to have kids!* I chastise, knowing it's true.

As we head west on the A259 towards Worthing, I let my mind drift. Gladys and Bob are in animated discussion about some political thing going on, and I am not interested in the slightest, people get so agitated about all that stuff. Life's stressful enough without barking on about what some fat cat in a suit has been up to.

I think about Rob and the fact that I still haven't heard from him, even after sending him a quick text in the car last night, and again this morning while I was frantically getting dressed, quite frankly, it's just rude not to reply and let me know he's ok.

Then I think about everything I discussed with George, finally letting him know about…I shut the door on that thought, but at least it's out there now, and I can start healing. I cross my fingers as I think about the upcoming hypnotherapy session, I really hope it works. I really do want to move on from all the crap that swirls around in my head, from all the insecure feelings that hold me back from really living life to the full, taking chances, being brave and not feeling so afraid all the time.

Thinking about it all makes me want to start the hypnotherapy straight away if I can. So, I pull my mobile out my bag and send a quick message to George, he instantly texts me back saying that Cindy Crosby is away for the weekend but he has left a message, so we should hear something back on Monday.

My stomach drops, what if I have to wait for ages? I don't want to do that? But I'm very much like that, once I get an idea in my head, I go for it full force. So I text George again asking if he thinks there's any chance I'll get in for a session next week. He says yes, but it will more than likely be a daytime slot that's free. I text him thanks and make a mental note of telling Joyce about it, I'm sure she'll give me the time off that I need.

And then my mind drifts again to Tristan - *Oh Tristan, Tristan, Tristan, what am I going to do about you?*

The dream comes back to me, and I'm instantly transported into my own little world, our little world. I still remember it all so vividly. The boat, the water, the beautiful scenery and Tristan looking like, well the sexiest man I have ever seen. But the feeling, *oh that beautiful feeling!*

I have never felt so serene in my entire life, so I have to question – Could I really have such serenity? Could I really feel that blissfully happy with Tristan?

And the resounding answer is – Yes, I could.

I swallow hard at that thought. My head starts to argue with me of course, all the usual stuff, that I'm not good enough, that I'm unlovable, that I'm a freak and how could such a gorgeous, successful man be interested in the likes of me. I'm nothing, I'm – "Stop!" I shout, scolding myself.

Malcolm slams on the break, and we all lurch forward, luckily there's no-one behind us, so we don't get hit.

"Sorry, sorry!" I frantically say, Malcolm pulls over and lets the car idle.

"Are you alright Coral?" he asks turning in his seat, appraising me.

I run my hands through my hair. "Yeah, I'm fine...I was just talking out loud. I'm really sorry, I didn't mean for you to..." I shake my head at myself. I can see he's trying to work out if I really am ok.

"Coral that was really silly," Gladys shouts. "You almost gave me a heart-attack, and we could have had an accident!" She bellows.

"I know, I know," I say feeling guilty.

Malcolm pulls back out into traffic, and I decide to keep a lid on my wayward thinking. But five minutes in, they continue their discussion on the economy and the state of the EU, and I'm drifting off again...*So what conclusion did I come to?*

I think all these stupid things about myself but should I let that stop me? Or should I just try and be brave and have a date with Tristan? My hands start to shake with nervous anticipation, just thinking about it being real makes me feel a little nauseous.

Ok, so maybe I could do that, but what about...sex? What about when that time comes, I made Justin wait way too long, would Tristan wait?

Somehow I doubt that then I doubt that doubt. If a man really cares for a woman and an attachment is growing between them, then doesn't he also have respect for that woman? And if he does, then wouldn't he want to go at her pace? *What are you talking about Coral? How many times have you imagined having sex with him?*

I finally admit the truth to myself, way too many times! *And did it feel, scary? Were you frightened?* In the fantasies – No, I wasn't, it felt good and close and intimate and...I feel myself starting to get turned on in a car with Gladys and Malcolm and Bob – *Ew! Stop!*

I sigh heavily and picture a load of doughnuts, so it takes the sexy, hot image of Tristan and I...*Oh, fuck its back!*

Ok, ok! Let's just think about all this logically.

You want him? – Yes.

So you're going to say yes to a date with him? – Yes.

Then I think it's going to be a whole month until I see him again, that's just too long. So how do I make contact with him without coming across and needy or desperate, which I'm not...I'm just...well totally hot for him – *Oh my God!*

Yep, I finally admitted it.

Then I think about what I said to George last night, that I love him, that I'm *in* love with him. I still don't understand how that can be, I hardly know him, then I think about what George said.

"Talk to him, tell him about yourself, bit by bit."

Can I do that? *You don't have any other choice, you want him to know you, understand you then you have to let him in, take the chance.*

My hands start shaking again, boy that's a scary thing to do.

Yep sure is! But let's face it you want to be on your own? You want to be a lonely old lady who looks back on her life with regret? And angry with herself because she was a coward who didn't face her fears, and live her life to the fullest? Is that what you want Coral?

I finally succumb to my own brutal words. No, no, I don't want any of that, no way. I want love and friendships and family and happiness!

Do you think you deserve it?

I'm still in two minds about that one, but I guess I'll soon find out. Then it comes to me – I have bought Tristan a painting, so I can just casually call him up, see if he got the house, and if he did, I could do what? Go round give him the painting? No seems too obvious. *Hmm*...I could help him move in? No, he'll have people to do that for him.

Ok, I could help him buy furniture for his new pad? I know all the best places. Yes! That could definitely work, I feel like punching my hand in the air, but decide it's best not to do that, Gladys will probably bollock me again!

My feet do a little tap dance all of their own, and a stupid grin spreads across my face. Then I remember Bob is sat in the back with me, but when I peek at him out of the corner of my eye, I see he is snoozing. *Phew, that was lucky!*

Feeling absolutely positive about my decision, I allow the dream to come back to me, I close my eyes and surrender to its beauty...

THE CAR STOPS PULLING me from my day-dream. I feel annoyed that I have to go back to reality. I hop out the car then run around it to help Bob out.

"Thank you, darling," he croaks, still a little sleepy.

As I turn us both around I notice a *For Sale* sign is up outside Debs house, that's odd, Debs hasn't said anything to me about moving, I instantly feel pissed off about it. *Why hasn't she told me this?*

I take hold of Bob's arm and help him up the steps to the front door, Gladys rings the bell. I cringe when I hear the screaming coming from the back garden. Scott opens the door and welcomes us all in. We all trail through the house and into the kitchen, looking out I can see the garden is already packed with adults and so many kids – Lily must be really popular at her nursery.

Gladys and Malcolm take Bob outside, and I'm about to follow when someone flicks my ear.

What the fuck? – I spin around and see Debs grinning at me.

"Hey trouble," she chuckles.

"Not funny!" I grumble back.

Debs pulls me into her and hugs me hard. "It's been ages," she says.

"I know." I roll my eyes and pull out of her hug. "So it's pretty packed out there huh?"

"Yeah…Lily's well happy," she says, her eyes glistening over.

"So what's with the sale sign?" I gripe.

"Scott got a promotion…we um….wanted a bigger place," she answers nonchalantly, but I can tell there's something more, something I'm missing, so I decide to probe.

"So you're just getting a bigger place in Worthing?"

"Well….no," Debs instantly looks flustered. Her cheeks blushing red is a sure sign she's anxious about something.

"What's going on Debs?" I snap, crossing my arms as I do.

"Nothing," she squeaks. "We probably will stay in Worthing, it just depends what we can get for this place." I scowl at her, for some reason I don't believe her.

"So why didn't you tell me?" I question. "I mean if it's no big deal why not just tell…" I trail off, suddenly thinking of Malcolm when Debs just saw him; it was as though they had met before. "You know!" I hiss feeling angry and betrayed that Gladys has done this.

"Know what?" She hisses back.

"About Malcolm," I growl quietly through gritted teeth.

"So!" She whines.

"What do you mean *so?*" I hiss even more vehemently.

"For god's sake Coral, why do you think Mom told me and not you, hmm?"

I glare back at Debs; we are almost nose to nose. "Why don't you enlighten me?" I growl more threateningly.

"Don't you dare look at me like that," she snaps, her voice wobbling slightly.

"Like what?" I hiss again.

"Like you want to punch me in the face, you really piss me off sometimes you know that. You and your effing temper!" Debs goes to storm off, but I grab her by the arm and stop her.

I take a deep breath and exhale. "Tell me why Debs," I implore.

Debs shakes her head and briefly closes her eyes. Then she looks back at me in the strangest way. "Because you over-react to everything," she sighs. "And Mom wanted to make sure what she had was going to be something permanent before she told you, maybe if you relaxed a bit more, weren't so wound up all the time she might have..." Debs throws her hand up in the air. "You know what; I can't be dealing with this at the moment. I've got a birthday party to run." She pulls her arm out of my grip; we glare at each other for a moment.

"Sorry, I didn't mean to scare you," I whisper.

Debs shakes her head at me and walks off into the sunshine. I turn away from the party and take several deep breaths to calm myself down, I'm about to go and have it out with Gladys when – "Aunty Coral!" A sweet little voice screams.

I turn just in time to catch Lily who has launched herself into my arms. *Why is she wearing a swimming costume?*

"Hey, kiddo, happy birthday," I say cheerfully.

"Thank you." She smiles sweetly at me and kisses my cheek.

"Have you opened any of your presents yet?" I ask.

"No. Mommy says later, after Daddy's burgers," she moans.

"Ah well, Mommy knows best," I tell her, not agreeing at all.

Lily scrambles down out of my arms and pulls on my hand. "Come see, come see!" she screeches tugging me along. We make our way outside, through the patio area, and into the hundred foot garden. *Whoa! How did I not notice that!*

A huge bouncy castle has been erected right at the far end,

and there's a massive paddling pool with a slide in front of it. "Wow!" I say to her.

"Mommy got me a bouncy castle," she says jumping up and down with excitement. Hmm food then bouncing up and down, I'm pretty sure some kids are going to be vomiting!

"That's great Lily." I beam.

"And a paddling pool," she screams, she's so over-excited. "Come and bounce with me Aunty Coral," she says, pulling me towards the castle.

"Um...Lily, I don't think it's for adults." I tell her, hoping she'll go play with her friends.

"But' – "It's ok Coral," Scott says, appearing from nowhere and grinning from ear to ear. "I had a go earlier, takes you back!" He chuckles and winks at me – *The bastard!*

Lily screams with delight and runs down the garden. "Great, thanks, Scott," I say grimacing at him and follow Lily down to the castle.

Kicking off my flip-flops, I climb up onto the castle in the most un-lady-like fashion and pull Lily up too. There are only a couple of kids on there, the rest of them seem to be enjoying the paddling pool, splashing about in the water. We start bouncing, and for a moment I am taken back.

Scott is right, this is fun!

Ten minutes in, and I am out of puff, bouncing is a work-out.

"More Aunty Coral, more," Lily shouts excitedly.

"Ok, a few more minutes," I puff.

I take hold of her hands and start bouncing again when all of a sudden my heart starts rapidly beating against my chest. For a moment, I think I'm actually having some kind of heart problem – then the butterflies kick in, swarming around my stomach, then that weird pulling sensation starts right between my chest and abdomen.

I frown hard wondering what the hell this is all about, knowing full well it only happens when I'm around Tristan, or thinking of him, and right now I'm neither!

Lily suddenly bounces around in a circle, and I'm the one facing the garden towards the back of the house. As I look up, I see the crowd of people part. I see Joyce, I almost go to wave, but instantly freeze because Tristan is walking in behind her… *Oh My God! What the hell is he doing here?*

I try my best to keep my concentration and not stare at him, but he's just too irresistible. He's wearing a pair of knee-length khaki shorts, a white polo t-shirt, and a pair of thick flip-flops, and his aviators are making his smile stand out a mile. *Oh wow…he looks hot!*

I can see he's searching the crowd looking for someone. Joyce distracts him and takes him over to Gladys and Malcolm, and then all of a sudden I see Gladys point in my direction. Tristan looks up, takes off his aviators and our eyes lock, all I can do is stare back at him, I cannot pull my gaze away. *Holy crap!*

My heart practically stops then begins frantically clawing its way out of my chest. I lose my footing for a second and just as I do, Lily bounces really high. I manage to tear my gaze away and look down, just as the top of her head connects with the bridge of my nose – *Oh fuck!*

Several things happen at once, my nose instantly gushes with blood. I moan with shock and collapse onto the bouncy castle. Lily screams in pain, and the other two kids start screaming too, making the castle bounce all over the place as they try to get off the castle.

The pain is beyond excruciating, I try to help Lily, reaching my hand out to her. I'm more concerned that she's ok, but the pain is knocking all my senses for six, I can't think or see straight. My stomach is rolling as I try to contain as much of the blood as I can inside the palm of my hand (I don't do so well with blood) my stomach rolls again, and I know I'm going to be sick.

As I try to regain my balance, and check Lily, several worried adults appear. Debs and Scott grab Lily and get her off the castle. At the same time, I see Tristan launch himself towards me. In the next breathe he's picked me up into his arms and it's almost as though the castle isn't bouncing, he's so strong and balanced – the speed and agility he uses to get me off that god damn thing is impressive.

"Jesus Coral," he says placing me down on the cool, non-moving grassy ground.

I lean forward trying to stop the pain.

"No, no, hold your head back," he tells me. So I do, but all I can feel is blood gushing down the back of my throat; its nasty taste instantly triggers my stomach. I roll on my side and vomit, blood and vegetable juice are splattering all over the green grass.

He reaches down and grabs all of my hair out of the way, making a makeshift ponytail.

"I think we need an ambulance," Tristan grimly states. I can feel him rubbing my back, trying to soothe me. When I finally stop being sick, I sit back up, and see that Gladys is there with something in her hand, she leans forward and presses it against my nose.

"Oh, Jesus!" I screech. It's so cold, and the pain of it touching my nose is so overwhelming, my eyes roll into the back of my head, I pass out…

I FEEL MYSELF SLOWLY coming back into consciousness.

"Ugh!" I blink my eyes open, everything is blurry *Oh Jesus!* The pain, I reach for my nose, but gentle hands are stopping me.

"Hey, careful now." I know its Tristan's voice, but I can't see him.

"Lily?" I whisper. It hurts to speak, to move my face.

"She's fine. She's got a bit of a bruise on her head, but she's fine. In fact, she's in the paddling pool right now," he chuckles. "Kids, they get over things so quickly," he adds.

I quickly assess – *Paddling pool, so I'm still at Debbie's?* I keep blinking trying to get my sight back to full capacity.

"Why are you blinking so much?" he asks, his hands gently brushing my hair away from my face.

"Everything's blurred," I whisper.

I feel Tristan tense beside me. "The paramedic is here Coral, you took a nasty bang to the nose it's not broken though, just badly bruised. Do you remember?" I want to scream of course I fucking remember! The throbbing in my nose and my loss of eyesight is enough to make anyone remember, but I don't.

"Yes," I squeak, my nose pulsing so strongly now that I feel like I'm going to pass out again. Then I feel something gets jabbed into my thigh, it really fucking hurts!

"Jesus!" I scream. "What the fuck was that?"

"Sorry," an apologetic voice I don't know answers. "It's Morphine, for the pain," he quickly adds. And it's at that moment I feel it flood my system, the throbbing in my nose quickly dies down to a numb ache. I feel my body relax – *Oh that's so much better!*

"Better?" Tristan asks. I feel his lips brush against my ear.

"Yesh," I say feeling quite drunk now. "W-hers Gladish?" I ask. *What's happened to my voice?*

"I'm here darling," she says. "Oh dear! Coral you're going to have such a bruise, what happened?"

"Shaw Trishtan," I answer honestly even though I don't want to. *Is this friggin truth serum?* I hear Tristan chuckle.

"Oh?" Gladys sounds surprised, and I know there'll be further questioning. *Great!*

"We'll need you to come in tomorrow for a check-up." The strange voice says.

"That's ok I'll take care of that," Tristan answers authoritatively.

"Oh thank you, Tristan, Malcolm and I had arranged to go out for the day, visit his daughters," Gladys says. *What no roast dinner? What the fuck!*

"What about Roasht Dinnerr?" And what about Debs already knowing about Malcolm, I want to say, but I know it's not something I want to discuss with other people around.

"Oh yes, sorry darling, I was going to tell you later. I'm off to meet Malcolm's girls tomorrow," she says full of excitement.

"Well thatts just greaaat," I slur.

"Oh dear!" Gladys leans over me, I can almost make out her face. "I'm sorry darling, I should have warned you earlier," she says.

I snort sarcastically forgetting that my nose is in a less than operative state, and splatter Gladys with tiny specs of blood.

"Oh!" she gasps trying to rub it off. "Never-mind dear," she says patting my head. "It'll come off." Then she leans down, kisses my forehead and disappears from view.

I instantly panic thinking I've been left alone. "Tristchtan?!" I whisper, reaching my hand out to him.

I feel his fingers grip mine. "Right here, I won't leave your side," he softly says, but I can hear the humour in his voice.

"S'not funny!" I tell him sternly.

"No, no. It's not," he says, the humour so evidently still there.

"Ok, Coral. I'm going to place this compress over your nose

now." The strange voice says, and something wonderful and cool is placed over my nose. "Don't let her fall asleep, and get plenty of fluids inside her. She can take Nurofen or Aspirin for the pain once the Morphine's worn off, but if the pain gets too much, you'll have to bring her into A&E for another shot."

"Will do," Tristan answers, I feel him stroking my forehead. *God, I feel so hot and sticky!*

"Aunty Coral." I hear a little voice squeak.

"Oh! Lily's that you?" I slur.

"Yes." I hear her start sniffling.

"S'okay," I say reaching my hand out to her.

"Want to try sitting up?" Tristan asks.

"Ok." I feel his arms push underneath my shoulders, his other hand gently holding my head up. And suddenly I'm upright; all the blood feels like it's rushing out of my head down to my toes.

"Oh!" I feel drunk, which makes me start giggling. Lily stops sniffling and starts giggling too, and my vision slowly starts to come back to me, I realise I'm in Debs living-room, on the sofa.

"Hey shweetie," I say to Lily. I can see her properly now, her cheeks are still stained from her tears.

"I'm sorry Aunty Coral," she sniffs again.

I reach my hand out to her and stroke her cheek, then pull her closer to me. "Shit with me," I say.

Lily giggles at me. "You said a bad word."

Tristan chuckles too and lifts Lily onto the sofa next to me.

"S'not your fault," I tell her. "Doesh your head hurt?" She shakes it left to right as she continues to chuckle at me.

"You're talking funny Aunty Coral." She giggles some more.

"Am I?" I ask.

"Yes." She squeals loudly, making it reverberate around my head. *Whoa!* "And you look funny!" She chuckles even harder, Tristan really starts laughing. *Great, magnificent!*

"Well, thanhks," I say trying to smile too, but the throbbing gets that little bit stronger when I do.

"I'm sorry I banged your nose," she tells me sweetly. "Mommy said to come and say sorry, but I was sorry anyway." *God, it's hard to believe she's only five.*

"S'okay, snot your fault, it was Trishtans." I smile inwardly because I know Lily will tell him off.

"Tristan," Lily scolds. "You hurt Aunty Coral and me; that's very naughty," she adds, pretending to smack his hand.

"I consider myself truly told off, I do apologise," he says.

"That's ok," she giggles. "Are you Aunty Coral's boyfriend?" *Holy Crap! Shut up, Lily!*

"Maybe..." Tristan answers. My heart instantly flutters.

Lily giggles. "Have you kissed Aunty Coral?"

Tristan laughs. "No, but I'm hoping to," he whispers.

Lily's eyes nearly pop out of her head. "You're handsome, like Daddy," she says, putting her tiny hand on his cheek.

"Why thank you," he croons.

"Are you going to marry Aunty Coral?" she asks all innocently.

Tristan sniggers again. "Maybe..." He whispers. *What?*

"I want to get married when I grow up," she says.

"Well, maybe I should wait for you," Tristan teases.

Lily throws her head back giggling in delight. "No," she squeals. "You're too old for me." *Ha! That told him, smug bastard!*

"Oh, my lady, you wound me," he says, clutching his heart.

"Aunty Coral hasn't had a boyfriend before," she says.

Ok, time for the kid to go!

"She hasn't?" Tristan questions, Lily shakes her head at him, but I'm saved from the conversation going any further by Debs walking into the room with a thunderous look on her face, she stops in front of me with her hands on her hips.

"There you are, Lily. Your friends are looking for you."

"Ok, Mommy." Debs lifts her off the sofa, she waves at me. "Bye Aunty Coral." I wave back - it's a very drunken sloppy wave.

"Henjoy your birfday, I hope you lick my preshent," I say.

"I will, bye Tristan, I really hope you kiss Aunty Coral better." With that she chuckles and runs off at full speed, I'm about to turn to Tristan to bollock him for mocking me, but Debs pipes up.

"It took five adults and six rolls of kitchen paper to get rid of all the blood," she says. "Jesus Coral, you gave me the fright of my life!" She adds scooping her long blonde hair up into a pony-tail. *Evidently, our little spat earlier is forgotten?*

"Cuase of Lily," I say knowing I'm right.

"No!" she barks. "You! I knew Lily would be fine, kids are always bashing themselves. They're over it in seconds," she huffs and plonks herself next to me - my nose throbs painfully at me again. "How the hell does someone bleed that much anyway? You got an extra stock-pile in there or something?" she adds.

I chuckle. "Yesh, vampire," I say trying to look scary.

Debs rolls her eyes at me. "Well I guess you'll be here for the night," she sighs.

"No, I'm going home," I tell her. "When the partiesh finished," I add.

"I don't think so," she huffs shaking her head at me.

"Yesh," I argue. "I am." I hate staying at Debs, her and Scott all loved up with their adorable little munchkin.

Deb's suddenly starts batting her eyelashes at Tristan. "You must be Coral's new boss?" She says in her most seductive voice.

"Yes, Tristan Freeman." He says holding his hand out to her.

"Debbie Fuller." She bats her lashes some more and shakes his outstretched hand.

This is not happening!

"Oh Coral!" I look up and see Joyce stood next to Gladys.

"Hi, Joyche," I answer, her mouth pops open.

"What's wrong with her?" She gasps.

"Morphine," Tristan answers.

I giggle at the whole situation, how ridiculous.

"It's good to see someone's having a good time," Joyce says sarcastically. "Oh dear, well I don't expect you to work looking like that young lady." I go to argue, and then I hear her proposal. "You can work from home until you're feeling better. I'll email your inbox to your laptop."

"Thanks, Joyche." I smile up at her. She smiles back at me; then starts sniggering like Tristan did. "S'not funny!" I bawl as loudly as I can.

The throbbing in my nose starts up again, I wince in pain, my eyes fill with tears, which start spilling down my cheeks, and everyone starts fussing.

"What do you need Coral?" Tristan asks, crouching in front of me.

Debs jumps up and starts patting my forehead, Gladys

gasps and grabs my hand, and Joyce does the worst thing; tries to readjust the cold compress.

"Ow!" I scream out in pain, everyone freezes.

Shit, shit, shit! – None of this seems funny anymore.

"Home!" I cry out. "Chake me home!" I want to stamp my feet, but I'm too out of it to do that. I look across at Tristan. "Aircondiching!" I whimper. "Pleashe…it's so hot!" I add, feeling more and more uncomfortable by the second.

Tristan passes me a bunch of tissues from Debs dispenser. I wipe my eyes and try to clear my nose, making it throb even more. "Pleashe," I beg again.

They all start arguing. Debs is saying she can't leave, Gladys wants to take me back to hers, and Joyce is insisting Gladys stays and she takes me back to her house.

"Want me to take you back to your studio?" Tristan whispers in my ear.

"Yesh," I whisper back.

"I'll do it," Tristan shouts – Everyone shuts up and turns to stare open-mouthed at him.

"Oh, thank you, Tristan." Gladys gushes.

"How very gallant of you Tristan," Debs says batting her lashes and smirking at him.

"Are you happy with that?" Joyce asks me.

"Yesh," I whisper – *I just want to get out of here.*

Tristan stands, pulls his mobile out of his pocket and makes a call. "What's the postcode and house number?" he asks.

Debs smiles coyly, and holds her hand out for his mobile, he passes it to her. "BN14 0AD, No 2," she says then hands him back his mobile with a coy smile.

Jesus I can't take much more of this!

"Got it?" Tristan asks. "Good, see you then," he says and hangs up, then he turns and sits next to me on the sofa again.

The room is silent. I look up and see Debs, Gladys and Joyce all staring down at me with smug looks on their faces.

"What?" I snap. They all glance at one another, then back to me, and across to Tristan.

Debs titters. "I better get back, I'll come and see you tomorrow," she tells me with a brief kiss on my cheek. Then she holds her hand out to Tristan. "Such a pleasure," she says shaking his hand for much longer than is deemed necessary, he smiles widely at her blatant flirting – *Debs!*– Finally, she lets go of his hand and bounces out of the room.

"I'd better get back to Malcolm," Gladys says, leaning down to kiss my cheek. "Take care of my daughter," she tells Tristan as she kisses his cheek too.

"Absolutely," he says, taken aback by her tone, and then she leaves too. Then I notice Tristan and Joyce stare at one another, exchanging some kind of unspoken conversation, then Joyce nods once at him and leaves the room.

"What's wash that all about?" I question.

Tristan looks across and smiles shyly at me. "Nothing," he says, but I know there was something there.

Joyce reappears with a glass of lemonade and a straw. "Here darling," she says popping the straw in the glass.

"Thanksh." I take it from her and take a long drink.

"Better?" She smiles – I smile back at her and nod, drinking more, I'm so thirsty.

Tristan's mobile buzzes in his pocket, he and Joyce stare oddly at each other again, then Tristan stands and takes his mobile out of his pocket. "Stu's here," he says.

"Shtuart's here?" I squeak – *Ouch! I'd better stop talking, it's too painful.*

"Yes," Tristan says throwing that beautiful smile at me. Joyce takes the glass off me and stands. Tristan holds his hands out to me, I lift up my arms and place my hands in his, he gently pulls me to my feet; but the room starts to bend and sway. *Whoa!*

Before I can fall one way or the other, he lifts me quickly and easily into his arms as though I'm as light as a feather. He smiles down at me and pulls me closer to his strong chest. "I think it's safer this way," he chuckles. "We don't want you getting into any more trouble," he adds dryly.

I pout back at him.

Joyce leans across and kisses me on the cheek. "Be careful darling, Tristan will take care of you, but if you need me, you know you only have to call, and I'll be there," she says smiling down at me.

I suddenly realise I don't have my bag or my keys. "Bag, Keychs," I say in a panic. Tristan frowns not understanding, but Joyce nods at me.

"Back in a second," she says.

Tristan starts walking me towards the front door then stops when Joyce comes back, she has my shoulder bag and something in a plastic bag.
"I'm afraid you were sick on your flip-flops darling."
And that's all I hear, I pass out again...

CHAPTER TWENTY-ONE

I AM DREAMING I AM on the boat again. Sunshine is flooding into the room, in fact, it's so bright it's almost hard to see. Tristan's hovering above me, he's gazing down at me in the most peculiar way, his soft fingers are lightly brushing my forehead, my eyes, running through my hair; it's so cooling and relaxing.

I'm astonished at the detail of the dream, this feels so real; Tristan looks so real.

His chocolate brown eyes are glistening with flecks of hazel, and I can see the laughter lines around those deep, soulful eyes. The skin on his face looks soft and warm, slightly tanned. I can see several freckles across his nose and his cheeks, I hadn't noticed those before.

I smile up at him, his answering grin is breathtaking, it makes my heart stop. My grin widens reflecting his. I love the way his dimples deepen, and his nose and eyes crinkle when he smiles like that; his smile is profoundly more beautiful close-up.

He has a five o'clock shadow running across his jaw, I've not seen him with stubble before, he looks even sexier if that's at all possible. I reach my hand up to run my fingers across it, see how real it feels.

Tristan frowns as I touch him. I scratch my short fingernails across his jaw and cheek, it feels so real. The peaceful feeling washes over me again, I feel so content, so serene.

"Heaven," I whisper. I place my hand against his cheek and run my thumb across his bottom lip, his breath hitches just as my heart takes flight.

I am astonished at how real everything feels. I reach my

hard around his neck, and entwine my fingers in his hair; it's just as soft as I thought it would be.

"Tristan," I whisper, and softly pull his head down so that I can reach his lips.

"I think that might hurt you." He tells me steadying my grip.

I freeze, my face inches from his – *Fuck, not a dream!* I instantly drop my hand and squeeze my eyes shut. I have no idea what to say – *Shit, shit, shit!*

"Coral, what's wrong?" His voice is low and husky, his breath on my cheeks.

I am mortified, swallowing hard, I look up and meet his steady gaze. He leans down, his lips almost touching mine. "That felt really good," he whispers.

I scowl in frustration, I can't believe that just happened. Now he's going to know I've been dreaming about him – *Fuck!*

He smiles at my expression, his dimples on full wattage – *Damn that smile!*

"I'm sorry," I mumble.

"What for?" he asks, gently stroking my cheek.

"I thought I was dreaming," I say, frowning at his touch. I close my eyes and try to reign in my disintegrated thoughts.

"Really?" I hear the glee in Tristan's voice – *She's been dreaming about me!* "Well, I don't know about you, but every night for me." My eyes dart open and meet his. "And all throughout the day," he confesses. "Literally can't get you out of my head," he adds.

"Well, that's not the same for me," I lie. "I haven't thought about you once." I pout.

"You wound me," he smiles. "But, that's ok," he sighs in a high pitch tone. "If I can't be in your waking thoughts, at least I'm in your dreams," he adds with a smug smile on his face.

I slap him playfully and smile back...*Ouch, what the hell?...*The events of earlier today start coming back to me in a blurry haze. Colliding with Lily, poor Lily, my nose bleed, the morphine. Then I realise I'm home, but I don't remember getting here.

"Careful," he tells me. "You look worse today."

"Thanks," I bite back. "How did I get here?"

"You don't remember?"

"Obviously, or I wouldn't be asking," I answer dryly.

Tristan cocks an eyebrow up at me disapprovingly. "You passed out at you're sisters, I bought you back to your studio."

"Why you?" I question. "Why didn't Gladys bring me back?"

Tristan tries to hide his smile. "Well, in your less than operative state you demanded to be taken home, they were all arguing as to who should take you. I asked if you wanted me to bring you home, you said yes."

I purse my lips at him. "I did?" I mumble.

"Yes," he smiles, his eyes twinkling – I get a flashback.

"What was going on between you and Joyce?" I narrow my eyes at him, remembering their weird exchange.

Tristan shakes his head. "Nothing." His tone is clipped, his eyes hooded – Evidently, he has something to hide, but I am in too much pain to try to work out what it is. "Are you in pain?" he asks mirroring my thoughts.

"Yes, and thirsty," I answer and slowly sit up, my nose throbbing with the movement.

Tristan walks over to my kitchenette and pours me a glass of water. "Here, take these." He crouches in front of me and hands me the water with a straw and two Nurofen.

I pop the tablets in my mouth and take a long suck on the straw then swallow hard – *Yuck I hate taking tablets!* I can't breathe through my nose – at all. *Great!* That's going to make eating and drinking such a pleasurable experience. Maybe there's a nose flush or something I can get at Boots?

"Better?" Tristan asks smiling wryly at me, which instantly irritates me.

"This is all your fault," I bark my nose protesting, throbbing painfully.

"Doubt that," Tristan argues.

"Yes, it is," I dispute childishly. "What were you doing there anyway?" Tristan ignores me and sits back on his heels, watching me with vague amusement. "What?" I snap.

"You haven't eaten since yesterday, I'm going to get some breakfast," he says, his tone soft but hiding his frustration.

"Yesterday?" I screech.

Tristan cocks his head to the side and frowns. "Yes, I've already told you that." He says his eyes narrowing, as he silently watches me. My head starts banging, I hold it still, trying to ease the throbbing.

"You stayed with me all this time?" I ask.

Tristan looks up at me, his eyes full of some emotion I can't quite understand. "Yes," he answers.

"Why?" I whisper.

He smiles warmly at me. "I wanted to make sure you were ok." He tells me, a secret smile playing across his lips.

"What?" I snap again.

"It was quite an eventful evening." He smirks – *Oh no... we didn't?...*

His face falls seeing my horrified expression. "You were sleepwalking and talking in your sleep," he snaps, running a hand through his hair. "Jesus Coral, what kind of man do you think I am?"

Oh no! – I place my head in my hands. "What did I say?" I whisper. "What did I do?" I am horrified, of all the people to do that in front of – I thought the sleepwalking stopped years ago.

He sighs heavily. "Later, I'm going to get some food," he says, his tone brittle. I think I've upset him. "Gladys tells me you were late yesterday and didn't have breakfast," he admonishes. "Which means you didn't eat all day," he adds darkly.

"I had my veggie juice," I whisper in protest.

"Yes, and as good as that is for you, it's not filling Coral." I shrug and try to drink more water then we both hear my stomach rumble loudly. Tristan cocks one eyebrow up at me. "Besides, you vomited that backup, if you remember," he adds sardonically. *Double crap, so embarrassed!*

"Yes," I whisper. "I do."

"I'm going to get a takeaway, anything in particular that you fancy?" He asks standing up sharply.

Yes, you! I scowl at the floor and drink more water, trying to decide. "Surprise me," I say panting from not being able to breathe, and shivering slightly because it's so cold.

Tristan frowns. "Are you cold?" he questions, his voice a little softer.

"No, it's the water," I say, drinking more because I'm so thirsty; I feel like I've been guzzling sea water and I need to get rid of the salt.

Tristan nods once at me and heads over to the patio door.

"Tristan," I croak, he turns back and gazes at me. "You will come back and have breakfast with me, right?"

He walks back over to me, crouches down and takes hold of my free hand. "Do you want me to?" he asks, his expression torn.

"Yes," I whisper.

He leans forward and plants a sweet, soft kiss on my forehead, making my stomach flutter madly; then stands back up. "I won't be long," he says, I look up and smile shyly at him, he smiles back, his face reflecting mine, then turns away from me. I watch his tall, strong stature walk out through the patio door. The moment he's out of view I close my eyes and grit my teeth…*what the hell have I done and said in my sleep?*

I groan inwardly, I'm not sure I want to know the answer to that. I look out the patio again and wonder idly what time it is, but I think my body has caught up with me now I'm awake – I'm suddenly bursting for a pee. I stand too quickly and wobble slightly, my head aching like I've been hit with a truck, not a five-year-olds head, and shuffle over to the bathroom.

Once I'm done, I carefully stand, using the sink for leverage. I slowly shuffle around, so I'm standing in front of the mirror. Taking a deep breath, I look up at myself. The cold compress that was put across my nose has gone, so now I can see the damage that's been done. My nose has a tiny split across it, and it's all caked in dried blood, the bruise running across it is light blue-ish, and I know it will eventually go purple – *Great!*

My eyes are slightly swollen, with the same colour bruising running underneath them and I have panda eyes from my smudged mascara, and streaks of it have encrusted themselves down my cheeks from my tears – *Ugh what a mess!*

I look like something out of a horror movie, and what's even more horrifying is the fact that Tristan's seen me like this – *Fucks sake!*

I grab a cleansing wipe and clean up my face, being as gentle as I can with my tender nose, then I clean my teeth, twice – *Ah that's feels so much better!*

Then I decide to try and unblock my nose, I can't breathe, and I hate that feeling. I pull a load of toilet tissue off and blow gently, but it hurts so badly that I don't risk doing it again, I sigh inwardly, I guess I'll just have to put up with it being blocked.

I slowly turn and shuffle back out of the bathroom. As I make my way over to the sofa, I notice the clock on the wall says 6.03am. *Whoa! I must have slept all day and all night!*

Didn't the paramedic say don't sleep? I shrug, I'm alive, and it was better than being awake and in that much pain. Reaching the sofa, I slowly sit down, then lie back and close my eyes.

I try to recall what was going on before the accident. I was mad with Debs, I remember that. Then I remember why – she already knew about Malcolm. Yes; I'm not happy with Gladys about that, we will have words, plus Debs is moving, and she didn't tell me.

My heart sinks into the pit of my stomach, Gladys has lied to me, and Debs has kept something important from me. It doesn't make me feel very good at all, and it certainly doesn't make me feel like I'm part of this family. I sit forward and grip my hands together, trying to understand why. It's so frustrating feeling like this.

Bob suddenly springs to mind, and I wonder if he got home ok? I'm sure Malcolm would have driven him back – *Holy crap, the car journey over to Debs!*

I remember something about it, something important. I made a choice, a very, very important, fundamental choice. I frown and try hard to remember, then it hits me – *Tristan!*

Yes, yes, I remember now. I was going to call him, see if he got the house, take him furniture shopping...tell him a little bit about myself, *bit by bit* – I hear George in my head and see his smile.

Ok, ok so I guess I got my wish, but why was Tristan at the party? I try to recall again, then I remember, right before I collided with Lily, Tristan walked in with Joyce.

So did Joyce invite Tristan? I shake my head, that doesn't make sense, why would she do that, they don't know each other that well, surely? Then I remember Tristan teasing me, asking if he could come to the party and me saying no, I was a real pain with him then.

That line of thought stops me in my tracks – How amazing, I feel so differently about him now; then I remember the dream. Yep, that's what did it. Then I remember this morning and cringe with embarrassment - *I couldn't put him off now even if I wanted to.*

As I look down at my twisted fingers, I notice my winter blanket from my bed is neatly folded next to the sofa, with one of the pillows from my bed on top of it, I frown at them both wondering why they are down here.

Did Tristan get them for me to use? I turn and notice my other pillow propped up behind me, it has dried blood on it (nice), and my quilt is all ruffled at the bottom of the sofa, I cock my head to the side. Did Tristan sleep on the floor?

That's unbelievable and crazy, he must have been so uncomfortable. Why didn't he just take me upstairs and sleep on the sofa, or use the bed with me? I scowl at my wayward thoughts. Tristan in your bed already? *Coral you Ho!* Well it's not like we'd have been humping all night is it? I argue back at myself.

I stop my thoughts right there, I'm in too much pain for my mind to be whizzing about like that. I just want food and some random animation, something to make me chuckle, so I don't curl up into a ball feeling sorry for myself.

I slowly lie back down, resting my head on the pillow, and close my eyes, the gentle whirring of the air-con is making me feel sleepy, which I can't quite understand. How can I want more sleep when I've already had so much?

The painkillers start to kick in, and the throbbing starts to ease - slightly. I feel myself drifting off, just as I slip away, I hear my mobile buzz. I groan inwardly, not wanting to answer it and let it go to voice-mail. Just as I'm drifting off again, I hear it start buzzing - *Grrrr!*

I get up far too quickly and the room sways, I sit back down for a moment and let my blood pressure adjust. When I feel like everything is where it should be, I find my bag on the kitchen side and fish out my mobile. I turn it over and see it's Rob. I can't press answer quick enough.

"Rob, are you ok? Where have you been?" I whisper.

"Sorry," he mumbles gloomily.

I shuffle back over to the sofa and gently sit down. "Rob, you've had me so worried! I'm really gonna kick your arse when I *finally* see you...*and* Carlos," I add – *I'm so mad at him too!*

"Coral...please," he pleads. He doesn't sound right.

"Ok, ok. So...?" I say waiting for his explanation. What I don't expect to hear is Rob burst into painful tears – *No!*

"Rob!" I gasp. "W-what's wrong?" It takes a few minutes, but he finally stops crying enough to answer me.

"I j-just called to see how y-you are?" he chokes out.

"What?" I ask totally dumbfounded.

He sniffs loudly then continues. "I called yesterday to say happy birthday to Lily, Debs told me what happened to you. So are you ok?" he croaks, sniffing some more.

"Better than you sound?" I answer softly. I've never heard Rob cry; whatever it is must be really bad. "Now tell me, Rob, what's wrong? Is it you and Carlos?" My leg starts jigging up and down, he starts to cry again. "Rob, you're really scaring me," I whisper.

"Sorry," he chokes, he sounds exhausted.

Just at that moment, Tristan comes through the door.

"Rob, please tell me?" I squeak.

"Another time." He sighs sorrowfully.

"No Rob now!" I bark. "You're my best friend, why won't you talk to me?" I ask bitterly. "We always talk about everything...please," I plead. "Tell me." I hear a funny noise in the background; sounds like an announcement at a train station, or an airport?

"I have to go" Rob sniffs. "Bye."

"No Rob wait' – He hangs up, I stare blankly at my mobile – *What the hell was that about?*

I grit my teeth in frustration and go over the conversation again. He didn't give anything away! How can I help him if he...I hear him burst into tears again, which automatically starts me off. I close my eyes and try to fight the tears that are now cascading down my cheeks...*god damn you, Rob, why won't you tell me what's wrong?*

"Coral!" Tristan gasps. I open my eyes and see his blurry figure dash over to me. He sits next to me and wraps his arm around my shoulder. I lean my head into the crook of his neck and try to choke back the tears – *It's official, I hate crying!*

Tristan squeezes me tighter and kisses the top of my head. It feels very comforting; and I know in that very moment I'm so, so grateful to have him here with me.

"What's wrong?" he whispers as he holds me tight.

"Rob," I choke. "He was crying...I...I've never h-heard him cry."

"Any idea what it might be?" Tristan asks; his voice full of concern.

"He... w-won't ... t-tell me," I growl.

"Want me to see if I can find out anything?" He softly says.

"L-like w-what?" I choke, looking up at him through my watery eyes.

"It's easy to find information, just have to know what to look for," he softly says, wiping a tear away with his thumb.

"He'll tell m-me when h-he's ready," I stutter and squeeze my eyes shut.

It takes a while for me to calm down, the sound of Rob bursting into painful tears keeps replaying in my head. I'm so frustrated, how can I help him if he won't talk to me? And now I'm starting to think Rob's got into some sort of trouble. All the worst case scenarios my over-active imagination can come up with play over and over in my mind – *Oh God, oh no, Rob!*

"Hey, hey...Coral, you need to calm down now. You sound like your hyperventilating," Tristan says lifting my head up which is now in full scale – somebody's got a gong next to it and is banging it repeatedly – mode. "Come on Coral, deep breaths." Tristan hands me the box of tissues from my side table.

I shake my head and shuffle out of his hold. "Help me to the bathroom?"

Tristan is instantly on his feet holding his hands out to me. I place my hands in his, and he pulls me to my feet, but the room sways again. So he lifts me into his arms, takes the few short steps needed, and places me down in the centre of my tiny bathroom. It's a tight squeeze with the two of us in there. Tristan shuffles backwards until he's outside the door. I glance across at him and see he looks so worried. "I'll wait right here," he tells me.

"No," I say waving him away. "Go eat before it gets cold."

"But' – "No buts Tristan, I won't be a minute." I sniff.

Ouch, that really fucking hurt!

I wince in pain and shut the door, then grab a load of tissue and clean myself up. Ok, so crying seems to have cleared my nose. *Grosse!* – At least I can breathe now. I wash my tear-stained face in the sink, then gently pat myself dry – *Jeez, I feel exhausted, and I haven't even done anything!* I hear Rob cry again in my head, I push back the tears that threaten to start up – *God Damn you, Rob!*

I take several deep breaths, and decide it can't be any of the really bad things I thought because Carlos would be worried and on the phone to me, so maybe it is those two? I shake my head at myself, I could be here all day trying to figure it all out. *There's nothing you can do about it Coral, come on, Tristan's waiting for you!*

Yes, he is. I shuffle over to the door and yank it open. I'm instantly hit with the smell of freshly made pancakes and coffee. My stomach growls in appreciation.

Tristan walks over to me and holds out his arms. "May I?" he asks.

"I'm ok," I croak and start to shuffle out. *I feel like a god damn old woman!* Tristan gives me his one hand to help balance me, and I gladly take it. "Thanks. Smells good," I say with appreciation.

"Tastes good too." He says helping me to sit on the sofa; then he sits next to me.

I see my pillow and quilt has disappeared and my coffee table is back to its usual place in front of the sofa. Tristan has laid out two plates, and there are knives and forks neatly placed on napkins, two tall take-out cups, and four Styrofoam white boxes, each has a small amount of steam oozing out of them.

"Cappuccino for the lady," he says handing one to me.

"Thanks," I say in appreciation.

"Now, I got several different types of pancakes as I wasn't sure which you would prefer," he says gesturing to the four different boxes. "So there' – "Pancakes?" I interrupt, purposely looking down-hearted.

"Um…yeah," Tristan shuffles slightly, looking very uncomfortable.

"But I don't like pancakes," I squeak, trying my very best not to let the grin that's pushing through appear on my face.

"I…Oh!" Tristan deflates, he looks lost. I can't take it anymore, I bump his shoulder playfully.

"Kidding!" I chuckle then stop – I shouldn't have bumped him, my head bangs in protest.

"Is your head really that bad?" He asks measuring my expression.

"I think yours would be too if you'd have had that happen," I answer dryly.

"True." He smiles. "You had me there by the way," he adds grinning widely.

I smile back at him. "I know it was good right? You really believed me!" I chuckle then stop – *The pounding really better stop soon!* Tristan is looking concerned again, so I quickly change the subject. "Good choice by the way. I haven't had pancakes in years!" I say cheerfully.

Tristan carefully opens each box, then turns and smiles broadly at me. "Tada," he says playfully. "Found this place just by chance yesterday morning, I got here really early, and I was starving, they are very good pancakes," he adds, looking very pleased with himself. "So, you have a choice of Chocolate Chip, Buttermilk, Cinnamon or Blueberry?"

"Wow!" I gaze down at the pancakes, they really do look delicious.

"So which will it be Coral?" I decide to go for the safe option.

"I'll take a buttermilk one, thanks." Tristan places one on each of our plates then takes the top off a little Styrofoam cup.

"Maple syrup?" he asks, his head cocked to the side, and a wicked glint in his eyes *Is he asking what I think he's asking?* I'm sure there's a double meaning there. I stop *those* thoughts in their tracks and clear my constricted throat.

"Sure." I watch him carefully drizzle a little syrup over each pancake, then I pick up my knife and fork and take a bite. "Mmm....delicious," I say, my stomach seems grateful too.

"They're good right?" he says demolishing his in seconds.

"Whoa! You must be hungry?" I say without thinking. I watch him take a Blueberry one and drizzle syrup on it.

"What makes you say that?" he says between mouthfuls.

I shake my head and carry on eating, too embarrassed to say.

"Ah come on Coral, I think we're past all the evasiveness by now, don't you?" He leans into me with pancake stuck to his fork and playfully shoves it into his mouth. *Ok, I can do this!*

"Well, I...sort of noticed on Tuesday that you, kind of, took your time with your food," I answer quietly.

"I was nervous." He admits.

"You were?" I gasp.

"Yes." Another mouthful, he quickly chews then swallows. "I so badly wanted you to say yes to a date, to something. It was putting me off my food." Another mouthful, he quickly chews and swallows. "And I'm never off my food," he adds thoughtfully.

"Oh!" Is all I can say to that.

"What about you Coral?" He asks, placing a chocolate pancake on each of our plates, then drizzling them both with syrup.

"I..." I take a bite. "Wow, really nice too. Good job I don't eat this kind of stuff too often, or I'll turn into a big fat bloater." Tristan chuckles.

"So what about you?" He repeats, taking a drink of his cappuccino.

"What do you want to know?" I ask.

"You didn't each much of your salad at lunch," he tells me. "Off your food too?" he asks. How very perceptive of him and for some reason, maybe all my inner-dialogue, I answer truthfully.

"Yeah...I guess I was," I say shyly. "I was nervous too...a-about how I was already feeling about you. I didn't understand it." *Ok, too much information.*

I take another mouthful before I can really put my foot in it.

"Do you understand it a little more now?" he asks. I instantly detect a hint of nervousness.

"Yes," I whisper nervously and eat some more.

"And?" He helps himself to another pancake, keeping his eyes locked forward.

"I don't know Tristan...what do you want me to say?" I try to think of something to tell him about myself. I come up with one thing, and before I can stop myself, it's out of my mouth. "I have a therapist."

Whoa! Shut up Coral, don't tell him that yet!

Tristan stops chewing and turns to gaze at me, I cannot look away from him. What is this power he yields over me? I feel like he's looking straight through me again. As he continues to stare, I notice his eyes grow darker, and his jaw tense a couple of times, finally he looks away, picks up his cup and takes a long drink.

I start breathing again, but my appetite has vanished - I knew it, I knew he wouldn't like it. Tristan stops drinking and frowns down at his plate, his whole body seems to have tensed up.

"Is your therapist helping you Coral?" He asks darkly.

"Yes," I whisper, feeling mortified I just shared that with him. "George is great...really, really great." Tristan turns to me and half smiles, it doesn't reach his eyes.

"If you ever feel like you want to try someone else, just ask me Coral, I'll pay for the best, whatever helps you." He says almost tripping over his own words.

"I...don't...err...thanks Tristan, but George is who I want," I say surprised at his openness. "You're not freaking out," I add.

"Freaking out? Why would I be...?" I see the penny drop. "You think because of that I wouldn't want to see you?" He asks a little high pitched.

"I...well, yeah," I admit shrugging my shoulders.

"That's crazy!" He says shaking his head.

"Well, I am seeing a shrink," I answer dryly, hoping he'll see the funny side. His head whips around, his face serious, then he sees my wide grin and automatically smiles back at me. I start laughing nervously, Tristan chuckles a couple of times then starts eating again.

Feeling thankful that he hasn't asked me anything about it, my appetite comes back, so I finish off the chocolate pancake and help myself to a Blueberry one.

"So can I ask you about that?" He asks, his voice cautious – *Damn it!*

"Sure." I swallow hard.

"How long have you been seeing him?" He asks his expression serious.

"Two years," I answer.

"How many times a week?" I catch him glance across at me, then quickly look away.

"Ok, Tristan," I stop eating. "Right now, my head is screaming at me that you're asking these questions because you're assessing if I'm right for the job. Is that the case?" I ask sternly.

"No," he scolds. "This is personal Coral. I've told you, your job is safe. This is just you and me, man and woman getting to know one another," he adds running his hand through his hair. I think he's frustrated.

"Oh, ok." I placate and take a bite of pancake, it's really

nice, but my appetite has vanished again. I place my cutlery down, pick up my cappuccino and curl my legs up onto the sofa.

"That's it?" He says. I frown back at him. "That's all you're going to eat?" he adds. I nod once and take a drink. His mouth sets into a hard line. "Two pancakes? That's not very much considering you haven't eaten for a couple of days."

I shrug. "I'm full."

"Somehow, I doubt that." He mutters to himself.

"I'm sorry Tristan, I won't ask about my job again. If you say I keep it, then I guess I'm just going to have to take your word for it. It's just so hard to explain what it's like being me, being inside my head. I always think the worst." I sigh and take a drink. "What was your question?" I ask.

He glances across at me again. "How many times a week do you see your therapist?"

"Well, normally once...on a Tuesday." I add smirking at him, he quickly works it out.

"Ah...so the other day...?" he says.

"Yes, I was due to see George." Tristan nods and finishes his pancake. "Why did you come to Lily's party?" I add.

A smile flits across his face. "I was desperate to see you again." That throws me, I wasn't expecting him to say that. I light up inside like a star on a Christmas tree.

"So Joyce invited you?" I whisper.

"No, I called her to say I'd closed the deal for the house and that I'd be down on Saturday – I invited her out for lunch." He adds.

"But you knew Joyce was going to the party?" I clarify.

"Of course I did." A slow, sexy smile starts to play on his lips.

"So you said that to get Joyce to invite you?"

"Yes, so I could see you again."

"Hmm..." I'm not really sure how I feel about that, using Joyce that way.

"I'm sorry. I guess that sounds really bad doesn't it?" He says echoing my thoughts.

I scowl at him. "Um...yeah, it kind of sucks actually, using Joyce like that."

"It won't sound so bad when you hear the rest though," he admits.

"The rest?" I question, picking at the cardboard around my cup.

"Yes, I thought it went so smoothly when I called Joyce, and she said she couldn't make lunch as she had the party, but then she invited me, it had worked perfectly. I was very happy because it meant I was going to see you again. Joyce asked me to meet her at her house, so I did. Only when I arrived, she marched me inside, sat me down and told me she knew what I was playing at and then she started grilling me about you."

"About me?" I squeak.

Tristan turns and sits face to face with me, tucking one foot under his butt. "Yep, that's why we were later than everyone else." He drains the last of his drink.

"Well, what did Joyce say?" I question.

"Basically she said that she feels just as responsible for you as Gladys does and that you haven't had it easy, and if I hurt you she'll break my legs, or some bones or something." Tristan smiles as though he's remembering something really funny.

My mouth pops open in shock. I can't believe Joyce said that.

Tristan leans forward and takes hold of my hand; instinctively I know he's not finished. "She said that if John were alive, he would have been the one saying that to me, but now he's gone, she feels it's her responsibility. Then she basically asks me why I'm interested in you. I tell her the truth, which is what I told you, she's shocked of course, but then I see her start to come around, she knows I'm not just some guy that's well, only interested in one thing. It's way, way more than that. We talked for a long time, and by the end of it, I think she's ok with it you know, if you do decide to see me, she's happy. Said you'd been on your own way too long..." Tristan stops and frowns deeply. "And I know just how that feels," he mumbles almost to himself.

"It sucks," I mutter.

Tristan smiles his sad smile. "Yeah it does," he says.

We sit gazing at one another again. I try to look away, but his eyes seem to have some sort of persuasive power over me. Tristan breaks away first. I flick my eyes down to my coffee cup,

I can't believe Joyce did that. I take a sip of coffee then stifle a yawn.

"Sorry," I mumble.

"You look tired." I scowl at him. I'm not ready to sleep, I have some questions. "Come on," Tristan gestures for me to move towards him. "You should sleep," he tells me.

I shake my head at him. "I'm not done," I tell him.

He cocks his head to the side. "Oh?"

"So what did I do and say?" I ask.

"When?" Tristan smirks. *He knows what I'm talking about.*

"Don't be obtuse Tristan," I threaten, his grin widens. "Tristan!" I scold.

"Ok!" He chuckles. "At about 1am this morning, you sat bolt upright and started typing, and you were talking, but I couldn't make out what you were saying. Then about an hour later you..." He drifts off, shaking his head.

"I what?" I whisper with wide eyes.

"You whispered my name." He says staring down at his hands.

"I did?" I squeak, scowling at myself in frustration.

"Yes." His frown mirrors mine.

"There's more?" I question.

Tristan nods solemnly. *Oh crap!*

"Give it to me," I say closing my eyes.

"You whispered..." The tone of his voice makes me look at him, he has his eyes closed.

"Tell me." I plead.

He swallows hard. "You said that you missed me, that you wanted me to stay and..." he breaks off again and opens his eyes. When they reach my shocked gaze, he clenches his jaw once then looks away.

"And?" I push.

"That's it," he croaks – I don't believe him, but I decide to leave it at that because I'm not sure if I want to know anymore and I have other questions.

"So you got the house?" I ask.

"Yes."

"Happy?"

"Not yet."

"Why not?"

"Waiting for you to move in," he says, grinning widely at me. My heart hammers against my chest, making me catch my breath.

"So have you picked up the keys?" I ask. *Breathe Coral.*

"Yep."

"Wow!"

Tristan laughs at my expression. "You really liked that house, didn't you?"

"Tristan, look around you. I live in this, which is great, but it's not a million pound house."

"I think this is nice." He tells me, his eyes all warm and soulful again.

"Oh let me guess, because I'm here, right?"

"Yeah..." He croaks in that sexy voice of his.

"Cheesy." I laugh throwing a cushion at him, his reflexes are fast.

"Hey!" He throws up his arm to protect his face. The cushion bounces off it and falls onto the floor, we both chuckle.

"So you need stuff to put in it right, the house?" I question shyly.

"That I do." He says.

"I was going to call you about that," I say looking anywhere but at him.

"You were?" He answers in amazement. I look back at him and silently nod. Then hold my head wincing. "We need to make our way over to the hospital at some point today." He tells me firmly.

"No." I bark. "I hate hospitals," I add grumpily.

"That makes two of us," he states. "But we still need to have you checked out," he argues.

"I'll see my doctor on Monday," I say, the pain making me wince again.

"You're local G.P?" he asks. "Is he good?"

I shrug. "I have no idea. I'm hardly ever sick, so I've rarely been. He might not even be there anymore." I muse.

"We'll see my private Doctor." He says.

"You already have a Doctor here?" I ask in shock.

"Yes." Tristan looks confused as to why I would find this shocking.

"You sure do move fast don't you?" I tease.

"You should see me in my car," he says, his eyes dancing with excitement. *Yeah, I bet it's loads of fun.* I have to laugh at his animated expression, but it makes my head pound, so I hold my head in my hands again.

"Ok enough talk." Standing to his feet, he walks a couple of steps over to the patio door, pulls the curtain across, and walks back over to me. Taking my cup off me, he places it on the coffee table and sits next to me.

Then taking me by complete surprise, he gently pulls on my upper arms so that I end up lying down, adjacent to the length of his body. I have my head on his chest, my arm across his torso, and somehow he managed to wrap his arm around me. His fingers start making smooth, soft circles on my shoulder – *Oh wow…this feels…amazing.*

"Sleep now Coral," he softly says.

"Hmm…" It's so lovely and relaxing that I start to drift off. Tristan suddenly moves his leg, trapping mine underneath his. I do not like that. I try not to panic because right now, everything else about this moment feels wonderful; and he's not to know that would freak me out.

I take a calming breath. "Tristan," I say trembling slightly.

He stills and looks down at me. "What's wrong?" I look up at him and meet his eyes, they are watching me carefully.

"Let go of my leg," I tell him. He instantly releases me. I put my head back on his chest. I can hear his heart is pounding. "Are you ok?" I ask. "Your heart's beating so fast?" I add.

"Yeah," he sighs, then puts his other arm around me and squeezes me tight for a moment. "Just trying to figure out what happened to you – who hurt you," he adds. I sigh inwardly. "I know someone did," he croaks, then goes back to rhythmically stroking me.

I say nothing. I'm not ready to share that yet, so I close my eyes and try to drift off. The peaceful feeling from the dream engulfs me, I revel in it. In fact, I can't quite believe this is actually happening. Then I question would this have happened if I hadn't had the accident with Lily? Would I be lying here peacefully in his arms, not feeling any kind of negative feelings at all?

The answer is no – I don't think I would be. Gladys has

always said things happen for a reason, that you might not see it's purpose at the time, but it all has meaning.

"Tristan," I mumble sleepily.

"Hmm..."

"Did you sleep on the floor last night?"

"Hmm..."

"Is that a yes?"

"Yes." He answers with that sexy, husky voice of his.

"Don't do that again." I scold.

"Ok." He chuckles, it vibrates through me, and I find myself smiling too.

"Why didn't you just take the bed?" I ask.

"Because you were incapacitated, and I wanted to watch you, make sure you didn't show any weird signs during the night. Plus, the bathroom is downstairs, it was just easier that way."

"Bathroom?" I squeak in panic, he instantly picks up on it.

He chuckles at me. "Relax, you were out cold, I didn't have to take you."

"Oh!" Relief floods through me, then I re-run his words, *'I wanted to watch you'* "You watched me all night?" I whisper.

"Yes," he huskily croaks. *How sweet is that?*

"Jeez Tristan, you must be exhausted?" He starts chuckling harder this time, then sighs in a high pitch tone.

"You're funny Coral," he says, then plants a soft kiss on my hair. It's such a sweet gesture, making my heart ache. Oh, what am I doing? *Falling hard, that's what you're doing!*

"Hey Tristan," I mumble. I can barely keep my eyes open.

"Hmm..."

"Thanks for everything. Looking after me...I'm really glad you're here." I tell him giving him a little squeeze of my own.

"Me too," he whispers, squeezing me tightly again, only this time he keeps both arms wrapped around me.

I am cocooned in a Tristan bubble.

A stupid smile starts to spread across my face.

I am officially in heaven...

CHAPTER TWENTY-TWO

I HEAR A STRANGE tapping noise. I sleepily open my eyes. *Oh, I'm still straddled over Tristan.* I crane my neck back to see his face, he's out cold. I watch him for a moment, peacefully sleeping. Then it hits me – *Holy crap!* I've been lying here sleeping with him, and I've had the best sleep ever, no nightmares! I never did that with Justin.

I sigh blissfully and put my head back on his chest. *Tap, Tap, Tap...* I frown at the noise and lift my head up. *What is that?*

"Aunty Coral?" I hear Lily's voice squeak. *Am I dreaming?* I look back at Tristan. I hope so, then *bang, bang, bang...*

Tristan's eyes dart open. "Did you hear that?"

"Yes," I groan. "I thought I was still dreaming," I add grumpily. Tristan and I gaze at each other for a moment, the reflection in our eyes saying the same thing – our blissful time has ended for now.

"Coral, it's Debs, you in there?" I hear her shout.

"Yes," I shout back, pushing myself up.

"I'll get it," Tristan says, stopping me from getting up off the sofa. I watch him walk over to the patio door, pull the curtains across, unlock the door, and pull it open. Lily comes bounding in first, followed by Debs who just stares open-mouthed at Tristan, then at me.

"Good morning Debbie," Tristan says.

"M-morning," she stutters, blinking rapidly.

"Aunty Coral!" Lily screeches throwing herself onto me. I quickly catch her so that she doesn't bash my nose again.

"Hey birthday girl, did you have a nice day?" I ask.

"Your nose looks terrible," she tells me.

"Thanks, how's your head?"

"I have a big bump," she says proudly, touching the top of her head.

I reach up and feel the lump. "Ouch!" I say.

"It doesn't hurt now," she says mockingly, as though I should know this.

"Oh good, my nose still hurts," I tell her. She goes to poke it with her finger, with lighting quick speed I grab hold of it just in time. "No Lily, you can't touch it, it's too painful," I admonish, trying not to sound too angry.

"Sorry," she whimpers, looking very forlorn.

"It's ok, just no poking!" I say, playfully widening my eyes.

Her big smile returns. "Ok!" she giggles. She looks so much like her Mom, long blonde ringlets, bright blue eyes, but she's got her Dad's smile. Then, she's up off my lap and pulling on Debs' hand. "Mommy, Mommy, let me show Aunty Coral," she says excitedly.

"Ok, darling." Debs bends down and takes something out of the big bag she's carrying.

"Look, look," Lily says running over to me. I see she has already half painted one of the Russian dolls from the set.

"Wow Lily, you did this already?" I ask quite astonished.

"It's her favourite present," Debs says winking at me.

"It is?" I say in surprise.

"I love it," she says jumping up and down with the energy that only a five-year-old can have. "Can I kiss your cheek?" she asks with big innocent wide eyes.

"Carefully Lily!" Deb warns.

"It's ok," I say and lean my cheek toward her, she kisses it lightly.

"Love you Aunty Coral, thank you for my present." Tears prick the back of my eyes. *Damn it!*

"You are very welcome." I sniff and softly stroke her cheek. *Stop crying!*

"Don't cry," she says, her little hand gently stroking my cheek again.

"I'm just so happy you liked your present, they're happy tears," I tell her. She looks a little confused at that one.

"Lily, let Mommy talk to Aunty Coral for a moment ok. Here, play with your tablet for a while."

Lily shakes her head. "I want to look at the boats," she says jumping up and down again.

"No darling' – "I'll take her," Tristan offers.

Debs and I look at one another, I nod to her.

"Ok, go with Tristan. But you hold his hand, and you don't let go young lady!"

"Ok, Mommy." She calmly walks over to Tristan and puts her tiny hand in his. Tristan smiles, then shrugs, and they both walk out the studio together. Debs crosses her arms and watches them walk away. Then she turns and looks at me, her one eyebrow cocked up.

"He's good with her." She says coming and sitting next to me.

"Lily's sweet, everyone likes her," I admit.

"Well, you haven't done badly there girl." She says nodding her head towards the window.

"It isn't like that," I say standing up and walking over to the kitchenette. "Tea?" I ask artlessly.

"I know what you're doing," Debs says coming and standing beside me.

"Really, what am I doing Debs?" I argue.

"Avoiding the fact, as usual," she says flicking her blonde hair back.

"Debs, seriously my head is banging, I feel like I've had a nose job. Can't you just..." I sigh heavily and begin making the tea.

"Alright, don't get your knickers in a twist." She huffs.

"My knickers are not twisted." I bark back.

"Well I would," she sniggers. "He's got a wicked, sexy body, a really cute arse, and he's pretty dreamy in the looks department too." She swoons.

"Debs! You're married." I gasp in horror.

"I am well aware of that, doesn't mean I can't fantasise." She says dreamily. *Ew!*

"You fantasise about other men?" I am shocked.

"Hey, there's no harm in looking!"

"But...you're happy with Scott though, right?"

"Of course I am. I still think he's the sexiest man ever, it's just...well, I would be going for it if I were in your shoes," she says teasingly.

I roll my eyes at her. "Right, duly noted," I say handing her a cuppa.

We make our way back over to the sofa, I carefully sit down.

"God Coral does it really hurt that much?" She says all big sisterly, reaching across and rubbing my back.

"Yeah, I was thinking about that earlier. I think it's so bad because as Lily bounced up, I was coming down, made more of an impact I think."

"You could be right," she says cupping my hair behind my ear. "You're going to the hospital today though?" She asks softly.

"No, I hate hospitals...you know that!" She goes to argue with me. "I am not spending all day in A&E just to be told to go home and take painkillers...besides, Tristan's taking me to see his doctor tomorrow."

"Is he now?" Debs grins widely. I roll my eyes at her again and take a sip of my tea. "So is there anything there?" I look at her wide-eyed expression.

"Maybe..." I finally admit. "But it's difficult. He's my new boss...so that doesn't make it..." I stop right there. I don't want her nagging me about it every five seconds.

"Ok, I get the hint. Just trying to find out the juicy gossip," she giggles and takes a sip of her tea. Just as I'm taking another sip of my tea, I get a flashback of us arguing.

"I'm still mad at you," I tell her.

"About what?" she asks, sighing heavily.

"You knew about Malcolm." I bite.

"For god's sake Coral," Debs says looking flustered.

"Is there anything else I don't know about?" Debs looks away from me, so I immediately know she's hiding something. "Is there?" I probe.

"No!" She barks, turning to glare at me.

"Hope not." I threaten.

"Look, I'm really happy for Mom, why can't you be?"

"Who said I'm not happy for her?"

"You're not acting like it." She snaps.

"You know, sometimes I don't think you know me at all. I think it's awesome, I didn't know Gladys was feeling lonely, I'm really happy for her. But that doesn't mean I'm not pissed at you both for not telling me." Debs looks away again.

"Well, we thought' – "We?" I interrupt. "So you all had a

nice little chat and decided best not to tell Coral, hardly seems fair, and doesn't really make me feel like I'm part of this family." I croak, feeling more hurt as I go on.

"Oh for god's sake!" Debs gets up and slams her cup into the sink. Then she turns and glares at me. "Maybe if you integrated yourself more with your family' she says making little speech marks to the word family. "Ever since you got this place you've just faded away. You hardly ever see me anymore, which means you don't see Lily either, and I know you only go to Mom's once a month now. What did you expect?"

I sigh heavily, everything she is saying is true.

"I know that, I just' – "Just what?" she barks, interrupting me.

I look up at her big blue eyes. "There's so much you don't know about me, Debs. It's taken me a long time to get over Justin, to...get some normality back, and then before I got this place I..." I break off. I don't actually want to spill too much to her, she walks over and crouches in front of me.

"What don't I know?" she softly asks, squeezing my one hand tightly.

I shake my head at her. "I'm sorry I stopped coming to see you so much." I offer.

"And I'm sorry I stopped calling and nagging you to come over," she says.

We finally smile at one another. "Can't blame you," I tell her. "I wasn't very good company," I admit.

"So, you're my sister. Always there for each other in hard times, right?" I nod my head and attempt a smile.

The truth is, Debs hasn't always been there for me when I've needed her. But I've always understood, it's not easy to go running off into the night when you have a husband and a child at home, they become your priority. I mean, we love each other as sisters do or should, but it doesn't necessarily mean we get along that well. We have nothing in common, and I've always thought she was pissed that I came along. Gladys gave so much of her attention to me that I think it caused Debs to reject me in some way. And with such an age difference, we rarely spent time together as kids. Debs was always with her friends, while I was always with Gladys.

"Listen Coral there's something..." Debs stares off into the distance, she looks odd?

"What?" I say trying to bring her back.

"Nothing..." She says smiling up at me, but it doesn't reach her eyes.

I frown back at her. "Are *you* ok?" I ask instantly feeling worried.

"Of course," she answers beaming even wider, but she's not fooling me. I decide when I next go to see Gladys I'll ask her if she knows why Debs is acting strangely. And why the hell she lied to me about Debs knowing about Malcolm.

"Well, we'd better get going." I put my cup down, and we hug.

"Thanks for stopping by," I say.

"What are big sisters for?" She hugs me a little harder, then whispers. "Shag his brains out!" *Ugh!*

I pull away from her and frown, Debs is still tittering as she picks up her bags. I walk out onto the sundeck with her. It's not as hot today as it has been, there's quite a cool wind blowing, and the sun is intermittent. I really feel like going for a walk, stretch my legs. I wonder if Tristan would like to come with me?

We spot Tristan and Lily in the distance, he has Lily up on the railing holding her carefully as he's pointing things out to her, she's laughing and giggling with him. Lily spots us and waves enthusiastically, we both wave back. Tristan helps her down, takes hold of her hand, and they start walking back over to us.

"I've never asked you this Coral, but do you want kids?" Debs asks watching Lily. It takes me by complete surprise; we've never had this conversation.

"No," I admit. "I don't think that's for me," I tell her.

"You'd make a great Mom," she says warmly. I frown wondering how on earth she has come to that conclusion.

"I doubt it, it's different when you don't have them all day...I don't think I'd really have the patience." I admit.

"You would," she says nodding her head at me. "They change you, so you become patient, it's weird how it works." I stare back at her wondering how Debbie became so wise and worldly.

Lily runs to Debs who picks her up, embracing her and

kissing her cheeks. I can't believe she's five already – I'm reminded for a moment what happened to me when I was five – I wince at the feeling, and try to focus on what's happening.

"Thanks, Tristan," Debs says warmly.

"My pleasure," he croons.

"Say goodbye then Lily." She puts Lily down, and I bend down and hug her.

"Bye Lily, be good for Mommy," I tell her.

"I will." She says sweetly and kisses my cheek, then surprising us all she turns to Tristan with her arms open wide, waiting for a hug. Tristan crouches down, and they hug, awkwardly on Tristan's part. "Thank you for showing me the boats." She sweetly says.

Tristan's cheeks flush. "You're welcome," he chuckles.

Lily turns her face and kisses his cheek, then she makes a funny face and rubs her lips. "You're prickly, like Daddy," she says.

Tristan rubs his hand across his face. "Yeah, I guess I am," he chuckles as he stands up.

"Come on then darling," Deb says holding her hand out. "See you, Tristan," she smiles, then turns and winks at me, Lily takes her hand, and I silently watch them walk down the concourse together.

I hear Tristan move to stand behind me. I feel the warmth of his body heating my skin; it's a clear indication of how close he is. I turn around and gaze up into his eyes, he gazes back at me. I hesitate for a moment feeling torn, I'm still not sure if I'm capable of anything.

"Well, I guess I better get going," he says, looking torn. *No, don't leave!*

"I was thinking about going for a walk, get some fresh air," I tell him decision made.

"Yeah...sounds nice." He says shyly.

"Care to join me?" I ask.

His amazing deep dimpled smile appears. "Love to." I can't help the grin that starts to spread across my face, giving my feelings away, we walk back inside the studio, Tristan closing the door behind him. "I'd like to get cleaned up first though," Tristan says.

"Yeah, I could do with a shower too," I say. Why am I feeling shy and nervous?

"Can I stay the night?" he asks.

My mouth pops open – *Is he asking what I think he's asking?*

"I'll take the sofa," he clarifies. "I just want to make sure you're ok," he says with his puppy dog eyes that instantly smoulder me – *Holy crap!*

"And so I can make sure you go to the doctor's tomorrow," he adds. I don't even have to think about it, now he's here, I don't want him to leave – at all.

"I'd like that," I whisper.

Tristan grins widely at me, making my stomach flip over again. "Good. Now stay here, and don't do anything. I'm going to dash over to the hotel, grab a change of clothes and then I'll be back."

My face falls, and my heart sinks. Tristan takes the couple of steps needed to be next to me and gently takes hold of my face between his hands. "Hey, I will come back," he says running his thumbs across my cheekbones.

"You will?" I tremble.

"Yes." He whispers. "Try keeping me away." His hands hold my face steady, as his eyes bore into mine. *Is he going to kiss me?*

I surrender and close my eyes. I feel Tristan gently kiss my cheek, then his hands disappear from my face. *Whoa!*

I open my eyes and watch him walk through the patio door, then disappear from view. I can't help wondering if I actually am still dreaming? My head feels light and giddy, my cheek is tingling from his kiss, and my stomach is full of butterflies. But more than that, the strange soul sensation that I've been getting whenever I think of Tristan suddenly feels empty and barren, just like I have always felt.

Strange – I didn't feel like that when Tristan was here. It's like, when he's here he fills me up and the emptiness kind of... disappears, and when he's gone...I decide I don't want to dwell on that too deeply. I look around my studio, this place looks a mess. I'd better do some cleaning up.

Clearing my coffee table, I throw the leftover pancakes in the bin, then I wash and dry up the cups. Picking up my quilt and pillows, I carefully make my way up the stairs, as I'm remaking my bed with my quilt, I catch my reflection in the mirror. I seriously need some heavy makeup to hide the bruises.

I quickly strip my clothes off me, throw them in the wash basket and pull on my robe. I need a shower and a change of clothes, that's for sure. I poke around in my closet and find my chocolate cords, my long sleeved fitted mocha t-shirt, and throw them on the bed.

Heading downstairs, I take a long leisurely shower, tenderly washing my hair so as not to start a headache off again. I don't want to rock the boat as my head seems to be improving.

As I'm rubbing my body with shower cream, I think about Tristan coming back. I think about us taking a walk together. I think about him taking my hand in his. I think about his tender kiss on my cheek. I think about what it felt like when my hand was in his.

My body flutters with excited tingles, literally from head to toe. I giggle and roll my eyes at myself. Now I'm the one acting like a love-struck teenager, not Gladys!

I wonder for a moment if that's what this is, some silly crush? But if I'm completely honest with myself, I know it's not that. After all, I admitted to George that I'm in love with him – I still can't work out how that's possible, but just being near Tristan makes me feel all warm and fuzzy inside.

Then I think about what George said to me about giving it a try, and how I argued with him that I'd self-destruct it, that all my fears and insecurities would come rushing to the surface, and in truth, I thought they would. I thought my own self-preservation would kick in, to protect myself from any further pain or hurt, but it feels like all that worry and anguish literally melts away when I'm with Tristan.

He makes me feel whole, normal...well as normal as I can be...

I AM SAT ON MY BED slowly drying my hair. I have showered, creamed my skin, cleaned my teeth, put on my makeup, deodorant and perfume, and dressed ready for the walk. I am almost feeling human again. I can't help sneaking a peek at the time on my alarm clock. Tristan's been gone an hour now. I hope he's ok? Just as I think that I hear the patio door slide open.

"Coral?" I hear the worry in his voice.

"Up here," I shout. Tristan darts up the stairs his eyes searching for me.

When he sees me, I can visibly see his shoulders relax, his eyes melt like butter. I notice his five a clock shadow is gone and that he's changed. He smells fresh, of shower gel and aftershave, but his own distinct smell is over-powering those, making me tingle all over again, and he looks good, really good! He's dressed in a pair of dark blue jeans that he's matched with a light beige t-shirt and a zip-up chocolate hoody over the top. He looks... *Irresistible!*

I switch the hairdryer off, I think my hair is dry enough.

Tristan crosses his arms and frowns down at me. "I thought I said stay put," he says, trying to look crossly at me.

I smile sweetly at him and shrug. "I get bored easily, and I wanted a shower. So that's what I did after I cleaned up," I say pulling on my Echo walking boots. "Besides you changed your mind didn't you," I quarrel.

"I did?" He questions.

"Yes. You said you'd be right back, yet you showered at the hotel." I pout.

"Ah yes! I did, guilty as charged," he says mockingly.

"What, my tiny bathroom not good enough for you?" I bite.

"Don't be daft. By the time I was there...well I just thought' – "You thought what?" I interrupt crossing my arms defensively, mimicking his body language.

"All my gear was already in the bathroom, it just seemed quicker that's all. I'm sorry." He says intently, his eyes searching mine.

"Don't do that again, you had me worried." I scold.

"I won't, I promise." *Ugh, I hate that word.*

"I don't want promises, Tristan, they can be broken. Give me your word."

Tristan frowns at me. "Alright, you have my word." He solemnly says.

I instantly forgive him and uncross my arms.

Tristan smiles, then comes and sits next to me on the bed. "You look beautiful," he softly says. "But you should have waited for me, what if you'd have hurt yourself or lost your balance?"

I gaze up at him and titter. "Tristan, I'm not made of glass, besides I'm feeling a lot better than I was earlier," I tell him, then I look down and notice he's wearing Echo boots too. "Snap," I say putting my left foot next to his right.

"They're good boots." He says nodding in agreement.

"Indeed they are. Did you want a drink before we go?" I ask politely.

"Right now I'm good, I had a coffee at the hotel," he says. "But I thought we could have something while we're out?" He adds.

"Like what?" I ask.

Tristan shrugs. "Whatever we feel like?" I smile back at him. He's so easy going, I really feel like I can be myself with him. In that very moment, as we silently gaze at one another, I decide to let him know a little bit more about me. *Bit by bit!*

We head downstairs, and I place my shoulder bag over my head. Checking I've got my keys, my purse, and some painkillers we make our way out.

"So where are we off to?" He asks.

"Somewhere I'm sure you've never been." I smile popping the keys in my bag.

"I think I've walked on a beach before." He drawls sarcastically at me.

"This isn't a beach walk." I retort dryly.

We head north towards The Master Mariner, as we reach it we turn east onto Undercliff Walk. It's a beautiful little gem of a walk, stretching right from the Marina all the way to Saltdean. As we reach the end of the Marina and carry on walking, Tristan stops and questions me.

"We're not going to the beach?" He asks.

"Nah, gets a little crowded when it's warm like this."

"So where does this lead?" He asks looking a little worried.

I chuckle and nudge him. Then I decide I could give him a little local history, turning around, so I'm walking backwards, I smile at Tristan and begin.

"Ok, so this is called Undercliff Walk, as you can see' I say playing air hostess with my arms to the right. "This is the seawall, in the 1930's the council decided they needed to do something with the cliff as it was eroding so badly, so the seawall was built. Of course to my left' – I fling my arms again like an air-hostess – 'you have the sea. It's so cool to walk along here in the winter, the waves really come up high and the spray soaks you." I chuckle.

"That sounds dangerous," Tristan says darkly. "You could get washed out to sea," he adds.

I roll my eyes at him and continue. "This bright white flat, concrete pathway goes all the way down to Saltdean, there's a really cute café at Ovingdean; we can stop there for a coffee if you want?"

"Sure." Tristan smiles shyly at me, places his hands in his pockets and gazes at me in that strange way of his like he sees straight through me.

I try to ignore it and continue. "So when the tide is out a sprawling city of rock pools are revealed, and the remnants of the old Volks Railway can be seen; it's tracks used to run through the sea. The train had spider legs that elongated, they rose up and up; its feet would be in the water and the carriage in the air."

"What happened to it?" Tristan asks animatedly.

"I know that a week after opening in 1896, a huge storm hit, and it collapsed. I remember reading they got it all up and running again, but it cost the company a lot of money and then I kind of remember something I learned at school about some groynes being built right near it and it damaged the track, and that it was too costly to move it all to another place. It didn't have electric motors so when the tide was in the whole thing would grind to a halt."

I shake my head in laughter. "Can you imagine being stuck eighty feet in the air with the sea beneath you, and not being able to get off for hours, because the damn thing won't move? They had some crazy ideas back then." I chuckle.

Tristan is gazing at me again.

"What?" I ask shyly.

"You look very beautiful and free with the wind in your hair, the sun making it shine when it comes out." I stop walking. Tristan doesn't, and as he reaches me, he picks me up and swings me around, making me giggle.

Then placing me back down, he puts his arm around my shoulders, squeezes me tight and kisses my temple. I wrap my arm around his waist and revel in the feel of it. It just feels so nice not to be walking on my own, and so comfortable with him. The conversation between us just seems to flow so easily.

We carry on walking, and I'm enthralled as Tristan tells me all about going to University, studying law and opening up his first company. I tell him about Joyce giving me my first job and how I liked it so much that I stayed. But as we walk along, I can't help noticing the looks we are getting. It's starting to make me feel self-conscious. *Maybe a walk wasn't such a good idea!*

Some of the women are really glaring at me, and some are looking at me as though they feel sorry for me. And I can see the men are sizing Tristan up, wondering if he's the one that's messed my face up like this.

"People are staring at us." I hiss, feeling utterly incensed they would be thinking that.

"Don't worry about it," Tristan tells me, but I can see from his countenance that he's hiding how uncomfortable it's making him feel. As if he would do anything like this to a woman. Those men, if you can call them that, are weak, soul-less, insecure jerks.

"How long until we get to the café?" Tristan asks.

"Thirsty?"

"No, just wondering?" He says casually.

"About another twenty minutes," I say looking out to sea.

"Tell me about yourself Coral?" *Oh Crap, here we go!*

"What do you want to know?" I ask, trying not to let my defensive wall come up.

"I don't know....stuff?" Tristan says shrugging.

"Tristan," I stop walking and turn him around to face me. "Why don't you just ask what you really want to know," I say, trying to put on as much of a brave face as I can.

"I don't want to rock the boat," he says grimly. "You're very defensive. And I'm sure you have every right to be' – "Tristan, just..." I run my hands through my hair. "Ok, when I talked to George about you, he said I'll never know what kind of potential we could have if I don't let you in, and that you'll always feel like you never know if you're going too far or saying the wrong thing..." I close my eyes, trying to balance myself and calm my scattered thoughts.

"Sorry, I've never been too good at getting out what I actually want to say, it just kind of sticks in my head and stays there." I shake my head to try and shake off the bad thoughts.

"Ask away Tristan, if it's too hard a question I just won't answer," I say hoping I've placated him.

Tristan holds my face in his hands again and strokes my cheeks with his thumbs. "Why were you adopted Coral? What happened to your parents?" He asks, his eyes searching mine, his expression intense.

"That's two questions." I breathe.

"Right, two," he says staring down at me.

My old instincts try to kick in, to get out of his hold, to run, so I don't have to talk about the past or deal with hard questions. So I fight them because I want Tristan more than I've ever wanted anyone or anything in my entire life. I nod slowly to him. Tristan releases me, then takes hold of both my hands, my breath hitches with the contact.

"Ok." I take a deep breath and exhale slowly, we are stood face to face my hands in his, this feels safe enough to talk about. "I was four when my Dad left, I think he'd had enough of my Mom. Of course, I was too young to really to know why, but I think it must have been the same for Kelly's Dad too, because he left when Kelly was six, or so she told me.

"I have this really weird memory of going downstairs because I was thirsty, and Dad had some woman in the house. Mom was a nurse she was working at the hospital, night shift I guess. Of course, now I'm an adult, I understand it completely. He was having an affair with her," I drift off for a moment remembering the woman, she was pretty, really pretty and she seemed like fun too, I remember them laughing a lot, Mom always looked like crap and hardly ever laughed.

"What did your Dad do?" Tristan asks staring at the concrete walkway. "Sorry, do you even remember?"

"Salesman, but I don't know what he sold. I think the woman he left my Mom for was his secretary, but that's usually how it goes right?"

"Why don't you call Gladys Mom?" He innocently asks.

I frown hard. "B-because I wouldn't...my *Mother'* – I hiss – 'was a waste of space, I wouldn't...no I couldn't call Gladys by that title, she is so much more than that to me. Angel would be a better word for her..."

"Why do you say that?" Tristan asks.

"Because she saved me, Tristan, in so many ways...she was

perfect for a girl like me. I'd be dead if it weren't for her. I'd have gone down the wrong path, you know drink, drugs, whatever it took to make the pain and the rage disappear." I shake my head remembering back then. "Gladys taught me how to deal with my feelings, my emotions, to the best of her ability. And she made me feel safe and loved. But above all she taught me how to laugh, she taught me that it was ok to be silly and childish, she gave me a way to deal with the problems, by using laughter." I let out a long breath.

"That's a damn good idea," Tristan says in surprise.

"Shall we?" I say, gesturing to walk on with my chin.

"Yes." Tristan releases one of my hands, but grips the other tightly, my breath hitches again.

"Do you see your Dad?" He asks innocently.

"No," I sigh. "When he left, he called a couple of times, but..." I shake my head at the memory. "Not long before I came to live with Gladys, my Mom told me I'd never see him again, that he had a new family. I guess it meant he'd had more kids." I shrug looking at the concrete walkway.

"Jesus, some parents are real assholes," Tristan says solemnly.

Just as he says that a woman walks towards us with a can of lager in one hand, and a cigarette in the other, the man that she's with is doing the same. Neither of them are taking any notice of the dishevelled looking toddler, who trips over and scrapes his knees on the concrete. He screams in pain, and instead of comforting him, they start shouting at him, then start swearing at each other – *Poor kid!*

Tristan and I glance at one another, no doubt both thinking the same thing. I want to help the child, give him some comfort, some stability, but I can tell by the parents that it could turn nasty. I shake my head and get back to our conversation.

"Yeah, they are. But as George reminds me when I get mad about it, that the past is the past, and the future is the future. You can't control, change or re-write either. Focusing on the present is the only thing that's important, the here and now. I can let my past dictate who I am, or I can take charge, and become the person I want to be.

"It's not easy, there are days when I really struggle, I think it's the why more than anything, well actually no, it's the how too. That's why I find it so bitter-sweet being around Lily. I mean

I love her, absolutely adore her, of course I know her parents do too. But when I look at her, I can't help thinking how any adult can have a child, and then abandon it? Surely there's like this protective thing that kicks in, you know like you want to protect that child, take care of it; teach it right from wrong. I can't wrap my head around it all." I say shaking my head again.

I look across at Tristan, he looks deep in thought. "Sorry, I'm waffling on aren't I. Ask one question floodgates open, Coral doesn't shut up," I titter, trying to make light out of darkness.

"No, you're not waffling," Tristan solemnly answers. "I'm just trying to imagine being in your shoes, and what it would have been like to go through all of that," he says staring blankly ahead; he looks a million miles away.

I smile shyly at him, he wraps his arm around my shoulder and squeezes me tight. Then he leans forward, making me think he's going to kiss me again, which he does, but it's a sweet, gentle kiss on my temple – I light up inside...

WE WALK IN COMFORTABLE silence for a while. It's felt really good to let Tristan in, to let him know some of my past. Ironically he's the one that seems to be more affected by it than I am. I spot the small lemon painted structure not far in front of us, we have reached the café. I hadn't even noticed how far we had come.

"Tristan?" I turn to look at him. But he still looks blank, like he's working out a really hard maths equation. "Hey," I stop walking and tug on his hand, so he has to look at me. "Pull out of it, or I'm not sharing anymore," I add and bob my tongue out at him.

He finally smiles back at me. "Anyway, we are here," I say pointing to the café like an air-hostess again. "Please feed and water me kind sir," I say with a strong Somerset accent.

"With pleasure my lady," he chuckles bowing grandly at me. I love that he just did that, the café is packed with people, and he simply didn't care.

I hear that little voice in my head telling me I need to be careful, that I'm falling hard for Tristan, but I shake the thought away and place my hand in his outstretched open palm...

CHAPTER TWENTY-THREE

WE ARE SAT AT A TABLE eating carrot cake and drinking coffee. Tristan said that he wanted to eat a *'proper dinner'* when we got back, as he didn't want to spoil his appetite. So I went along with it, knowing that my very strict diet has been thrown out of the window this past week. But I'm rarely naughty, so I stop nagging at myself and enjoy the cake.

"You want to ask another question don't you?" I say, licking my lips after taking the last mouthful of cake.

"Your mother?" He says.

I stare out to sea and take a deep breath. "Her," I spit. "She doesn't deserve the title of mother. A mother is someone who should love you unconditionally. A mother is someone who puts her child's needs before her own." I snap, then I lean back in my chair and twiddle with the dessert fork.

"Will you tell me about her?" He asks tentatively.

I glance at Tristan from the corner of my eye then look back out to sea. Do I really want to talk about her? Is she worth my breath? Deciding I'll tell him, I close my eyes and begin.

"She...she was a drunk, a hopeless, useless drunk. It wasn't long after Dad left, and Kelly died, that things really went downhill' – I shiver internally – 'She stopped going to work, I guess she was on the dole. I'm not really sure. I remember feeding myself, that's if I could find anything to eat," I snap and grit my teeth. I still remember how my belly would swell and then the pain would start. I shake my head at the memories and glance at Tristan again, he looks mortified.

"She tried to kill herself. I called 999, police and ambulance came, and I was taken away. I did see her a couple of times after that, but....." I trail off, I don't want to say anymore.

Tristan takes my hand that was playing with the fork and squeezes it tight. He looks so sorrowful, then he slowly brings my hand to his lips, and kisses the back of it. "I'm so sorry Coral...I...I don't really know what else to say to that."

I lean forward and using my free hand I softly stroke his cheek. "You don't have to say anything Tristan." I feel the pull between us again, I want to kiss him. It takes me by complete surprise. Just as I'm leaning closer to him, we are rudely interrupted by an elderly woman, who pokes Tristan with her walking stick.

"You should be ashamed of yourself," she croaks. She looks incensed like she wants to attack him.

"For what?" he asks innocently, staring up at her wild, angry face.

"That!" She says swinging her stick, so it points at my face.

Tristan and I both smile, which turns out is the worst thing to do.

"Oh! You think it's funny young man?" She raises her stick in the air, I think she's going to hit him with it. Tristan throws out his arm to protect himself, I launch out of my seat and grab her stick, just as she brings it down.

"Hey lady," I hiss, glaring at her. "I got this from playing bouncy castle with my niece." She frowns back at me then narrows her eyes at Tristan, so I continue. "I would never let a man do this to me. That man' – I point to Tristan – 'has more respect for women than any other man I've ever met. He happens to be the most kind, gentle, loving person I have ever met," I say feeling the weight of my own words. "So put down your stick and be on your way." I put my hands on my hips and glare at her. I'm not sure if she believes me, because she narrows her eyes at Tristan for a few seconds then walks away, muttering to herself.

"Wow," Tristan chuckles. "My Heroine."

We both burst into fits of giggles. I see the lady look back at us shaking her head, but I don't care if she believed me or not. I was not going to let her attack Tristan for something he hadn't done.

"Shall we start walking back?" I say glaring back at the woman's retreating figure.

"Yeah..." he replies.

I don't think Tristan can quite believe that a little old lady would have the courage to say that, but then I see Gladys doing something exactly like that when she's old and doddery...

WE STAND AND START heading back towards the Marina. Tristan silently reaches for my hand, I place it in his, and I immediately feel that same sense of peace that I got from the dream. I feel very relaxed but also tired, the long walk has worn me out, and my head and nose are starting to pound again.

"Can I ask you something?" I roll my eyes at Tristan, waiting for his question. "Don't take this the wrong way, but why don't you have guys lined up Coral? I mean you're stunning, mesmerising, yet you're not dating? You should be beating them off with a stick."

"I've told you, Tristan, fuck up," I say tapping the side of my head. "Look it doesn't matter how pretty or attractive someone is on the outside. If you felt vile, ugly and repulsed about yourself on the inside, then you're not really in the right state emotionally or mentally to be getting involved with someone. Are you?"

His mouth pops open in shock. "I couldn't say...I don't know what it is to feel like that. I take it you do?" He adds, swallowing hard.

"Not so much anymore, George has really helped me develop a healthier internal relationship with myself. I guess he's worked wonders really. It's only been since the beginning of this year that I've been able to look at myself in the mirror without turning away in disgust...." I stare out at the ocean, I don't want to see Tristan's reaction to that.

"So is that why you were so adamant that we shouldn't see each other because you have issues...well...you know...I mean, that came out wrong..." He stops walking and runs both hands through his hair. He's flustered.

"Tristan, it's ok. You can say that you know. I do have issues. I like to think of myself as a work in progress." I look up at him, he looks a little lost for words, which is fair enough, I think I'd be having the same reaction if the roles were reversed. "I still stand by what I said though, I really don't know if I'm capable of having a normal, healthy, long-term relationship," I add.

Tristan gazes back at me. "I think you can," he whispers, taking a step closer. "You just don't want to get hurt again." He leans down and softly kisses my cheek, it takes my breath away.

The sheer proximity of him is enough to make my heart pound and my head feel woozy...I smile shyly at him.

"I don't think it's such a good idea to eat out tonight," I chuckle trying to lighten the mood. "You know, just in-case you get attacked again." I burst out laughing at my own joke.

"Oh ha ha!" Tristan wraps his arm around my waist and playfully swings me around. "So what do you want to do?" He asks.

"Well, I'm feeling pretty worn out, so a movie sounds good." I like the idea of that, curling up on the sofa next to Tristan.

"Yep, I'm up for that, but what about food. You want to order in?" He asks.

"No, no takeaway, I have eaten far too unhealthily already this week. How about a roast dinner?"

"Sounds great, but I don't think you're really up to cooking Coral, you should be relaxing."

I roll my eyes again. "Tristan' – "I can cook," he interrupts, shrugging his shoulders.

"You can?" I say rather astonished.

"Don't look so surprised. My Grandmother taught me, I can make a mean roast dinner," he says smugly.

"I'm impressed," I chuckle – secretly thanking the heavens for sending me a man that can cook, and fend for himself. "Well, when Gladys doesn't do a roast I have to admit I cheat, I buy everything premade, chuck it in the oven, then serve it up for Bob and me."

"You and Bob?" he says. I watch Tristan's face twist with anxiety as he tries to remember. "Yeah Bob...you know...my next door neighbour?"

His whole body sags with relief. "Oh right, yeah...I remember. Bob." He says nodding to himself.

"You thought it was my secret boyfriend." I chuckle. Tristan shrugs nonchalantly, but I can see that I'm right, I laugh out loud again and continue. "So every Sunday night I make one up for him and take it around. If I've been to Gladys's I bring one back for him, on occasion, he comes along."

"That's sweet Coral." I shake my head wishing I hadn't, it's hurting again.

"I don't think so. Bob's all on his own, I like looking after him. I make him fresh meals after work too," I say. "He eats too much canned food," I add, which he does. It's not healthy.

"Coral." Tristan stops us walking, and stands opposite me. Slowly his hand reaches up and strokes my cheek. "It is sweet," he says, his eyebrows knitting together.

I gaze up at him, my heart starts to hammer against my chest, I really want to kiss him. I want to know what those full lips will taste like, what they will feel like brushing gently against mine. I think Tristan's feeling it too because he leans into me, his lips inches from mine, but just at that moment, his mobile starts ringing. Tristan mumbles something under his breath and pulls away from me.

"Sorry." He says looking exasperated.

"It's fine." I breathe, although I'm totally gutted.

"Tristan Freeman." He answers politely, though I can see he is agitated, then he walks a few feet away from me. I walk over to the seawall to give him a little privacy. Whatever the call is about looks important, his expression is seriously intense, he doesn't look happy.

As I lean against the wall and look out at the ocean, my mind starts wondering to Rob and Carlos, and my decision to go see them after Lily's party. It keeps nagging away in the back of my mind, and I know whatever it is that he's upset about must be bad – him crying like that, it just wasn't right. I know I have only known him a couple of years, but I feel like I've known him all my life. So I decide to make it my mission after seeing Tristan's doctor, to go over to their place and find out the truth, beat it out of him if I have to.

Then I think about Debs and Gladys, and the fact that they kept Malcolm a secret and how hurt I feel because of that. Then I think about what Debs told me about how I've seen less and less of everyone – of course, she thinks it's all to do with Justin, but it isn't at all. Yes, he broke my heart, but that was nothing compared to being raped, forced upon. And she is right after that happened, I alienated myself from the world – not just my family.

Rob's the one that really got me out of my studio, and got me socialising again, I couldn't have done it without him, I know that. Which is why I have to repay the favour, get over there and see him. But I don't know what to do about Gladys not telling me, no matter how distant I've been. I still don't understand why she didn't just casually say that she's seeing someone.

But then I've always thought Gladys and Debs are the closest, much more than she and I. But maybe that's because Gladys had Debs from the very beginning, when she was a baby, they say a deeper bond forms when you have a child from scratch.

Maybe that's why I've always felt out of the loop? I mean I know Gladys loves me, deeply, but it's just not the same. I just can't stand lies and secrets. It drives me up the wall and makes me feel insecure. Like there's a bomb about to go off, and I'm the last to know about it.

"Hey." I feel Tristan's arms wrap around my waist, his body pressed against the back of mine. I should panic at this kind of embrace, it's never felt safe or comfortable to me. It's one of the many things Justin used to moan about to me, that I wouldn't show affection towards him. He called me cold, but then he didn't know me, not really.

Tristan knows more about me in the short amount of time I have spent with him than Justin did in the two years we were together. Yet, with Tristan, this feels...normal, right, as it should do – *I wonder why that is?*

"Hey yourself," I say twisting my head round to smile up at him.

Tristan smiles warmly at me and kisses my cheek, then gazes out to sea. "That was my doctor, you're in for 8.15am tomorrow," he tells me.

"Ok," I say.

"Not too early for you?" I silently shake my head, revelling in the feel of his arms around me. And for a long time, we just stay there like that, both deep in thought...

AFTER A VERY FUNNY shopping experience, we make it back to the studio with bags full of food and wine, which Tristan insisted on carrying. I feel totally whacked out again.

"You look tired." Tristan guesses.

"Yeah, my nose is really hurting again," I answer feeling guilty that all I want to do is sleep for a while.

"Why don't you have a cat nap on the sofa, I'll get dinner in the oven." He says, reading my thoughts.

I smile sleepily at Tristan. "You don't mind?" I say stifling a yawn.

Tristan smiles at me. "No, not at all. I think I would be feeling the same if my nose was nearly broken," he responds sweetly, kissing my forehead.

"I feel guilty leaving it all to you," I say running my hands through my hair.

"Don't." He demands strictly.

"Yes, sir." I titter and head over to the sofa.

Taking a glass of water with me I down a couple of painkillers with difficulty, trying to get my throat to open is a real pain in the arse sometimes.

"You have difficulty taking tablets?" Tristan vigilantly assesses. *Is there anything he doesn't notice?*

"Yeah..." I lie down on the sofa, resting my head on the pillow.

Tristan kneels down in front of me. "Why?" He asks. I roll my eyes at him, he smiles back at me and moves my hair, tucking it behind my ear. "Tell me," he pleads.

I sigh inwardly and begin rattling it all out at top speed. "I was off school with flu. Gladys went out to get some shopping. I woke up, took the cold and flu tablets she left on my dresser and well, they kind of went down the wrong way. I was scared to death, I couldn't breathe, I was on my own and..." I feel my throat tightening up on me as I recall it. "I was ok, obviously, in the end." I chuckle, trying to make it seem more light-hearted.

"That must have been scary." He says with dark eyes.

I reach my hand up to his face and stroke his cheek. "It was at the time, now it's just really annoying that my throat closes up on me whenever I need to take a tablet," I answer yawning again, my eyes feeling heavier and heavier.

"Sleep Coral," Tristan says kissing my forehead again.

And just like that, I slip into unconsciousness…

I WAKE UP TO THE smell of roast beef, roast potatoes and Yorkshire puddings. I smile broadly, keeping my eyes closed I stretch deeply. I feel rested, and my nose is no longer throbbing. When I open my eyes the first thing I see is Tristan sitting on the end of the sofa, my feet are on his lap, and he's gently kneading them – *No wonder I slept so well!*

Then I notice he has an e-reader in his hand, he's evidently enthralled by whatever book he's reading.

"Hey," I say sleepily.

Tristan puts down his e-reader and leans down towards me. "I'm glad you're awake." He whispers. "I was missing you."

I lean up on my elbows so that we're almost nose to nose and smile broadly at him. "I missed you too," I tell him sweetly, my heart racing against my chest. "I didn't know you liked reading?" I add.

Tristan loses his grin. "My grandparents wouldn't let me watch T.V. Gran used to say it rots your brain, so I was given books, lots and lots of books. She said that reading would help expand my mind and help me to become more creative, I guess it kind of stuck." I cock my head to the side, he seems pissed off about it. *I wonder why that is?*

"I read a lot too," I say trying to work out his expression.

"What kind of books do you like?" He asks.

"Oh, all sorts. I can read anything from Anne of Green Gables, which was my favourite as a kid, to Chris Ryan's The Kill Zone, you?"

"I've read that' – "Anne of Green Gables?" I giggle interrupting him.

"Oh, very funny!" Tristan chuckles. "No, The Kill Zone," he says poking me playfully.

"Who else do you like?" I giggle.

"Dan Brown, Clive Cussler, Lee Child, Michael Crichton, the list goes on." He smiles, waving his hand in the air.

"Me too, Lee Child writes the Jack Reacher books, right?"

"Yes, he does," Tristan answers with his heart-stopping, deep-dimpled smile.

That soulful feeling deep within me expands again,

spreading through me; I swear it's getting bigger by the day. It really feels like the more time I spend with Tristan, the closer I get to him. That never happened with Justin either, it always felt the same. *Breathe Coral!*

"Have you seen the Jack Reacher film? You know that one with Tom Cruise in it?" I ask, trying to ease the enormity of the moment.

"No, I haven't actually." He says, his head cocked to the side.

I swallow hard. "Me neither, want to rent it tonight?"

"Good idea." He beams, inching towards me.

"You know what they say, great minds think alike," I whisper.

Tristan leans closer and closer, I can feel his breath against my cheeks. I stop breathing, all I call feel is an overwhelming burning passion for Tristan bubbling under the surface. I lean even closer to his lips, and stare deeply into his warm brown eyes, I see no hesitation.

I close my eyes ready for the feel of his lips on mine – *Bing!* – The oven chimes warning Tristan that dinner is either ready, or something needs checking.

I open my eyes and see Tristan close his in frustration. It seems we are being held back by random events. I wish I had more confidence, I really want to kiss him, but I'm just not forward enough to just launch myself onto him, that just wouldn't feel right.

"So what are you reading now?" I say pulling in a ragged breath as Tristan walks over to the cooker, turns over the roast potatoes and pops them back in.

"John Grisham's, The Racketeer." He answers thoughtfully.

"He's really good too, I've read quite a few of his books. We seem to have a lot in common, don't we?" I add sounding hoarse, so I pick up the water and glug a load back.

Tristan turns and smiles at me. "We certainly do," he agrees. "Would you like a glass of wine?" He asks as he puts the beef on the side to rest.

"Please." Tristan gets two wine glasses out of the cupboard. He looks so at ease in the kitchen. Then he gets the rose wine out of the freezer, pops the cork and pours two ice-cold glasses. As he reaches the sofa, he passes one to me.

"How did you know?" I say taking a sip.

"Know what?" He answers looking a little confused.

"That I..." Then it hits me, I don't remember telling him that I like really cold wine, so he must like it like that too, I chortle and shake my head.

"What?" He questions.

"Nothing I just thought...you like your wine cold?" I question.

"Um...yeah, I..." His face drops.

"Relax, I do too." I smile.

Tristan perks up again and takes a drink, I suddenly remember the gift that I bought him.

"Oh hey, I got you something," I beam. "It's kind of two presents in one though, a housewarming gift and a thank you for the air-conditioner." Tristan's eyebrows shoot up in surprise. I put my wine down and stand up. "Stay where you are," I order.

"Yes Ma'am." Tristan places his wine on the coffee table then leans back against the sofa.

"And close your eyes," I add.

Tristan grins like a kid on Christmas Day, its pure joy to see. As I run up the stairs to get his painting, I suddenly feel really apprehensive. *What if he doesn't like it?* Ok, so I can say that first, that if he doesn't, we can exchange it.

"Ok, eyes closed?" I shout at the top of the stairs.

"Yes." he chuckles. I carefully make my way back down the stairs. Tristan peeks with one eye. "No peeking." I scold. His grin widens, he's so cheeky. "So, I thought if you don't like this we can exchange it ok? Above all be honest." I tell him forcefully.

"Honesty is my middle name." He assures me.

I stand in front of him holding the painting against my body. I almost decide to hold it up above my face so I can't see his expression, then I change my mind.

"Hurry up," he says jigging up and down. "The suspense is killing me," he adds. He's really smiling now, his dimples deep. I swoon at him for a second then snap myself out of it.

I take a deep breath. "Ok, open your eyes."

Tristan peeks with one eye for a tenth of a second, then both eyes burst wide open in what, shock, surprise, horror?

"E-type?" He says breathlessly.

"Um...yeah," I answer glumly. "If you don't like it, we can exchange it," I repeat.

"Shut up..." He drawls staring up at the painting – *Ok, maybe he likes it?* A grin from ear to ear starts to spread across his face.

"You like it," I say jumping up and down on the spot. Tristan looks up at me with wide eyes. I can't quite read the expression on his face. Is it awe, gratitude, surprise?

"Coral, you shouldn't have," he gasps. "This must have cost' – "Tristan!" I scowl. "It's a double present anyway," I reiterate. The last thing I want is him telling me I can't spend my money on him.

"I don't know what to say." He answers softly, still gazing up at me with that look.

"Thank you would be nice," I say dryly, cocking one eyebrow up.

Tristan stands, takes the painting out of my hand, places it against the sofa, and launches me up into the air and into his arms, swinging me around as he does.

"It's perfect, just like you." He whispers.

My mouth pops open. *He thinks I'm perfect?* He really doesn't know me that well, must have rose coloured spectacles on.

He chuckles at my shocked expression. "I love it," he adds excitedly.

"You do?" I breathe.

"Yes." He chuckles back, placing my feet back on the floor. We are face to face again, so I reach up and run my fingers through his hair; it's so soft.

"I'm glad." I croak. *Breathe Coral, breathe!*

Tristan closes his eyes and leans his forehead against mine. It's a heady feeling, literally. I've seen it happen in so many movies and shouted at the T.V for the couple in question to get on with it and kiss, but now it's happening to me, I finally see the beauty in it. I see the romance, the longing, the passion, I close my eyes and melt into the moment.

"Coral," Tristan's voice is so low, it's barely a whisper. I open my eyes and see he's looking at me that way again like he sees straight through me. My breath catches with the intensity of the moment. "Tell me you want this?" He whispers.

I let out a ragged breath. "I want this, I want you," I say

stroking his cheek again. Tristan squeezes me harder against his body. I wet my lips in anticipation – *Bing!*

We both sigh loudly then burst out laughing – *This is getting god damn ridiculous!* – Tristan lets me go, shaking his head as he does – *Grrrr, the irony!*

"Hungry?" he asks checking the meal. "Because it's ready," he adds.

"Kind of lost my appetite now," I say as butterflies are flying around like fighter jets in my stomach.

"Coral, you have to eat." He softly admonishes.

"I know," I whisper.

He walks back over to me and pulls me close to his body. "I really want you to eat something," he says. "You haven't eaten much over the past two days."

"Well, you probably haven't either," I argue.

"Good point, I haven't had much, which is probably why I want to demolish this meal."

"You're hungry." I guess.

"Yes." He says, smiling at me. I frown at the floor. "What?" He says lifting my chin with his thumb and forefinger – *Be honest Coral.*

"Don't I have any effect on you? We nearly…and you…you just want to eat?" I stutter.

"You have no idea the effect you have on me," he whispers. "I'm hungry, for you and for food."

Oh, bugger me that's….that's the sexiest thing I've ever had said to me. I blink rapidly at him. I've lost the power of speech.

"So, shall we? If we leave it any longer it'll be ruined," he adds.

I nod my head in acceptance. "I'll set the table," I squeak.

"Marvellous. Shall I serve?" He asks, his playful smile is back.

"Yes please," I whisper.

Tristan walks back over to the kitchenette, while I pull out my tiny little fold up table and two chairs. I unfold the chairs and place them under the table, then I walk over to the kitchenette, bumping Tristan with my hip as I do, which he chuckles at. I open the drawer and pull out two placemats, coasters and two sets of knives and forks. This feels really weird. I, of course, normally pull out just one, unless Bob eats with me, but he prefers to eat alone. I smile as I place them opposite each other, then I pick up our wines and place them on the table too.

I stop for a moment and take stock of how natural this all feels. Tristan serving up dinner after a lazy Sunday afternoon walk, me setting the table; it feels like we're a real bonafide couple that's been doing this forever. It feels so god damn good to eat a meal with someone, so nice.

Tristan has done a magnificent job. We have Roast Beef with Yorkshires, Roast potatoes, mustard mash (my favourite) a vegetable medley of broccoli, kale and peas and roast carrots and parsnips, topped with delicious thick gravy, this could out-do Gladys's roasts.

There are three plates laid out, and the portions are perfect. Not too over-loaded like Gladys's, she thinks I'm skinny and need fattening up. So after many arguments, she now lets me serve up my own plate, even though she always rolls her eyes at my small amount.

"Wow, good job," I say beaming up at him.

"Why thank you." Tristan grins sexily at me, making me lose my train of thought for a second.

"Um...I'll take Bob's round to him." I pick up one of the plates. "Oh careful with the table, it's a bit rickety," I tell him as I walk out the patio door, moments later I am back. Tristan has placed our plates on the table and is sitting down waiting for me, how gentlemanly.

"You waited." I beam as I sit down.

"It's good manners to wait." He says taking a sip of wine.

"Your grandparents taught you well," I say, then regret it. I doubt he wants to be reminded of them. I take a big whiff of the meal, and my appetite comes back with a vengeance. "Mmm smells delicious."

"Cheers." Tristan raises his glass, I pick up mine, and we clink glasses.

"Cheers." I take a sip, place my wine down and start eating. "Dig in Tristan, don't let it go cold," I add. I'm so used to eating on my own that I don't think anything of it as I munch away without any conversation until Tristan's chuckling brings my attention back.

"What?" I ask feeling as though I'm blushing.

"I just had a flashback of you eating that muffin," he chuckles, filling his fork back up again.

"I was mortified you caught me," I confess, cringing inside that he's brought that up.

"I know you were, that was half the fun of it." His eyes twinkle wickedly.

"Tristan!" I scold.

"I know it's bad, right?" He chortles.

"I'll get you back." I gripe sulkily.

"Doubt it." He answers, his eyes sparkling some more. I have to smile back. It feels as though the moment I see his smile, my face automatically reacts and smiles along with him…

WE LAUGH, TEASE AND talk our way right through dinner, the time actually flies by. What felt like five minutes was actually an hour.

"Want to put this film on?" Tristan asks pouring us both more wine. I feel so content, full belly, no nose pain, and a gorgeous man named Tristan to ogle at for the rest of the night.

"I'm not fussed," I say dreamily, taking another sip.

"Good. Because I have a surprise for you." Tristan gets up and switches the oven back on. *More food?*

"Tristan, what are you doing?"

"Oh, you know in the supermarket we were comparing puddings?"

"Err…yeah," I say sceptically.

"Well I snuck one in," he says, grinning like a naughty schoolboy.

"Tristan," I moan. "Seriously?" I sigh heavily in resignation. "Healthy diet, window gone," I grumble, then I narrow my eyes at him. "You're not pulling a Gladys on me are you?" I question.

"What's a Gladys?" he says sneaking something into the oven.

"She's always saying that I'm skinny, but I don't think I am, do you?"

Tristan shakes his head at me. "It wouldn't bother me what weight you were Coral," he says, sitting down opposite me.

"That's not an answer." I huff, feeling annoyed.

"Ok, I think you look amazing as you are. If you lost

weight, I would be worried you had an eating disorder, if you gained weight it wouldn't make any difference to how I feel about you. But you probably do look very slim to Gladys, she's pretty plump." He says cheekily.

"Not as plump as she was," I mumble to myself. "So you bought a pudding to surprise me, not fatten me up?" I finally let the grin spread across my face.

"Precisely," he says sipping more wine. "Happens to be my favourite too you know. It's was my Grandmothers speciality," he says smacking his lips together – *I wish he wouldn't do that, they already look tantalisingly good!*

We gaze at one another, the atmosphere charging with electricity again. Tristan leans forward and takes my hand.

"So is it safe to say I can ask you out on a date?" I frown. "Is that a no?" He smiles cheekily, his dimples deepening.

"No, it's not a no. I just hate that word." I grumble.

"What word?" He asks, cocking his head to the side.

"Date," I say taking a gulp of wine. "It has so many hidden implications," I sigh.

Tristan frowns. "I really want to wine and dine you Coral, spoil you rotten."

I lean back, take my hand out of his and run it through my hair. "I don't need you to do that," I argue.

"Then what do you need Coral?" He asks his expression serious.

"Tristan, I think we're past all that kind of stuff...I think it's quite evident how we both feel." I frown even harder, hearing myself say that out loud is weird.

"Tell me what you want?" He says huskily.

"This is nice," I whisper placing my hand back in his.

Tristan's eyes darken as he rubs his thumb over the top of my hand. "Yes, it is," he agrees. The oven chimes again, pulling us both out of the little bubble that seems to surround us...

CHAPTER TWENTY-FOUR

I AM SAT BLOWING COLD air onto my steaming bread and butter pudding. I really want to dig in, but it's just too hot.
"Your turn," I say to Tristan.
"My turn?" He questions.
"Yes, tell me about your upbringing and your Grandparents."
Tristan shrugs. "There's not much to say really." I roll my eyes, but I can see it's not really something he can easily discuss. *Tough!*
"Ok, I'll help. Where were you raised?" I ask cheerily.
"Maidenhead," he replies.
"Ooh, very nice," I answer playfully.
"You?" I cock one eyebrow up at him. "I mean before you came here," he adds.
"Somerset," I grumble.
"Ever been back?" he questions. I decide not to answer that one.
"Hey, this is meant to be my twenty questions," I argue, Tristan grins. I can see what game he's playing, but it won't work. "So did you go to your Grandparents, or did they relocate for you?"
"No, they had lived in Maidenhead all their life, so it was logical for me to stay with them." I nod as I listen to his reply.
"So how old were your Grandparents when you went to live with them?"
"Granny was fifty, Gramps was fifty-five."
I shake my head in amazement. "I bet they didn't think they'd be doing it all over again at their age." Then I realise how

awful that sounded. "Sorry," I whisper. "That didn't come out right." I scowl in frustration at myself.

"It's ok," he frowns. "It hit them pretty hard when my mother died, of course, I was a newborn, I had no idea. But they said having me, helped them both deal with it. You know lost a child gained a grandson." I nod solemnly.

"So what was it like being raised by the previous generation?"

"Good mostly, they were very kind, patient people." I can tell it's still painful for him to talk about them, I can see it in his face, although he's hiding it well.

"Tristan, I'm sorry, this must still feel so raw to you. We can talk about something else?" I offer feeling guilty.

"No, no, it's ok really. I miss them, but I also like remembering them too. You can ask me questions about them." He prompts.

I smile tentatively at him and continue. "What was it like growing up an only child?"

"That was difficult at times, but again my Grandparents were really open, honest people, they didn't hide anything. They would talk about their past, their mistakes. So if I got something wrong, or I didn't know how to deal with something, they were always there for me with open arms, they never judged me."

"They sound like they were awesome," I say smiling as I do. Then I frown wishing I'd had that kind of start in life.

"With that kind of stuff they were," he says trying to hide something, but I'm getting to know him better, I can see through his facade.

"So what were the negatives Tristan, there has to be some?"

"There were, but they weren't bad enough to make it, so my childhood seemed traumatised." He bites – *Was that a dig at me? Ouch, that hurt!*

"Damn it Coral, I didn't mean…" Tristan sighs heavily and runs a hand through his hair. "I…I was bullied….a lot." He picks up his wine and takes a large gulp.

"You were?" I squeak in surprise, he's such a tall, big, manly man. I can't imagine him ever being bullied.

"Yes, until Gramps found out and he taught me to box." He adds, grinning widely.

That's it! – I knew it! I knew there was something else there, something I couldn't put my finger on. And now I know. I instantly feel even more protected, if that's possible. I was right; Tristan can look after himself, which means me too.

"Ok, back up why were you bullied?"

"Boys will be boys," he answers, then takes a spoonful of pudding and eats it.

"What, you went to a boy's school?" Tristan nods. "So did you get the bully back?" I grin hoping he'll say yes. I hate bullies. I take a spoonful of pudding too.

"Oh yeah, he never came after me again, and neither did his mates. I was so mad and so tired of all their bullshit." Tristan scoops some more pudding.

"What bullshit?" I take another spoonful.

"Kids are kids, right? Whatever they can take the piss out of they do, so they took the piss out of the fact that my parents were old, they took the piss out of my clothes' – "What was wrong with your clothes?" I squeak, my spoon frozen in midair.

"They were awful, second hand and definitely not in fashion."

"Oh." I frown trying to understand him, what he went through.

Tristan continues. "I was one of those quiet kids, you know. I didn't cause trouble, I paid attention in class, but I was a loner, always have been, I guess I always will be. I didn't really feel the need for friends, so I guess that made me a sitting duck because I wasn't like them. They needed each other for validation, but I didn't need anyone but my folks. Besides what good were friends that bully you, make you feel like shit, to me that's not a friend."

I look down at the table, trying to imagine what that felt like as a kid. "What else did they bully you about?" I nervously ask.

Tristan sighs. "Clothes, shoes, bag, coat, pencil case, you name it they took the piss out of it."

"Why?" I question, trying to understand.

Tristan shrugs. "We didn't have much money." I can tell there's more there, but I decide to leave it be.

"That sucks," I say frowning hard.

"Yeah, but I kind of didn't care." Tristan eats more pudding.

"Why?" I eat more too.

"Because I knew I had better parents than them."

"How did you know that?"

"Because I was…happy," he says simply.
"And they weren't?" I conclude.
"Nope, the leader, his Dad was…" Tristan trails off and looks down at his pudding.
"Was what?" I ask totally enthralled in his story.
"An alcoholic," he answers still looking at his pudding.
I sigh heavily. "Yeah…I guess there are a lot of parents around like that," I say bitterly. We both eat more pudding, but I want to know more, so I chew quickly and swallow, Tristan's on a roll I want to keep him going.
"So his Dad was a drunk? Bet he was having a hard time at home." I muse.
"You on the bullies side now?" I look up from my pudding, Tristan is stony-faced.
"No, of course not," I gripe. "I just…never mind," I say shaking my head. "So what about the other kids?"
Tristan shrugs. "I don't know, I could just tell the other kids didn't have it easy either. It was a tough school you know, working class kids, rough parents. I don't think any of them made anything of themselves."
"Except you," I say proudly.
"In the business world, yes," he grins. I frown at him. "I got expelled," he chuckles.
"Expelled?" I gasp. "Well that makes two of us," I add, wondering how much more stuff is going to come up where Tristan and I seem identical.
"You…expelled," he chuckles.
"Um…yeah, I kind of had anger issues." Tristan loses his grin. "Anyway enough about me, you were expelled for fighting I presume?"
"Yes, well that's how they saw it. Gramps saw it differently, of course, he went to the education board, they agreed to allow me be homeschooled. Gran was my tutor." I throw down my spoon. "What's wrong?" He asks his spoon halfway to his mouth.
"Nothing, it's just weird how many similarities we seem to have. Gladys homeschooled me." I tell him.
"Ah," Tristan eats more pudding.
"What age for you?" I ask totally intrigued.
"Nine."
I gasp aloud. "You were nine?"

"Um...yeah, you?" Tristan doesn't understand my surprise.

"Fourteen, I did the last year at home."

"Wow."

"Yeah." We sit silently for a while, enjoying our puddings. "Did you like it, studying from home?" I ask.

"Yeah I did, no more crap from other kids. But I got a little lonesome sometimes, for company my own age I mean."

"Like a buddy to go hang around the woods with, or go on a bike ride with?"

Tristan shakes his head at me. "There weren't any woods, and I didn't have a bike."

"Well, what did you have?" I ask.

Tristan sighs. "See this is what most people can't get their head around' *Most people?* 'All those things that you're talking about are material possessions right?"

"Yeah?" I say hesitantly.

"Well I was raised to understand from a very early age that it means nothing, sure it's nice to have things, but to put anything like that against a loved one, was, well...shallow."

"It's not shallow to want a bike when you're a kid Tristan," I argue.

"I know that, but I didn't feel the need for one."

"Why not?" *This is weird.*

"I just didn't. I wasn't like other kids Coral. I hadn't been brought up that way. I mean, I get what you're saying - Didn't I ever want to play? Yeah course I did, and when I wanted to I did, with my dog, we'd play in the garden for hours." Tristan looks frustrated. "Look, I was always with either Grandparent. At weekends I'd either be learning how to cook or get a coal fire going with Gran, or I'd be learning with Gramps how to make things like chairs and cupboards and..." he trails off and stares into space.

"He was a carpenter?" I ask calmly.

"Yes." His answer is clipped, he seems pissed?

"And your Gran, did she work?"

"No, she wanted to be a housewife." Another clipped answer.

"I'm sorry Tristan. I wasn't knocking you or the way you were raised, just trying to get in your head, so I know how you feel, that's all."

"Know the feeling," he retorts with sarcasm.

I sigh heavily. *Why are we arguing?*

"What was your dog's name?" I ask brightly.

"Max."

"What kind of dog was he?"

"Border Collie."

"They're cute and really intelligent, right?"

"Yep." Tristan seems to have withdrawn into himself, I don't understand it at all.

"You know, I understand my reasons for clamming up about my past, but I don't understand yours?"

"Nobody gets it that's why, and I always get *'the look'* it's very annoying." I tense up feeling the frustration rolling off Tristan.

"Am I giving you the look?" I ask sullenly.

Our eyes finally meet after what seems like a long time, Tristan silently shakes his head at me, and I don't know why, but I get up from my chair and walk round to him.

"Turn around," I say. Tristan moves so his legs are in front of him, I take a seat on his lap and wrap my hands around his neck, his arms slowly snake their way around my waist.

"I think it's beautiful the way you were raised because it's made you who you are today. And who you are right now....it's almost as though it's all pre-ordained. Like I was meant to go through what I went through, and you were raised like that, so one day when we met, and we would be perfect for each other. I love that you are who you are. You're the only straight guy I've ever…felt…" I trail off, then I go into a mini panic. I just used the word, Love. *Fuck!*

"I think what I'm trying to say is that your upbringing turned you into a great man, a really wonderful, kind, loving man. The kind that's perfect for me…" *Breathe Coral.*

"None of my exes thought that," Tristan says, surprising me again. "And I'm far from perfect," he adds glumly.

"Well, I'm glad they thought that because it means I get to have you." *Am I really saying this?*

"Well according to my exes I'm boring, predictable…oh and too nice." He says. I see the sadness in his eyes, buried deep inside.

"I'm sorry Tristan, but that's bullshit. If anyone's boring, it's me." I scoff.

"Believe me Coral, you are the opposite of boring." He says gazing up at me.

I close my eyes for a second then lean my forehead against his. "Well, just for the record, you are not boring or predictable. You're dependable and sweet and charming and well-mannered, which I love. And as for being too nice, that's just crap...you really must have dated some hard-hearted bitches, who evidently wanted to get themselves hooked up with some shallow, vain, bad-boy that would treat them like crap."

I open my eyes and take a deep breath, exhaling slowly after my little rant.

Tristan smiles warmly at me. "I think you have more to offer than you could ever imagine Coral, but that's probably because you don't seem to see yourself very clearly – or think you're worthy." He adds. *Whoa! Nail on the head Tristan.*

I take a deep, ragged breath. *What am I doing?*

"You know, I never thought I would meet someone like you, maybe it's the age difference, I don't know? The point is, I love that you have all those qualities and more. I will always know where I stand with you. There's no pretence, no bullshit, no secrets. You're a straight up guy Tristan, and for me, that's like a dream come true..." I gaze down at his lips. "I'm glad all those women let you go," I say breathlessly.

He's seeing straight through me again. I can feel the pull resonating from him, my heart is hammering, my stomach is swarming with butterflies, and my soul feels like it's just expanded a thousandfold.

"You know I'm in love with you don't you," Tristan says his voice all low and husky.

My mouth pops open in shock. Did he really just say that? I scowl at him. He can't be, we don't know each other. *This is weird.*

Tristan shakes his head. "I know that sounds odd, coming from someone you hardly know, but I felt it the moment we met. There isn't anything in the world I wouldn't do for you, whatever you want, it is yours."

Holy fuck! I let out a raspy breath, lean my forehead against his, and close my eyes. I feel his hands make their way through my hair, his thumbs stroking my cheeks, and at that moment I know I have to tell him, I have to let him know. I pull my head up from his and open my eyes.

"I'm warning you, Tristan, I don't really know how to be close to you…I don't even know if I can be…intimate." I say, my voice sounding raspy and breathless.

Tristan closes his eyes and exhales slowly. "Coral, don't you know?" he whispers huskily, opening his eyes as he does. "Just being with you is enough – more than enough. I want to be your man baby, you just have to say yes, and I'll show you, I'll show you how you can build trust with me, how I'll protect you. We can take this really slow, day by day. I'm yours," he adds, gently stroking my hair as he does.

I place my hand against his cheek. This feels so deep already, it's really scaring me.

"Hey," Tristan lifts my chin. "I don't want to frighten you off. Did I just do that?" He questions.

"Kind of…" I whisper, trying to pull my gaze away from his.

"Shit!" Tristan runs his hand through his hair in frustration.

I instantly feel bad, I'm sat on his lap telling him how great he is, which he is, and then I'm half running out the door when he declares himself to me – *Fuck it!* – I have to stop all this bullshit.

I place my other hand against his cheek, run my thumb across his bottom lip and stare down at his parted lips. I will be brave. I will kiss this man and see once and for all, if I can really do this, the moment is just too beautiful to pass by.

I lean down, my lips inches from his – "Hello?" *Knock, knock, knock.*

"You have got to be kidding me," I hiss. "It's Gladys," I add gritting my teeth. Tristan nods, understanding that like it or not, she will be coming in.

I feel myself deflate like a balloon. I get up from his lap, walk over to the door, pull the curtain across and open the door to Gladys and Malcolm.

"Ooh, do I smell Roast Dinner?" She slurs, leaning in to kiss my cheek. *Oh great!* She's tipsy, which means she'll have her talkative head on. *They'll be here all night long!*

"Yes," I sigh, smiling tentatively at Malcolm. "Hi, Malcolm."

"Hello Coral." He leans down and kisses my cheek as they

both walk in. Gladys stops in her tracks as she notices Tristan standing to his feet.

"Oh! I didn't think you'd have company?" Gladys says looking at me, and then Tristan in total surprise.

"Hello, Gladys," Tristan says, leaning in he kisses her cheek then shakes Malcolm's hand.

I close the door and walk over to the kitchenette. "Would you like a glass of wine or coffee' – "Ooh wine please." Gladys interrupts me plonking herself down on the sofa.

"Malcolm?" I ask as I give Gladys a small glass of wine.

"Coffee thank you Coral. How are you feeling?" I smile at Malcolm, how sweet of him to ask.

"Much better thank you, I've been in very good hands." I smile shyly at Tristan, he smiles shyly back at me, in fact, I think he looks a little uncomfortable.

"That's good to hear, although your nose still looks very sore," he adds.

"It's getting better. Did you have a nice time with your daughters?" I hand him his coffee as he sits next to Gladys. Malcolm briefly tells me about his daughters, their husbands and their children, so he's a Grandpa too!

I pick up my wine and sit next to Gladys. I'm trying not to glare at her, even though I want to have it out with her as to why she didn't tell me about Malcolm when she told Debs. Tristan makes his way over, and sits next to me on the arm of the sofa, I love that he wants to do that, be so close to me.

"So, what have you two been doing today?" Gladys slurs. I go to answer, but Tristan beats me to it and launches into an animated story about our day. Gladys is mesmerised, blinking rapidly as she watches Tristan – *So it's not just me.*

"Tristan, I have to say thank you again for looking after Coral so well," she says hugging and kissing me, Malcolm narrows his eyes at my uncomfortable reaction.

"Tristan, I have a business question, would you mind?" Malcolm says, and gestures for Tristan to follow him.

Tristan looks surprised. "Not at all," he says, and they walk over to the patio door. *Subtle Malcolm, very subtle!* – They begin chatting away, so I use it as my opportunity to probe Gladys.

"So Debs came round today," I casually say.

"Oh, how lovely, you two rarely see each other anymore."

"Kind of difficult when she's got a kid and a husband to look after," I bite. "Which reminds me, she let it slip that she already knew about Malcolm," I add.

Gladys's face falls, I can see she's trying hard to hide her true feelings, to put a mask on.

"So you want to tell me why she knew and I didn't?" I ask. Gladys is silent. "Mom," I say, using that word feels wrong. "I'm really upset she knew, and I didn't," I add softly, I don't want to upset her, but she needs to know what she did was wrong.

Gladys takes hold of my hand and squeezes it. "I'm sorry darling…it's just…well you don't take too well to change," she says.

"I know that, but just because you started seeing someone doesn't mean everything has to change," I answer. A guilty look appears on her face. "And now I know Debs is selling up too, you both are. Is there something else I don't know about?" I ask just as I did with Debs.

"No, no…o-of course not," she stutters looking totally uncomfortable, which just confirms there is.

"Please Mom, tell me," I whisper. "I won't freak out," I add.

Our eyes meet, and I know in that instance I am right. Something big is going down, and I don't know about it, she's having the exact same reaction as Debs.

"Oh, darling it's lovely hearing you call me that," she squeaks. "Anyway how about you and Tristan?" she whispers so he can't hear, and totally changing the subject. "He's a real dish darling, you've done very well there. Are you going to start seeing each other?" she asks.

I sigh heavily, she's not going to tell me. "Yeah…" I answer glumly.

"Oh that's wonderful dear," she beams enthusiastically.

"Yeah…he's really…" I can't think of the right word to describe who he is to me.

My anchor, my north, my south.

In such a short space of time, he's become my home.

"Well, you just be sure to take care of him. Men need looking after just as much as us girls," she tells me. I nod silently in response.

Gladys drains the rest of her wine and stands up. "Well, we'd better be off," she says nervously.

I frown deeply at her odd behaviour and look across at Tristan, the moment our eyes meet he frowns too, he knows something's up.

"Already darling, but we've only just got here?" Malcolm argues.

"Malcolm!" Gladys warns. "I'm tired, please take me home."

Malcolm blushes a little. "Of course darling." He places his coffee in the kitchen sink and walks over to me, holding his hands out to me, I use them to pull up off the sofa.

"Thanks." I squeak.

"Bye Coral," he says kissing me on the cheek again. "Sorry, it was such a short visit."

I try to smile at him. "Don't worry about it," I mumble.

Tristan comes and stands next to me, placing his arms around my waist as he does. It feels so good that he's here next to me.

"Bye darling," Gladys gushes kissing me on the cheek. I show no enthusiasm. Malcolm looks confused from me to Gladys to Tristan. "Nice to see you again Tristan," she beams kissing him on both cheeks. "Look after that daughter of mine," she adds.

"I fully intend to," he offers and shakes Malcolm's hand again.

We walk the few steps to the patio door, Tristan pulls it open and lets them out, they both wave, then turn and walk out of view. I try to control the anger I feel rearing up inside of me.

So, to try and take my mind off it I decide to clean the kitchen up. As Tristan shuts the door, locks it and pulls the curtain back across, I'm already at the kitchen rinsing everything off before I start washing up.

"Hey," I feel Tristan behind me. His arms wrap around my waist, his head rests on my shoulder. "You want to talk about it?"

I shake my head rapidly. "I....not now," I answer my voice wobbling with anger.

"Coral, it's not good to bottle things up' – "Tristan please, I'm trying really hard to use all the techniques I've learned in therapy, so I don't let the anger take over. Please give me some space, let me calm down." I beg.

"Oh ok," he says. "Shall I dry?" I know he's smiling.

I stop what I'm doing and turn my head around, I can't help smiling back at him.

"How about some music?" I say.

"Ok," he chuckles.

"My MP3 player is on the side, next to the amp." I gesture with my chin.

As I'm filling the sink with hot soapy water, UB40s Can't help falling in Love starts playing. It instantly lifts me. *I wonder if Tristan picked this one on purpose?*

Tristan is back just as I've washed the first plate up.

"Tea towels?" he asks.

I point to the cupboard next to me, I watch him bend down and pull out a clean one. I can see all the muscles in his back ripple through his t-shirt. It sends shock waves down to my nether regions, I clamp my legs together and try to ignore it.

"You like reggae?" Tristan asks taking the plate from me, but my mind is already undressing him. Kissing him all over and wondering what he will taste like, and whether he will fit me like a glove; like he was made for me.

"Coral?" He prompts.

"Hmm?" I turn and lock eyes with him.

"You ok?" he chuckles.

"Uh-huh." I can't seem to make my brain work properly.

"Reggae?" he asks again.

"Oh right, yeah...I really like it," I answer dreamily...

IT DOESN'T TAKE LONG to clean up the kitchen, and as I check myself, I notice my anger at Gladys has completely dissipated. Tristan must be some kind of drug to me or something. I think I'm getting very, very addicted.

"So what would you like to do now?" he asks. *Oh boy!*

I wish he hadn't just asked that question. How about I'd like to rip your clothes off and make passionate love to you? But I know I look hideous at the moment and I want it to be right, to be special.

"Coral." Tristan takes my face in his hands. "Where are you?"

I clear my throat and try to settle my rapidly beating heart.

"Sorry...I just..." I smile up at him. The room fills with that same bubble of electricity. I feel the pull from him, so I lean up on my tip toes so I can reach his lips.

Tap, tap, tap – Who the fuck is it now?

"I'll get it," I say gritting my teeth. As I pull the curtain across I, see it's Bob with his empty plate. "Hey Bob," I say as I open the door.

"Delicious as usual Coral, just like you," he croons.

I smile shyly and take the empty plate off him. "You want to come in?" I ask.

He shakes his head at me. "No thanks, I've got Top-Gear recorded," he says his eyes twinkling.

"Oh ok, enjoy," I smile. Bob leans forward, and for the first time ever, he pecks me on the cheek. "Aren't I the lucky girl," I giggle. His cheeks blush as he smiles back at me, then he clocks Tristan inside and narrows his eyes.

"Looks like I've got some competition," he croaks.

I glance at Tristan and raise my eyebrows, trying my best not to burst into a fit of giggles.

"I think you may have Bob, but don't worry you'll always be my favourite," I say squeezing his wrinkly hand. Bob looks back at me in the most peculiar way. I think he is actually serious, and in fairness, if Bob was my age I think I would be hard-pressed to ignore him. He was a real dish in his younger days. "Want me to get you anything?" I ask.

"No darling you've done enough," he smiles and walks off. I watch him get inside his studio, then I shut the patio door, and pull the curtains across.

"I think he's in love with you." Tristan pipes up.

"Don't be daft." I choke, laughing nervously.

"I'm dead serious," he argues.

My face falls, all humour instantly dissipating within me.

"Are you kidding me?" I squeak, suddenly wondering if I've actually been leading a lonely old man on. I run my hands through my hair. "Do you think I need to have a talk with him?" I ask.

"I'd leave it as it is," Tristan answers. "Maybe having the fantasy of you is what's keeping him going."

I frown at that one, pick up my wine glass and finish it off. "More?" I ask Tristan.

"I'll get it. We still have time for the movie, how about

some popcorn to go with it?" He smiles, but it's a little off. So he wants to watch the movie with popcorn? Boy, I'm going to feel bloated tomorrow, nothing but salad.

"You ok?" I ask as I put the bag in the microwave.

"You really meant it didn't you, about not liking yourself." Tristan is frowning deeply as he fills up our glasses.

I feel myself close up, shut down - withdraw. I shrug my shoulders at him.

"You should see yourself more clearly," he adds.

I glance across at him then find my big bowl out of the cupboard for the popcorn. As we both sit down on the sofa, I feel myself tense up, and I don't know why.

"Coral, relax, you want to talk about what went on earlier?" He softly asks.

I nod, feeling glad I have someone to talk it out with.

"Debs is leaving, her house is up for sale, and she didn't tell me, and she knew about Malcolm ages ago. I asked Gladys why she didn't tell me, but she avoided the subject. I asked them both if there's something else going on, they didn't deny or confirm it. I know they are both hiding something, I just don't know what. And with everything else going on, Joyce leaving, my job, Rob not talking to me, the last thing I need is to find out my own family are..." I stop so I don't burst into tears. "I'm so glad you're here Tristan, and I'm not just saying that because I feel lonely," I exhale heavily. "Weird really, it's like all this crap happened just as you turned up...Shit, that sounds bad, I mean' – I shake my head – 'I don't know what the fuck I mean." I blurt running my hands through my hair in frustration.

"Hey," Tristan rubs my back. "I'm glad I'm here too," he tells me softly.

I turn and look into his deep soulful eyes. "Sorry, what I meant was, it's like you turned up at the right time, to be here for me while all this is going on. Does that make any sense?"

"Yes it does," he chuckles then leans closer and wraps his arm around my shoulder.

"I'd be freaking out if you weren't here, I know I would," I mumble.

"I don't think you would be," Tristan argues.

"Oh I would, you might not see it on the outside but'- I tap my head - 'on the inside I'd be cracking up."

Tristan sighs heavily. "Who do you go to when you're upset or worried about something?"

"It used to be Gladys, then I met Rob," I answer immediately.

"So if he were around to talk to, you would be ok about everything else?"

"Maybe, Rob helps me. He says I take life too seriously. He helps me look at life from a different perspective and helps calm my wayward thoughts." Tristan smiles so deeply his dimples are on full wattage, he cocks his head to the side as though he's worked something out.

"What?" I mumble.

"That night at Iguana's, you were with Rob?"

"Yeah?" I frown wondering where he's going with this.

"And you told me you don't normally go out drinking on a weeknight?"

"Yeah?"

"Oh to be a fly on the wall and hear what *that* conversation was about, but I have a pretty good idea," he says smugly.

"Well, a fly in a restaurant is not a good idea," I answer dryly hoping he doesn't ask me.

Tristan chuckles hard. "You did not know where to put yourself when I turned up."

I sigh, caught out. "No, I didn't," I answer taking a gulp of wine.

Tristan stops laughing and moves so close to me, I can feel his breath on my cheek. "You were discussing me," he whispers in my ear. My heart starts manically beating. "I knew you felt it too, that moment when we met in reception," he adds.

I slowly turn and meet his heated gaze, it's deep and so soulful. His eyes have dilated, his cheeks are flushed, his breathing heavy, and he's radiating sexiness.

"Yes," I whisper my breathing just as hard.

Tristan leans forward, I think he's going to kiss me, my mouth instantly goes dry, he's so close – "What happened to you Coral?" I frown back at him. "In the car, you told me you find men creepy. I can understand you being the way you are because of your parents and their complete lack of care for you. But something else happened, what is it?" I clam up inside. "Coral!" He admonishes.

I slowly turn away from him trying to keep as calm as

possible. "I c-can't..." I look back at him. "Tristan I...it's really not something I want to..." I sigh heavily. "I'm not even sure if I will ever tell you, I just don't know," I add.

"I wish you would, was it your Dad? Did he beat you' –
"Stop!" I place my finger over his lips. "I don't want retribution, it happened, and there's nothing I can do about it except live my life to the fullest, the best way I can." Tristan glares back at me.

"I mean it, Tristan. This may sound strange to you but..." I take a deep breath, I'm not even sure if I want to tell him. Whenever I think of what happened to me, I think Karma, what goes around comes around. I'm pretty sure those people that did those things to me will get their comeuppance, someday.

"Tell me Coral, what are you thinking?" He asks running his fingers through my hair.

"Karma," I whisper, staring straight ahead.

"Karma?"

"Uh-huh." Tristan pulls on my chin, so I have to turn and look at him.

"Karma, you believe in it?" I nod silently. Tristan stares blankly ahead. "What goes around comes around," he mumbles to himself, then turns his penetrating gaze on me. "What else do you believe in?" His face is unreadable, so I decide to go on.

"Spirit, the universe, that we are all connected," I whisper feeling silly for sharing my beliefs with him - I've never shared them with anyone.

"I like that." He says brushing his thumb across my bottom lip. "Can you teach me?" he asks.

"Um...well, I can give you books to read. I think you have to come to your own conclusion about what it all means to you." I answer feeling as though I'm blushing.

Tristan smiles his deep dimpled smile. "I'd like that." He takes my hand in his and kisses it. And I don't know why, but I feel as though I want a really long hug.

"Will you do something for me?" I whisper.

"Anything," he answers in his husky voice. I put down my wine and stand up giving him my hand as I do, Tristan takes hold of it. I pull him to his feet, then fling my arms around him and squeeze him tight, my head resting against his beating heart.

"Is this what you want?" He asks sounding a little confused.

"Yes," I whisper.

Tristan's arms envelop me, and I sink into the peacefulness of the feeling. I feel safe, secure and so content. I wish I could stay like this forever, it feels so wonderful. I notice the music is still playing in the background and that it has flipped onto the next album. Dionne Warwick's This Girl's In Love With You is playing, it's one of the old mixed tapes that I transferred to my player. It's been years since I've listened to it.

"This is a favourite track of mine," Tristan softly says. I look up at him. "Well the Herb Alpert one, you know...the guy in love..." He smiles.

I nod, knowing the song. "Let me guess, your Grandpa?"

"Yep, big fan."

"Yeah, Gladys likes Dionne, kind of gets you into it, doesn't it?"

"It does indeed." Tristan pulls away from me, and I am momentarily gutted until he holds out his hands to me. "Dance with me?" He asks.

"Here?" I question, blinking up at him.

"Yes." He has his hands held out waiting for me.

"What old style?" I squeak.

"Yes." His face is dead serious.

"I-I...don't know how to do that," I whisper.

"I'll show you." He says. Tristan takes my left hand and places it on his right shoulder, then wrapping his right arm around my waist, he pulls me in so that our bodies are touching. He clutches my right hand with his and places them against his chest. Then he gazes down at me and starts to slowly move us around my tiny studio. *Whoa!*

Tristan moves with grace and such fluid movements that it's evident he's done this before and does it very, very well.

"You've done this before," I say dreamily.

"Yes," he croaks huskily. "My Grandparents went to a dancing club every Wednesday and Saturday evening, I went along with them."

"Oh that explains it," I answer as Tristan twirls us around some more. "Why do you think people stopped dancing like this? It's really nice."

"I don't know. Maybe the music changed, so it changed people styles."

"I like the old way, men taking women out dancing, I bet it used to be really fun."

"It was also a great way for men to check out the women they were dancing with," Tristan adds.

"How?" I question.

"Well....you know," Tristan smiles shyly. "My Gramps told me it was a way of checking out a woman's figure," he grins cheekily.

"Ah," the penny drops. "I suppose it was. And if I were in a dress like back then, what would you be surmising right now?" I tease flirtatiously.

"I'd be thinking I was the luckiest man on the planet, and I'd be thinking of all different ways to impress you, so you would say yes to another date." His dimples go to full wattage as we grin widely at one another.

"Good answer," I say.

"It was, wasn't it," he says, his cheeky grin appearing.

I chuckle and shake my head at his reply. The next song comes on, Ray Charles, You don't know me. It's one of my all-time favourites. Tristan stops moving and stares down at me, his expression intense.

"How is it that all the songs I like, you have?" He asks moving us around again.

"You know this one?" I ask incredulously.

"Ray Charles is one of my favourite singers," he tells me.

"And this song?"

"It's what I heard playing in my head when you came walking into reception, then all through the meeting, and when I drove back to the hotel."

I gasp in awe. "You did?"

Tristan nods solemnly at me.

"Tristan," I whisper placing my head under his chin. "Don't ever leave me," I whisper so quietly I'm not even sure he heard me. I close my eyes to my own words, feeling the power of them and the enormous effect Tristan has over me.

"Not a chance in hell," he whispers back. *So he heard me!*

I open my eyes again and stare up at this amazing man that has entered my life like a whirlwind. A powerfully profound urge to kiss him overtakes me again. I lean up onto my tip-toes, entwine my fingers through his hair and lean into him.

Tristan tentatively leans down, and his lips finally reach mine. He kisses me gently, carefully, and his lips are just as soft as I imagined they would be, but something is happening to me, I feel like I'm on fire.

Desire explodes inside me, desire for this amazing man.

Tristan has ignited a flame that is now burning so intensely, that I don't think twice about my actions, all rational thoughts have disappeared.

I jump up and wrap my legs around him, forcing his lips apart so I can taste his tongue, kissing him with all the passion and fire that's been burning up inside of me. Our lips mesh together in perfect symmetry, as our tongues lash against one another in heated passion. Tristan moans a deep sound of longing, which makes me whimper out loud, I want him so badly, but I know I need to be careful, I don't want him to think the obvious is going to happen.

As we continue to kiss with heated passion, our tongues lashing and probing against one another, my nose suddenly starts throbbing angrily at me. I think I must have bumped it as I got lost in the moment.

"Ow! ow...ow!!" I moan and gently slide down his body, his hands gently gripping me, keeping me balanced. I reach my hand up to my nose to try and protect it, but I can't see as my eyes have filled with watery tears – *God damn it!*

"Oh, baby." Tristan wipes the tears away that are rolling down my cheeks.

"Sorry," I whisper keeping my eyes closed so I can try and concentrate on pushing away the pain.

"Don't be, come, sit down Coral." He gently ushers me to the sofa, I carefully sit down. I hear Tristan walk away, then I hear the tap running, within a moment he is back.

"Open your eyes baby," he softly says. As I do, I notice him crouched in front of me with a folded tea-towel in his hands. "Here," he places the cold towel gently across my nose. "Keep it there I'll get you some painkillers."

As I watch Tristan walk away, I notice he's trying to hide his erection. I try not to chuckle.

"What's funny?" He says as he re-appears in front of me with the tablets and a glass of water.

"Nothing," I say trying my best to hide my smile. Downing

the tablets with the water, I lean back on the cushion, close my eyes and wait for the throbbing to settle down. "I think I caught my nose there," I tell him.

"Yeah...I think you did." I can hear he sounds concerned.

"Maybe I bashed it on your erection." I chuckle to lighten the mood.

"Shit!" He hisses. I chuckle even harder and open my eyes. Tristan looks mortified, I stop laughing. "Tristan, it was a joke." I admonish.

"It was just a kiss, I should have had more control," he barks, condemning himself.

"Er...no you shouldn't, I think we can safely say that was definitely more than a kiss." I'm really trying not to laugh. I grab hold of his t-shirt and pull him down to me, then kiss him on the lips. "That was just a kiss," I titter. "There was a bit of a difference, don't you think?"

Finally, he relents, his shoulders relax, his eyes crinkle at the corners, and his lips twitch trying to hide the smile. "Admit it, that was a funny joke," I giggle.

Tristan finally chuckles too. "Very funny," he chortles leaning his body against mine and kissing me gently on the lips again. "Sorry about that, I freaked out there for a second. I just don't want you to think you have to, or that that's all I'm after, or' – "Tristan shut up," I chuckle. "You couldn't be more gentlemanly if you tried, that was passion, it happens," I say, my eyebrows raised in amusement.

"Well no more for now," he tells me. "I don't want you in pain," he adds authoritatively.

"Me neither," I agree my nose pounding again.

"Right then, the movie it is." Tristan stands and switches the music off, just as Ruby Turner starts singing Stay With Me Baby.

I pick up the controllers, find the movie and purchase it. Tristan leans back into the sofa and pulls me into him. I rest my head on his shoulder, and that same peaceful feeling swells inside me. So much so, that I have to fight back the urge to cry. But I have another feeling, one that's just as strong, and it's screaming at me to end this, to never see this man again. Because it will, inevitably, go wrong. And I know I won't survive that, my stomach churns.

I look up at Tristan and sigh inwardly. *What am I getting myself into?* I close my eyes and push the negative feelings aside, then I snuggle closer to him.

How can I let him go? I've finally found the answer to the empty ache I've always had, I know it, I feel it.

He is here. I finally found my home...

CHAPTER TWENTY-FIVE

I WAKE FROM THE MOST peaceful sleep, surprised to find I'm in my bed. Then I hear soft breathing next to me, I panic for a moment and turn my head only to find Tristan fully clothed, sleeping next to me. I can't help the smile that spreads across my face. I think I could stare at him forever and never get bored of his beautiful face.

His long eyelashes are gently resting against his lower lids making him look cute and sexy at the same time. I want to stroke his eyebrows, his cheeks, his full lips, but I stop myself, I don't want to wake him – besides my bladder is protesting.

I slip out of bed as quietly as I can and tip-toe down the stairs, as I'm making my way to the bathroom, I can't help thinking how rapidly life is changing for me and how good it feels to have Tristan in it.

Once I'm done, and I'm washing my hands at the sink I stare up at myself. My nose looks better, the bruising under my eyes has almost disappeared, all that's left is very slight yellow markings. *Thank-god for that!*

I sleepily make my way back up the stairs, trying not to make them creak, but as I reach the bedroom, I see Tristan is wide awake watching me.

"Hey," I whisper. "I didn't mean to wake you." I climb back into bed facing Tristan.

"You fell asleep, missed the end of the film." He tells me as he strokes my cheek.

"You put me to bed?" I stare at his lovely sleepy eyes.

"Um...yeah," Tristan frowns.

"It's ok, I could get used to this," I say snuggling closer.

"Me too," he croaks and kisses me lightly. Now I feel wide awake.

Tristan chuckles at me. "What?"

"Nothing I just..." I shake my head.

"Tell me," he urges.

"When do you have to leave?" I ask knowing he's going to at some point.

Tristan sighs heavily. "Wednesday." I close my eyes for a second. "I'll come back Friday," he tells me stroking my cheek, looking at me in awe.

I suddenly feel really scared, and I have to ask myself. Is that normal? Should I feel so enraptured by this man? Is this what love feels like? Or is this something else? Is it that I'm just hanging onto him because I don't have anyone at the moment?

"I'll miss you like crazy," he tells me. "I'm not really sure how I'm going to get through one day to the next."

I stroke his cheek. "I'm scared, Tristan."

He wraps his arms around me and grips me tightly. "Of what?"

"You," I tell him softly. "Of how I feel for you, I'm afraid of being close to anyone in case they leave me," I admit.

"I'm not leaving you." He tells me, and I can see he's sincere.

"Have you ever...felt like this before?" I ask hoping and praying he'll say no.

"Never," he answers shaking his head to emphasise his point. "Coral...I know you want to take things slowly, build trust with me, but I give you my word, I'm not going anywhere. You have no idea how long I've waited for you, longed for you... if I..." Tristan breaks off, sighing heavily.

"What? Tell me," I whisper.

"I swear to god I'd marry you tomorrow if that's what it took to prove to you that you have me for the long haul." I gasp in shock.

"M-marry me?" I stutter. I can see Tristan is regretting what he's said.

"You don't want to marry, do you?" He says spookily reading me.

"I don't know," I answer truthfully, staring down at his chest.

"Coral." He lifts my chin to look at him. "Whatever you

want, however you want this to work is fine with me. As long as I get to be with you, that's all that matters." Tristan strokes my cheek, instantly calming me.

"Marriage is just a piece of paper to me. I'm sorry Tristan, I can't help feeling like that. What I feel for you is far stronger, more eternal than that." I tell him.

"I understand," he tells me, softly kissing my lips again. "I just want you Coral, forever."

I smile back at him. "Forever," I say.

We kiss each other softly again, and I have to admit, I am building trust so fast with Tristan that it's taking my breath away.

"Stay with me?" He asks.

"Huh?"

"At the house, spend the weekend with me?" *Is that such a good idea...too fast?*

"Only if you want to. I don't want to push my luck, or scare you away," he adds, but he looks lost. His face mirrors my feelings completely, I can't bare to think about him leaving.

"Ok." I smile broadly at him.

"You will?" He beams.

"Yes." I chuckle, then I remember he's only just got the keys. "Wait, do you even have any furniture in there?"

"No," he grins cheekily at me. "But if I remember correctly, you said you were going to help me with that?"

I sigh. "Yes, yes I did."

"So will you?" He asks.

"Yes." I murmur against his lips.

"Good." He says kissing me lightly. I smile sleepily at him, then I involuntarily yawn. "Boring you?" He chuckles.

I punch him lightly on the shoulder. "Shut up." I chuckle then groan. Back to work tomorrow.

"What's up?" He asks.

I sigh heavily. "Back to work tomorrow, back to reality," I grumble knowing our little bubble will be burst.

"Well, this morning actually." Tristan smiles, my eyes widen. "It's 5am," he adds.

I suddenly remember I have Will tonight. "Oh no!" I'm not sure if combat training is such a good idea at the moment.

"What?" Tristan asks worry etched across his features.

"I have Will tonight," I tell him.

"Will?" He questions, his expression torn again. I think about winding him up but decide against it.

"Yes. My trainer at the gym," I tell him. I can see the relief in his eyes.

"I'm not sure that's such a good idea," he says echoing my thoughts.

"Me neither. I'd better go see him first thing and let him know."

"Doctors first," Tristan admonishes. "I want to make sure you're ok," he adds.

"Yes, sir." I tease saluting him.

"Very funny," he sulks.

"Yes, I am aren't I," I answer smugly.

"Yes you are," he chuckles. I yawn again. "Sleep baby." He says.

"I don't think I can, not with you here," I answer pressing the length of my body against his.

Tristan squeezes me even tighter. "Yes you can, you've been sleeping all night. Now close your eyes." I do as he asks, then his fingers start gently stroking my eyebrows, it's very relaxing. Then he starts humming, I flick my eyes open in astonishment, I know that tune.

"Some Enchanted Evening?" I whisper in shock.

"Yes, now go to sleep," he murmurs.

"But' – "No buts, you can ask me later," he softly scolds. I close my eyes and smile, Tristan knows yet another one of my favourite tunes. This is starting to get a little spooky, I keep feeling as though I need to pinch myself, see if I'm not dreaming.

"Tristan?" He's still humming and stroking.

"Hmm?"

"Am I dreaming all of this?" I ask.

I feel him chuckle, it vibrates through me. "Why would you think that?"

"B-because…it feels too good to be true, and I don't really get why…?" I break off not really wanting to tell him.

"Why what? Tell me Coral, I want to know what you're thinking."

"I…I just feel like…" I stop myself again.

"Like what?" he asks his voice all husky again.

"Like…well…I don't get it." I say my eyes meeting his.

"Get what?" He asks leaning up on his elbow, his face inches above mine, concern etched into his features.

I close my eyes for a second. *Come on Coral, you can do this!*

"Why me?" I ask opening my eyes and gazing into his. I want to see his reaction, see if his eyes tell the truth.

Tristan frowns as he stares down at me. "I don't think any of us really have a choice who we fall in love with Coral." I frown, my heart sinking.

"So...so if you had a choice, it wouldn't be me?" I squeak.

Tristan puts his hands either side of my cheeks and shuffles down, so we are nose to nose. "That's not what I meant," he tells me sternly.

I sigh heavily. "I just...you're too good for me," I blurt staring down at our bodies. "I want to say I believe that you'll stay, but...deep down I feel like you'll get fed up with me and leave me for someone who's..." I want to say more fun, but I know I'm fun to be with, well most of the time.

"Look at me, baby." I pull my gaze up to meet his. "Don't you know? Nothing in life is for certain, not love, not the economy, the weather, things change, people change." Tristan takes a deep breath. "Have you ever read Captain Corelli's Mandolin?"

"No," I whisper. *What's that got to do with this?*

"It was one of my Grandmothers favourite novels," he tells me. "When I was seventeen, I got dumped by a girl who I thought I was in love with' – "Tristan," I interrupt I don't think I want to hear this.

"Bare with me," he says. "So I go to my Grandmother, and I say 'how am I supposed to know Gran? How will I know when I've met the right girl?' She took one look at me, stood up, went over to her bookcase and pulled out a novel. She sat me down and quoted a passage from the book. It's what the father had told the daughter. I don't know why, but it made sense and stuck with me. Do you want to hear the quote?"

I nod silently, totally enthralled by his story.

"Love is a temporary madness. It erupts like volcanoes and then subsides. And when it subsides, you have to make a decision. You have to work out whether your roots have so entwined together that it is inconceivable that you should ever part because this is what love is. Love is not breathlessness, it is not excitement; it is not the promulgation of promises of eternal passion, it is not the desire to mate every minute of the day. It is not lying awake at night imagining that he is kissing every cranny of your body. That is just being 'in love', which any fool can do. Love itself is what is left over when being in love has burned away, and this is both an art and a fortunate accident."

I take a few moments to let it sink in. But it's no good my head is spinning with so many questions and doubts.

"But how are you supposed to know that once the in love part has gone that you'll want to stay with me? From what that quote says, you only really know once the in love part has passed, and we haven't even begun…" I say weakly.

Tristan kisses me again, his eyes pleading with me. "Because I already know, I don't know why or how I just do. I knew the moment I met you that we had something so strong, so profound that no matter how hard you pushed me away, it was inevitable that we would end up together. I was never going to give in, and I will never stop fighting for you. I'll never stop showing you how much I want you in my life, with me, by my side, through the good and the bad. I'll never stop trying."

"Why?" I ask incredulously.

"Because I couldn't imagine spending the rest of my life with anyone but you," he croaks huskily again.

"You know it's forever?" I ask. "You're totally sure, one hundred percent?" I whisper.

"Yes," he whispers back. "And I'll remind you every day, for the rest of our lives if that's how long it takes to convince you."

I place my hands on his cheeks and rest my forehead against his then close my eyes. I want to believe, I really do. And maybe Tristan is right, I just need to build trust and keep believing that he'll stay.

"My Grandfather said he knew," he whispers, I open my eyes and lock onto his. "He met Gran at a dance, he told me he knew the moment their eyes met that she was the one. She said no, of course, gave him the run around for ages. Apparently, he was a bit of a bad boy back then, always flirting with other girls, so Gran told me, and she knew she didn't want to be with a man that cheated. Then one day she said yes to a date and well history tells the rest.

"Gramps told me on that first date he knew he would never get to be with her unless he changed his ways, that it was time to grow up, be a man, so he did. And from that day on he only had eyes for Gran." I nod solemnly. Their story is a lovely one, but I doubt either of them had anything close to the fears and the issues I deal with.

"How do you feel?" He asks.

"Overwhelmed," I answer honestly.

"One step at a time," he whispers.

"Yeah," I gush. "I...I guess I stopped believing in happy endings a long time ago. I really struggle with it Tristan, it's taken years for me to believe I'm even worthy of love, let alone getting my dream man in my life."

"I'm your dream man?" He beams.

I shake my head at him playfully. "Oops! Guess I shouldn't have told you that one." I smile shyly at him.

Tristan shrugs. "You're my dream girl, so I guess we're even."

I raise my eyebrows in surprise. "Your dream girl is a nutcase like me?" I ask dryly.

Tristan's eyebrows knit together, his gaze staring down at the bed, then he takes a deep breath and meets my worried eyes. "You *are* loveable Coral, and just as worthy of love as everybody else. So start believing it baby, cause you're going to be getting bucket loads of it, better get used to it," he chortles kissing me hard on the lips, then, again and again, laughing as he does.

I can't help giggling back and playfully kissing him too until we are rudely interrupted by an alarm beeping. Tristan leans over, picks up his mobile and switches it off.

"Back to reality, I guess." I go to get out of bed, but Tristan stops me.

"Five more minutes. I kind of like all that kissing," he chuckles.

I lean into him again, pressing my lips against his and we continue where we left off...

I AM SAT DOWNSTAIRS waiting for Tristan to come back from the hotel, he insisted he gets ready there, I don't know why? But before he left, he made me a cup of tea, which I am sat drinking, and it's perfectly done. But he did insist that I showed him how I like it made, and wouldn't you know it, turns out we both like it made the same way. Three squeezes of the tea-bag, a drop of milk and no sugar. *Crazy eh!*

I take my mobile out my bag and check to see if I have any messages, although I didn't hear it beep last night. I'm still hoping I'll hear from Carlos or Rob – *Niente! Damn it Rob Text me!*

Tristan said I should just give him some time, and that he's sure to come around when he's ready. I sigh heavily and against my better judgement, I type up a text.

Hey Robster. Are you ok? Please let me know. I'm really worried about you. I'm working from home so pop round if you want to. Love Coral xXx

I press send and hope that I'll hear back from him soon, it's really bugging me what it could be. I hear the patio door slide open, so I put my mobile in my bag and stand up ready to leave, but all the air gets knocked out of me when I see Tristan. He's suited and booted in his dark blue pin-striped suit, the very same one he was wearing when we met.

"Going somewhere sexy?" I exhale, feeling my blood pumping through my veins. Damn, he looks hot, much hotter than the first time I saw him wearing that! *Maybe it's because I know him now?*

Tristan's eyebrows raise, and his sexy smile appears. "Sexy eh?" He says reaching me. He smells so good, aftershave, and Tristan scent mixed together. It's so potent.

It should be classed as a hazard to women!

He leans down his lips brushing mine softly, and I realise that I've missed him. He's only been gone half an hour, and I've missed him, badly. A sinking feeling spreads within me, this isn't normal, surely? How the hell am I going to feel when he's gone? Feeling empty and deprived of him even though he's stood in front of me, I deepen the kiss, forcing his lips apart and finding his tongue.

He tastes of toothpaste and coffee, and I'm glad Tristan hasn't pulled away, afraid of hurting my nose again. It's a very long, amazing, wonderful kiss, I feel like I'm on cloud nine, all heady and light.

"You really shouldn't do that," he says his cheeky grin spreading across his face.

"Do what?" I ask breathlessly.

"Kiss me like that, or we'll never make it out of here."

"Sounds good to me," I wrap my arms around his neck. Tugging on his hair, I push his lips harder against mine.

Tristan pulls back, I frown. "Careful baby, your nose."

"It's fine." I gripe and pull his hair again. Tristan takes hold of my hands and brings them down in front of me, I sigh heavily and stare at the floor.

"Hey," Tristan lifts my chin. "We have all the time in the world for that." He grins broadly at me and kisses me once more, but it's a quick, soft tender kiss.

I sigh inwardly. *I'm not so sure about that.*

"Come on, or we'll be late," he says, tugging on my hand.

Stepping outside, I notice it's yet another scorching hot day. I'm sure Tristan is just melting in that sexy suit of his. Just as I'm locking the patio door, my mobile starts ringing.

Pulling it out of my bag I notice it's Rob – *Yes!*

"Hey Robster, I'm so glad you called," I breathe.

"Coral, I'm just calling to let you know that Carlos and I will be away for a couple of weeks," he states grimly.

"W-why, where are you going?" I ask feeling shocked by this news.

"To his parents," he answers.

"In Spain?" I gasp.

"Yeah…" He sounds tortured.

"Why? Oh, Rob won't you tell me' – "I'm coming to see you when we get back." He interrupts.

"You are?"

"Yes, there's going to be some changes…I…" Rob chokes up again. I feel myself start to crumble. Something is really, really wrong.

"I'm here for you always, whatever it is," I tell him my voice trembling.

"I know," he whispers.

"I'll miss you," I tell him.

"Me too," he croaks.

"Tell Carlos I miss him too won't you?"

"C-Coral..." He whispers, his voice laced with pain. My heart constricts for him.

Oh Rob, please tell me what's wrong!

"I'd better go," he quickly adds.

"Ok, love you, Rob," I say fighting against the lump in my throat.

"Love you too." He croaks.

"Safe flight," I whisper.

"Bye." He hangs up. So something major is up, I was right all along. I turn to Tristan and wrap my arms around him, he grips me tightly.

"Did he say?" I shake my head.

"They're going away for a couple of weeks." I frown hard trying to figure it all out. Why would they go to Spain? They don't even get on with Carlos's dad that well, he's very old-fashioned, doesn't really understand that being gay is nature, not nurture. He thinks Carlos is doing this to piss him off.

Tristan squeezes me tighter and kisses the top of my head. "We have to move Coral."

I pull out of his arms and swipe at the tears that have fallen. Tristan takes my hand, and in a daze, I walk along the concourse, deep in thought. As we reach the Gym, I'm about to ask Tristan how we'll be getting to the Doctors when I see Stuart pull up. Tristan opens my door for me, and I slide in the backseat.

"Morning Stuart," I sniff.

"Miss Stevens," he nods. "Are you feeling any better?" he politely asks as Tristan slips in beside me.

"Yeah, much better thanks. It was agony at the time."

"I bet it was," he answers pulling out onto the main road.

As the car moves smoothly through traffic, I notice Ed Sheeran's Lego House is playing on the radio, I love this song. I turn and smile at Tristan.

"I love this song," he says.

"Me too," I smile back at him – How we think and feel, it seems so synchronised, we seem so in tune with one another, Tristan picks up my hand and kisses it.

I shake my head and gaze out the window. I'm trying so hard not to fall for this guy, but I'm starting to think it's too late...

I AM SAT INSIDE A VERY upmarket examination room. Tristan is sitting in the corner, flicking through a newspaper, while I'm sitting on a very high tech examination table, being examined by a man called Dr Andrews, he really isn't what I was expecting at all. He looks younger than me, has jet black hair, deeply set brown eyes and is quite frankly, a hunk as Debs would say. In fact, he reminds me of Keanu Reeves – *Bet he's gonna get all the ladies after him!*

"Well Coral, you're healing up nicely." Dr Andrews smiles.

"Good." I smile up at him.

"Are you getting any dizzy spells, blurry vision?" I shake my head. "Good, any headaches?"

"No, my nose is just tender from being bumped so hard..." *And when Tristan is kissing me.* I glance across at him. I really could ogle at him all day and not get bored.

"Yes, that's to be expected. Just take some Aspirin or Ibuprofen, but if anything changes come back and see me straight away."

"Ok." I look across at Tristan again. I feel ridiculous in my jeans and t-shirt while he sits there looking like a gazillionaire.

"Well, you're all done." Dr Andrews says.

"Thanks," I say and jump down off the examination table.

"Ready to go?" Tristan asks.

"Yep." I swoon at him again.

Tristan shakes Dr Andrews hand. "Thank you for fitting us in at such short notice."

"It's my pleasure," he says reaching his hand out to me – *Fuck it, he doesn't seem slimy!*

I take his hand in mine, and we shake. I sigh with relief, his hand is cool and dry. He hands Tristan a card, and we leave his very plush office.

Tristan takes hold of my hand again. "Why do you do that?" I ask.

"What?"

"Hold my hand?"

He shrugs. "I like it." I'm sure there's more to it than that, but I decide to let it go. Whatever those reasons might be, I don't care. It feels really, really, good. Tristan hands me Dr Andrews card, I shove it in my bag.

"Did you like him?" Tristan asks frowning down at me.

"Who?" I ask, bewildered.

"Dr Andrews."

I smile up at him. "What makes you ask that?"

"You shook his hand," he says darkly.

"Oh…well, he…he didn't seem slimy," I whisper, frowning at the floor.

"Hmm." Tristan doesn't seem convinced.

"Tristan, if you're jealous, I'll tell you now. You have no need to be."

He smiles wryly at me, squeezes my hand, and we continue walking out of the plush building, and into the blinding morning light. Stuart pulls up outside the building, Tristan opens my door for me again, and just as I'm about to lean down I freeze – *Was that Rob's car?*

I instantly straighten up, trying to get a better view over the roof of the Jaguar, but I can't see where it went, and I couldn't really see if it was Rob driving.

"Coral." Tristan touches my elbow bringing me back to him. "You ok?"

I nod and frown in the direction of the car park. If that was Rob's car, what is he doing here, in the hospital car park? I slide into the Jag in a daze. I can't decide whether to text him or not, to find out if he was there, then I think even if he was, would he deny it?

My stomach drops then turns over. What if Rob's sick? I shake the thought away. No way, if he were, he would tell me. Maybe he was visiting a friend or something if it was him at all.

"Coral, what's on your mind?" Tristan says pulling me from my musing. I notice we are on the move again.

"I thought I just saw Rob's car," I whisper, frowning at my own thoughts.

Tristan is watching me with worried eyes. I think about how I would be reacting to Rob's behaviour if Tristan wasn't with me. I'd be climbing the walls, I would have to know. I would have knocked down his door by now to get to the truth. I pull out my mobile, and I'm about to text Rob when it starts ringing, it's George.

"Hi, George."

"Good morning Coral. I thought I'd let you know that I've

spoken to Cindy, she can get you in for a regular session with me on Tuesdays at 5pm."

"So I'll see her tomorrow, before you?"

"Yes."

"Where?"

"My place."

"Really, that's great George. You're an angel, thank you so much," I gush feeling utterly grateful.

"You're more than welcome," he says. "Did Lily have a nice birthday?" I groan and tell him all about our little coming together, which makes me think of the hospital, then seeing Rob.

"Hey George, you haven't heard from Carlos or Rob have you?"

"Not directly, but we had friends over last night. Apparently, they're off to Spain for a couple of weeks, it's alright for some isn't it," he laughs.

"Yeah," I smile not really feeling it reach me. "Did they see them before they left?"

"No I don't think so, well they didn't really say. Why?"

"Nothing I just' – "Coral don't think the worst," he admonishes, interrupting me.

"I know," I sigh. "It's just not like Rob..." I stop myself. I can go through all of this tomorrow night. "George, you're an angel, thank you for organising that for me. I'll see you tomorrow."

"Yes, see you tomorrow." I smile down the line.

"Bye George." I hang up then send a text to Rob.

Did I just see you at Montefiore's? xXx

I pop my mobile back in my bag and look up at Tristan, he looks deep in thought.

"Coral, I'm sorry, but I've got to go into the office for a couple of hours." *Ah, so that's why he's suited and booted!*

"Stuart will take you in to see Will, and get you back to your studio," he tells me.

I burst out laughing. "No, he won't, no offence Stu," I say, glancing at him in the rearview mirror.

"Coral, please don't be difficult," Tristan replies, exasperated.

"Difficult?" I question.

"Yes," he snaps. I don't know why, but Tristan's demeanour seems to have changed since George called.

"Tristan...?" He holds one finger up to me.

My mouth presses into a hard line. I can't help gritting my teeth at him. A minute later Stuart pulls up outside the office. Tristan nods to him and leaving the engine running, Stuart steps outside.

"What's that all about?" I ask.

"He's giving us some privacy," he answers.

"Oh!" I swallow hard.

Why do I feel like I've done something wrong?

Tristan turns in his seat, so he's facing me and takes my hand in his. "I really want Stuart to' – "Tristan don't. I'm quite capable of getting myself home from the gym. Don't treat me like an injured animal, it'll just piss me off!"

"Ok." Tristan holds his hands up in the air in defeat.

"Is that all?" I snipe feeling annoyed at him. Tristan stares ahead contemplating what he's got on his mind. "Oh for heaven's sake Tristan, just spit it out!"

"You have your therapist tomorrow?"

"Yes."

"And someone else?" *Why oh why did he have to hear that.*

I sigh heavily. "Yes."

"Who?"

"What?"

"Coral, I want to make sure you're' – "She's a hypnotherapist," I blurt in frustration.

"A...a hypnotherapist?" he stutters. "Why would you need one of..." Tristan trails off and stares into space. Finally, he turns to me, and runs a cool, soft finger down my cheek, then takes my hands in his and entwines our fingers. "Give me your word that you'll tell me....one day," he adds.

"I...I can't Tristan, I can't guarantee you that," I croak.

"Why not?" he asks, his voice low and husky.

"Because I don't want to let you down," I mumble. "I don't know if I have the courage to..." I stare down at our entwined fingers. "Can we talk about this another time, I'd like to get home," I say.

My nose hurts, I'm hungry, and I don't want to assess how I'm really feeling about Tristan. He wants so much from me, and

I don't know if I can give that back to him. I pull my hands out of his, cross my arms and pout.

Tristan purses his lips then frowns deeply and narrows his eyes at me. "Coral, why do I get the feeling that you're going to say goodbye, and I won't see it coming?" He asks, his voice shaking slightly. *Shit!*

I shake my head and run my hand through my hair. "I don't know," I lie, turning to stare out of the window. I can't look at him, if I do I'll crack, and I don't want him to know the real depravity of my feelings.

I'm deeply scarred by the events of my past, and he doesn't know how deep those scars run. I feel like a have an internal battle raging within me, and I already have enough battle wounds. I don't think I could take any more, and falling for Tristan is starting to make me realise how deep those wounds go.

My heart is broken, torn in two, it needs stitching back together, but I don't know how to do that. I'm not even sure if it will ever heal completely, and I'm starting to realise that if I really let Tristan in, and it goes wrong, my heart will snap in two and I'll never repair from it. I'll be a broken fuck up, just like my mother, and I just don't think I can take that risk.

"I'll be back at lunchtime. Can I pick you anything up?" His voice is low and strained.

"Sure, a salad would be nice," I whisper.

"Done," he answers.

I can feel him watching me, waiting for me to look at him.

"Coral," he whispers.

I turn and look up at him, he looks lost and as though he's in pain. I squeeze my eyes shut for a second, feeling guilty for making him feel like this.

"I'm sorry Coral, I' - I move forward and press my lips against his. "Don't be, you're curious. I would be too." I kiss him softly, trying to ease his anxious look.

He gazes back at me and gently strokes my hair. "I have to go," he says.

"I know," I whisper and sit back in my seat.

"See you later?" I nod at him and pull my lips up into a semblance of a smile.

He narrows his eyes at me, leans forward and gently kisses

my forehead. His kiss sears me, changing my mind again. *What the fuck am I doing?*

Tristan steps out of the car. I watch him walk over to Stuart and chat with him for a moment, then Stuart hops back in the car. "So just to the Gym," he clarifies, smiling broadly at me.

I nod silently, already lost in thought...

TEN MINUTES LATER I have said goodbye to Stuart, and I'm walking into the Gym. I have no idea if Will is even here this time of day. I don't know if he's a full or part-time fitness instructor, so I decide to ask at reception. As I stand waiting to be seen, I'm eyed speculatively by the two girls that are serving clients. I roll my eyes at them, and I'm about to say something when I'm tapped on the shoulder. I turn around and see Will's mouth gaping open in shock, and before he even asks me a question, he's tugging me along and pulling me into a small office.

"Coral!" *Jeez, he looks really angry!*

"This isn't what it looks like!" I say raising my hands in the air to stop him.

"Oh really' – Will crosses his arms – 'Denial, it's always the first step," he barks.

"Will, my niece, did this to me," I snap, he scowls back at me. "I swear to you," I add, then tell him how it happened, but he still doesn't look convinced.

"Will," I whisper closing my eyes as I do. "I would never let anyone do this to me." I open my eyes and continue. "I came in here to tell you I can't do tonight, and that I'll see you on Thursday, my nose should have healed up by then."

He sighs heavily. "You know you can always tell me if anyone' – "Will!" I bark. "I get that you care about me, and I really appreciate that you do, but I'm telling you my niece did this!" I snap, feeling annoyed at him.

"Alright Coral," he nods, but I'm still not sure he's convinced.

I shake my head at him and walk over to the door. "See you Thursday," I grumble wrenching the door open. *I don't need this shit! I've got enough going on.*

I march out the gym and all the way home...

THREE HOURS LATER I have caught up with all the work that Joyce sent over this morning, and resent it for her to print and sign. I have welcomed the work; it's taken my mind of Tristan, and the raging battle that's going on. I'm so confused from all the fucked-up-ness that goes on in my head.

I sigh inwardly and sit back on the sofa. I look up at the time, Tristan will be back soon. I shake my head at myself. *What am I going to do?* It all feels like it's going so fast. I take a deep breath trying to calm myself, but all I can smell is Tristan, his scent is all over this place now. It was a bad idea letting him stay here, building memories with him.

I wish I could talk to Rob, he would help me rationalise it all. Maybe I could tell him why I'm like this, tell him the truth. I could tell him all about my past, maybe then – My mobile buzzes at me, pulling me from my musing, I pick it up and see there's a text.

I scramble to open it, hoping it's a reply from Rob.

HEY MY SEXY, GORGEOUS GIRL ;-) WHAT KIND OF SALAD WOULD YOU LIKE? TRISTAN xXx

I grin like an idiot. I instantly feel lifted from my sombre thoughts. He's so hard to resist, not only does Tristan think I'm gorgeous and sexy – which is a very heady feeling in itself – but I got a wink too, I press reply and send one back to him.

I'M STARVING AND MISSING YOU, HURRY BACK. SURPRISE ME BABY xXx

His reply is immediate.

I DO APOLOGISE SOMETHING CAME UP. MISSING YOU TOO, SEE YOU SOON GORGEOUS xXx

Just as I'm about to text back a witty reply my mobile rings.
"Hi, Joyce."
"How are you feeling darling?"
"Oh fine, can I come back tomorrow?"
"Not until your bruising has gone." She answers sternly.
I frown at her reply. "Why?" I question.
"It just...well doesn't look good on the company darling,

and do you really want all the girls gossiping about you? Which they will," she adds.

"I don't care." I snap.

"Well, I do." She retorts.

"So you want me to take the week off?" I question in horror.

"There's no rush Coral, when the bruises have gone, come back in."

I sigh heavily. "Ok, if that's what you want," I mumble.

"Darling, use the time productively. Why not spend some time with Tristan while he's here?"

I'm speechless. Then I remember what Tristan told me about their little chat.

"I'm finishing myself now so you won't get anything else sent across today. Take some time off Coral, you deserve it." *Why do I get the feeling Joyce is pushing for this too?*

"Um...sure ok," I mumble.

"I'm doing the same tomorrow, a few hours in the morning and then I'm off again." She tells me.

"Oh, ok." I have to wonder what Joyce is up to. "Do you need me to help you with anything?" I ask hoping she'll say yes. I'm going to go mad sitting around when Tristan's gone.

"No, I'm fine, thank you Coral."

I shrug and sigh. "Ok, I'll see you soon," I grumble. "Bye." I'm about to hang up when Joyce stops me.

"Oh Coral, Lily loved the dress, thank you for choosing it for me."

"Anytime," I smile, feeling momentarily better.

"Bye darling." Joyce hangs up.

I check my mobile for a reply from Rob, still nothing. Guess I'm just going to have to be patient and hope that I'll hear from him soon...

TWENTY MINUTES LATER Tristan comes waltzing into the studio looking sexy as ever, gone is the suit – I guess he went back to the hotel and got changed –now he's in a pair of dark blue jeans, and a black t-shirt that fits snuggly against his muscular torso – *Uh-Oh! I didn't think he could look sexier than the suit, but he does!*

I swoon at him for a second then snap out of it. "Hi," I squeak.

Without a word, he places the take-out bag on the coffee table, pulls me into him and kisses me so forcefully, I almost fall backwards. And I would have done, had it not been for his strong arms wrapped around me. But there's something more, something behind the kiss, a hint of desperation maybe, I don't know.

"What was that for?" I ask breathlessly.

"Does there need to be a reason?" He asks, staring down at me with anxious eyes.

"I guess not," I whisper.

"Your salad my lady," he smiles his deep dimpled smile.

"Thanks." I sit down on the sofa, open the packaging and see Tristan has ordered my favourite. Green leaf and avocado with black olives and sundried tomatoes.

"How did you know?" I beam as Tristan sits next to me.

"I'm observant, and I listen," he muffles.

I look across and see he's demolishing his food again.

"Hungry?" I chuckle.

"Yes." Tristan gobbles his chicken salad down in no time at all, but I'm struggling again, all I keep thinking about is his hands on my body, his lips against mine and what it's going to feel like when he's finally inside me, making love to me.

Then I think about it happening for real, and I start to freak out, my heart starts hammering against my chest, making me feel nauseous.

"Will you tell me?" He softly asks.

"Tell you what?" I mumble as I pick at my salad.

"Why you have Hypnotherapy?"

"Tristan," I moan putting my fork down, my appetite completely vanished.

"Please?" He begs.

"For god's sake man, let me eat!" I admonish.

Tristan frowns back at me but he doesn't push it, he nods once, stands and walks out onto the decking, I can hear him chatting away to Bob. I take the alone time to try and eat the rest of my salad. I concentrate hard on chewing and swallowing, keeping my mind clear of all thoughts.

"Fancy going over to the house today?" He asks making me jump. I hadn't noticed him come back in.

"Sure," I say finally finishing my salad, which was delicious.

"Will you tell me now?" He asks solemnly. I know what he's asking.

"No!" I bark.

Tristan sighs heavily then nods in resignation. "Ok, well I thought we could go to the house, choose what kind of furniture we would like, where it can go, and then go and see if we can find it."

Ok, I think this is going way too fast!

"You don't want to do that?" he says, his eyes narrowed, his brow furrowed. He runs his hand through his hair in frustration. "What's wrong Coral?" He barks.

I sigh inwardly. Why is he asking about furniture shopping, when he knows I have work this afternoon, unless...*Joyce has already told him?* Then I think maybe Tristan has told Joyce about staying over and thinking back on it, she wants me to spend more time with Tristan...

"Did you ask Joyce to give me the day off?" I question, my eyes narrowed.

Tristan instantly looks guilty.

"You did!" I screech. "Tristan," I scold. "You shouldn't have done that," I add, feeling agitated that I am losing all sense of control.

"It wasn't like that," he tells me sheepishly.

"Really? Enlighten me, Tristan, how exactly was it?" I growl.

I'm so pissed at him.

"Coral, it was very innocent, we got talking, and I told her that.....well, we seem to be really getting along and that you're going to spend some time at the house with me this weekend. She knows I'm leaving on Wednesday' – Tristan sighs heavily – 'I told her about your offer to help me find some furniture, she thought it was a nice gesture, so she offered to give you the afternoon off so we could' – "Ok, I've heard enough." I interrupt.

I have to get away from him.

I stomp my way up the stairs, and when I get to my bedroom, I plonk myself down on my bed and close my eyes, trying to work out why I'm feeling so pissed about it. Is it because I feel as though my life is being planned for me? That I'm losing control? Or am I just annoyed by it all? I wanted to go back to work.

I like having that sense of normality, routine, and for the first time ever it's been taken away from me – without my approval!

I hear the bottom stair creak. "Can I come up?" His voice sounds torn.

How can I deny him? "Sure." I open my eyes and sit cross-legged on my bed.

Tristan runs up the stairs, then tentatively walks the couple of steps needed to be next to me, and hesitantly sits down. His face is as white as a ghost; he looks lost, torn.

"I'm so sorry," he whispers. "I thought that you would like it, spending more time with me, and so did Joyce."

"It's not that," I grumble.

"Then what is it?" He softly asks.

"I just...don't I get a say?" I gripe.

"I...I thought' – "Tristan," I lean in closer to him, I need him to understand. "I need my routine, having a stable job to go to every day gives me a sense of purpose. And with all the madness that goes on in my head, for that to just be stripped away from me without any say' – "That's what it feels like to you?" he interrupts.

"Yes," I whisper in exasperation.

"Most people would love being given time off– "Don't," I tell him. "Don't go there, I've already told you I'm not like other people."

"So you don't want to spend more time with me?" He questions.

"It's not about that!" I shout. "Don't you get it? I crave control Tristan, and having this job gives me that. Having two people I thought cared about me conniving behind my back, so I can't go to work feels like entrapment to me." I bellow running my hands through my hair in frustration.

"I...I didn't know you felt that way." He says, frowning at the floor.

"That's because you didn't ask!" I shout, my temper getting the better of me.

"I think I should go," Tristan says standing up sharply.

I almost go to agree with him, it's my chance to let him go, but something deep within me tugs at my heart, it feels like it's being crushed again – by the steel hand.

"Tristan," I whisper, instantly regretting my little rant. "Please stay."

"I don't think that's a good idea," he tells me.

Shit! What have I done? I don't want him to leave!

I scramble to my feet, stand in front of him and tug on his hand. "Please, don't go," I beg leaning my forehead against his chest. "I...I'll tell you more," I barter.

"More?" He questions.

"Yeah...a-about me," I stutter.

"You don't need to do that Coral. I just thought you'd be happy to spend more time with me, that's all."

I look up at his face, I can see I've hurt him – *Damn it!*

"I do want to spend more time with you. Its just...it would have been better being done a different way, that's all. Like you and Joyce actually asking me instead of telling me." I say throwing my hands in the air.

Tristan frowns again, deep in thought. "I apologise," he says, 'I didn't mean to make you feel that way Coral. It won't happen again. I give you my word."

"I'm sorry too," I whisper.

We stare at one another again. I'm not sure if it's Tristan or me that starts smiling, but either way, I feel lighter for it. The argument is is already forgotten.

"Do you have a problem with authority?" Tristan titters lightly.

I smile widens. "Yeah...I kind of do," I say.

"I'm betting you were a real pain in the ass as a teenager," he says taking my face in his hands and running his thumbs across my cheekbones.

"You have no idea!" I chuckle lightly, Tristan joins in.

"So are we going shopping?" He asks playfully.

"Yes." I beam, reeling at the thought of helping him furnish his house.

"Ok." He leans forward and kisses my forehead.

"I need a few minutes," I say.

"I'll wait for you downstairs," he says, then softly strokes my cheek.

As Tristan scuttles back down the stairs, I stop and think for a moment about the future, which I know I shouldn't do, but I can't help it. I envisage my life without him, going to work, the gym, seeing Rob occasionally. It makes me realise how deeply Tristan's got under my skin, in just a few short days. I think about how scared I am, and how quickly this is all going. I know he wants me to move in with him, that he wants to marry me, but I'm just not there yet.

I close my eyes and imagine saying goodbye to him, walking away…A huge crater opens within me, it's dark and barren, torn and twisted, and it hurts like hell.

I quickly think of the flip side.

Tristan's house is what I see. I'm sitting outside on the decking, soaking up the sunset with a glass of wine. I look back inside and see Tristan is putting the finishing touches to the meal he's made, I watch him walk towards me, a big dimpled smile spread across his face.

The image shifts. I'm alone in the house taking a soak in the bath, I hear Tristan come home, then he's next to me, he's naked, and he's joining me in the bath, he starts massaging my shoulders, it feels wonderful –"Coral, are you ready?" Tristan shouts.

I jump feeling startled, then giggle at myself for getting so lost in the dream.

"Coming!" I shout back. I find my wedges, pull them on and run down the stairs to Tristan.

"So where to?" he asks.

"Depends what kind of furniture you're looking for?" I say.

"What do you think?" he asks.

I narrow my eyes at him. "Tristan, this is your house, not mine."

"Hmm, did you like how it was furnished?" He asks.

"Yes."

"And the rooms? Keep them as they are?"

"Why are you asking me this?"

"I want you to be happy there." He says shrugging slightly.

"Liar!" I blurt, teasingly.

His mouth twists trying to hide his smile. "Alright, I do have an ulterior motive…but I think it's too early to say anything," he says, looking nervous.

"Say it." I push. He shakes his head at me. "Tristan!" I warn. "You won't build trust with me if I know you're hiding something."

"Fine! I was going to ask you to move in with me when you're ready. It's in the future, I know that but I would have it instantly happen, and I want this place to feel like it's just as much your home as it is mine."

My mouth pops open. "Move in with you?" I whisper.

He moves forward and gently strokes my cheek. "One day, not now," he says calming me. "I just want to know what you thought of the furnishings, the layout."

"Perfect," I answer, his eyebrows shoot up in surprise.

"Really?" He questions.

"Yes, I thought all the rooms were perfectly appointed. The office, the library and as for that big sofa…" I drift off.

"So basically replicate what we viewed?"

"Yes, if that's what you like too?"

"Oh, baby…" He crushes me to him, inhaling my hair, my scent like I've done with him. "Perfectly matched," he whispers.

Ok, now I'm excited. If we can get that house looking like it did, that would be awesome. Tristan smiles down at me and kisses me softly, then taking my hand in his, we head out into the blazing heat of the afternoon…

THE FOLLOWING DAY, I find Tristan waiting to pick me up from my session with George. I smile tentatively at him and slip inside the Jaguar. My head is spinning. Hypnotherapy with Cindy, followed by a gruelling session with George, I feel like I've been rattled to pieces. Not that I was honest with him – which he won't be happy about if he happens to find out.

"How did it go?" Tristan asks, clasping my hand in his.

I feel a little hesitant to answer him, and I don't want Stuart to overhear our conversation.

"Good," I answer, not wanting to give away any more, and gaze out of the window.

Yesterday when we had finished our mad shopping spree, Tristan asked me if I wanted to stay at his house while he's away, but I declined. Seeing it again made me remember how I was feeling about him when we first viewed it; how scared I was, I still am if I'm honest. In fact, the more I think about it, the more I can feel myself spiralling down, withdrawing into myself, shutting myself away from him. Just thinking about him leaving tomorrow is filling me with dread.

I swallow hard and try to chase away the horror.

Of course, I didn't tell George any of this, because I know what he will say, that I'm self-destructing the relationship. But I don't think he'll ever understand me, not truly, but he did say that Tristan leaving was probably a good thing so I can get some perspective, some distance. I frown at that thought, I'm not sure I actually want distance, but at the same time I do – I'm so confused, why can't I just feel fucking normal, for one day?

"Coral?" Tristan prompts.

"Hmm," I turn and look at Tristan, he looks worried.

"How did it go?" He asks again.

"Good," I repeat.

I hope this isn't how it's going to be – Tristan drilling me every time I come back from a session, because I just can't take that, and I don't want to open up too much to him. Things are going so well at the moment, and I don't know why, but I keep getting the feeling that he'll run a mile when he finds out about me, I know he will.

I sigh inwardly. As much as George keeps telling me I can heal and repair, I'm not so sure I can, or will, being scarred so badly as a child changes everything. When you're a kid, you should be able to trust the adults that are around you, and when you realise you can't, your whole worldview changes, completely.

Tristan laughs sarcastically at me. I glance across at him. "So full of information as usual," he bites.

"I know what you want," I tell him staring out the window, watching the world go by.

"I don't think you do," he argues.

"You want to know everything," I retort.

Tristan sighs heavily as Stuart pulls up outside the gym. I watch him jump out and walk around to my door; he pulls it open and holds out his hand to me.

"I want you to open your heart to me," he says as I place my hand in his.

I step out the car and stare down at the floor. "I'm trying Tristan, but the more you keep asking, the more I'll pull away."

He lifts my chin, leans down and gently kisses my lips.

"Tristan," I whisper wrapping my hands around his neck. "What if I can't ever tell you? Would you be satisfied with that?"

He softly kisses me again. "I wouldn't really have a choice, would I?" he says. "Let's not fight," he adds, wrapping his arm around my shoulder. "I'm leaving tomorrow, this is our last night together. Want to go through more booklets for furniture tonight?"

"Sure." I smile tentatively at him, and we walk arm in arm towards my studio.

What I really want to do, which I can't tell him, is to go straight upstairs and try on the one and only skirt I own. I want to know if the Hypnotherapy has started working.

I unlock the patio door, walk inside, and without looking back at Tristan, I walk straight up the stairs. Reaching my closet, I start pulling the neatly piled clothing out to get to the skirt at the back of the shelving, but I can't reach it.

God damn it! – I'm right on the tips of my toes, my arm stretched to breaking point when I hear Tristan behind me.

"What are you doing?" he asks.

I stop stretching and turn to look at him. I can see he's looking around at all the clothes strewn all over my bed, trying to work out what I'm doing, and I don't know why, but I suddenly feel really shy, I look down at my knotted fingers.

"Are you looking for something?" He softly asks.

I nod my head at him.

"Need some help?" – *Please God, don't let him ask why? Or any other questions!*

I finally look up at him. "Yes please."

Tristan takes the few steps needed to reach me and smiles softly at me.

"There's a Jane Norman bag at the back, can you see it?" Tristan looks up, then leans forward and effortlessly pulls the bag out. He silently hands it to me, I can see he's dying to ask what's in the bag.

"Thanks," I mumble.

"Want some help putting these away?" he asks politely.

I really want him to leave, but I know my short arse can't reach up to put it all away.

"Please." I carefully put the bag down, so it doesn't reveal what's inside, then I start passing the clothes to Tristan who neatly stacks them.

When we're done, we end up gazing at one another again.

"I'll leave you to it," he says a look of concern etched across his face. Tristan leans down and without touching me at all, he softly presses his lips against mine. I close my eyes surrendering to the sensation. When I open my eyes, I see he is gone, and I didn't even hear any of the stairs creak.

Nervously, I pick up the bag and sit on the edge of the bed. *Well here goes nothing!*

Pulling my jeans off, I pull the skirt out of the bag. Closing my eyes for a second, I hug it to me and say a little prayer that I won't freak out. Standing up, I undo the zip and step my first foot in, then the second. Slowly and hesitantly I pull the skirt up and around my waist, then carefully pull the zip up.

Taking a deep breath I prepare for the panic attack, for the shaking, for the palpitating heart, but a couple of minutes in and my breathing is normal, my heartbeat is slow, and I'm not having hot or cold flushes.

I fall back onto the edge of the bed and choke back tears of relief, saying a silent prayer of gratitude to Cindy and George, if it wasn't for them – then an image flashes in my mind's eye!

No! – My five-year-old self is sat on that man's lap.

I squeeze my eyes shut, trying to push the image away and yank the skirt off. Ok, Ok so it's going to need more work, but that's never happened before, I've never been able to put a dress or skirt on without my body going into freefall, and it didn't, I just got the mental image!

Good, this is good! I can tell George and Cindy about it all.

Putting the skirt back in the bag and hiding it under my bed, I pull my jeans back on and skip down the stairs. Tristan is sitting on the sofa with his laptop on his legs, I can see he's concentrating hard, so I stand staring at him for a moment. *What the hell have I done to deserve this man?*

Suddenly, he looks up and smiles warmly at me. "Hey," Tristan shuts his laptop and pats the sofa next to him. I grin like an idiot and walk over to him. "I'm missing my kisses," he says, pulling me onto his lap.

He kisses me hard, scattering all thoughts. I chuckle lightly at his ardour.

"What?" He smiles deeply at me.

"Nothing," I say shaking my head.

"So do you want to go through some more books?" he asks sweetly.

I don't think I do, we have already seen so much furniture and have so many items ready to be delivered on Saturday. Tristan has given me his word he will be back Friday night, I'm missing him already.

"I have a better idea," I say and pull his lips to mine…

CHAPTER TWENTY-SIX

It's Friday afternoon, and I'm at work. I cannot stop jigging up and down in my seat. I'm so excited to see Tristan again, but also very nervous. I've had lots of time to think while he's been away. I've tried to rationalise my feelings for him, but the harder I try, the more I keep coming to the conclusion that I am, for all intense and purposes, deeply and irrevocably in love with him. Which scares me to death, I don't feel like I'm ready for this, it's just all happened so fast.

Yet, when he left on Wednesday morning, I felt like the hole that has always been there in my chest had been torn wide open again, and I just wanted him back in my arms to fill it back up. George told me that might happen; that it is one of the consequences of falling in love.

Me, in love? – It's still so hard to believe.

I've tried to feel excited about it, I mean most people do when they fall in love, but instead, I have felt lost, no compass, no bearing, like I'm a tiny blip in the ocean, never to be found again. Maybe that's because I have missed him so much, I feel like he's been gone for three months, not three days.

It actually hurts to think about him, and when I do the ache becomes more prominent, so I've been trying and failing badly not to picture him, or feel his arms around me, or his gorgeous full lips kissing mine. I knew the moment I watched him walk out of my studio, after kissing me goodbye for so long, that I wanted him forever. But the more I think about that, the more I feel myself withdrawing, it feels safer like that, I can't get hurt again. But being with Tristan has also made me realise what I've been missing, how good love can really feel.

I have pictured his face a thousand times as I try to tell him goodbye, and every time I do, it literally cripples me.

I have been back at work since Wednesday. Against Joyce's wishes, I caked my face in makeup so you couldn't see the bruising, marched into work and demanded she let me come back. I couldn't stay at my studio, it reminds me of Tristan too much. His smell is everywhere, and I keep picturing him sitting on my sofa, smiling his sexy smile at me. And every time I try to do something to take my mind off him, like reading or watching a movie, I get fidgety and restless.

It's driving me crazy, literally.

I close my eyes and remember back to Wednesday night, I thought it was going to be the hardest night of my existence, turns out it wasn't. Tristan called me, and we spent hours on the phone. I eventually fell asleep to him humming Some Enchanted Evening to me – again. I'm never going to be able to listen to that tune without thinking of him, but maybe that was his plan?

My phone rings pulling me from my musing. I answer it in a daze, it's the call Joyce was expecting so I pass it through to her.

Picking up my handbag, I pull out the set of keys Tristan gave me and start fiddling with them, I'm so restless. When I agreed to take delivery of his bed yesterday, I didn't expect to feel so odd when I arrived at his house. It took the delivery guys ages to get the king-size bed up the two flights of stairs, which gave me too much thinking time.

I wandered around the house in a daze, checked out the pool and cinema room, which I hadn't seen, and then drifted back upstairs. I walked past the kitchen, and straight out onto the rear terrace. I was so lost in my own thoughts that the delivery guy had to touch my arm to get my attention; that did not go down well, I almost had a meltdown.

When they had left, I did what I vowed to myself I wouldn't do, and I went upstairs. As I reached the master bedroom, I stared down at the big, empty bed and tried to imagine myself living there with Tristan. Waking up with him, making love to him – My throat tightened at the very thought of it, and I questioned it again – Is it because I was raped that I'm feeling like this? Or is it fear of commitment, of being loved and giving love?

I stood there for ages trying to work it out until I realised I wasn't going to get the answer, not without George, so tonight I have to be honest with him, whether I like it or not.

When I got home last night, I ordered a king-size quilt and covers online, which turned up today at work, and it's huge. It normally takes me half an hour to get to George's from work, but with this lot to carry, and the heat, I'm definitely going to get a taxi.

I look up at my screen, click on the images of Tristan and gaze at him. *What is it about you that has me in knots?* I shake my head at myself and try to get back to the now, to what's going on in my life other than Tristan.

I've still not heard from Rob or Carlos, and Gladys and Debs haven't given me any new information. On the upside, I tried the skirt on again last night. I wanted to leave it a couple of days to see if it made any difference, and it didn't – which I was pleased about. I'm really looking forward to next Tuesday, and I'm excited to see how far we can take this Hypnotherapy. Maybe it will heal me? I hope so, I want to feel pretty, feminine, sexy – I don't want to feel like a freak anymore.

I look up at the clock on the wall again, only another minute has passed.

My stomach fills with butterflies again, and I fight against the grin that involuntarily spreads across my face. Honestly, one minute I'm smiling like a fool, the next I'm feeling lost, sombre and empty – I wish Tristan would hurry back. I need to know if this is what missing someone is like, or if I'm feeling like this because I'm freaking out?

I want Tristan, I want to bed him, I want to be as close to him as two people can get, but the very thought of it keeps sending me into a nervous frenzy.

I sigh heavily. *Concentrate Coral!*

Ok, I'm back to my routine of swimming in the morning, and I had my session last night with Will, I think he finally believed me about the bruising because I kept getting flashbacks of Tristan and no matter how hard I tried, I couldn't wipe the stupid grin off my face.

When Will asked for the fourth time why I was so happy, I relented and told him all about meeting Tristan, he seemed genuinely pleased for me...

THE CLOCK ON THE wall finally chimes four o'clock. I shove Tristan's keys back in my bag, dash out of my seat, and knock on Joyce's door.

"Come." I fling the door open.

"Need anything before I go?" I ask in a rush.

"No but...going somewhere?" Joyce smiles coyly at me.

"I...um, I have a session tonight," I tell her not wanting to get into talking about Tristan.

"Oh," Joyce's face falls.

I smile at her, I can't help myself. "Then I'll be seeing Tristan," I whisper.

Joyce beams with pride and jumps up out of her seat. "Darling girl," she chokes and hugs me hard. I hug her back. "It gives me such great pleasure to see you so happy..." Joyce breaks off choking back the tears. "Reminds me of how giddy I used to feel when I had a date with John, you know before we married. They are precious times, make the most of it," she says rubbing my arm.

I feel mortified that I've been walking around feeling so happy while Joyce has been in hell, I frown hard at my own behaviour.

"I'm sorry Joyce, that's really insensitive of me," I murmur.

"Nonsense." She smiles, dabbing her tears with her handkerchief. "It gives me such joy to see you so happy, and he's a lovely chap Coral, you've done really well there," she says almost proudly.

"I don't think I really did anything," I answer feeling shy.

Joyce smiles warmly at me. "Always so modest."

I snort and stare at the floor.

"Are you alright darling?"

I make myself smile. "Yes, of course."

Joyce frowns at me. "Want to talk about it?" I shake my head at her. "You've been very up and down since Tristan left," she muses.

Damn it! I thought I was hiding it.

"Sorry Joyce," I mumble.

"No need, take a seat." She points to the deep green leather sofa. Reluctantly I walk over and sit down with her. "Now then, let's get this show on the road."

I frown at her. "S...sorry?" I stutter.

"Missing him?" I scowl at my twisted hands. "Alright, going too fast?" My eyes dart up to meet hers. "I see, Coral, if that's how you feel, you need to tell him this," she says. "Tristan is older than you, and I know he's ready to settle down. Evidently, you're not. So the two of you need to sit down and talk it through." I nod back at her.

"I have to say Coral, I am surprised. You've met a handsome, eligible man, who's fallen deeply in love with you, yet you're walking around as though you don't know what to do with yourself?"

How does she know this?

"I can tell dear," she says, patting my hand. "Coral, you probably don't know this, but when John and I first met, we fell madly in love. My parents said it wouldn't last because we fell so hard, so quickly, but we did last. I want you to know this, so you don't feel so afraid of it working out so quickly."

"I just…" I stop, not knowing what to say.

"Do you think the two of you have a chance at working this out?" *Shit!*

"I…I'm not sure," I whisper, staring at my hands.

"Do you love him?"

"Yes…but…" I break off again, I can't even begin to tell Joyce how I really feel; we'll be here all night.

"He's a steady, hardworking man, a good man. You could do a lot worse," she scoffs.

"I know," I softly say.

"Then why are you so reluctant?" she adds in a softer tone.

"I don't know," I whisper. "I just am."

"Well, I can't really push you in one direction or the other, I'm sure you know what you're doing," she adds.

"Thanks, Joyce." I know she cares, truly I do, but she hasn't got a frigging clue.

"Well, go on then, off you go," she says ushering me out of her office with her hand.

"Night Joyce." I want to say have a nice weekend, but I don't think she will, not for a long time.

"Goodnight dear," she smiles tentatively at me.

As I walk out of her office, I think back on our conversation. Part of me knows she's right, that most women would be jumping for joy at meeting such a great guy, a smart, kind, eligible bachelor, but I'm not like other women, god knows she should know that. As I walk over to my desk and start to close my computer down, I think back to her words.

"He's a good man, you could do a lot worse."
"He's older than you, he's ready to settle down."
"He's deeply in love with you."
Oh, Tristan!

Suddenly, the pain of losing him grips me, and I don't mean us ending, I mean him dying; like John did. What if I take the risk and that happens to me? What if Tristan suddenly dies? What the hell am I meant to do? It's too unbearable to even think about – I grip my stomach to stop it from turning over, and that's when I make the decision. I have to tell him tonight, I have to. I can't hold it back any longer, it's time for some truths. Ordering a taxi, I pick up my handbag, my overnight bag, the quilt and the bedcovers and struggle down the hallway…

AS I REACH GEORGE'S house, I take a deep, steadying breath and knock on the door.

Phil answers it, as usual. "Hi Coral," he beams, he's got the phone in his hand. "Oh my God! No, he didn't!" he gasps. *He's such a gossip!*

"Hey Phil," I drag my feet into the hallway and plonk the quilt, bedcovers and my bags on the floor.

"He won't be long, make yourself comfortable," Phil says, covering the handset.

"Ok." I walk through the hallway, past the open plan kitchen-dining area, turn left and walk into George's study. The room is empty, and for a fleeting second, I think about opening up his notepad to see what he's written about me.

"And how are we this evening?" George says as he enters the room, making me jump – again!

"I'll be fine once I've got over the heart attack," I say with sarcasm and sit on the sofa.

George chuckles at me, sits in his chair, takes out his notepad and waits patiently for me to start.

"How do people do it?" I muse.

"Do what?" George asks looking over his glasses.

"Get over the person they love that has died. Joyce seems as though she's coping so well, but I don't see how...if I lost Tristan, I don't think I'd cope at all..." I say shaking my head.

"Time is a healer," George tells me.

"That may be so George but what about day to day stuff, just getting up' –"Coral," George holds his finger up to me, I stop talking. "Remember we have talked about this, worrying about future events that may or may not happen is a complete waste of time. Besides, for all you know, you both could lead a very happy, healthy, long life together. Try to concentrate on that."

I relax a little, my shoulders coming down from my ears.

"Better?" He asks.

"Yeah," I take a deep breath.

"Good, now several things to go through tonight. Firstly, I'd like to know if you found any difference in yourself this week. Do you think the Hypnotherapy has helped?"

I nod and smile.

"How?" He asks taking notes again.

"Well...when I got home I tried on a skirt, and I didn't freak out!" I beam.

"Really? That's interesting...So, no palpitations, heavy breathing, hot or cold flushes?" I shake my head at each question. "That's wonderful," George beams.

"There was one thing though, I may not have got any of the emotions that go with it, but I got an image," I say darkly.

"Go on." George urges.

"Him," I whisper. George looks confused - How is he not getting this? "The guy....you know, the first time I was abused, *him*," I say in a rush.

George takes more notes. "Has that happened before?" he asks.

"No, I just used to get the feeling before," I say twiddling my fingers in my lap.

"This could be a long process Coral, it's not an overnight cure."

"I know," I answer. "George, I'm doing what you've advised me to do, I'm really pleased so far, and I'm really eager to keep going."

"Good." George closes his pad and crosses his legs. "Have you noticed anything else, any other subtle changes?"

I narrow my eyes at him. "Why, what else did she do? I thought we were just working on the dresses?" I say in a panic.

"We did, but having Hypnotherapy can help in other areas too Coral, without it being a conscious effort." He softly says.

"Oh! Well...I'm less anxious I guess, but I'm not sure if that's Hypnotherapy or...." I break off. I don't really want George to know how bad I've got it for Tristan, he's all I can think about.

"Or Tristan?" he smiles.

I shake my head and laugh.

"It's good to see you smiling Coral," George says grinning widely.

"It feels good," I tell him, then frown.

"Let's discuss." He adds.

"Tristan's...well wonderful. He's good for me, almost too perfect really, but I've felt really up and down since he left. One minute I'm smiling because I'm happy, you know, he's great, I'm in love and the next minute...I just feel like it's too heavy, too quick. He wants so much. I know he wants me to move in with him, he wants marriage, and I know he wants answers. He wants to know what happened to me and I don't think I'm ready for that, for any of it."

George nods as he makes more notes, then he stops and looks up at me.

"Coral, love can feel very scary. We govern more with our hearts than our minds, so when our head interjects, we think of all the reasons why we shouldn't, why we should hold back, run, or even end the relationship. Is that what you want, to end it?"

I shake my head, then I shrug.

"Alright, well as for moving in and marriage are concerned, from what you've told me Tristan is ready for that, but I know you're not, so as we discussed on Tuesday, take it at your own pace and tell him how you feel. You've already revealed more to him than you have to any other person. Have you actually told him that?"

I think about it for a moment. "No, I don't think I have, it just kind of came up in conversation," I tell him.

"Well maybe a little nudge in that direction," George smiles. "Now, we spent all our session on Tuesday talking about Tristan," he says a little disapprovingly. "I'd like to go through other aspects of your life tonight."

I shrug nonchalantly.

"Work?"

"Fine," I answer simply.

"Elaborate please Coral," George replies, his tone full of sarcasm.

I hide my smile. "There's not really much to say, I was working from home as you know. I went back into the office on Wednesday, everything was normal. Susannah's coming next week to train me." *Ugh! Leggy Blonde, so not looking forward to that!*

"So you're no longer feeling anxious about working with your new boss?"

"Tristan's assured me no-one will know about us. And as far as the office goes, he's my boss, and he'll hardly be there." I answer my hands flying up.

"So you'll be seeing less of him?" George frowns.

"No, what I mean is…Tristan has said that he will work from home so…" I shake my head and laugh. "Sounds silly doesn't it," I add feeling awkward.

"No it doesn't, please continue." George is furiously making notes again. *I wish I could see what he writes down.*

"Tristan….well, when he lost his folks he worked a lot from home, he said it sort of stuck and he realised he wasn't needed in the office as much as he thought he was. He has really great people in place to do most of the work for him."

"And you're comfortable with that?"

"Of course, I get to keep my job, and Tristan has said he will work more from his Brighton home, so I get to see him weeknights too."

"Good. Gladys and Debbie?" *Crap!*

"What about them?" I snipe still reeling from their dishonesty.

"Have you spoken to either of them?"

"No, I plan to do it this weekend," I tell him sombrely.

"Still convinced they are holding something back?"

"Yes," I state firmly.

"Alright, tread carefully Coral. You know how protective Gladys is about you. I'm sure that if she is holding something back, it's in your best interest."

I raise my eyebrows at that little speech. "Whose side are you on?" I grumble.

"No one's Coral. I really do hope you're wrong, and there is no big conspiracy." George eyes me speculatively.

"Sorry George," I sigh feeling guilty.

"No need. Rob and Carlos?" he adds.

My eyes instantly fill with unshed tears – *God damn it!*

"I hate that he won't tell me what's going on and has gone off leaving me in the dark," I sniff.

George hands me the box of tissues. "Thinking the worst again," he scolds.

"You would be too if you heard him." I tremble. "I've never heard him like that George. He sounded as though…as though he was in shock. Like something really bad had happened to him." I croak, pulling out several tissues.

"Let's discuss." I sigh heavily and blow my nose. "Even if something terrible has happened, what difference do you think you can make?" George asks.

"I don't know," I say feeling angry at that question. "Rob's my best friend. He's helped me out and been there for me when I've been sad, lonely or just a bit down, he's always been there," I stare out the window. "I just want to know he's ok, and if he's not, I want to be there for him. Is that such a crime?" I blurt.

"No, but getting yourself into a frenzy about it is. Coral you have to start to learn to let go of control, you want to know what's going on, so you feel you have some sort of control over the situation because you hate feeling in the dark. But it is inevitable that whatever it is, good or bad you have no control over it, the only thing you can do is be there for Rob if it's bad news. You can't take it away from him, you can't make everyone around you happy and have them be in your life without any problems, life is not like that."

I clench my hands into fists in exasperation. I know George is right, but how the hell do I stop worrying about it?

"So you're saying, just continue with my life as if nothing's going on, and not think about Rob at all, pretend like I don't give a fuck about him, or what he's going through? No! I can't do that!" I snipe, shaking my head.

"No that's not what I'm saying at all." George swaps his legs over. "Whatever he is going through right now is….No, let me try it this way. Do you think worrying about whatever it is, is going to make any difference to the outcome?" *Whoa, hadn't looked at it like that!*

"I...I guess not, no," I answer sheepishly.

"Good because it won't. What I am trying to suggest is to try and continue with your life as you normally would and then deal with whatever it is when he comes back."

"But if it's bad, I'll feel guilty for having a good time while he's been having a bad time."

George shakes his head in frustration. "Coral, don't you understand? It is obviously something he wanted to go through with Carlos - if there is anything. If he wanted to tell you, he would have, and I very much doubt he's going to be angry with you for continuing with your life while he's been away. Goodness me Coral!"

"Ok, ok I get it," I scowl.

"Thank goodness," George blurts falling back into his chair as though he's passed out. It's a little over exaggerated, but funny. "So," he says lifting his head. "Have you got anything nice planned for the weekend?" I squirm in my seat. "Out with it!" George says.

"I....well, it's private," I whisper feeling embarrassed.

"Coral, how many times do I have to tell you? You are in therapy, nothing is private!"

"Fine," I hiss. "I'm going to sleep with Tristan tonight." *Holy hell, this is beyond uncomfortable.* I look up at the ceiling, so I don't have to look at George.

"How are you feeling about having sex again?"

"Fine," I answer keeping my eyes up.

"Coral, please look at me," George says in his softest voice. Reluctantly, I do so. "What?" I say all innocently.

George cocks one eyebrow up at me. "You are not fine. So come on," he prompts.

I sigh inwardly. "I...I thought it would...I thought I wouldn't ever want to again, but Tristan's..." I swallow hard. "Tristan makes me feel safe. And it's like you said, prolonging it can sometimes make the act of doing it again even worse, it gets exasperated in your mind. I'm in love with him George, so sex is just the next, most natural step, right?"

"Yes, it is. So why do you look so worried?"

"Ok, ok, so I'm a little apprehensive that I think I'll be ok then I'll freak out, then he'll think I'm crazy..." I drift off.

"I very much doubt that. And my advice to you would be if you do *freak out* to tell him the truth."

I blow out my cheeks. "That's pretty heavy stuff to tell someone you hardly know," I say.

"Do you trust him?" I think about that one, and I think I do.

"Yes, I think so," I whisper.

"Then tell him, he won't go anywhere." I nod silently, I'm going for not freaking out, but if I do, I'll deal with it at the time.

"So that's a wrap?" George asks.

"Yes." I take my mobile out and call a taxi. "Thanks for seeing me tonight George. Can we keep the extra sessions going?"

"Yes, of course." George smiles fondly at me.

As we both stand, I give George a big hug, and he chuckles at me. "It's good to see you so happy Coral," he says.

"Joyce said that too, was I walking around looking miserable all the time or something?"

"No, not really. You just didn't smile much, that's all."

"Oh! I see." I walk with George to the front door and pick up the bedding and my bags.

"Coral, let me help you," he says.

I smile warmly at George and pass him the quilt and bedding. "Thanks." I see the taxi pull up and beep his horn, we walk out into the warm summer evening. George pops my items on the back seat, and I place my overnight bag next to it.

"Thanks, George, have a great weekend," I smile up at him.

"You too. Good luck for tonight," he whispers, softly squeezing my arm.

I swallow hard and throw a fake smile at George. Turning around, I get into the passenger seat and clip my seatbelt into place. When I checked out Google last night, it said it would take three minutes to get to Tristan's, I think more like five, either way – it doesn't leave me much thinking time.

"Where to love?" The driver asks.

"The Cliff," I answer.

"Very nice," he muses.

I wave at George as we pull out of his driveway. We head south down Wilson Avenue, take a left onto Roedean Road, then a right onto Cliff Road and an immediate left onto The Cliff.

"What number love?" The driver asks.

"It doesn't have one." He whistles at that answer and keeps driving. "See those wrought iron gates?" The driver leans forward and gazes up at the big trees. "That's the one," I say, my voice shaking slightly. He pulls up, and I pay him, then I pull the bedding and my bags out the car, then stand waiting for him to drive away.

When I know he can't see me anymore, I bend down and lean my hands on my knees. My heart is racing, my hands are shaking, and I know it's because I want to make it happen tonight, but the closer it's getting to the actual event, the more nervous and panicky I'm getting – *Ok, deep breaths Coral!*

I slowly breathe in and out, trying to bring my heart rate down. I notice a couple strolling across the road, they both turn and look at me; suddenly she stops and walks over to me.

"Are you ok?" The woman asks. I nod to her, trying to think of something to say. The man calls her back over to him, she starts walking away, and as she does she keeps looking over her shoulder at me. *Come on Coral, get a grip!*

Ok so maybe I'm putting too much pressure on myself? I decide that I am and I just need to play all of this by ear, see how I feel when I'm back in Tristan's arms.

Happy with my decision, I turn and walk over to the keypad. I punch in the code for the gates and they smoothly open. I pick up my bags and the bedding, take a deep breath and awkwardly walk down the driveway. When I reach the front door, I use the keys and open it up.

Stepping inside I shut the door behind me, and punch in the code for the alarm. Then I let my bags and the bedding drop to the floor. I take another deep breath and stare at the empty, barren house, the enormity of what I'm going to do tonight takes over, and I sink to the floor – *Come on Coral get a grip!*

I try to swallow, but my throat feels thick and dry. Standing up, with my legs still shaking, I head into the kitchen and pour myself a glass of water, and drink it down in one go, then I pour another glass and still myself.

"You can do this!" I say out loud, trying to convince myself that I can.

Taking another deep breath I look around the huge expanse, this place is so frigging big and empty that it actually feels kind of spooky.

"Echo..." I shout, my voice instantly echoing through the empty rooms.

Shaking my head at myself, I walk back over to my bags, pick them up with the bedding and awkwardly make my way up the two flights of stairs, and into the main bedroom.

I take a look at my watch, it's 5.30pm. I figure it will take me an hour to shower, shave and pamper myself in all the right places, and Tristan might get back earlier than anticipated – I better get a move on.

I quickly open the quilt and lay it out on the floor, so it can flatten out. Then I make the bed up with the bottom sheet and the pillowcases. Then last but not least, I put the quilt cover on and lay it on top of the bed – *There, now it's starting to look more like a bedroom!*

Time for a shower. Finding my wash-bag, I march into the en-suite, stripping my clothes as I go, then finding my razor, shower gel, shampoo and conditioner, I step into the huge shower...

I AM STOOD IN FRONT of the double sink, staring at myself in the massive mirror that's above it. I look ill, my cheeks are sunken. *That's not eating for you!* I castigate, but it's not like I can help it, the moment Tristan left my appetite vanished with him.

My eyes are as wide as saucers, and as I take a closer look, I can see the fear behind them. I try not to think too much about that. On a more positive note, the bruises have gone down significantly, and my nose feels completely healed, the only thing left is very light yellowish bruising underneath my eyes, I intend to cover them up with concealer.

I look down at my naked body and try to imagine Tristan's hands touching me, caressing me, but the fear keeps taking over, making me feel nervous and breathless. Maybe it won't happen tonight? Maybe I'm just not brave enough? I know I have the fear to deal with after what happened two years ago, but add on top of that the fact that I'm not entirely confident about myself, it's not really the best combination for a sexy night together.

And I can't help wondering if I'm sexy enough for Tristan? I shake my head at that thought – *Get on with it Coral!*

I start putting my makeup on, foundation, blusher, powder and my favourite eye-shadow - it's a copper-brown mix - then some nude lip gloss. Picking up my mascara and opening it up, I suddenly notice how badly my hands are shaking, I can feel the adrenalin pumping through my system, making me feel woozy – I close my eyes and breathe deeply for a while.

When I feel calmer, I open my eyes and start to apply the mascara, but I'm still shaking so much that I've nearly poked my eye, three times.

Come on Coral relax! This doesn't have to happen tonight!

I keep repeating my mantra as I make the finishing touches. When I'm done, I take a satisfied look at myself, my skin is buffed and creamed, my hair has dried naturally, curling into soft waves and my makeup looks nice – *Ok good!*

Making my way back to the bedroom to get dressed, I feel a little annoyed at myself that I didn't pick something up that's, well... sexy! Even if it was just a silk pyjama set or something – But oh no, I was too chicken to do that, so I have my only decent pair of fitted dark blue sweats and my white support vest. *Great!*

I slip into a pair of lacy boy shorts, then my sweats. Pulling my vest over my head as carefully as I can so I don't ruin my makeup, I suddenly get a random thought of Justin – *"Why don't you ever wear anything sexy for me? You know I like stockings and suspenders."*

I shake my head and push the thought of him away, back then I was far too shy to do anything like that, wear provocative, sexy clothing. Now I wish I had, so I would at least have something to wear for Tristan.

My hands are shaking again. As much as I'm trying, I just can't seem to get rid of my nerves – *Alcohol!* – I decide that's the key. Padding down the stairs, then down the next set, I make it into the kitchen – *Maybe we need a mini fridge upstairs?*

I walk over to the built-in fridge and pull out the cold bottle of Chardonnay that I put in there yesterday. Luckily, I remembered at the last minute to bring a bottle opener with me. I pour myself a small glass and glug it back in one go then I pour another.

Placing the wine back in the fridge, I immediately feel it flooding my system. I really should have had lunch today. I have tried to eat, but nothing has any taste, it all seems so boring and bland. I make my way back up the stairs so I can tidy up the mess I've left behind, but just as I reach the door to the bedroom, I hear my mobile ringing.

I dash over to it and see that it's Tristan.

"Tristan," I gush, feeling a settling warmth flow through me.

"Hello, beautiful." I smile deeply.

God, it's so good to hear his voice again!

"Look, I know we said Pizza tonight, but I fancy a steak. How about you?"

My stomach grumbles in agreement. "Yeah that sounds good, but may I remind you we have nothing to cook with." I point out.

"I like the sound of that," he says huskily, sending shivers down my spine.

"The sound of what?" I ask confused.

"You said '*we*' have nothing to cook with," he tells me.

"Oh," I breathe.

"Yeah, oh!" he titters. "So I've checked it out, and I can order at this Italian and pick it up when I get there. That's if you want to eat straight away?"

"Yeah sure, I don't mind," I tell him, my stomach tightening – *Jesus Coral that's it, not tonight!*

"You ok?" He asks sounding concerned.

"Yeah...just missing you, hurry up!" I tell him playfully.

"I will. I'll see you in say...half an hour?"

"Ok," I squeak a little high pitched and hang up...

I AM SAT OUTSIDE ON one of the bean bags we bought on Tuesday. I'm really trying not to, but I'm counting the seconds down until he arrives, I wish he'd hurry up! I've nearly finished my second glass of wine, and I'm feeling pretty wobbly, not a good impression to make. And the more I sit here, the more the nerves keep re-appearing, and my stupid leg won't stop jigging up and down. I hear a noise behind me. I dart up, almost falling over, and make my way inside, then I hear the front door shut.

"Coral?" Tristan calls out. My whole body relaxes in response to his voice. I close my eyes for a second savouring the exquisite feeling.

"In here!" I call my voice all raspy, I swallow hard and pull my hand to my throat.

As I walk into the kitchen, I see him placing his bags down. *Damn, he looks good!* He's in a pair of light grey suit trousers, a crisp white shirt and a deep blue tie. He looks up with a smile on his face that immediately disappears – *Uh-oh!*

Tristan marches into the kitchen, puts down the take-out bag and pulls me into his arms, squeezing tightly.

"What's wrong?" He asks, his voice sounding husky and dry.

God, he smells divine!

"Nothing," I lie and reach up to kiss him, Tristan reciprocates, but he still looks concerned.

"You look nervous," he tells me softly. "Should I be worried?" He asks.

I shake my head. "No, I just...I missed you," I tell him wrapping my arms around his waist, leaning my head against his chest.

Tristan tightens his hold on me and kisses the top of my head. "I've missed you too," he whispers.

"You sound thirsty." I look up at his warm eyes and smile.

"Thirsty, hungry and in need of a shower," he tells me. "You started without me," he says gesturing to my glass of wine. *Guilty as charged!*

"Yeah...sorry about that," I answer feeling all my fears from earlier coming back to the surface.

Tristan frowns down at me. "Hard day at work? Or a difficult session with George?" *Is there anything he doesn't know about me?*

"Um...no, not really," I answer honestly, then castigate myself for it.

"Ok, you talk, I'll get a drink." I sigh heavily. Tristan walks over to the fridge and pours himself a glass of wine, then turns and strangely gazes at me. He walks over to me, places his wine down and runs his finger down my cheek.

"You're so beautiful," he whispers.

I frown – *No way am I that!*

"You are," he tells me firmly, as though he can hear my inner dialogue.

I laugh nervously in response, his frown deepens. "Coral' –"Let's eat," I interrupt, "before it goes cold." I walk over to the cupboard and take out two plates and two sets of cutlery, thankfully we picked up a set on Tuesday. Otherwise, we'd be eating with our fingers!

Tristan is watching me, assessing me but thankfully, he doesn't question me. Instead, he opens the bag and starts dishing it all up, it smells so good. When he's done, I look down at my plate. I have peppered steak smothered with Dianne sauce, chips, peas, mushrooms and half a grilled tomato.

"Where the hell did you get this from?" I ask in astonishment. Tristan has already started eating – *He must be really hungry!* – He smiles and taps his nose at me.

I chuckle and start eating, but each time I go to swallow my stomach tightens with nervous anticipation...

WE EAT IN COMFORTABLE silence. I top our wine glasses up half way through the meal, I'm drinking far more than I should - I know that, but I'm hoping it'll help me relax. Tristan has already finished and is quietly watching me as he sips his wine.

"Why don't you go and take a shower," I tell him. "I'll be finished by the time you get back." Tristan gazes at me for a moment then looks down at my plate. *I'm eating so slowly tonight!*

"Off your food?" He asks I nod feeling awkward. Tristan stands and kisses my temple, then grabs his bags and makes his way up the stairs. The moment he's out of view I exhale loudly – *Why do I feel so relieved?*

I decide I don't want to dwell on that too deeply and try to eat some more, but two thirds into my meal, I decide I'm too full to finish – I hate wasting food – I guess my stomach must have shrunk with not eating regularly.

I stand, feeling exhausted for some reason, and start clearing everything away. Maybe it's the adrenaline that's been pumping through my system for hours? Or maybe it's the wine? Or maybe it's the fact that I have hardly slept at all? I just can't seem to get

Tristan out of my head, and the few hours sleep I have had, I've dreamt of him.

Just as I'm washing the last plate, I hear Tristan coming down the stairs.

"That was quick," I say breathlessly. He looks so good, he's in a pair of loose black sweats that hang in the right way on his hips and a light grey vest, I haven't seen his bare shoulders before, they're big, beautiful, and look very strong.

He quickly reaches me, his scent knocking me for six, then, slowly he reaches out and takes my face in his hands. "Ok spit it out, why are you so nervous? Have I done something wrong, or not done something?" He looks really worried.

"No!" I bark feeling angry that he thinks that, but I can't get my words out either. The only way I feel I can explain it to him is to show him.

I move his wine glass out of the way and prop myself up onto the breakfast bar, opening my legs I pull on his vest, so he reaches me, then I wrap my legs around him and kiss him, hard. Tristan moans in response. I feel his erection grow between my legs and freeze – *Fuck!*

I pull back from his lips, trying not to show him how much I'm panicking, but my breathing has escalated, and my heart feels like it's trying to break out of my chest – *Fuck!*

"What is it?" He whispers, trailing soft kisses down my neck.

"Tristan...stop!" I bark. His head snaps back up, our eyes locking onto one another. "I'm sorry, I can't..." I move him out of my way, jump down off the breakfast bar and walk towards the terrace, but Tristan catches me, wrapping his arm around my waist, my back to his front.

"What was all that about?" He whispers in my ear.

I lean my head back against his chest and close my eyes. I feel stupid and angry and pissed off that I thought it would just naturally happen. I freaked out, and I want him so badly – Fuck! What do I do?

I hear George's voice in my head – *Tell him Coral!*

I turn around and look up into his worried, anxious eyes. I stroke his cheek, his day's stubble has disappeared, but now I'm really looking, I notice he looks tired.

"You look tired," I say.

"Don't change the subject. Tell me what's wrong?" He orders in a deep, flat voice.

"No!" I bark. *I can't tell him, I just can't.*

"Coral, what just happened?" He pushes, I can tell he's getting angry, frustrated. He takes hold of my upper arms and grips them tightly. "Tell me, baby, you should know you can tell me anything," he adds, his eyes pleading with mine.

And at that moment, I don't know why, but all my fears, doubts, worries, and inhibitions come rushing to the surface – And I know…in that very moment, I know – I can't do this anymore.

I mean, who have I been kidding? *Myself that's who!*

I can't do relationships, I can't do intimacy, and I can't do this – not anymore. I know I'm self-destructing it, but I self-destruct everything, people, places. The only thing I have ever held onto in a long-term sense is my job.

I've even spent most of my life waiting for Gladys to leave, even though I know she loves me, deeply, and I love Tristan, more than I've ever loved anyone, which is why I have to go. I can't continue like this, knowing full well that one day I'll just up and leave.

"Tristan, please let go of me." He instantly releases my arms. "I can't do this," I mumble staring down at the floor.

I feel his stature freeze before me. "What?' – "I have to go, I can't do this anymore," I whisper, keeping my eyes fixed on the floor. If I look up at him I know I'll stay and I can't, I can't do this to him, or me.

"Why?" he gasps. I shake my head unable to give him an answer. "You're just running because you're scared!" he barks.

"Yes, I am scared, but I still need to go," I croak.

"Coral, no, please…don't do this," his voice quivers.

"I told you, Tristan…" I whisper. "Right from the start, I…" I shake my head, unable to articulate my feelings.

"Please…Coral I don't want you to go," he whispers.

I frown at the floor. "I think it's better this way, to leave now…before we get too involved."

Tristan snorts sarcastically at me. "Too involved?" He shouts.

I look up at him, he's gripping his hair with his hands, a look of despair on his face. "I think we've gone way past that, don't you?" he barks, his voice shaking, his cheeks flushing, his eyes darkening and widening in horror – *Fuck!*

"Tristan..." I close my eyes and try to get my words out. "You don't....I'm not..." I break off again.

"Baby....please, don't do this..." He says, his voice trembling. "We can take this slow...go at your pace. I know we can work this out."

He tries to reach out to me, but I take a cautious step back.

"Please, Tristan, don't make this any harder than it already is." I look up at him, he looks broken, like the world is falling from beneath his feet, I instantly squeeze my eyes shut. "I have to go," I whisper, and without looking at him, I turn around and make my way up the stairs.

Reaching the bedroom, I silently pack my bag, when I'm done I throw my weekend bag over my shoulder, grab hold of my handbag, stuff my feet into my trainers and march down the stairs – I feel numb.

Reaching the kitchen, I take a hesitant look at Tristan. He's sat on one of the bar stools, a deep frown etched into his features, totally lost in thought. I almost change my mind – *No! Coral you have to leave, you're not good for him!*

The truth of the matter is that I'm not strong, and I'm not capable of this. I have nothing to offer him. Nothing but fears, doubts, insecurities, and now I know – I am incapable of love.

I march over to him, take my keys out of my bag, unhook the set he gave me and silently place them on the breakfast bar. I take another hesitant look at him; he looks broken, totally and utterly broken – *God that hurts, knowing I've put that pain there!*

Tears swim in his eyes as he looks up at me – *Oh fuck!*

"Don't go...please," he croaks.

My heart sinks to the pit of my stomach. "I'm sorry," I squeak and dash towards the front door.

I yank it open, close it behind me and speed walk down the driveway, keeping my eyes fixed firmly ahead - I don't stop, I can't stop, I won't stop.

I walk in a zombie-like state all the way back to my studio. I feel nothing, just an empty hollow feeling that's always been there. Only now it feels a thousand times more profound, more empty. Reaching my studio, I unlock the door, step inside and let my bags fall to the floor - *Coral, what have you done?*

I ignore my own thoughts and make my way up the stairs. Reaching my bedroom, I kick off my trainers and collapse on the bed. In one fail swoop the enormity of what I've just done comes crashing down on me, and I howl in pain. Angry tears begin spilling down my cheeks.

What is this?

I grip my stomach trying to make the empty ache disappear.

God, please make it stop!

This is torture, I can't take it. I rock myself back and forth as I try to make it all go away. The pain I feel at never seeing Tristan again is indescribable, I feel it everywhere. In my head, my heart, my soul, my body, it even feels like it's with me in the room – And I know that's because he was here, in this place, with me.

What have I done?

The right thing, I tell myself.

I'm not good for him, I can't give him what he wants, what he deserves. I am not capable of this, of love – I'm a twisted freak.

I cry even harder as I digest these thoughts. I grip the quilt closer to me, hoping it will bring me some sort of comfort, some solace, but it smells of him. I take a deep, ragged breath, and I'm instantly knocked over by his scent, it's deeply ingrained in the quilt, which makes me howl even harder – *Will this ever end?*

I curl up into a ball and really let go, crying so hard I'm not sure if I'll ever be able to stop. I picture his face as I left him, so hurt, so broken.... *Tristan.*

END OF PART ONE

Hi There!
Did you enjoy this book?
If so, you can make a big difference.

Reviews are the most powerful tools in my arsenal when it comes to getting attention for my books. Much as I'd like to, I don't have the financial muscle of a New York Publisher. I can't take out full page ads in the newspaper, or put posters on the subway. But I do have something more powerful than that, and it's something that those publishers would kill to get their hands on.

A committed and loyal bunch of readers.

Honest reviews of my books help bring them to the attention of other readers like you. If you've enjoyed this book I would be very grateful if you could spend just five minutes leaving a review (it can be as short as you like) or simply rating the book on Amazon. I wholeheartedly thank you in advance.

Find Out What Happens Next In…

Freed By Him
Darkest Fears Trilogy Book Two

When the past felt too big to bear, Coral Stevens walked away from the burgeoning love between her and Tristan Freeman, handsome mogul – and her new boss. Heartbroken, yet resolute, she feels she has made the right choice… too bad Tristan doesn't.

Their confrontation forces Coral to re-evaluate her choice, and gives her the chance to follow her heart. Trusting him may be the hardest thing that Coral has ever done, yet the love that has grown between them cannot be denied – nor can the flammable passion that explodes whenever they touch.

Slowly but surely, Coral opens her heart to this enigmatic man, revealing her soul, her pain… and eventually her past, even though she fears it will drive him away.

Instead, Tristan proves to her that she is worth it, regardless of her revelations – and shows her what a real, loving relationship can be like.

Then just when Coral thinks that things can't get any better, danger weaves its way around them, finding the vulnerable crevices of desperation, desire and obsession. Tristan, loving and trusting man that he is, can't see the evil lurking – but Coral can. She has known malice before and she feels it now. With her happiness and their very lives on the line, how far can she go to protect the one she loves?

<u>Reviews for Freed By Him</u>

"The term 'Never let me go' was never so aptly used as it was in this, on both their counts. I truly loved and connected with how this played out. I'm kind of a wreck as I wobble on the final book. Can't wait…" **5 stars - Goodreads**

"Hot! Hot! Hot! This author knows how to write hot steamy sex! Plus, it was just as gut wrenching as the first book. I really love Coral and Tristan. I laughed and I cried, and then the climax at the end was just awesome. This trilogy is going to go far in the romance world, and this author is going to have a stellar career…" **5 stars – LibraryThing**

"Brilliant sequel to the first book, I was as equally hooked into the story. After the end of Fallen For Him, I couldn't wait to get into Freed By Him. It's one of my most memorable reads for years…" **5 stars – Amazon.co.uk**

"Coral and Tristan share an amazing chemistry together, but Tristan's past hides an enormous secret that threatens their future together, it was a joy to read. The steamy parts were well written and I loved the dialogue. Thumbs up…" **5 stars – Amazon.com**

"Intense and very engaging romance, I was so easily pulled into the steamy relationship between Coral and Tristan. Another great read that delivered on both the dramatic and erotic fronts. Love the characters and the story. Looking forward to the conclusion in Forever With Him…" **5 stars – Amazon.com**

"One of the best series I have read in a long time. After finishing the first book, I just had to read the second. I loved the love scenes and how powerful the story was. This book was just as good as the first and I cannot wait for the third…" **5 stars – Barnes & Noble**

Join My Mailing List

Join my mailing list via my website www.clairdelaneyauthor.com for exclusive offers and competitions and to keep updated with future releases.

Connect with me

Also, you can connect with me via social media. Or contact me via the email address below. I would love to answer your questions, or simply read your feedback and comments.

FACEBOOK - Clair Delaney Author
TWITTER - @CDelaney_Author
INSTAGRAM – ClairDelaneyAuthor
PINTEREST – Clair Delaney Author
WEBSITE - www.clairdelaneyauthor.com
EMAIL - clairdelaneyauthor@gmail.com

ABOUT THE AUTHOR

CLAIR DELANEY is a former P.A who currently lives in rural Wales in the UK. From a very young age, Clair would always be found drawing pictures and writing an exciting story to go with those picture books. At five years of age she told her mother she wanted to work for Disney, that dream didn't pan out, but eventually, she found the courage to put pen to paper and write her first romance novel Fallen For Him. She is also the author of Freed By Him, Forever With Him and A Christmas Wish, Darkest Fears Christmas Special. When she is not writing Clair loves to read, listen to music, keep fit and take long walks with her dogs in the countryside.

Fallen For Him - Copyright © 2018 Clair Delaney

THE MORAL RIGHTS OF THE AUTHOR HAVE BEEN ASSERTED. ALL CHARACTERS AND EVENTS IN THIS E-BOOK OTHER THAN THOSE CLEARLY IN THE PUBLIC DOMAIN ARE FICTITIOUS AND ANY RESEMBLANCE TO REAL PERSONS, LIVING OR DEAD IS PURELY COINCIDENCE - ALL RIGHT RESERVED. THIS E-BOOK IS COPYRIGHT MATERIAL AND MUST NOT BE COPIED, REPRODUCED, TRANSFERRED, DISTRIBUTED OR USED IN ANY WAY EXCEPT AS SPECIFICALLY PERMITTED IN WRITING BY THE AUTHOR, AS ALLOWED UNDER THE TERMS AND CONDITIONS UNDER WHICH IT WAS PURCHASED OR AS STRICTLY PERMITTED BY APPLICABLE LAW. ANY UNAUTHORISED DISTRIBUTION OR USE OF THIS TEXT, MAYBE A DIRECT INFRINGEMENT OF THE AUTHORS RIGHTS, AND THOSE RESPONSIBLE MAYBE LIABLE IN LAW ACCORDINGLY.

Printed in Great Britain
by Amazon